About the Author

Melodi Bac is an award-winning novelist, screenwriter, and script consultant with a BA in film and television and a UCLA master-level certification in screenwriting. She is best known for writing fantasy and science-fiction novels, stories, and screenplays. Literary critics declared her "Turkey's J. K. Rowling" when she was only sixteen. As a young novelist with seven published books and three international awards, nowadays Melodi Bac focuses on writing novels, screenplays, and finishing her latest novel for her best-selling book series *ANKA*.

Website: melodibac.com
Instagram: @melodibac & @melodibac_author
Facebook: @melodibackitaplari
TikTok: @melodi.bac

Return of Anka

Melodi Bac

Return of Anka

Book I

Olympia Publishers
London

www.olympiapublishers.com
OLYMPIA PAPERBACK EDITION

Copyright © Melodi Bac 2024

Maps created by Anay Kharade

The right of Melodi Bac to be identified as author of
this work has been asserted in accordance with sections 77 and 78 of the
Copyright, Designs and Patents Act 1988.

All Rights Reserved

No reproduction, copy or transmission of this publication
may be made without written permission.
No paragraph of this publication may be reproduced,
copied or transmitted save with the written permission of the publisher, or in
accordance with the provisions
of the Copyright Act 1956 (as amended).

Any person who commits any unauthorised act in relation to
this publication may be liable to criminal
prosecution and civil claims for damage.

A CIP catalogue record for this title is
available from the British Library.

ISBN: 978-1-83543-021-7

This is a work of fiction.
Names, characters, places and incidents originate from the writer's imagination.
Any resemblance to actual persons, living or dead, is purely coincidental.

First Published in 2024

Olympia Publishers
Tallis House
2 Tallis Street
London
EC4Y 0AB

Printed in Great Britain

Dedication

To my dear mother, Gulgun, father, Candan, my husband, Will, and my dog, Nalu… Thank you for always believing in me. I couldn't have done it without you…

Acknowledgments

The book is translated from Turkish by Oyku Gizem Gokgul. Polished by Melodi Bac.

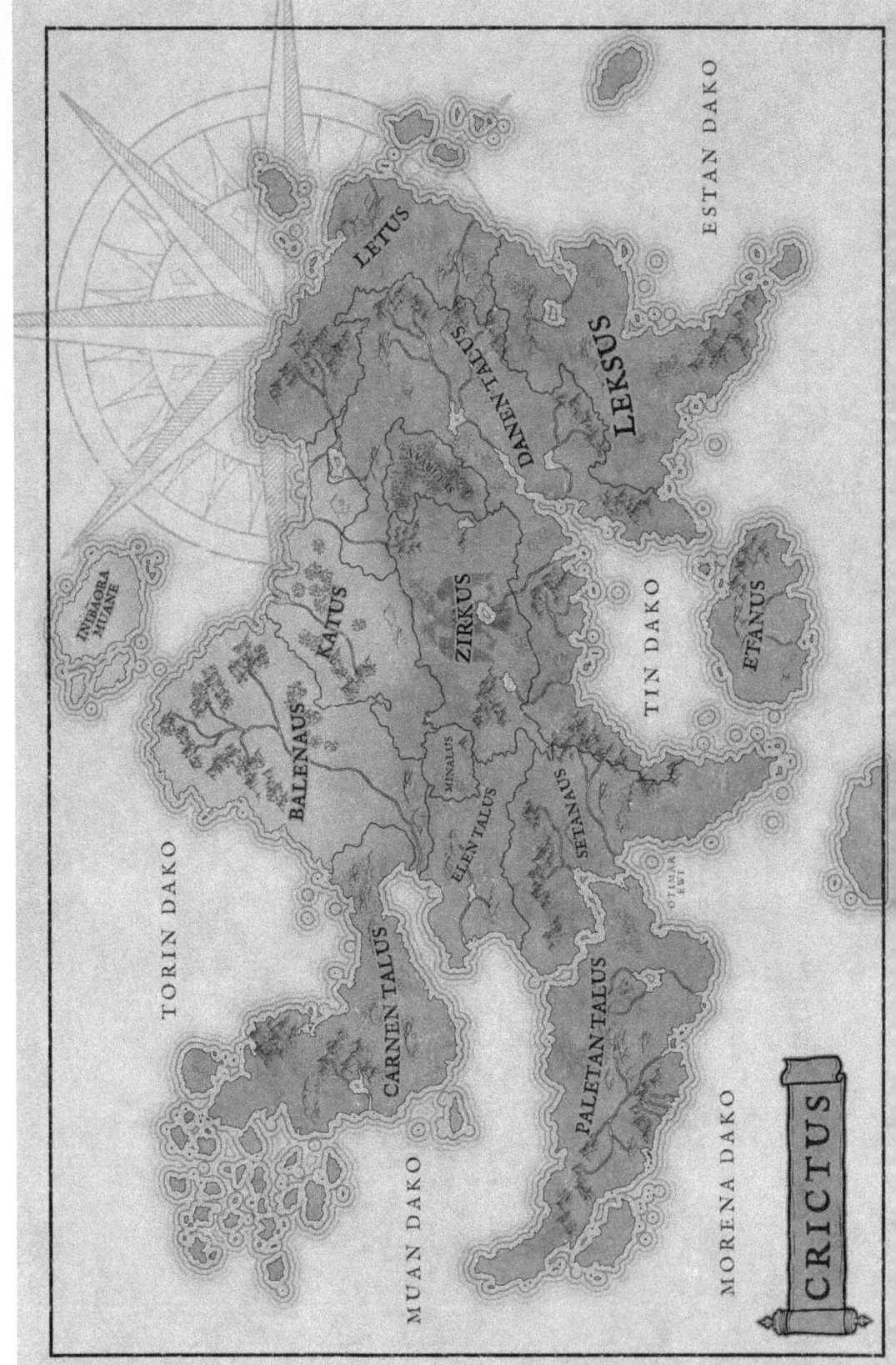

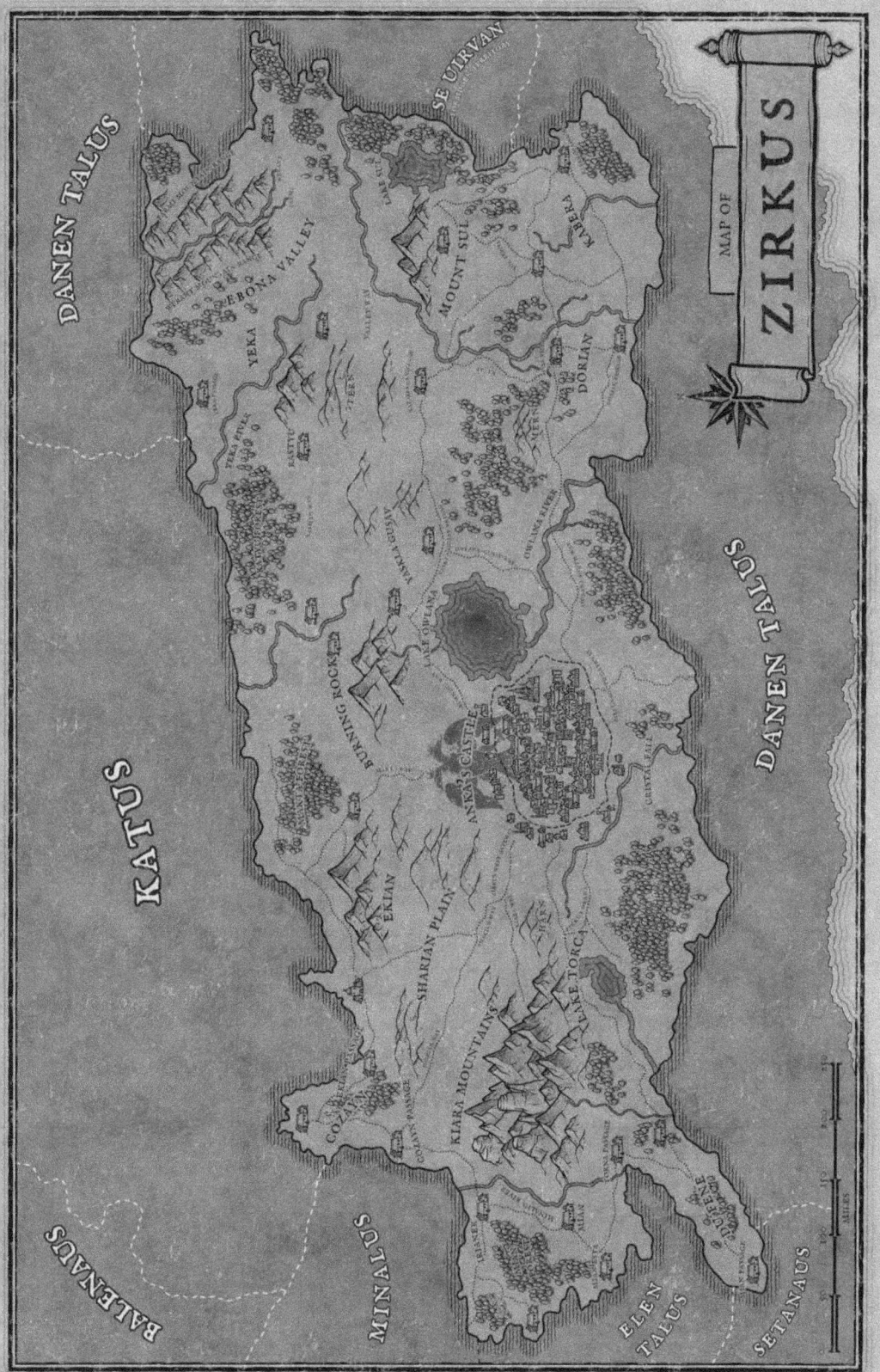

0

The guards holding Carmen dumped her right in the center of the hall, directly in front of the throne. Carmen collapsed to her knees. She was breathing heavily. Carmen raised her head slightly off the ground. The throne was in front of her; it was splendid, with exaggerated golden inlaid legs, and it mocked her. The throne assumed a dark aura with light seeping through the two frosted windows behind. There it is, Carmen thought. The reason for her very existence was standing in front of her. Fearlessly displayed in its glory, it taunted her as if it was staring pitifully at Carmen. Carmen recalled her thoughts from a few weeks ago when the closest she had been to the throne was while she cleaned the corridor leading to the throne hall. Though she was mere steps from it, it had never seemed so far away. *Isn't it ironic?* She thought. The throne was still staring sarcastically at her. Nobody in the room was talking. Carmen stared defiantly at the throne. *It was supposed to be mine, but it's too late now,* she said. Hope, hope... Where are you? She was looking for a grain of hope in herself, but there wasn't any. Soon the door would open, the Soul Hunter would enter, and she...

She thought about the times when her life was simple. She was an average girl on Earth. When did this all happen? How did she end up here? She looked at the glorious throne again. There was nothing else left to do but wait...

1

A FEW MONTHS AGO

Anka... Anka... Anka...

Carmen opened her eyes in a flash. She could've sworn someone had called her name. Gathering her wits, she straightened up a bit in bed and glanced about the room. She then peered at the clock that was a present from her grandfather perched up on the nightstand next to the wall. As she couldn't cope with getting up so early in the morning, she had to set the alarm so she wouldn't be late for school. Glancing at the clock, she noticed it was set to go off in ten minutes. Carmen rolled grumpily out of bed as she pressed the alarm button. At that moment, she was looking forward to the end of the school year. It was May and school would soon be out for the summer. What a relief! A fine vacation chock full of surprises awaited her. Carmen was ecstatic about it.

She stood up. The clothes she tried on the day before to get ready for school were lying on the floor. Carmen was quite untidy. She promptly stepped on them as she went over to her closet to throw on a pair of jeans and a strappy blue blouse instead. Then she parked herself in front of the mirror and carelessly combed her brown hair. Getting all dolled up and putting on fancy clothes was not really her cup of tea. After combing her hair for a bit longer, she went over to her school backpack sprawled out on the floor like a rag and threw it together. Then, as she slung it onto her back, she went back over to the mirror one final time. Although she was not so popular at school, Carmen was an attractive and smart girl. Carmen's hazel eyes practically matched her hair, enhancing her beauty. Her well-shaped pink lips curled slightly. She shrugged her shoulders.

She walked down the squeaky wooden staircase to the kitchen. While her mother was whipping up a quick omelet for Carmen in the kitchen, her father was sitting at his usual spot, reading his daily paper. As soon as Carmen entered the kitchen, her mother looked at her.

"Good morning, dear. Boy, you're early today!"

Carmen went over to the wooden table in the middle of the kitchen. She put her bag on a chair and sat on the next one over.

"Yeah. And guess what, I had the same freaky dream again."

"Oh, really?"

One couldn't help but notice the edge in her mother's voice. Her father raised his head over the top of the paper slightly and looked at his wife. Carmen could not sense the unease in her mother's voice. She went on from where she left off.

"Yeah, I saw the same woman again. She was blabbering about some gibberish I didn't quite understand." She paused as her mother set the omelet in front of her. After taking a bite, she went on talking, "What I don't get is why this woman keeps calling me 'Anka.' I don't even know what it means."

Carmen's mother fidgeted nervously.

Her father said calmly, "It probably means nothing."

Carmen shrugged and continued her breakfast.

During her school lunch break, Carmen went out to the quad and headed over to the table where her friends were sitting. The weather was quite warm, and it was hard to sit still in class in such heat. She sat beside her friends.

"I think I hate our history. Why does it have to be so boring?"

"Oh, Carmen, don't you know all our presidents lived such boring lives so we could die of boredom. I'm surprised you didn't know that."

Liz, who was Carmen's best friend, was a very charming girl with short brown hair and big eyes. They had known each other for five years. She responded to Liz's little joke with a chuckle. Then silence dominated the table as they started dining on their meals.

Anka... Anka...

Suddenly, Carmen raised her head from her tray. She had heard that voice again. She looked at her friends. They looked calm.

"Did you hear that, too?"

"Hear what?" asked George.

"That voice."

"I didn't hear anything," Liz replied.

I must be out of my mind, Carmen thought, and sighed. Instead of saying it aloud, she mumbled, "I must have misheard it" to change the subject.

And yet, Carmen was still pretty sure she had heard it. After Carmen had said that, silence reigned supreme. George broke the silence after a while.

"Do you have any plans for tonight?"

Carmen gazed at George in astonishment. She knew that George had feelings for her, but she didn't want to be any more than friends with him.

"Actually, I have to study for a test tonight, George."

Liz jabbed her under the table. Liz wanted Carmen to date George, even more than George wanted to date Carmen. She insisted that George and Carmen would make a great couple. George was blond with green eyes, and could attract the attention of all the girls, but he just couldn't manage to attract the one girl that was the object of his attention.

"But I think you're free tomorrow evening, aren't you?"

Carmen gave Liz a resentful look. Liz just couldn't keep her trap shut.

"Yes, why not?" Carmen said.

As a matter of fact, George could be a really good boyfriend for her. They had a great time whenever they got together, and George was really handsome. Nevertheless, Carmen still didn't feel anything for him.

"That's great," said George gleefully.

Carmen sighed. She disliked hurting him.

Carmen felt beat when she went home that day, but as she had informed George, she needed to cram for an exam. She went to her room in a huff. Carmen was always annoyed with the fact that her life was mundane. She was sixteen and hadn't even been beyond the coastal town where she lived. It was nothing more than houses interspersed in the forest by the seaside. Carmen hated this town. Her biggest dream was to get away from here one way or another. She knew that it wouldn't be easy to leave a place where she had spent sixteen years. All the same, she desired to go out and travel the world and meet new people, but it was impossible. Her father had already started to pressure her to work at his business. But the last thing in the world Carmen wanted was to be involved with mathematics when she got older. She despised math and tried to tell her father thousands of times that she had absolutely no desire to become an accountant, but she failed to make him understand.

The next day Carmen returned to her humdrum life and went to school. The math lesson passed interminably. Liz sat two desks away from her and they kept throwing paper wads at each other and finally stopped when the teacher admonished them. At this point, the lesson was too boring to cope with. Carmen could no longer focus on her lesson. Instead, she was looking out the window.

Suddenly, she gasped for air with a terrible spasm on her heart and let out a shrill scream. She felt like she was drowning. Her eyes abruptly blacked out as she sensed bucketfuls of water were pouring down her throat. She was underwater… she saw a young man. He had a blue emerald on his heart, shining in a dazzling light. It seemed the emerald was puncturing his heart. As the young man screamed and shouted, a horrific pain simultaneously conquered Carmen's body, then it stopped instantly where it had begun, in her heart. Everything happened too fast. Putting her hand on her heart, she looked around dumbfounded with no idea of what had happened. She was out of breath, and her hand was still on her chest. Her vision restored; she was back in class. Ms. Kead was standing in front of her, looking at her anxiously.

"Carmen, are you okay?"

It took some time to regain her wits. She looked at her classmates' faces, stammering, and then looked to the side where the question had come.

"I… I'm okay, Ms. Kead. I felt a brief twitch in my heart. That's all."

"Are you sure? You can visit the nurse's office if you like."

"No, no I am really fine." Carmen had no desire to explain whatever the hell it was.

Ms. Kead hesitantly turned her head back to the board. Carmen was still trying to regulate her breath. Just then, she heard the same voice again.

Anka… Anka…

She didn't know what it meant, but it was beginning to scare her. For a second, she thought she was really going mad.

At lunch, she sat and chatted with her friends in the wooded part of the campus. Carmen was brooding because of what had happened to her. She couldn't make sense of what had come over her recently. The voices out of nowhere, heard by nobody else, strange dreams and now this. *Perhaps it is time to visit a doctor* Carmen thought.

"Carmen?"

Carmen cringed when she heard her name called. It was Liz.

"Yes?"

"Are you all right? You've been looking a bit strange since class." Liz appeared concerned. Carmen gulped faintly.

"I'm good."

"Really, what happened to you back there in class?" Liz asked.

"I just…" In fact, she had no explanation for it. She wasn't sure, either. What she saw, what she felt… Carmen took a deep breath. "I just felt a twitch in my heart. I was out of breath for a moment. Nothing serious."

Everyone at the table went silent. While Carmen was put off by the introduction of this matter, it was George who broke the ice.

"What time would you like me to come and pick you up today?"

Carmen had forgotten all about their date until George mentioned it. She was still dwelling on what happened in the classroom. Still, she didn't let on that she had forgotten.

"You can come around seven," she shrugged.

"Great," George said happily.

Carmen flashed a fake smile at him. The bench was joyous again as everyone picked up the conversation where they left off. After a while, Carmen joined in as well. Just then, the same voice reverberated in her ears once again.

Anka… Anka…

Carmen suddenly stopped laughing at the joke her friend made. She pricked up her ears to the voice.

Dirnsk Ekis…*

(Come to me…)

The voice whispered, echoing in her mind. It was as if the voice was inside her head. She looked around while her breathing quickened.

Xoro tue…*

(Find me…)

Not knowing why, Carmen stood up suddenly instinctively. The whisper was in a language she could not comprehend, but somehow, she knew what it meant. *Something was beckoning her*.

"What are you doing?" Liz asked.

Without even responding, Carmen started walking toward the woods adjacent to the school. She had no idea where her feet were taking her. She could neither resist nor make sense of what this was all about. She was only heading to where she believed the voice was emanating from. She heard a friend calling out her name, but she couldn't react. They were saying things behind her. They were asking where she was going but she couldn't answer them. She couldn't call for help as she felt her heart beating faster. She was afraid, and she couldn't possibly make sense of what was happening. The voice in her head spoke in that language again.

Anka... Ekis... *

(Anka... Come...)

Carmen was heading toward the voice. She was trying to control herself and her feet but to no avail. She thought, *Where am I going? I don't even know what 'Anka' means. I'm not even 'Anka'... Why can't I control my feet?*

Carmen merely proceeded toward the voice in a state of hypnosis. She was pretty much inside the wooded area now. Apprehensive with her destination unknown, she soon spotted someone in the forest. She was walking toward this person who was a rather tall and unattractive guy in his 30s. He was holding a small rock that resembled crystal. When he saw Carmen, he put the rock down. Without knowing why, Carmen got closer to the man, and picked up the crystal he had just put down. She leapt up instantly as if struck by an electric shock. The voice in her head disappeared. Silence… Confounded, she looked at the stone in her hand and then at the person grinning nonchalantly. She took a few steps back.

"Ray kemas!" *

(Hello sister.)

"Wh… who are you and what am I doing here?" Carmen said, not understanding where she was and what was happening.

The look on the man's face turned into a fake sadness.

"Oh wow. This is deeply upsetting… You really don't know who you are."

Carmen was happy to ascertain he could speak her language. She chuckled at what he said. She was quite good at being frivolous even in serious situations.

"I know who I am. I'm Carmen and I really don't know what I'm doing here."

"I summoned you here, Anka."

Carmen spoke in a slightly annoyed and defiant way. "I'm not Anka.

Are you deaf? My name is Carmen, I told you."

The man softly laughed. "All right, *Carmen*. I'm Inca. I'm pleased to meet you. Thanks to you, I will rule the whole Crictus and make everything easier for the next-generation Incas. They won't have to hunt the Anka."

Carmen grimaced without understanding. "Are you high? What are you talking about?"

Inca continued unperturbedly. "I summoned you here so you can help me. I'm going to ask a small favor from you, sister."

Carmen crossed her arms on her chest. "What help! I am not going to help you. Leave me alone!"

As Carmen attempted to leave, Inca's smile grew larger. "Your death. That's what I want."

The know-it-all look on Carmen's face disappeared. "What are you talking ab—"

Before completing her words, a powerful beam emanating from Inca's palm knocked her into the tree behind her. The crystal rock fell from her hand as Carmen emitted a high-pitched shriek. Her chest was in agony.

"How do you—"

Once again, before even finishing her sentence, she realized that Inca was going on the rampage, and ducked down. The beam hit the tree, which began to shake violently. Scared out of her wits, Carmen stood up and hurriedly tried to flee the scene. Meanwhile, Inca picked up the rock from the ground and went in hot pursuit of Carmen, who was double-timing it out of there. She had never been more frightened in her life. She breathlessly began to zigzag amongst the trees, and looking behind her for a moment, she noticed the beam of light coming after her. As she looked ahead again, she suddenly found herself in someone else's arms. Her scream echoed in the forest.

"It's okay. Calm down, Anka. I'm here."

Carmen couldn't comprehend what was happening around her. She stuttered while trying to catch her breath.

"Help. A man… he's after me… he wants to kill me."

Carmen was utterly petrified. It was that young man! The one she saw underwater! Involuntarily, she took a step back.

"I know. I'm here to help you."

Carmen was quite stoked with fear.

"You… You were underwater—" Then she heard Inca's footsteps, and she looked toward the voice coming from behind her. Inca was there.

"That's him!" she said, pointing at Inca.

The boy shoved Carmen behind him. Inca was breathless, huffing and puffing, but still wore a grin on his mug. Meanwhile, Carmen's limbs were trembling with fear.

"I see you're the bearer of the water emerald. I was expecting someone... better," Inca said.

"Don't worry, Inca. I'm quite capable. You haven't seen nothing yet."

Just as he said that, Inca attacked without compunction. The water emerald suddenly generated water out of the ground. The airborne water created a shield that hindered the light from striking her and the water emerald, as Carmen took a few steps back out of confusion and fear.

"Oh my God! What are you people?" She couldn't understand what was happening around her. The water emerald looked behind and shouted to Carmen. He was also trying to avert the beam coming at them.

"Anka! Get out of here!"

Carmen was ready to argue. "I'm not Anka."

The water emerald shot right back. "Go!"

Carmen knew that it made no sense in protesting such a situation. She turned back around and began sprinting away as fast as she could. After a long run and out of breath, she spotted a few houses in the distance and began running toward them. It wasn't long before she reached the houses on a street. There were some folks outside. Should she ask them for help? Then again, nobody would believe her about the water suspended magically in the air, lights emitting from a hand that caused such atrocious pain... Carmen continued running without pause and was even afraid to look behind her. As she lived in a small town, there were no taxis around. She didn't intend to wait around for a taxi anyway. She mustered her strength and ran all the way home.

Meanwhile, Ron the Water Emerald was still trying to fight off Inca, who was flabbergasted for letting Carmen get away. Thus, he attacked with all his might. Ron began to lose his patience against Inca. He sent his ground-generated water flying in Inca's direction with all his strength. A dazed Inca hit the deck forcefully. Ron looked at the stone Inca had just dropped. He had to take that stone which posed a mortal danger to Anka. With a deft move, he reached for the stone, but Inca's lunge pushed him back. Inca was crawling on the ground to reach the stone. Having fallen down, Ron reached for the stone in the same way. He was able to grab the stone, but in doing so, he didn't realize Inca was attacking again. Ron groaned softly but managed to get a grip. He quickly stood up and looked to see that he was holding the crystal stone.

"You'll have hard time reaching Anka without this."

"Give it back to me!"

Grinning maliciously, Ron took a few steps back, and disappeared inside an enormous beam the moment he closed his eyes. Inca stood up with rage.

"No!"

He couldn't stand failing. Everything was messed up. He had wasted his one and only opportunity to kill Anka while she was defenseless.

Carmen arrived home just then. Locking the door behind her as soon as she got inside, she leaned her head against the door. She was finally feeling safe. She was breathless and sweating buckets as her chest heaved. Just then someone touched her from behind, causing her to scream.

"Carmen, it's just me!"

It was her father. Seeing him in front of her, Carmen has never felt this happy before... She threw herself in his arms.

"Dad, you wouldn't believe what just happened."

She released her father as her mother came in from the living room. Carmen breathlessly began to tell them.

"There was a man and a stone. And then, the man told me that he was going to kill me. We were in a forest. I couldn't ask for help from anyone." She stopped and made a face: "Then... Then this light came out from his hand, and I ran away, and then there was a guy. He could control water coming out of the ground with his hand. It was unbelievable and he saved me. Then, I escaped and came here. I know it sounds like nonsense but believe me, it's all true. I saw them all with my eyes..."

Carmen's mother, Susan, put her hand to her mouth. She looked very concerned. Ryan, Carmen's father, touched his daughter's arm.

"We believe you, Carmen."

Ryan looked as sad as Susan.

"But you should believe me..." She paused. "Hold on a second. Did you just say that you believed me? How is it possible? Even I'm having a hard time believing what I just saw."

Carmen was still out of breath. Susan embraced her. She sounded tearful.

"I didn't know they would come so soon. She's only sixteen."

Carmen quickly left her mother's arms.

"What are you talking about?"

A teardrop set free and fell down Susan's cheek. They headed to the living room together and sat down. Carmen was still waiting for an answer, but no one said anything. Silence dominated the house, but Carmen needed to learn the truth. So many strange things had happened to her since the morning but now to top it all, her mother and father were keeping a secret from her.

"Will you tell me what you're talking about?"

At that moment, the door rang. Ryan went to open the door. There was a young man standing in front of him. He had dark hair, brown eyes and a fair complexion. He had a shapely and handsome face.

"Hello, I am Anka's water emerald. You must be her family?"

A big frown appeared on Ryan's face.

"Yes," he said, forcing himself.

Ron extended his hand.

"I'm Ron."

"Hi, Ron. C'mon in," Ryan said, shaking his hand.

Ron came in and directly headed toward the living room. As soon as Ron came in, Carmen pointed at him.

"That was the boy who was controlling the water with his hand!"

She couldn't hide the astonishment in her voice. When Ron came in, Susan talked while her voice was trembling.

"Have you come to take her?"

Ron nodded in consent. Although he was surprised that Anka's parents knew who he was, he didn't show it.

"Yes, ma'am. I'm grateful you've protected her for all these years, but now I have to take her back."

Carmen couldn't believe what she was hearing. She couldn't fathom what they were talking about.

"Just a second here. I'm not going anywhere," Carmen said, objecting.

Ron sat on a vacant seat. His outfit belonged to Middle Ages, so he certainly didn't fit well in this modern-day house setting. It was actually bizarre that he was sitting on a modern chair. Everybody in the room could see it. He stared at his surroundings for a second but then he directed his gaze at Carmen. She was the reason he was here.

"I know this is hard for you, but you have to come with me to Crictus." Carmen looked blankly. A pregnant moment and Ron felt the urge to explain.

"Your planet."

Carmen burst into impulsive laughter. In the meantime, Ryan went to Susan, sat next to her and hugged her.

"Say what? Are you saying I'm an alien?"

Cause that would explain a lot, she thought to herself sarcastically.

Ron pretended he was contemplating in a know-it-all manner.

"Yes, I certainly think so."

"Well, I've never heard anything so ridiculous in my entire life," Carmen said and continued. "It's obvious you are one, but you're dead wrong about me."

As she was saying that, she moved her hands the way Ron moved his when he brought the water out of the ground.

"Mom, Dad, tell him something," Carmen said, looking at her parents.

Ron turned his gaze to Susan and Ryan.

"You haven't told her yet, have you?"

"Told me what?" Carmen jumped in.

Ryan stirred a little in his seat.

"Carmen, we've been waiting for the right moment to tell you this. We should've told you earlier, but we couldn't find the courage to do it. I think it's time for you to learn now."

Carmen felt that she was running out of patience. Her mother continued the talk. Her eyes were filled with tears.

"Do you remember we once told you we couldn't have children and then we had you after many attempts...?"

Susan wiped her tears. Carmen had the feeling that something bad was coming. Ryan continued.

"Yes, we had a baby after so many attempts, Carmen, and that baby was... not you."

The room was completely quiet. Carmen couldn't believe what she was hearing. She could barely speak. She was having a hard time breathing and felt that her tears were about to pour down.

"It wasn't me? Then who was that baby?" Ryan responded.

"That baby… died just after Susan gave birth. We lost it."

Carmen was looking at her mother and then her father with questioning eyes.

"Once we were out of the hospital and came back home, we found the most beautiful baby in the world left at our doorstep. You were a gift to us."

Carmen leaned back, trying hard to breathe. It was hard to take in what she just heard, and she didn't want to believe. She took a deep breath and put her hand on her face.

"No, it can't be. Tell me it's not true!" she said, looking at her parents in despair. Was she adopted? Had she been living a lie all those years? She wished her parents would tell her they were joking but they maintained their reticence. Her mother was silently weeping in her father's arms.

"Then where is my real family?"

It was really hard for Carmen to say this.

"We looked for them. We searched all the birth records but we couldn't find any trace of either you or your parents. Then, a woman started to haunt our dreams. She told us many things about who you were, what you were, and that you were only entrusted to us, and when the time came, you would return to your true task and where you belonged."

Carmen gave them an incredulous look.

"You saw her in your dreams?"

"Yes," Susan said, her eyes and face were moist.

"Juliet…"

It was Ron who spoke. As soon as she heard that name, Carmen recalled her dreams in which there was a beautiful woman with brown hair and dark brown eyes, wearing a white and gold dress. This was what she said when she first saw her in her dream…

Hello, my daughter. I'm Juliet… Your mother…

Carmen's eyes filled with tears. She looked at Ron.

"The woman you saw in your dreams was Carmen's real Mother, Juliet. The previous Anka," Ron said.

"But…" Carmen gulped.

"At first, we didn't believe it either. We thought it was just a dream…"

Susan completed Ryan's words.

"But then we realized we were having the same dreams over and over again." She looked at Ryan when she said, "We were even in the same dream once."

It was clear that she was not feeling at ease with magical events.

"Juliet tried everything to convince us," Ryan added.

"This can't be…" Carmen was shaking her head.

Susan went over to Carmen and embraced her.

"I don't care. I might not be the one who gave birth to you, but you're still my daughter."

Carmen couldn't believe what was happening. Her world had turned upside down in a single day. After Susan let go of Carmen, Ryan continued to talk.

"She haunted our dreams and told us where you had come from and who you really were." He stopped.

Ron continued the talk. He was looking directly at Carmen. "You came to life at Anka's castle in the capital of Crictus."

Carmen stood up in revolt.

"All of this is a bunch of nonsense… How could you expect me to believe in what you just say! You can't just come here as you please and tell me that I'm an alien!" Carmen spilled all her hatred out on Ron, and then turned to her parents. "And you can't expect me to believe in a stupid dream! This is absolutely daft!"

Ron looked into Carmen's eyes. They were full of rage. He talked in his calmest voice.

"Please calm down and have a seat. I'm going to explain everything."

2

SIXTEEN YEARS EARLIER – PLANET CRICTUS

Shouting voices were emanating from within the castle as screams ricocheted off its walls. Juliet was fighting for her life in her chamber. Her fire emerald, Caleb, was waiting for her outside the room. It was frustrating to wait at the moment. He couldn't endure Juliet's suffering. Juliet's husband, Richard, was outside as well, pacing up and down in front of the door.

"Almost there, my queen, one last push…" the midwife said.

Juliet pushed with all her strength one final time and all of a sudden, her agony ended. A cry was heard. It was the voice of a little princess. However, Juliet passed out before she could take the baby in her arms. She was hemorrhaging heavily. The midwife inside shouted.

"The queen has fainted!"

Another healer went inside to intervene immediately. Richard and Caleb also couldn't endure it any longer and went in as well. The midwife took the baby to her father.

"Congratulations, My Lord, you have a beautiful daughter."

The Father looked at his daughter and said, "Later…" Then, he approached his wife. Anka Juliet was in agonizing pain. The midwife whisked the baby quickly off to the baby's room and left her alone there to attend to Juliet. Anka Juliet's life was certainly more important than anyone's life, but a baby shouldn't have been left so defenseless.

Anka Juliet finally opened her eyes three days later. Caleb was waiting by her side.

"Juliet, you're awake!" Caleb practically shouted out. Anka Juliet smiled slightly and tried to straighten up a little. She was still in pain.

"Where is my baby?"

Caleb suddenly became serious and tried to get Anka Juliet to sit down.

"You haven't recovered yet. She is fine," he said.

Caleb had been Juliet's guardian emerald for five years. He had protected her since she became the Anka and hadn't lied to her even once. So, it wasn't long before Anka Juliet sensed Caleb was lying.

"Is there a trouble?" There was a note of dread in her voice. Caleb gave Juliet a furtive look. Juliet repeated persistently.

"Caleb, I want to see my baby."

Caleb was looking at Juliet hesitantly. Juliet straightened up in fear.

"Where is my baby?"

Caleb wavered.

"You need to rest."

"Caleb! I want to see my daughter right now."

Juliet's voice was panicky. Caleb remained reticent.

"What happened to her? Did she…" Juliet felt that she was breathless for a moment.

Caleb put his hand on her arm.

"No. She's alive, but you need to rest."

"I want to see her now. Bring my daughter to me."

Caleb gritted his teeth. He didn't want to say anything that would upset her.

"I can't."

Juliet looked at Caleb with questioning eyes. Caleb didn't know how to tell her. He spoke, keeping his voice calm.

"They took her."

Juliet hastily straightened up in fear.

"Who?"

"The Soul Hunter."

Horrified, Juliet tried to get up as Caleb tried to placate her.

"Juliet, please be calm. Richard is trying to find them."

Juliet started sobbing.

"What if they do something to her… I need to find her, Caleb. Please let me go."

Caleb spoke, trying to calm her down. He was having hard time restraining Juliet.

"No, you have to rest. You are still in recovery and the Soul Hunter's only goal in kidnapping her is to attract you to him. I'll never allow this."

Juliet answered sullenly.

"You can't force me to stay here. As my emerald, I'm ordering you to do your job and leave me."

"I'm sorry, Anka, but today you will obey my orders. My duty is to protect you. The Soul Hunter only wants your soul, namely the Anka itself… If he captures it, this will end everything. Now please be calm and try to rest."

Juliet tried to calm herself. She knew that Caleb was right, but she was hurting deep inside. Her daughter was in the hands of her enemy. After a while, she calmed down. Caleb had managed to sedate her with a hug. Juliet stopped struggling in his arms. She leaned backwards hopelessly. When Caleb was sure that she was calm, he stood up.

"I'm going to see Richard. I'll be back in a few hours. Wait for me here. We'll find her." Before leaving the room, he looked at Juliet once more. "Please don't do anything stupid."

For the last couple of hours, Juliet merely sat and stared up at the room's ceiling. It was hard for her not to do anything stupid. She wanted to find her daughter and kill that abominable man, but she was powerless and had no idea where to go. She trusted Richard and Caleb to find her daughter. Still, having her hands tied was driving her nuts. Her three-day old baby… In the hands of her enemy… Defenseless… Juliet was about to go insane, so she tried to free her mind from such thoughts. At that very moment, she heard that voice.

Anka… Anka…

Juliet intently listened to the whispering voice of her stone. She used its potent magic to call someone. When your name was read on the stone, it summoned you and you would simply obey the voice without being able to resist. A content smile appeared on Juliet's face knowing she would reunite with her baby. Without further ado, she stood up and began heading to the spot where the voice emerged from the forest situated at the rear of the castle. Juliet used the secret tunnels to come out of the castle then started walking toward the forest. Caleb sauntered into her room just as Juliet had reached the forest.

He rushed back out of the room, screaming, "No!"

He questioned those who had seen Juliet, trying to track her down. By then, Juliet had reached the whispering stone. She picked it up off the ground and regained her wits with the sudden shock wave. Looking around, she noticed a relatively large lake to her side. The Soul Hunter and his assistants were on opposite sides. The Soul Hunter was holding Juliet's baby.

"Edmund…"

Juliet said this name in disgust.

"I'm glad to see you, too, Anka," Edmund said to Juliet.

Juliet looked at her baby, who was gazing about in curiosity. She had the face of an angel. Juliet felt a pang inside.

"Leave her be. I am the one you want."

Edmund looked at the baby.

"Yes, you are right, but I would really love to taste the soul of this little one. She is strong. I can feel her soul."

Juliet clenched her fists.

"If you touch her, I'll make you regret the day you were born."

Edmund looked at Juliet in defiance.

"How does it feel to fear the loss of your family?" Juliet was despondent. "You slaughtered my entire family, all my acquaintances. I'm the only one left of my kind. It was a mistake to keep me alive. Finally, I'm gonna make you pay for your sins."

Juliet darted forward.

"Your family threatened me, they wanted to take my soul. I had no choice…"

Juliet had all the Soul Hunters killed off to protect Anka's soul. During her reign, Juliet's only problem had been the Soul Hunters. That's because Inca was imprisoned in a grave many years ago and it was very difficult to get out from there.

"They were my family!" Edmund roared. A pregnant moment. Edmund continued to talk, looking at the baby in his arms: "How would you feel if I took your family from you now, too?" Lightning flashed in Edmund's eyes.

"I'm begging you. Please let her go."

Juliet was truly pleading. A grin appeared on Edmund's face.

"I will leave her, but as you may surmise, I get something in return."

Juliet gulped.

"Whatever you want." She knew exactly what he wanted.

There was a cruel tone in Edmund's voice.

"I want Anka."

Soul Hunters could only survive by stealing other people's souls. All the souls they collected would help them become much more omnipotent. Exceptionally strong and old souls like Anka and Inca would make a Soul Hunter unassailable.

Juliet didn't intend to give her soul to him.

She exclaimed. "I can't do that," shaking her head.

Edmund looked at the baby in his arms.

"It's a pity." He raised his hand slightly and started to move it over the baby.

"Such an innocent soul," he mumbled.

Juliet could no longer endure it.

"Stop! Please. I will give you what you want."

Edmund looked at Juliet smiling.

"Here's the answer I've been waiting for…"

He put the baby down, raised his hand, and moved it as if he was pulling something out of Juliet. Juliet looked at the baby on the ground one final time. She suddenly felt a terrible pain and collapsed to her knees. Just then, as a big fireball crashed down upon him, Edmund lost control, and his clothing caught fire. This was the work of the fire emerald Caleb. He quickly went to Juliet and helped her get to her feet. Having just recovered, Juliet stood up.

"My baby!"

She rushed over and picked up her baby.

"Let's get out of here!"

After Caleb had tossed fire over Edmund's men one last time, he started running with Anka and her baby with all his might. Edmund threw himself into the lake to douse the fire.

"What are you waiting for! Go and catch them!" he ordered his men as he walked out of the lake.

Juliet was running with her baby as fast as she could. Caleb looked behind him to see what was happening. Just then, an arrow struck him on the right side of his chest, throwing him down.

"Caleb!"

Juliet's cry reverberated in the forest.

"Run Anka! Run!"

"No, I won't leave you!"

As she said this, she leaned over Caleb, grabbed the arrow and yanked it out of his chest. Caleb struggled fiercely not to scream. She then helped him to stand up and tried to carry him, wrapping her hand around his waist. By then, the Soul Hunter caught up with them, and used all his might to focus on Juliet. Juliet uttered a scream and let go of Caleb. The baby had started to cry upon her mother's scream. Juliet fell on her knees and calmly laid her baby on the ground. Both she and her baby were still screaming. Then, Juliet's scream stopped suddenly as her lifeless body dropped to the ground. Anka—Juliet's soul—was now suspended in the air. Fire emerald Caleb had almost blacked out due to the pain. But upon seeing Anka in the air, he expended all his energy with a desperate effort to shoot Edmund. While Edmund was distracted, Anka broke free from the air for a moment and got inside the only body, the purest, most impartial body where it could take refuge, that of Juliet's baby. The baby's cries grew more incessant. She must have been hurt. Normally, Anka was supposed to enter an adult's body, but these circumstances were different. It was perilous for Anka to wander near a Soul Hunter in the form of a soul. Caleb touched the baby, and using his ability to change dimensions, possessed only by Anka, Anka's emeralds, and Inca, he sent her to Earth.

"No!"

This was Edmund. Spitting nails, he was looking at Caleb. Caleb grinned with the contentment of having saved Anka.

"What did you just do?"

"I sent Anka somewhere you can never reach. It is safe now."

With a terrifying expression on his face, Edmund sauntered toward Caleb, who was lying on the ground.

"But you are not safe."

"I don't care. Take my soul. I won; you couldn't lay your hands on Anka."

Caleb was acting courageous, but he knew his end was nigh. Even though he lost Juliet despite everything, he had managed to keep her soul and baby alive. As an emerald, he had completed his mission of safeguarding. Caleb was breaking out in a cold sweat as he had lost a lot of blood.

Edmund said, "I don't need your miserable soul, but your heart will just do fine," and deftly removed Caleb's heart in the blink of an eye with a stiletto. Caleb's terrible screams ended soon after.

Edmund examined the crimson, blood-soaked emerald intently. The emerald's glow died down. Edmund smiled faintly and turned to his back.

"Now let's march to the castle and take what's mine."

3

TODAY – CRICTUS

Ron approached the log cabin in the forest. He knocked on the door three times, waited, and knocked three more times. The door opened.

"Brother."

Ron tousled his younger brother's hair. An agile boy at the age of fifteen, Mason was three years younger than him. Although they looked remarkably alike on the exterior, they had entirely divergent personalities.

Releasing his brother, Mason said, "You've managed to come back." They went in together. It was small and dusty inside. The old man inside was Ron's grandfather. He was almost ninety years old, and Ron and Mason were entrusted to him.

"I'm home. Hi Grandpa…" Ron said, smiling. The old man nodded. He had never liked what Ron was doing. Not caring for his grandfather's standoffish behavior, Ron turned to Mason, who looked excited.

"So, tell me, how many people have you beaten?" he said, whispering. He didn't want his grandfather to hear it.

"A lot of people. Mason, I told you I can't count it."

Mason's eyes got bigger.

"Wow."

Ron leaned forward and got closer to his ear.

"I'm going again soon. We're going to blow up one of the Soul Hunter's armories." He paused. "Of course, after taking what's inside first…"

A fascinated Mason was listening to his brother. After a while, he was startled as if something had come to his mind.

"Ron, they say that Inca is back. Are you planning to do something?"

"Yes, but neither the emeralds nor Anka are around, and we don't know how to beat Inca."

Seeing how disappointed Mason was, Ron added, "But we'll definitely find a way."

Mason slightly smiled. Ron was about to stand up, when Mason stopped him.

"Ron…"

"Yes?"

"I wish I could come with you today."

Ron touched his brother's shoulder.

"You stay with Grandpa. Take care of him."

Mason turned up his nose. He wanted to imitate Ron, but his grandfather had told him it was too dangerous. Ron was a rebel. He was from the group who rejected being dominated by the Soul Hunter and believed the castle where the Soul Hunter had been living for the past sixteen years belonged to Anka. The throne was empty as neither Anka nor Inca was around. The throne was the Soul Hunter's right as he was the one who had killed Anka and the last fire emerald. While Ron and people who thought like him believed that the Soul Hunter could not stake a claim on the throne, these people were in the minority. Most people thought that the last Soul Hunter, Edmund, was the most powerful person after Anka and Inca, and the absence of Anka and Inca made Edmund a king. Nowadays there was a rumor going around that Inca was back, which was deeply undermining Edmund's authority. Ron and other rebels wanted to give the throne back to Anka, who was living on Earth without a clue as to who she was or the power she had inside herself. That's why she couldn't come back. The only way was if she were to be brought back by an emerald. Nevertheless, the last Soul Hunter had killed off the last emerald sixteen years ago. Still, Ron and people with similar thoughts never gave up, and they would never give up on Anka. So, they were at constant war with Edmund.

Ron's grandfather didn't want him involved in dangerous activities, but Ron was on Anka's side, and would even risk his life for this cause.

Ron lived in the Crictus capital, Zirkus, where Anka's castle was located, and his name was mentioned in every attack made against the castle. As one of the rebel leaders, his reputation was known by one and all.

That day, after saying farewell to his family, Ron headed toward the secret headquarters. He along with the other rebels set out after they completed the plan on how to infiltrate the armory in detail. They decided to attack in the morning, as there would be fewer security guards then. Located a few miles from the castle, the armory had extraordinary security measures in place. The day was a big advantage for them. Hiding behind the bushes, Ron was counting the number of guards. They needed to get the job done without making a sound. If they made any noise, the plan would be in jeopardy. Moving forward with a few people, Ron crouched behind other bushes. Waiting for one of the guards to approach the bushes, Ron knocked him unconscious by throwing a stone at his head.

"I'm going in," Ron whispered. As soon as he said that, he ducked out from the bushes and went into the armory. The armory looked like a normal wooden house. Sunlight penetrating the woods was enough to lighten the interior of the armory. Inside were hundreds of chests stacked on top of each other. Ron went over to one of the chests and opened it. He noticed it held more than a hundred swords. A smile spread across his face. Just then, he leapt up with the blare of a siren. Shouts were coming from outside. The door flew open with a powerful kick blow. Ron instantly began defending himself with a sword he grabbed from the chest. Managing to deal the attacking guard a few blows, he then went out. Most of his friends were fighting the guards, but some of them had already lost the struggle. Ron quickly sprang to their defense but then had to duck behind a tree due to an attack coming from above. He looked at his other friends. The arrows were raining from the roof of the two-story armory.

"We need to get out of here! There are too many of them!"

This was Ron's friend, Eddie. Although Ron didn't want to listen to him, he did what Eddie told him.

With the order of "Retreat!" all the rebels began running for their lives into the forest. Ron and Eddie sprinted in the same direction. Two archers and two guards were in hot pursuit. They were almost darting behind the trees in order to escape the arrows. The chase went on until they came to a clearing, where an arrow found Eddie's back. Ron had no choice but to continue running without looking. At the end of the clearing, there was a cliff and an old bridge to cross over to the other side. He was about to head for the bridge when he looked behind. It was his end. An arrow hit his heart. Ron stopped. He was right on the edge of the cliff. He collapsed to the ground and pulled out the arrow lodged in his heart with all his might. He was hemorrhaging as he lay writhing on the ground. A guard approached and leaned over him.

"Let's see where you'll escape now."

He had a disgusting grin, and his breath smelled foul.

"Go to hell!" Ron said with his last breath.

"What shall we do with him?" said another one behind him.

The archer said, "Let's just throw him down."

The guard towering over Ron spoke, "Good idea."

As he said this, he gave Ron's belly a swift kick and he started to fall down the cliff, groaning. The cliff was not so high and there was still water below. Ron dropped at a great pace and crashed into the water. He was still alive, as the cliff was too low for him to impact the water like a chunk of concrete. He didn't resist after crashing into the water. He was already in horrific pain as he started to sink. As he reached his demise, he never supposed he would die during an uprising but sure enough, it was happening as he continued sinking. He could no longer breathe, and he didn't have the energy to attempt swimming up to the surface. His pulse had slowed, and his eyes were closing. Just then, he noticed a glow from beneath the water. *How nice...* he thought. It was a *light blue emerald,* and it was shining. Ron was descending onto it. The emerald glowed brighter as Ron approached it. Ron looked at the emerald one last time and started to close his eyes. He was now ready for death. At that moment, his body fell over the emerald. The emerald shone with a glow illuminating all the water. The emerald was superheated, and Ron could feel the warmth in every inch of his body. All of a sudden, Ron felt a terrible pain he had never felt before. Hopelessly screaming under the water, his lungs were filled with water. While his entire body convulsed with pain, the emerald slowly burned his skin and prepared itself to replace his heart. The pain was excruciating. Meanwhile on Earth, Carmen, who was in her math class, simultaneously felt the same pain, not knowing what was happening. *Thus, a new emerald was born.*

Looking down at the water, the guards standing next to the cliff couldn't believe their eyes. The water was lighting up everything. A beam of blue light reached the sky instantly. Everybody saw the light that broke the sky apart. In his castle, the Soul Hunter also saw the birth of a new emerald.

Suddenly, water began rushing up at full speed. The guards drew back in fear. On top of the water was Ron, whom they had just thrown over the cliff. Ron raised his hands and directed the water at the guards with all his force. The water completed its mission by swallowing up the guards, then quietly reverted back to its previous shape. Shortly afterwards, Ron found himself on the ground out of breath. He placed his hand over his heart, which was still beating. He could only figure out what had happened after a while. His heart had been replaced with the water emerald. *He was now one of the new guardians of Anka.* The first one in sixteen years.

Soaked to the skin, he was barely able to straighten up. Looking around, it was difficult to believe what had just transpired. He smiled softly. His soft smile soon turned into a chuckle. He was totally in high spirits. He stood up with difficulty and headed home. It was now time to find Anka and bring her back to Crictus. Everything was starting anew.

THE DAY BEFORE – CRICTUS

The Soul Hunter's brother Derick was sitting in his room. He was nearly twenty-eight years old and he truly hated his brother. He wasn't a Soul Hunter like his elder brother Edmund as he didn't have such genes. That's why he always considered himself a useless person. He cringed when he heard a knock on the door. A servant came in.

"My Lord, King Edmund has summoned you."

Derick got up, grumbling, and went off to see his brother. Being obliged to go to see him when summoned was something he could hardly deal with, but he went to see him anyway. After all, he was the king and the most powerful person on Crictus.

"You called for me."

Edmund looked at Derick.

"Yes… I couldn't decide what to wear for the ball I'm going to host this weekend. You know, merchants from all the cities are coming. As their king, I must be presentable."

Derick glanced at the two outfits smoothly laid out on the bed.

"You summoned me here for this?"

Edmund shrugged. Then, he looked treacherously. "That is, of course, if you've got nothing else to do."

Derick knitted his brows. Edmund treating him like a useless person bugged him to no end. He wanted to become an important person too. He wanted to rule Crictus and be a king, as well. But this was impossible while Edmund was still alive, and Derick's hands were tied. Derick turned his nose up. He spoke, showing the outfit he didn't like.

"Wear this."

Edmund looked at the outfit.

"You have such terrible taste," he said.

Derick gritted his teeth. He got a few steps closer to Edmund.

"You know what, Edmund? No matter what you wear, you still can't hide your repulsiveness."

Edmund knitted his brows. Derick was more handsome and younger than Edmund. The nearly fifty-year-old Edmund had grown so ugly that no woman would want him. Without waiting for an answer from Edmund, Derick went out of the chamber, got out of the castle, and began walking straight toward the forest. He couldn't bear to stand in his brother's presence or his castle one more second. While walking, he muttered to himself.

"He thinks I don't have anything to do, that I have bad taste. Who does he think he is, anyway? He's just an ugly soul sucker!"

As it was getting dark outside, Derick kept walking, but he had no intention of going back. The truth was, if he vanished today, no one would have missed him. That's why he was going to go back eventually. By now he had reached the end of the forest and was still walking. Night had fallen and Derick had been walking without a break for a long time. Again muttering, he took his revenge by kicking a stone on the ground. The stone flew fast, struck something in the air then fell to the ground. Derick was petrified to see the stone he kicked hit something invisible in the air. He looked around and wanted to make sure that what he saw wasn't a figment of his imagination. He picked up a stone and tossed it in the same direction. This stone also hit something in the air and fell to the ground. Derick gawked at the space in astonishment. He headed over in that direction cautiously and reached out his hand in fear. In doing so, he felt he had touched something. The thing he touched suddenly became visible. When Derick got scared and retracted his hand, it disappeared again. Derick touched it once more. This was a door. It was an enormous double door with golden script on it. He couldn't read the script. This was the ancient Anka language. It was one of the first languages spoken on Crictus. He went on touching the door and decided to give it an inward push. The door seemed quite heavy. This time Derick heaved at it with all his strength. The door opened slowly. Derick hesitantly took a step and went in. Behind it was a long staircase that descended to the ground. While Derick was very curious about what was inside, on the other hand, a fear welled up inside him. He looked hesitantly at the forest behind him. One thing was for sure and that was he had no desire to return to the castle. He was tired of being regarded as useless. He looked at the stairs. At least he had nothing to lose. He started to go down the stairs. It was stifling inside. It was as if nobody had visited for centuries. He cringed when he heard the door closing after him. He was caught in a trap. It was pitch-black all around him, but he continued his way into the unknown. He was breathing heavily. He was about to faint because of the stuffiness. Touching the walls, he was going down by making his way blindly. The ground was slippery. As he descended, he saw a light. After continuing a little further, he reached downstairs and was taken aback when he saw a grave in front of him. There was nothing else around it. He approached the grave cautiously. There was a glass coffin on top of the marble stone in the center of the small chamber. There was dust on the glass coffin. He removed the dust layer gently with his hand and took a step back when he made eye contact with the black soul in it. The soul looked very terrifying; it was flying like black smoke in the glass coffin. Apparently, it was trapped. Even though the black smoke was frightening, Derick couldn't help but to feel drawn to it. He thought, perhaps he should try to save it, but the thought was not his own thought. He stepped toward the coffin as if the black smoke had power over him. The soul was moving in the glass coffin. He hesitantly put his hand on it. The soul was writhing as if trying to reach Derick. It headed toward Derick's hand. Derick was looking at the soul incredulously.

Ozve tue…*

(Save me…)

Startled, he whipped his hand back. He couldn't believe the voice he heard. The soul had spoken to him. It was incredible. Derick paused for a moment. He wasn't sure whether he should open the glass coffin or not. For some reason, Derick wanted to help it. The soul was writhing in the glass coffin, trying to get out. Derick took a deep breath. He didn't know if what he was doing was right, but he still held the handle of the coffin and tugged it with all his might. The lid of the glass coffin suddenly fell down. The soul inside was freed. The soul shuffled to and fro like crazy inside the tomb. Derick watched in horror as the soul revolving madly around him. A second later, it entered Derick's mouth. Derick was breathless. He soon found himself on the floor. He opened his eyes in fear. It took some time to understand what happened. He could only stand up after some time. Getting to his feet, he looked at his hands. He was feeling different. He made a fist with his hands. A big smile extended on his face. He now knew what he had just done. *He had just set Inca free, and Inca had chosen him.*

Derick went straight back to the castle and went up to Edmund's room right away.

As soon as he saw Derick, Edmund started to scold him.

"Where the hell were you!"

Derick was grinning without paying any attention to him. He went near Edmund. Edmund's eyes suddenly widened.

"Can you feel it?" Edmund was looking at his brother in astonishment.
"This can't be."

"But it happened, brother. Now I am the chosen one" Derick said.

Edmund had felt the soul inside Derick. When one of two of the most powerful souls on Crictus was next to him, it was impossible for a Soul Hunter not to feel it. Inca's return changed everything. This would undermine Edmund's authority. But he knew his brother well and he knew his weaknesses, as well. He could use him before capturing Inca. After remaining quiet for a while, a smile appeared on Edmund's face. He put his hand on his brother's arm.

"Now we'll really have fun…"

TODAY – CRICTUS

King Edmund was absolutely livid, seeing the blue light beam ascending to the sky. He had to see his brother right now but this time he didn't have the chance to summon him like before. Derick was now Inca. He was one of the oldest eternal souls. He had to get on well and, like it or not, even collaborate with him. He still couldn't grasp how an invisible, immortal soul could choose his useless brother, Derick.

Quickly passing through the corridors, he entered Derick's chamber.

"To what do I owe this visit?"

"The water emerald is back," Edmund said at once.

Derick straightened up on bed. This drew his interest. He was chosen by Inca only a day ago. The unexpected arrival of the water emerald couldn't have been just a coincidence. *Mighty Phoenix plays with faith*, he thought to himself. Derick was suddenly alarmed.

"What should I do?"

It was to Edmund's benefit that Derick was unaware of the extent of his powers and had poor planning skills.

"Now, it's time to find and kill Anka. You must kill her before the water emerald reaches her."

"How will I do this?"

Derick said this while Edmund took a crystal stone out of his pocket. He went over to Derick and gave it to him.

"The whispering stone…" Derick said.

"Yes. When you whisper Anka's name to this stone, it will bring Anka to you."

Derick turned the stone over and over. He found it strange that Derick gave him such a valuable stone. He too was powerful now. Edmund touched his brother's shoulder slightly.

"Now brother, go to Earth, find Anka and kill her. That way, Anka will never be able to return. But remember, this might be the only chance you find her defenseless. We have to take advantage of the situation."

Edmund was right. If the body that Anka had borrowed died on Earth, it wouldn't be possible for Anka to enter another body, and its soul would be entrapped on Earth. That's because Anka could only enter someone from Crictus.

4

TODAY – EARTH

"What? Am I a queen?"

Carmen still couldn't wrap her mind around what was happening and what Ron told her. There was no way anyone would believe this malarkey anywhere anyhow.

Ron repeated himself.

"Yes, Carmen, for the tenth time, you're a queen."

"But I don't get it. What will happen now?"

"I'm going to take you to Crictus and give you back your kingdom."

"Crictus is your planet, isn't it?"

"Yes, Carmen, it's my planet."

Ron was getting mighty frustrated by now. For the last few hours, he had been trying to explain to Anka that she was Anka.

"That's fascinating," said Carmen, slightly knitting her brows.

Ron clapped his hands.

"Yes, it is. Can we go now?"

"Wait a minute… I'm not going anywhere. I have a life here."

She looked at her mother. Her eyes were swollen since she had cried her heart out. Then, she remembered that she wasn't her real Mother. Carmen didn't know what to feel or how to behave. Finding out that she was adopted didn't change her feelings toward them in any way. Yes, she was miffed with them. They should have told her earlier she was adopted, but despite everything, they had brought Carmen up for so long. Even if they weren't her biological parents, they were still her real parents.

"I can't just leave my parents, my friends, everything and run off to the unknown."

"Carmen, if we don't leave now, Inca will find us, and I might not be able to protect your parents. You have to do this for your parents," said Ron.

Carmen looked sadly at her family. Then, she turned her gaze to Ron. *Going with a stranger…* she thought. *Finally, getting away from here… But should it be like that?* Carmen was wrestling with her thoughts. It was quite hard to believe what she had experienced a few hours ago, but she herself witnessed what had happened. There really was a light coming out of that man's hand, and it hurt a lot. The handsome young boy with dark hair sitting across from her could really control water. The crystal rock really called her in a language she didn't know, and she could remember the woman in her dreams, Juliet. She had been a witness to all of this. On the other hand, she couldn't help thinking it was a camera prank. Even if it wasn't so, this boy was asking for something impossible from her: going to another planet! Who would accept such an offer? It was inconceivable! What a bunch of nonsense! There was a so-called planet named Crictus…

Carmen sulked.

"I can't do this!"

Everyone in the room looked at each other. Ron didn't know what to say. He had to convince her. It wasn't safe here for Anka.

"Carmen, if you stay here, you will risk your own life and, more importantly, your family's life. Look, you saw the man in the forest. He's ready to do anything to achieve his goal, and his only goal is to kill you," Carmen gulped. Ron continued, "If you stay here, I'll stay, too, and do anything in my power to protect you, but he will go to all lengths to reach you too." With his head, Ron pointed at Carmen's family. "And that includes killing your parents."

Carmen's eyes got bigger. She looked at her family with fearful eyes. She couldn't lose them. She couldn't imagine that they would die, or that they would die because of her.

"You don't want that to happen, do you?"

Carmen looked at Ron. Shaking her head, she said, "No."

"Then, you've got to come with me."

"Hey, you don't understand. I can't just leave my life here behind at a moment's notice and wander off like that. I haven't finished school yet. I have a life here and you expect me to toss it all away, come with you to a world that I'm not even sure really exists, embark on adventures and become a queen. Doesn't it all sound a bit insane to you, too?"

She sounded mocking. Her mockery always came into play in serious situations.

Ron sighed.

"I know, what I want from you is very difficult. But if you stay here…"

"I get it, it's dangerous," Carmen interrupted Ron.

"Look, coming with me now doesn't mean that you can't return here. If you don't like it, if you don't want to stay there, you'll always have the chance to come back. Whenever you want, you can visit here."

He was speaking in his most serious tone of voice. Of course, Ron wasn't exactly serious about all that he said. When Carmen became the queen, she would have to stay on Crictus. She would be able to visit Earth, but she would have to live on Crictus. In fact, he was sure that Carmen would love Crictus. The only hitch was to convince her to go there. He thought that knowing she had the chance to come back to Earth anytime would put her at ease. And he was right.

Carmen knitted her brows.

"I can come back here any time, right?"

"Of course."

Carmen looked at her parents desperately. It was too much. Everything was changing so fast.

Meanwhile, Ron was looking at Carmen's parents, and begging for help from them with his eyes.

Ron spoke, "Think of it as if you were getting away from here for some time. Like you were going to a different place in the world."

Susan spoke, "Anyways, you've always said you wanted to get away from this town and see other places."

Carmen grimaced. "Do you want me to go?"

Susan started to cry again. Ryan spoke, hugging Susan.

"We knew this day would come. We were prepared for this."

Carmen looked at her crying Mother, making a face.

"Looks like you were not so prepared after all."

Ron broke into the conversation with Carmen's weak attempt at cracking a joke.

"Carmen, you need to make a decision now. Time is of the essence. We must go to Crictus soon."

Carmen gulped.

"So, it will be to protect my family, right?"

"Yes," said Ron quickly.

"And I can come back *anytime* I want?"

"Yes."

"What about school?" Carmen said, looking at her father.

"Don't worry, we'll handle that."

Carmen sighed. She didn't want to leave her parents and friends behind. But she also sort of wanted to. She was confused. Her dream was to get away from this town and travel the world. Now she had the opportunity. But she would travel to another planet, not around the world. She laughed nervously. All that was happening was nonsense. Still, she could think of it as a vacation. Besides, she would become a queen. She gave Ron a quick look.

"I'll be able to come back whenever I want, right?" she asked again.

Ron knew he was finally close to persuading her.

"Yes. You can come here whenever you miss your parents and friends."

"But wouldn't it be dangerous?"

Ron shrugged.

"Since Inca knows that you're here right now, Earth is dangerous. If he thinks you're on Crictus, there won't be much risk when you visit here. I still wouldn't suggest you spend too much time here. I'll always be with you and protect you, but I can't protect everyone at the same time."

Carmen turned up her nose. She looked at her parents again.

"Mom? Dad?"

Susan swiftly broke loose of Ryan's arm. She hugged her daughter. She smelled her hair.

"I knew this day would come." She pushed Carmen a little away from herself. "Don't even think about us. I know it's a tough decision, but even if we don't want you to go, we know that you have to. That woman prepared us for today."

Carmen looked hesitantly at her father.

"We trust you."

Carmen smiled gently, but she still had a lot of qualms. Now she had the opportunity she had been anticipating. Finally, she could escape this ghastly town. But why was she wavering? Because she was scared, that's why. She was frightened of the unknown. But her parents trusted Ron. They approved. They would never do anything that would be bad for Carmen. If they didn't trust Ron, they would show it. Carmen was looking at them in their eyes and waiting for them to say, "Don't go," but they didn't. It was impossible to make eye contact with her mom because her eyes were beet red from crying. On the other hand, her dad seemed confident. Carmen sighed deeply. She looked at her parents one last time. Ryan touched her daughter's shoulder.

"Sweetheart, you gotta go."

"But Dad…"

"Don't worry about us. Do what you gotta do."

Carmen was stuck in dire straits. She secretly wanted to leave, but her dream was to travel the world, not to travel to a planet called Crictus, which was not even in her solar system. But she was impressed by what Ron had said and promised. Being a queen really sounded very nice. Moreover, up until this very morning, she had been complaining about how boring her life was. Now everything could be changed. Taking a deep sigh, Carmen looked at her parents. She was secretly pissed off with them, but she still didn't care. They had lied to her for all these years… Yes, it wasn't fair but now was not the time to dwell on it. She could be angry with them later. After all, they would be safe here. That was what Ron said, at least. Now she had to make a very important decision. She still couldn't believe what was happening around her. It all felt so unreal, as if someone would suddenly come up and say, "April Fools!" But if what Ron said was true, if she was really a queen, this might be the only chance she had to get away from this mundane life.

Carmen looked at Ron again. She took a deep breath.

"Okay, I'm in."

Ron suddenly jumped to his feet.

"Finally…"

Carmen looked at her parents. They both stood up and hugged their daughter.

"We'll miss you very much."

"I'll miss you, too."

Her mother was trying to wipe her tears.

"I don't care if I was adopted. You're my parents and I'll always visit you."

Carmen never thought that she would abandon them so soon, but she never imagined all of this, anyway. She turned to Ron.

"Do I need a suitcase?"

"No, I don't think so," said Ron calmly.

He was looking at Carmen's strapped blue blouse and jeans. Carmen looked at her parents, sighing. She was trying hard not to cry, but part of her was dying to go on an adventure with Ron. She couldn't make sense of that part inside her. Where did all of this come from? What was she doing? Where was she going? She felt uneasy in her heart. But strangely, a part inside her, the part she couldn't make sense of, was telling her to go. *At least, I'll have the chance to come back,* thought Carmen.

She went to Ron. Ron held Carmen's hands.

"Now I need you to focus on me."

Carmen glanced at Ron and began to scrutinize him. Ron was a really handsome guy. She hadn't realized it in all that commotion, but now that he was sitting in front of her, she noticed how attractive he was. She came to her senses when Ron admonished her.

"Carmen, please focus."

"Sorry," said Carmen, and really focused this time.

"I'll be helping you for this first time, but from now on, you will be traveling by yourself on this journey."

"What journey?"

"An interdimensional journey," said Ron as he shut his eyes.

Unable to make any sense of what he had just uttered, Carmen shut her eyes too. A dazzling light swiftly enveloped them, then Carmen opened her eyes with a sudden shudder.

Carmen's parents watched their daughter as she disappeared inside a bright light. Just then, the door rang. Puzzled, they looked at each other. Ryan cautiously approached the door. After looking through the peephole, he answered the door.

There, George was standing with a huge smile on his face.

"Good evening, sir. I am here to pick up Carmen."

Ryan just stood there and stared at him blankly, not knowing what to say.

Far away from Earth, upon opening her eyes, Carmen lost her balance with a horrendous headache and held on to Ron.

"Are you all right?"

"Yes, I think so," said Carmen and raised her head.

They were no longer in the living room. There was neither the sofa set nor the TV nor her family around them. They were in a forest. The trees were just like those on Earth.

"C'mon," said Ron.

Carmen was walking, examining what was around her.

"This place is real…" she murmured to herself.

Ron looked at her, smiling. Only after they walked together for a while, did Carmen realize they were on the side of a hill. When she suddenly raised her head, the scenery almost made her swallow her tongue. A lot of small shining houses were scattered in the forest… An enormous castle ascended to the sky like a guardian… The vast forest continued and a river behind the castle, flowing gently, quietly… Hundreds of ponds and rivers inside the forests adorning the vast hills… Carmen was looking at the scenery before her, without believing her eyes.

"Wow."

"Welcome to the capital of Crictus, the city of Zirkus, my queen."

Carmen looked at the scenery with wondrous eyes.

"It's beautiful…"

"And this is all yours …"

Unable to take her eyes away, Carmen gazed at the scenery while taking a deep breath in. The air almost felt lighter in her lungs. As if, she was meant to be here all along.

Pointing to the magnificent castle with his index finger, Ron added.

"When this is all over, that will be your home."

She was startled when she thought that enormous castle would be her home. It was incredible.

"Well, what about this Inca you mentioned? Isn't this also his home?"

"I know, there are plenty of things you're curious about. So, I'll take you to my grandpa. He'll tell you the story."

Carmen grinned slightly.

"You're going to introduce me to your grandpa? What's the rush?"

There was sarcasm in her voice.

"Excuse me?" Ron said, not understanding her joke.

Carmen sighed heavily.

"It's nothing, forget about it…"

"Let's go."

Carmen sighed. This sigh was not full of trouble but hope. She had a good feeling about this place.

They set out together. They were going directly to Ron's grandfather's cabin. It was almost dark, but there was still sunlight. Proceeding beneath the last rays of the sun, they finally arrived at the cabin.

Ron knocked on the cottage's door three times, paused then knocked three times again. It was Ron's grandfather who opened the door. The old man cracked a smile like he was smiling for the first time in years.

"What took you so long?" Then, he turned to Carmen. This time, he had a sincere expression on his face. "Welcome, Anka. It's so nice to see you again…"

Carmen knitted her brows slightly and smiled.

"This is actually the first time you're seeing me." Pretending not to hear that, the old man went inside. "He must've mixed me up with someone else," Carmen said to Ron silently.

Ron gently smiled in response and made way for her to go inside. After he scanned his surroundings, he went in after Carmen. Inside, Carmen and Ron sat around the table.

"Would you like anything to drink?"

"No, thanks," said Carmen.

The old man eyed Carmen from head to foot. He ignored her and went on to grab her a tea-like drink from the pot in the kitchen.

"You look a lot like your mother."

The smile on Carmen's face vanished.

"Did you know my mother?"

"Of course. Everybody knew her. She was our queen."

The expression on the old man's face turned to pity.

"Poor Juliet. She lost her life at such an early age."

Though she had never known her real Mother, Carmen saw her in her dreams almost every night. Of course, it was sad that a woman whom she had never known lost her life at an early age, but it was her mother in question.

"I told her how her mother was murdered, but I haven't told her the legend of Anka and Inca," said Ron.

The old man stared at Carmen with demeaning eyes.

"Such a pity. It's a terrible thing that an Anka doesn't know how great her power is…"

Carmen looked at Ron as if asking for help.

"Can you tell us, Grandpa?"

The old man put the drink in front of Carmen, slowly sat on a chair, and took a deep breath.

"Very well. Long time ago, Queen Kayra was the ruling monarch. The queen had twin sons, Anka and Inca. As Anka was born before Inca, the throne would be his birthright in the future. The two brothers grew older, and they began to fight amongst themselves. As days and months passed, the love between them dissipated to be replaced with animosity, anger, and hatred.

Other than the hatred they had for each other, the two brothers had many things in common. They both had an insatiable thirst for ambition. Both wanted to always be the best and the strongest. Both were natural-born leaders. They could never beat each other in martial arts. Apart from that, of course, they also had their differences. Anka was known as the 'good twin,' whereas Inca was called the 'evil twin.' People loved Prince Anka greatly. This would annoy and make Inca jealous of his sibling. These two power-hungry brothers also had some other characteristics in that they both could display their inner energy in ways unbeknownst to them…"

"Inca's beam of light coming out of his hand," exclaimed Carmen.

The old man gave Carmen a withering look. Carmen buried herself in her chair.

"Yes… Anyway… Where was I? Aha… These twins didn't know the source of their power, but the answer was simple." Queen Kayra was unable to conceive a child. Thus, one day she did the unspeakable. She walked into the forest. This forest wasn't any ordinary forest, but rather the one in the forbidden place *Se Uirvan, the house of the Mighty Phoenix, where he rose from his ashes over and over again till eternity.*

It was a place no one would dare to step foot. It is said that this was the deadliest place on Crictus. But Kayra dared to do this simply because she had no choice. Her aim was to find the Phoenix and plead with it. The Phoenix is known to be the master of all creatures and animals. When Kayra got tired of walking in the forest, she encountered the Phoenix and pleaded with it, "Oh, Mighty Phoenix, grant me a child…"

The Phoenix said it would be impossible without paying a price. Kayra implored it. She said she would give anything it wanted. The Phoenix agreed but had one condition in return. The newborn would be his child. Kayra accepted without hesitation.

The Phoenix touched and everything changed.

With one touch of the Phoenix's wing on her belly, Kayra got pregnant. Nine months later, she gave birth to twins, the babies touched by the Phoenix. Kayra named them Anka, and Inca.

The brothers grew up fighting each other. They were the strongest princes of Crictus. While Anka used the powers granted to him by Phoenix, for good Inca used them for evil.

Another talent given to the twins was the ability to conduct interdimensional voyages. Since the atmospheres of Earth and Crictus were very similar, Anka, Inca and the emeralds could only travel between these two planets. Anyway… Let's get back to the subject.

One day, an unfortunate event happened, and Kayra died. While most people wanted Anka to ascend the throne, there were many others who wanted Inca to become the king. However, the throne was the right of the older twin, even if he was just slightly older. So, Anka ascended the throne. Unfortunately, Inca didn't intend to remain a mere spectator. Inca mercilessly killed his brother on the day Anka ascended the throne. But the Phoenix had granted another power to the twins. The legend of the Phoenix says, it's born, it lives, it dies in fire, and it is reborn from its ashes. It's an unbeatable immortal creature. The Phoenix had granted the princes this power. It didn't make their bodies immortal, but their souls remained undead. After Anka's physical body was killed by Inca, Anka found another one to inhabit and set out to ascend the throne once again. This situation continued like this for centuries. As the two brothers killed each other, they entered other bodies and fought for the throne. Until one day. On that day Inca courageously visited his father, and made a wish to the Phoenix, "Divide Anka's power, so that I will be stronger than him, so that I can stay on the throne forever…"

At first, the Phoenix didn't accept this wish, because they were both its offspring. Then, it listened to Anka's wish, "Make such a grave for Inca's soul that, when I imprison it, it can never come out of the grave until the one who will be the carrier saves it…"

"The Phoenix reviewed both siblings' wishes. It made an invisible tomb for Inca. No one knows where it is, except the Phoenix itself. Thus, Anka got his wish, a tomb where he could put his brother to eternal sleep. But the Phoenix fulfilled both siblings' wishes, so it divided Anka's power into four separate parts and placed them into four emeralds, representing fire, water, air, and earth, and sent them to different corners on Crictus. When these emeralds are all together by Anka's side at the same time, Anka's power becomes equal to Inca's power.

Thus, the struggle between two siblings continued under these conditions..."

Carmen abruptly interrupted the old man and asked, "So, how do Anka, Inca, and the emeralds choose their carriers?"

"Good question, Anka. These immortal souls choose those who take sides with them and who never hesitate even once during their lifetime. For example, your mother... Juliet was like an Anka even before she became Anka. Anka chose her, because it had not sensed any hesitation at all in her."

"What about me? It chose me when I was just an infant. So, did it choose me because I didn't wet my pants?"

Carmen laughed lightly at her own joke, but when she saw that the old man didn't find anything amusing at all, she had to pipe down.

"No. When Anka was removed from Juliet's body, it hurriedly entered the nearest, purest body, which was you. It was pure luck it had chosen you. Normally, the sequence goes from a woman to a man, and so on. And usually... Or more precisely, it had never entered an infant's body before. So, you're pretty much the exception and an accident."

"Well, thanks..." Carmen said coldly.

Ron joined the conversation.

"You were saying how emeralds are chosen, Grandpa."

Ron looked more excited and eager than Carmen.

Carmen leaned back. The matter was interesting, but she still hated history lessons.

"Yes, you're right. Emeralds... Choosing an emerald is more difficult. An emerald doesn't go to its bearer, its bearer should go to it. This is quite difficult and a matter of random luck... As its owner approaches the emerald, it begins to shine and warm up. When the emerald touches the person it chooses, it replaces their heart. Legend has it, it is quite painful."

"It certainly was for me..." Ron said with a bitter smile.

Paying him no heed, the old man went on.

"Anka also feels this at the same time, because the emerald is a piece that was split from Anka."

Suddenly, Carmen put the puzzle pieces together. She remembered the boy she saw when she felt that terrible pain in her heart in math class today. That was Ron. Now everything was beginning to fall into place. It was that very moment when the emerald replaced Ron's heart and Carmen had felt this. Carmen looked at Ron in amazement.

"It all makes sense now."

At last, Carmen started to comprehend what was happening around her, but it was all still hard for her to believe. It all happened in a single day and apparently, the day wasn't over yet.

"The story hasn't ended young lady," said the old man harshly.

Carmen went on sitting in her place.

The old man cleared his throat slightly.

"Anyways… There are things you should know about emeralds. First of all, the emeralds are Anka's guardians. They risk their own lives to protect Anka from all danger."

Saying this, he looked at Ron. Ron nodded in agreement.

"Secondly, besides controlling the elements given by the emeralds, they have other abilities. For example, son, you can sometimes see the future on the water. The air emerald can easily hear distant voices. The earth emerald can listen to plants. The fire emerald can understand if a person is lying or not and feel close by bodies."

"We're lucky we don't have a fire emerald," said Carmen, tactlessly.

When she saw that no one laughed at her joke, she buried herself in her chair again.

The old man went on.

"Anka and Inca also have some abilities, of course. For example, Anka can see in her dreams what's happening at that very moment."

"But it's not a very beneficial skill. Everyone sleeps at night."

"Then, try sleeping in the morning," said the old man to shut Carmen up. Carmen frowned.

"Inca has a talent, too. It can walk into Anka's dreams with a special magic."

This startled Carmen.

"That's creepy."

The old man ignored Carmen again and turned to Ron.

"Is there anything else you want to learn?"

Carmen raised her hand as if she were in class.

"I do."

"Ask away."

"What do I have to do now?"

The old man sighed deeply.

"This is unacceptable. As Anka, you should already know what to do.

It is your eventual duty to destroy your enemies…"

Ron shot his grandfather a calm warning, "Grandpa please. Give her a chance…"

Grandfather turned to Carmen, somewhat patiently.

"Your purpose is to ascend to the throne again… For this, you have to remove the Soul Hunter and Inca out of your way."

"Hold on a second, the Soul Hunter? What do you mean, 'Out of my way?' What are you talking about?"

"For centuries, Soul Hunters have been chasing the most powerful souls, namely yours and Inca's souls. They are abominations created by a powerful ancient tribe, the Werth tribe, to bring down Anka and Inca's reign. Your mother managed to beat all the Soul Hunters during her time, but she missed one. The Soul Hunter who killed your mother is Edmund. He's been on the throne for the past sixteen years while you were trapped on Earth. Now you must depose him and ascend the throne. Meanwhile, Edmund is also holding the fire emerald. This prevents the fire emerald from finding a host, and thus it restricts your powers. I suggest that you recapture the fire emerald first. Then, your mission should be easier. There is a rumor in the city that Inca chose Edmund's brother, Prince Derick as a bearer. So, you must keep him out of your way by killing him."

Carmen glimpsed at the old man in bewilderment.

"Sorry but I don't know how to do all these things and when I decided to come here, no one told me that I'd be killing people."

While saying this, she didn't hold back herself from looking incriminatingly at Ron. Ron simply shrugged.

"Allow me to remind you that you bear Anka's soul. Even if it had chosen you accidentally, this doesn't change the fact you're carrying its soul, thus you are the rightful heir to the throne… And as Anka, you must complete your purpose, ascend to the Crictus throne. Your soul comes with responsibilities. That includes killing anyone that stands between you and your eventual purpose."

Carmen jumped up to her feet.

"You can't just demand that I kill people. Sorry, but I'm not a murderer."

"Anka and Inca have been doing this for centuries. You can't change your destiny. If you're not up to it, it means that you don't deserve the soul you're carrying."

"That's quite enough, Grandpa. Don't push her. She's already gone through a lot today," said Ron as he stood up. Ron's grandfather got to his feet with difficulty.

"Enough of this conversation. I shall get some rest." While he was about to enter the next room, he paused and looked at Carmen. "It was a pleasure to see you again, Anka," he said as he left the room.

Carmen looked at Ron wearily.

"Would you be offended if I said I found him annoying?"

"He is pretty annoying," said Ron, shrugging his shoulders as he grinned. Carmen responded with a smile.

"In fact, he's not always like that, but he's become grumpier as he grows older."

Both sat on their chairs again.

"How long have you been living with him?"

"I was three when my father died in a riot and two years later my mother got sick and passed away," he shrugged. "All that's left of my family are my grandfather and my younger brother Mason."

A sad expression appeared on Carmen's face.

"I'm very sorry to hear that."

Ron sighed. There was a brief silence. It was Carmen who broke the ice.

"You said your father died in a riot?"

"After Anka died, the Soul Hunter came to the forefront and most people were distressed by this. In these circumstances, riots arose. My father was one of the leaders of these riots when he was killed. The number of rebels has since decreased and now you can say that only a few of us are left."

"You mean you also followed in your father's footsteps?"

"Yes, I took part in almost every riot."

Ron said this proudly. Carmen reflected for a moment.

"Many people must have died. I had no idea," she said with sorrow.

"It is not your fault. This is a war." Ron stopped and leaned toward Carmen. "And your arrival is going to change everything."

A forced smile spread over Carmen's face, but her smile also showed hesitation. She had no knowledge about being a leader, let alone being a queen. She was a person who vomited whenever she saw blood, and the idea of killing a person made her feel queasy in the stomach. The best thing she could do in a fight was to run away. Carmen was scared out of her mind about what Ron and his grandfather had told her. She had no idea about how to go about doing all of that. While all of Crictus citizens were counting on her, she wasn't sure if she would end up disappointing them or not. Carmen sighed painfully. What was she getting herself into?

Just then, there was a knock on the door as if there was a secret code. Ron got up and opened the door. It was his brother Mason.

"Hi, Ron," said Mason as he put down the basket full of food. As he turned away from his brother, he looked at Carmen sitting at the table. A crooked smile appeared on Mason's face.

"Hey, I didn't know you were busy. Is Grandpa outside again?"

Ron rolled his eyes.

"She's not what you think, Mason."

Mason passed by Ron with a flirtatious look.

"Is that so?" he said as he removed the hat hiding his dark brown hair in front of Carmen. "I'm Mason. Pleased to meet you."

Carmen smiled. Mason's behavior was funny. Ron covered his face with his hands and laughed. Ron took a step forward and went over to Mason and Carmen.

"Mason, let me introduce you. This is Carmen, the bearer of the noble soul, Anka."

No sooner did Ron say that than Mason recoiled as if he had been slapped in the face. He looked carefully at Carmen. The clothes she wore weren't those of Crictus. How could he not see? Astonishment and awe replaced his crooked smile.

"I'm sorry, My Lady. I mean, my queen. I… I had no idea. Forgive me."

Carmen burst into laughter. Throughout her sixteen years of life, nobody has called her "my lady" or "my queen." Carmen stood up.

"No need to apologize, Mason. I think it was cute." Carmen extended her hand to the bewildered Mason. "Nice to meet you too."

Mason hastily shook Carmen's hand in astonishment.

"It's a great honor to meet you…"

Carmon looked at Ron with an expression that sensed she thought Mason was exaggerating. Ron laughed. Mason was still holding Carmen's hand, still surprised. As Ron cleared his throat, Mason finally retracted his hand.

"Mason, go and spread the word." He stopped and looked into Carmen's eyes:
*"Anka ay miana."**
"Anka has returned."

5

Mason ran right out of the house, grinning from ear to ear.

Carmen stared at Ron blankly.

"What did you tell him?"

"I told him to tell everyone Anka was back," Carmen blinked.

"Why did you do that? Didn't you say that Inca shouldn't find us?"

Ron picked up the food from the floor his brother had brought and put it on the table.

"Yes, I did but nobody knows what you look like." Ron looked at Carmen's clothes. Carmen was still wearing her strapped blue blouse, jeans, and a pair of black Converse. He finished his words, saying, "I mean, your clothes are not really suited to here, but we'll take care of that…"

Carmen crossed her arms on her chest and looked at Ron with questioning eyes. Ron was taking the food out of the basket.

"I still don't get why you did that."

"Because, if people find out that you're back, they'll start questioning the integrity of the Soul Hunter."

There was a wide smile on Ron's face. Carmen pondered a bit and then spoke, "Wise…"

Now she was smiling, too.

Once he took all the food out of the basket, Ron went over to one of the rooms.

"Let's see… Will I be able to find anything that suits you?" After a couple of minutes, Ron entered the room carrying some garments. "Try these on," he said as he handed them to Carmen.

Carmen unfolded the clothing items Ron gave her. They were dark in color but at least they matched. For a moment, she looked to see what Ron had on. Carmen didn't care much about what she was wearing, but she had never worn such depressing clothes either. Ron was wearing duds that were as dreary as what he brought for Carmen to wear. The gray sleeveless T-shirt on Ron was the lightest shade on him. For a moment, Carmen looked at Ron again and realized he was burly. He had visibly muscular arms. She suddenly shifted her gaze so that Ron wouldn't notice she was staring at him.

"So, uh, where can I get dressed?"

Ron showed her to an empty room. A few minutes later, Carmen went back to Ron with her new clothes on. Like Ron's, Carmen's T-shirt was sleeveless, but it was blackish purple in color. She had short comfortable trousers, and everything fit snugly. Carmen tried to reach her back.

"Well, they're a bit itchy."

Ron smiled.

"They look great on you."

Ron was sincere in saying this. When he went to Earth to find Anka, he didn't expect Anka to be so... Beautiful. Before he left, he knew Anka was a young girl, but still, what he had expected was completely different.

"Whose clothes are these? They're exactly my size." Before giving Ron the opportunity to answer, Carmen crossed her arms on her chest. "Or do they belong to one of these girls your brother mentioned?"

There was a mischievous expression on Carmen's face. Ron smiles, somewhat embarrassed.

"Believe me, it's not so easy living with my Grandpa."

Carmen laughed. Ron cleared his throat.

"They were my mother's."

This halted Carmen's smile.

"You don't have to give them to me," said Carmen. She felt awkward for a second.

"No worries, nobody's wearing them anyway. You can wear them."

"Thank you," Carmen said gently.

While Ron was preparing dinner, Carmen looked about the house from where she sat. There was a center table and chairs that took up most of the space in the small room she found herself in. A countertop resembling a kitchen with large pots was in a corner of the room. In the other corner was a bookcase with dusty ancient books. There were two doors, one each at both ends of the room. One of them led to Ron's grandfather's room, while the other opened into Mason and Ron's room. The house was as small as a box.

While Ron was setting the table for dinner, Mason finally came home. Soon after their grandfather came and the four of them took seats at the table. There was an animal Carmen had never seen before on the dining table. It was clearly indigenous to Crictus. Everyone reached for a cooked animal on the table and was pulling pieces from it. Carmen eyed them, trying to understand how she would eat it. Ron noticed Carmen's stare and he gave her a piece he had pulled off. After Carmen took a bite, she laughed oddly.

"Hey… This tastes like turkey."

The old man took a look at Carmen.

"This is not turkey. This is 'Klaush.'"

Carmen quickly responded to the old man, "Well, then, I love 'Klaush.'"

Carmen smiled when she said that, and she was happy to see the old man smile at her, too. *One day maybe I'll be able to get along with this old man too,* she thought.

There was silence for a while. Everyone was famished. Breaking the silence, Ron made a sound as if he remembered something and started talking before swallowing his bite.

"Tomorrow we have to work on your fighting techniques. We better find out what and how much you know."

Carmen abruptly stopped. She swallowed her bite with difficulty and drank some water to wash it down.

"Did you just say 'fighting'?" There was an expression on Carmen's face, like she had put her foot in her mouth.

"You do know how to fight, right?"

Ron gave Carmen a skeptical look. Mason leaped up to answer Ron's question.

"Of course, she knows, brother. She's Anka."

Oh my God, these people are expecting too much from me, Carmen thought. Mason looked at Carmen with hopeful eyes. Carmen smiled evasively and turned away. This time she caught Ron's glance. Ron was looking at Carmen questioningly.

"Do you know how to fight?" he asked Carmen again.

His voice sounded as if he was questioning her. Carmen gulped.

"I might know a few things…"

Ron placed his food on the table. He somehow managed to look understanding and fed up at the same time.

"You don't know, do you?"

There was a punctuated pause. All three pairs of eyes at the table were riveted on Carmen. Feeling the pressure, Carmen went on the defensive.

"Well, okay, I don't know exactly, but please keep in mind I've been living on Earth for sixteen years, and don't expect me to keep up with everything so fast. It's only been a few hours since I came here."

The disappointment on Mason's face was very evident.

"But you're Anka…"

Carmen glanced at Mason with a weary face.

"Yes, but I only learned I was Anka just a few hours ago, and I don't even know what that means yet."

Ron lightly touched Carmen's hand on the table.

"Don't worry. Everything will fall into place."

Carmen looked at Ron, thankful for his support. After Ron responded to Carmen's smile, he turned to Mason and his grandfather.

"Please let's not rush her. She's already gone through more than she can cope with today."

Carmen took what Ron said in. Everything was so different when she woke up this morning. She had a family, a school, friends, and her own house. Even her future was secure. But now she found out she had been adopted by her parents, and even worse, that she was an alien. Here she was on a planet she had no idea about with people she didn't know, eating something she wasn't familiar with that tasted like turkey, not to mention the fact that her future was most uncertain. She wasn't even sure what awaited her tomorrow. All this in just one day was too much for her. Her life had been turned upside down. All of a sudden, she discovered everything she knew was wrong.

Carmen tried to sum up the day in her mind. First, someone attacked her, then she found out she had been adopted, and she was from another planet called Crictus which she traveled via an interdimensional voyage. Then she learned that she was a queen and that she had to prepare for an ultimate battle in order to reclaim her rightful throne. Carmen sighed in distress. She was feeling very depressed and hoped that her day would end soon. That's because she might not be able to cope with one more thing.

Carmen suddenly stood up, and all eyes turned to her.

"I want to get a little rest, of course, if you don't mind."

Ron slowly got to his feet.

"Of course, we don't mind. Let me show you where you'll be sleeping."

After bidding everyone goodnight, she went into the adjoining room with Ron. He gave Carmen Mason's bed. Carmen lay down on the bed, which was up against a wall in the room. Ron's bed was against the opposite wall. After Ron said goodnight to Carmen, he went back to his grandfather and Mason. As soon as Ron came back, his grandfather started to talk.

"Unacceptable. We cannot possibly rely on a sixteen-year-old girl who doesn't know how to fight and isn't even aware of her powers. We need someone who can end this war, not a child. I assume this must be Anka's worst host choice. But after all, Anka had to make this choice to save itself from being eaten by the Soul Hunter."

Ron gave his grandfather a stern look.

"Please, don't talk about her like that. I'll teach her everything."

Ron sat in his chair at the table while saying this.

"Indeed, you are. It is natural for you to protect her… You're her emerald, but you must not be this blind. She doesn't have any right skills to end this war."

This time Ron protested more harshly.

"If I hadn't trusted Anka in the first place, the emerald wouldn't have chosen me and she is, in fact, a very talented person. You'll see. She'll overcome both the Soul Hunter and Inca."

Ron sounded very determined. He didn't have any doubt. After all, this was the reason why the emerald chose him. His faith… Ron believed in all he said, but he also knew that time was needed for all this. With some patience, they could handle anything.

Ron went to bed half an hour later. His brother would sleep on the floor in the living room that night. Ron wanted to turn in early, because this was the first day he had spent as an emerald, and he had successfully completed his mission by managing to keep Anka alive. A near death experience and making inter-dimensional journeys twice in a day had tired him. A lot had happened that day, and it was too much to handle in one day.

Ron tiptoed into the room and closed the door behind him. He was trying hard not to make any sound as he got slowly into bed and drew the quilt over himself. Carmen was still trying to sleep at that time but was unable to do so. It was as if her distress was growing inside. When she heard Ron coming in, she closed her eyes and pretended to be asleep. Carmen tried to sleep for some time but couldn't do it. There was no sound around.

It was pitch dark except for a light glimmer coming inside. Carmen turned a little in her bed. The bed was hard. She turned her face to the side where Ron was sleeping. Ron's eyes were closed.

"Ron, are you asleep?" Carmen whispered.

Hearing that, Ron opened his eyes.

"I thought you were," he said.

Carmen slightly shrugged.

"I tried to sleep but couldn't."

Ron straightened up slightly in his bed.

"Is there something wrong?"

Carmen sighed and she straightened up a little. She leaned her back on the wall behind her.

"All of this is very odd. I can't even believe I'm not on Earth anymore."

"I know. This is too much for you, but you'll get used to it over time."

Carmen gave Ron a weary look and then turned her head to the window. The light from a planet she didn't recognize was reflecting on her face. It was like the Moon but larger.

"What I don't understand is how this place looks so much like the Earth. Almost everything is the same…"

Ron shrugged.

"I don't know very much about Earth. I only read about it from the books written by the previous Anka, Inca, and Emeralds, but I know that it is quite similar to Crictus. Centuries ago, there was an Anka like you who spent a lot of time on Earth and brought many innovations back here. For example, the language we're speaking is a reform accomplished by the previous Anka. The Anka language is still used, of course, but even Inca supporters adopted the reformed language."

"I see." Carmen paused for a brief moment, then continued.

"I wonder… Since he had spent so much time on Earth, was he also as incompetent as me?"

"You are not incompetent."

Carmen looked at him and chuckled.

"Thank you for your faith in me, but you might change your mind after tomorrow."

Ron laughed quietly.

"Of course, if we can get out of bed tomorrow. It's late and we are both exhausted. We deserved to rest a bit."

"You're right..." Carmen said as they both lay down on their beds.

Carmen turned once or twice in her bed. She tried falling asleep, and at last, she was defeated by fatigue. In the same way, Ron fell into a deep slumber.

ANKA'S CASTLE

"What do you mean you lost them? It was your only chance, and you blew it..."

Edmund's voice was booming in the castle, resonating down the corridors. For a moment, he had forgotten he was talking to Inca. Inca glared at his brother.

"How dare you yell at me! If you'd given me that damned stone when I became Inca, we needn't have had to worry about Anka now, would we? But, no, what did you do? You waited for an emerald to show up!"

"I had no idea the water emerald would emerge so soon."

Edmund went behind the throne and grasped it. The throne room was empty. Light seeped in from the big frosty windows to the right and left of the throne. The room was lit with torches hung on the wall. Edmund looked at his brother who looked furious. Edmund didn't want to make him angry but was defeated by his own fury. According to his plan, his brother was going to find and kill Anka on Earth. Anka's soul would then be trapped on Earth, and he would have been rid of Anka forever. And once Derick came back from the Earth, he would possess Inca's soul, thus allowing him to maintain his authority. Now his plan was tainted. He needed another plan. He turned his back and began to look out the window. He knew that it wouldn't work to capture Inca at the moment. He had to be smart. Anka was powerful, but Edmund would be more powerful if he acted with Inca against her. Only when Anka was completely annihilated could he possess Inca's soul. A treacherous smile appeared on Edmund's face. He wiped the expression off his face so his brother wouldn't notice. He turned slowly and approached his brother.

"I apologize for my behavior. It wasn't my place to yell at you."

He had a downtrodden look on his face when he said this. Derick was not really expecting Edmund to apologize. So, he couldn't hide his astonishment.

"It's quite all right," he said reticently.

Edmund put his hand on his brother's arm.

"It's not a big deal you couldn't nab Anka. We… We will overcome this together and we will…" he said, as he pointed to the throne, "… rule Crictus from this throne together."

Inca Derick smiled. The throne was always Derick's dream. Learning that he would possess it one day uplifted his spirits, but he didn't intend to share the throne with his brother, no way and no how. When the time came, after Anka died, he must have the throne to himself.

RON'S GRANDFATHER'S CABIN

"C'mon, get up." Ron had woken up some time ago. While it was his habit to get up early in the morning, what Carmen loved most was to sleep in, and she hated waking up early. She moaned in bed, burying her head further beneath the pillow. Laughing at Carmen's behavior, Ron spoke again. "C'mon, rise and shine. We've got a lot to do today."

Carmen moaned again.

"Mom, just five more minutes… I don't have any important lessons today anyway."

At that moment, Ron understood how tough it was for Carmen to undergo such a radical change. For an instant, he felt really sorry for her. This was Carmen's fate, and nothing could change it. Ron went over to Carmen's bed and leaned down.

"Carmen, your mother's not here, and you really need to get out of bed now."

Carmen raised her head a little and looked at Ron. She looked around a bit in a confused manner and then it dawned on her. It wasn't all just a dream. She was really on another planet. She put her head back on the pillow with a weary face. Without raising her head from the pillow, she spoke in a hoarse voice.

"Okay, I'm up."

After getting up out of bed, Carmen ate breakfast with Ron and his family. Carmen really liked the food on Crictus. The food tasted so familiar. After finishing her meal, she and Ron left Ron's grandfather's cabin. It was nestled somewhere in the forest, isolated from the small houses near the castle with no other structures around. When Ron and Carmen emerged from the cabin, they began hiking in the forest. After walking for a long time, they came to a waterfall. The pond where the waterfall was pouring into was full of crystal rocks that glittered in the sunlight beneath the water. It was impossible to pick up these crystal stones. The water descended at a great volume. For many years, plenty of people tried to pick up these stones, but unfortunately, it always ended badly for them.

Approaching the edge of the waterfall, Ron took out a crystal stone from his pants pocket. It was the same stone he had taken from Inca yesterday.

"Where did you get this stone?" Carmen said, looking at it curiously.

Ron looked at the stone.

"I took it from Inca yesterday." Carmen looked at the stone for a while. Then, she stared at Ron as if she was expecting an explanation. Ron felt like he had to tell her. "This is the whispering stone. When you whisper someone's name to the stone, it summons that person." Ron turned the stone over and over in his hand. "This stone is very dangerous for you." Saying that, he threw the stone into the waterfall with all his might.

Carmen screamed.

"What are you doing? This stone could have helped our cause."

"The stone is a danger to you. No one should ever have it. That being said, now nobody can reach it here. It's impossible to distinguish it from the crystal stones below and no one has been able to reach down there so far."

Carmen gazed at the bottom of the waterfall curiously. She could see thousands of crystal stones at the bottom of the waterfall. As Ron said, it was impossible to find the whispering stone now.

Carmen looked at Ron again.

"Well, did we come all the way here just for this?"

Ron chuckled.

"Of course not. We are here to train."

Carmen sighed. She didn't know anything about fighting. The only thing she knew was that in fighting movies, men could blow kicks in the air and that they were impossibly swift. As for Carmen, she would make a fuss even if her fingertip bled.

"I don't think I know anything about fighting," she said timidly.

"I think you should first learn to use your Anka powers. They'll be your biggest assets."

"But I don't know how to use them."

Ron shrugged.

"It is really easy. I didn't know how to use the water either, but this is something that comes from within… It's like… You instinctively know all of it…"

Carmen looked at her hands. There was despair in her face. She spoke, looking at Ron, "I don't think so."

Ron got closer to Carmen.

"Just calm down and focus on the tree over there." He was pointing at a tree in front of them when he said this. Carmen looked at the tree desperately. "Just believe in yourself."

Ron's words reassured her, even if just a bit. She took a deep breath and visualized the scene where Inca attacked her. Inca raised only one of his hands. Or maybe Carmen missed the actual point since she was too busy trying to escape. Still, she decided to try, and she extended one of her hands forward. After she stood like that for some time, she slightly pushed her hand forward. Nothing was happening. There was no light coming out of her hand, nor did the tree she aimed at shake. She was just making a fool of herself.

"This is nonsense. I am not… magical. Don't you think I would have known it by now if I had magic," Carmen grumbled.

Ron turned to Carmen.

"You wouldn't be able to. Your emeralds carry your power. When the water emerald chose me, your powers were triggered and what you have is more than magic. The power you possess is a reflection of your immortal soul who has lived a thousand lives. You have to believe in yourself. You need to feel the energy within you and direct it out. Feel your soul. Feel Anka."

While saying that, Ron was acting as if he was pushing something with his hands. Carmen imitated Ron.

"Okay, I'll try."

She took a deep breath and rubbed her hands together. She looked for something inside her, some energy… So, she shut her eyes. Her eyes were shut for a bit, but Carmen couldn't feel anything. Focus, she said to herself in her mind. She was really trying. Failure was not her thing. She took a few deep breaths. She imagined there was a light inside her. In her imagination, she directed this light toward her hands and opened her eyes. As soon as she opened her eyes, she rapidly swung her hands fast toward the tree. A powerful light beam came from her hands just next to the tree, but at the same time, Carmen was pushed back with the force of the light and instantly struck her back onto the tree behind her. Carmen groaned.

"Carmen, are you okay?" Ron sounded very worried.

"Yes, I just broke all my bones."

Ron helped Carmen get to her feet. Excitement and happiness now replaced the worry on his face.

"I told you; you could do it." Carmen paused for a moment. She'd really done it. She started laughing, too. "Now, if we can just work on aiming, everything will be fine."

Carmen felt excited for the first time ever since she arrived in this bizarre world. They went on with the training. The only break they took was to quickly eat the snacks they had brought along with them. While Carmen was working on aiming at the trees, Ron was working with the waterfall. Carmen was really doing well in using her abilities. After a while, she excelled at releasing her power. Just as Ron had said, it was like an instinct she never knew she had. Still, she was having a hard time controlling this power. Most of the time, she found herself on the ground or at the foot of a tree.

It was already getting dark when their training was done for the day. An exhausted Carmen and Ron headed home under an orange and red evening sky. Every muscle in Carmen's body was in agony. In her real life, she was too lazy to even exercise. But since the morning she had been mauling herself by tossing herself on the ground. The first thing Carmen did when they got home was to throw herself on her bed. She was certain she would sleep better today. And she did. After dinner, she fell asleep the moment her head hit the pillow.

The next day, Carmen got up early again at Ron's command. Her entire body was aching. Working so much had not been good for her muscles. When she heard Ron's plans for the day, she felt her muscles suddenly ache even more.

"Today, we're doing some sword training."

"Sword? You gotta be joking. I've never even seen a real sword in my entire life."

"Well, you'll be seeing one today then."

Ron had already worked out the training plan. He wanted to make Anka as powerful a fighter as possible, but he was aware that was easier said than done. Carmen had never even been in a fight in her whole life. Unfortunately, Ron didn't intend to give up trying to turn her into a warrior. A good queen must be always the strongest warrior.

That day she wore the same clothes she wore the previous day. After a long trek, they approached the crystal waterfall. This was a good place for their training as there was nobody around who could see them. It was also quite far from Anka's castle, which was held hostage by the Soul Hunter. Carmen's legs had already started to ache by the time they reached their training spot, but she still knew that she couldn't change Ron's mind about the sword training. During the three days she had known him, she understood how stubborn Ron was.

Whining, she sat on a big rock.

"At least let me catch my breath a bit."

Meanwhile, Ron put the bag he brought with him on the ground and removed two swords from the bag.

"No. A good queen has to be a good warrior."

"But I am not a queen yet."

"But you will be," Ron said, looking at Carmen in a know-it-all manner.

Carmen stood up anxiously. Ron lowered one of the swords to the ground. He turned the other over and over in his hand and held it toward the sun. This majestic sword glinted under the sun. After examining it closely for a while, he handed it to Carmen. The moment Carmen took the sword in her hand the tip of the sword fell forward.

"Hey, you didn't tell me it would be so heavy?"

"What did you expect?" Ron chided.

Carmen frowned. Ron got near Carmen. In the meantime, Carmen could merely lift the sword using both hands.

"Let me show you how to hold it."

"Maybe you should show me how to lift it first."

Ron smiled. He showed Carmen the position. Carmen imitated Ron, but she was really having a tough time keeping it in the air. Ron went and took his sword in hand. He tried to show Carmen a few moves. Carmen was trying to perform them, but she was not very successful. Still, Ron was trying to offer her support. Carmen was moving the sword in the air with all her might. Though she tried performing all the footwork Ron had shown her, it was impossible for her to keep all of it in mind. She was not a good memorizer. Which is why she hated her history class.

After some more training, Ron stood up against Carmen. They clinked their swords, trying to make the right foot move. Ron was very good at teaching as he demonstrated great patience with Carmen. Whenever Carmen made a wrong move, he showed her how it was supposed to be over and over again without ever getting frustrated.

At the end of the day, Carmen's muscles were in serious pain. Exhausted, she slumped down to the ground. She didn't even have the energy to walk to the rock behind her.

"I don't think I'll be able to walk back."

Ron looked at Carmen smiling and took the sword from her hand.

"You did a great job today."

Carmen was out of breath. She didn't think that she had done well. On the contrary, she felt that she disgraced herself in front of him. She asked curiously, "How can you be so patient?"

Ron looked at Carmen, smiling. "Don't be too hard on yourself. You were pretty good for someone who's seen a sword for the first time."

Carmen perceived the irony in his voice.

"Hey." Ron burst into laughter.

Carmen joined him after a while. Ron helped Carmen to her feet, and they set out to the cottage together.

Both were exhausted when they arrived at the cabin. Carmen threw herself into a chair. His grandfather came out of his room carrying soup.

"Is everything all right?"

Carmen looked at the old man wearily.

"I'm exhausted. I don't think I can make another move."

Carmen had already learned how sharp-tongued the old man could be, but still, she was honest with him. The old man came over to Carmen and grabbed a chair.

"Turn around."

Carmen turned her back trusting him fully. The old man put his hand on Carmen's back. He started to mutter something.

"*Gins vaire yori, raasfayar toy. RaSe tia toy peane, qienne…*" *

(My hand is the cure that heals her. It takes her pain and ache…)

With these words, Carmen felt warmth on her back. After some time, the old man took his hand away. Carmen looked at the old man in astonishment. All her pain was diminished.

"How did you do that?"

Ron answered the question on behalf of the old man.

"My grandfather's an old warrior and sorcerer."

"Magic? Are you serious?"

"Yes. He was once one of the finest sorcerers."

The old man smiled in response to the compliment.

"Oh, stop it you. There were better sorcerers than me." The old man stood up. He went to the oven, put the soup on the stove and started to work on the mixture next to it. Ron sat next to Carmen. "Now I'll prepare you a brew. You'll both feel better than before."

Carmen couldn't believe that magic existed. In fact, it should not have been too hard to believe it after she saw the light beam coming out of her own hand and having made an inter-dimensional journey. Still, it had been only three days since she arrived on Crictus and she was having difficulty comprehending everything that was going on around her.

Carmen glanced at Ron in amazement.

"Can you also do magic?"

Ron shrugged.

"Maybe. I haven't tried before."

Carmen's amazement increased.

"But why?"

"Because all the magic books were pulled off the shelves during your mother's time."

"Why would my mother do such a thing?"

"Because magic drives people mad."

Meanwhile, the old man left the pot and came over to them holding two bowls. He gave them the bowls.

"Ah-ha. Magic is a dangerous craft. Your mother did the right thing. That power… It may drive people insane."

What Carmen heard made her shudder.

"But you have just performed it?" Carmen couldn't hide the inquisitive tone in her voice.

"There are many kinds of magic. The one I just performed is Alti

Magic, which is one of the simplest. Some of them are harmless; doesn't it always start like that? Now drink this."

Carmen looked at the brew in front of her without objection, leaned over, and sniffed it. The brew's odor made her face wince. It smelled awful.

"It smells like dead rat." Carmen was feeling sick.

"Then drink without smelling."

In the meantime, Ron chugged down the brew. He quickly put the bowl back on the table. He winced and swallowed the brew with difficulty. He coughed a few times. All the while, Carmen was watching Ron. After a while, she plugged her nose and followed suit. It tasted like nothing she had tasted before. It was as if she was drinking raw sewage. After swallowing the brew, she coughed a few times like Ron, even retched but managed not to vomit.

Later in the evening, the brew started to have an effect on them. Carmen was now feeling very vigorous. As the old man had said, she was feeling much better than before. That night she had difficulty falling asleep. She felt as if she had drunk three energy drinks before going to bed. They talked for a long time before sleeping, because Ron was feeling the same way. After their talk, they decided that they had to get up early in the morning and tried to sleep.

That morning, instead of going to the waterfall, Ron decided to take Carmen to the city center. Carmen was seeing the city for the first time. This place resembled a big village. There were houses of different sizes mixed in with stores on each side. The ground was made of stone. While the roofs of some houses were covered with straw, others were tiled. It was evident that the owners of such houses were richer. There were inscriptions on the doors of the stores she couldn't read. It was easy to understand this was the regional language here. Carmen and Ron encountered lots of people as they proceeded down the street. Carmen was examining their clothing, behavior, walking, etc. They all looked like people on Earth, but their clothes seemed from an older period.

After a few minutes of walking, they reached their destination. It was the workshop of a blacksmith. Ron pushed the wooden door open and entered. It was dusty and extremely hot inside. Upon entering, they saw a middle-aged and slightly chubby man with a bald spot forging a sword on a stone. Noticing somebody had entered the shop, he quickly dropped what he was doing when he saw Ron. A small smile spread across his old face.

"Ron! It's nice to see you…" he said while embracing Ron.

"It's great to see you, too, Rudolf." Ron turned to Carmen. "He's my father's best friend."

Carmen kindly extended her hand and introduced herself. Rudolf was looking at Carmen attentively as he lightly elbowed Ron.

"What a beautiful young lady. Am I to assume you are finally settling down?"

Carmen looked away in embarrassment. Ron chuckled.

"You'll never change Rudolf, will you? This is Carmen. I'd like you to forge a sword for her."

This time Rudolf glanced at Carmen as if he was scaling her. After looking at her for quite a while, he spoke.

"I shall begin at once."

And without losing time, he headed to his furnace. In the meantime, Ron and Carmen sat on two chairs and watched the sword master at work. For a while, nobody talked. Rudolf glanced at Ron once in a while as he mopped his brow.

"Hey Ron, I heard something about Anka being back. Do you know anything about it?"

The gossip Mason started had spread very quickly. Ron winked at Carmen.

"No, I don't."

Carmen fidgeted nervously.

"Huh. I thought you'd know something about this." He turned and looked at Ron. "You're sort of the head of the rebels. I'm surprised that you don't know anything."

"If in fact Anka is back, I've got no doubt she'll ascend to the throne soon."

Rudolf smiled slightly at him.

"You've always been like your father. He truly believed in Anka too, but things are far more different now. Anka ought to face a great challenge. May Phoenix has mercy on our souls."

This time it was Carmen who spoke, "What do you mean by great challenge?"

Rudolf looked at Carmen. There were beads of sweat on his face.

"You know. The Soul Hunter was already quite dangerous, but now

Inca chose his brother. With Anka's mortal enemy by Soul Hunter's side, I don't know how Anka can survive the threat. She doesn't have an army; the rebels are weakened in many years." Rudolf returned to his work again. "I don't think Anka stands a chance this time."

Carmen and Ron glimpsed at each other. This was the last thing Carmen needed to hear. She sighed in distress. She knew that it would be hard to ascend the throne, but Rudolf' swords caused her to think twice.

After some time, Rudolf took the sword from the furnace and started banging on it. Each stroke made Carmen even more uneasy than before. Rudolf shaped the sword for a while and then made a final retouch. He attached the hilt to the sword and lastly, he put it into the bucket near him. Smoke started to come out of the sword. After a while, he removed it from the bucket and handed it to Carmen. She stood up and held the sword from its hilt. This one was lighter than the one she used for practice. She gripped the sword easily and tried to perform some of the moves Ron had shown her. She was able to perform the moves faster.

Ron stood up and came over to Carmen. There was a big, hopeful smile on his face.

"Now we can do some real practice."

After they finished their business in the city center, they went directly to the cascade and immediately started to practice. Carmen was trying to perform each move Ron showed her one after the other. She stopped upon Ron's warning.

"Don't use the sword like a weapon, Carmen."

"How else am I supposed to use it?"

Ron swung his sword gently in the air. He was performing the moves he taught Carmen. The sword was moving naturally in the air rather peacefully.

"See the sword as an extension of your arm. Treat it as if it is a part of your body."

Carmen watched Ron in complete rapture. His sword was floating like a feather in the air. But when Carmen performed the same movements, her sword was practically tearing holes in the air. Carmen tried doing what Ron said. It was tough at first.

"Treat it gentler. As you treat your arm…"

Carmen was now making gentler moves. Although she still needed a tone of practice, after a while, she started to perform the moves gentler and quicker.

It had gotten dark when they finally came home. Both were as exhausted as they had been over the past couple of days. The training was really straining Carmen. And she lied about feeling well because she didn't want to drink that disgusting brew again.

Carmen and Ron continued to practice during the subsequent days. Sometimes, they practiced her Anka powers too, but they were usually training with swords and in one-on-one combat. Ron didn't spend much time on Anka powers because they were inherent in Carmen. And he was right about that. Carmen was already using her powers extremely well after practicing just a few more times. After long training sessions, Carmen was returning to the cabin worn out.

On one such day, Carmen's entire body was wracked with pain. Her ankle in particular was aching since she made a wrong move with the sword while exercising. She was planning to go to bed without even having dinner, but after listening to Ron's grandfather's advice telling her that "eating would make her stronger," she agreed to sit down to dinner with them at the table. She even joined their short conversation after dinner. When she felt that she couldn't endure the pain anymore, she asked for permission and went to the bedroom. Ron accompanied her too. Both went to their beds.

Carmen was looking at the ceiling. It had been just a few minutes since they went to bed, and she was sure that Ron wasn't sleeping.

"I could never have imagined this."

"Imagined what?"

Still keeping her eyes on the ceiling, she replied.

"I had very different dreams." Turning in his bed, Ron looked at Carmen. She was still staring at the ceiling. "I was going to leave my town and start traveling the world after I graduated high school. Whenever I needed money, I would work daily jobs, and keep moving on." She looked at Ron. She continued to speak, "Then, maybe, I would move to a big city. Like Istanbul, New York, Paris, London, Sydney, something like that. Maybe I would start a family," she sighed. "Now look at me. I'm on a planet I don't know, I'm millions of light years away from my family and I won't be able to make any of those dreams come true."

Ron smiled slightly.

"Perhaps, you will have a new dream. A bigger one."

Carmen sighed in distress.

"Like being a queen of Crictus?"

"Like changing the world to make it a better place. Any world…"

Carmen couldn't help but smile at what Ron said. Then her smile vanished.

"I miss my family."

This time, there was sorrow on Ron's face.

"I'm sorry you can't go against your fate."

Carmen looked at the ceiling again. Even though her mother didn't give birth to her, they had been Carmen's mother and father for sixteen years. After all, they were Carmen's parents, and she missed them a lot. It was the first time she had been away from them for so long. In fact, it was not only her family she missed. She even missed the town that she hated so much. She missed her friends, and maybe even her classes. She deeply resented having to leave the place where she had lived for sixteen years so suddenly. And yet, what she wanted most in her life was to run away from that town, and now she had done it. Still, she couldn't believe she was missing that town. She sighed. The significance of change being good or bad didn't matter, since change was always a great challenge itself. There was no return now. *Maybe, it's better this way…* she thought. Maybe, if she didn't have such a chance, she would never be able to leave that town. She closed her eyes a little, and in just a few minutes, she was overwhelmed by fatigue. Difficult times awaited her ahead.

6

ANKA'S CASTLE

As the days passed, rumors about Anka's return spread through the grapevine until at last they reached Anka's castle. Edmund and Derick were much disturbed by this rumor that they knew to be the truth. While everyone knew the throne was Anka's right, this rumor severely undermined Edmund's authority. Nonetheless, Edmund didn't intend to let this happen and he had to find a way to force Anka out of his way. Unfortunately, he had lost the whispering stone that allowed him to reach Anka. Whispering stones were very unique and it was nearly impossible to find them. Losing it didn't bode well for Edmund.

Edmund sauntered to his brother's chamber and knocked on the door. Then he barged in without waiting for a reply. Derick stood up from his desk when he saw Edmund. Since he became Inca, everyone treated him like a real prince, and now he was even allowed to be involved in government business.

Before Edmund closed the door behind him, he gestured to the maid to leave the room. When the two brothers were alone, they started talking.

"What troubles you?" Edmund eyed his brother.

"Anka, of course…" Edmund said, as if summarizing the whole problem.

Derick sighed.

"You still couldn't find her?"

"No. I don't know what she looks like, and rumors of her return have already spread far and wide. This is going to destroy both of us. We've got to stop her immediately." Edmund said.

A thoughtful expression appeared on Derick's face. He looked at his brother, stroking his stubbly beard.

"What do you suggest?"

Derrick had no plan as usual. Edmund knew very well that he had to benefit from this situation. Taking a few steps, he went over to his brother.

"Since you saw her and her emerald, you'll be participating in the search personally." While saying this, he was also poking Derick's chest with his index finger. Derick didn't want to be Edmund's puppet.

"On one condition. You'll take part, too."

Edmund grimaced. He knew that opposing Inca wasn't a good idea. So, he agreed.

"First of all, we've got to come up with the source of the rumors. Whoever spread this rumor must know something."

THE CRYSTAL WATERFALL

Two weeks have passed since Carmen left Earth and arrived on Crictus. During this time, she had practiced with the sword and one-on-one combat with Ron with nary a break. They had their hands full every day. They got up early every morning, went to the crystal waterfall, and spent the whole day practicing. Carmen was getting better every day. Still, two weeks of training wasn't enough to transform her into a warrior.

Carmen was just able to stop a sword thrust Ron made by deftly performing one of the moves Ron taught her.

"That was impressive."

Carmen smiled. "I know."

Meanwhile, Ron went back to the attack position. They practiced only defensive moves that day. Ron was parrying Carmen with light but rapid thrusts. Most of the time Carmen managed to ward them off because Ron was striking lightly. However, she would get distracted and find herself at the tip of Ron's sword other times.

They decided to finish practicing and headed straight toward the cabin as the sun began to set. While they were walking back to the cabin, Carmen was relating some funny things that happened to her back on Earth. Ron couldn't help laughing.

"And you put that creature called a frog in your friend Liz's bag?"

"What else could I do? There was no other place to hide it."

Ron burst into laughter. They had almost arrived at the cabin, which had come within visual range. Ron glanced toward the cottage and noticed a few men were loitering around it. He suddenly stopped laughing. With a rapid move, he grabbed Carmen, and as he ducked her out of sight, he clamped his hand over her mouth so that she wouldn't make any sound.

He gestured to Carmen to remain silent and let her go. Carmen looked at the cabin and spotted two well-dressed men waiting outside the cabin. There were a lot of guards near them. She immediately recognized one of the well-dressed men. He was Inca. She turned to Ron in worry.

"What are they doing here?" She kept her voice as low as possible.

Ron nodded as if to say, "I don't know."

"How could they possibly find us?"

"I don't know…" Ron repeated himself.

At that moment, two burly guards manhandled Mason out of the house, pinning him by his arms. Then, two guards got the old man out of the house. They shoved Mason and the old man down to the ground in front of Edmund and Inca. Ron looked at Carmen. Carmen had a dreadful look on her face. They went a little closer, hiding behind another tree to better hear what was being said. After advancing by a few more trees, they could easily hear them and hide themselves as well.

"So, you haven't seen Anka?"

This was Edmund. He was questioning poor Mason. Mason was shaking like a leaf.

"N… No, sir. I really haven't seen her."

Edmund shouted, "So, why did you spread such rumors?"

Mason was shaken. "It wasn't me. I swear."

Carmen looked at Ron in haste.

"We have to do something."

Ron paid no attention to what Carmen was saying. He went on watching the terrifying event unfold before his eyes. Carmen did the same thing.

Edmund was starting to believe the boy shaking in front of him. He suddenly turned to the old man. He was livid.

"What about you? Have you seen her?"

The old man looked very calm unlike Mason, and there was no sign of fear on his face.

"I haven't seen her, but if I had, be sure that I wouldn't have told you anyway."

Rage was written all over Edmund's face. Ron bemoaned himself.

"Oh grandpa…"

Edmund leaned toward the old man.

"You have a death wish, haven't you?"

Ron gritted his teeth. He was furiously watching Edmund behind the trees. Carmen looked at Ron, begging.

"We have to rescue them, Ron. We have to do something."

Again, Ron didn't hear what Carmen said, but this time Carmen insisted. "Ron, I'm begging you… We've got to stop them, otherwise they'll kill them both."

Ron replied, keeping his eyes on Edmund, "I know."

Despite saying this, Ron didn't make a move. Appalled, Carmen looked at Ron and went on watching what was happening.

The old man looked at Edmund's face.

"Do what you want to me, you coward. One way or another, Anka will dethrone and destroy you. Even knowing this is enough for me."

Edmund's eyes got bigger with anger. He looked at Mason again.

"If you want this old man to live, you better tell me where they are."

Mason looked in hesitation at his grandfather.

"I don't know…"

He sounded defeated. There was desperation on his face. Ron gritted his teeth when he saw his brother's expression. Inca slowly went over and touched his brother on the shoulder.

"They don't know anything."

"No, they know but they're hiding it."

While saying this, he didn't move his eyes from Mason even for a second.

"Then, finish them off. If they helped Anka, they deserve to die."

Inca's voice was merciless. Edmund liked his brother's attitude. He slowly approached Mason, who was still trembling in fear. He was about to cry. Watching the proceedings from behind the tree, Carmen turned to Ron in horror.

"Ron, what are you waiting for? He's going to kill your brother." Ron was still looking at Edmund with a faintly bitter expression on his face. Carmen couldn't bear it any more. "Well, if you won't do anything, I will."

When Carmen attempted to step out from behind the tree, Ron grabbed her and pinned her back to the tree.

"No, Carmen, I can't put your life in danger."

Carmen started to struggle to control her emotions. "I don't care. We must rescue them."

Ron was in agony, but he kept holding Carmen tight.

"I can't. I must protect you."

"Please Ron."

"No."

Ron was having serious difficulty saying this. A loud shriek was heard just then. Carmen wriggled from Ron's arms and looked at Edmund. Edmund had raised his hand. It was Mason who screamed, writhing like a live wire. Carmen couldn't look anymore and threw herself into Ron's arms. Ron embraced her, but unlike Carmen, he went on watching this violence. After a while, Mason's dead body dropped to the ground. The Soul Hunter turned to the old man.

"Are you sure you still don't know anything?"

A tear fell down from the old man's eye. He could barely speak.

"May Phoenix's curse rain upon you."

The Soul Hunter raised his hand and motioned as if he were inhaling something. The old man started to scream. After a while, he stopped screaming as his soul left his body and his body fell to the ground. Ron hugged Carmen who was crying in his arms tighter and closed his eyes. He was clenching his teeth. He desperately wanted to march there and kill the Soul Hunter, but he couldn't do it. He couldn't put Carmen's life at risk, as she was the most important thing on Crictus.

As he looked at the corpses on the ground, the Soul Hunter made a sound indicating he was relieved.

"I think we're done here."

After a while, they moved slowly away from the cabin. Ron and Carmen stayed hidden amongst the trees until they were gone and came out into the open when the men disappeared completely from sight. Carmen crept over to Mason and knelt down. His eyes were still open. Ron came up to Carmen. For a long time, he looked at Mason's innocent face and eyes. Then, he bent down and shut Mason's eyes. Carmen couldn't stop crying. She then looked at Ron's grandfather, his eyes cold and dark. Ron went to his grandfather, bent down toward his head, and shut his eyes, too, then stared at him for quite some time. The track of the last tear flowing from the old man's cheek was still visible on his wrinkled face. Carmen quickly wiped her tears. Immense rage welled up inside her. She looked at Ron.

"Why didn't you help them?"

Ron stood up.

"Because I can't put your life in danger."

Carmen looked at Ron with blaming eyes.

"They were your family…" she stopped. "You could've saved them, but you didn't! Why not!"

Carmen was shouting now. She was spilling out her hatred against Ron.

"Because, Carmen, you are the most important being on this planet and it's my duty to protect you! If they noticed us, they would have killed us too! I couldn't fight all of them on my own! I had to choose you!"

"They didn't have to die!"

"Carmen, we're in a war, and in war people die! You'd better get used to that!" Ron stopped and went on shouting angrily. "Also, it's no use holding me responsible for their deaths! I didn't kill them."

Carmen went on screaming at him desperately as she cried.

"You could've helped them! But instead, you chose not to even lift a finger!"

This time, Ron shouted at Carmen more furiously.

"They were my family! Why would you care!"

Carmen froze upon Ron's words. Anger was flowing from Ron's eyes. Maybe his anger wasn't focused on her, but like Carmen, he was taking it out on her instead of the Soul Hunter. Ron quickly went into the cottage, which was in total disarray. He quickly grabbed a shovel, went out and started to dig into the ground. Carmen was watching Ron.

"What are you doing?"

Ron was still angry with Carmen. That's why he gave Carmen an angry look.

"I have to bury them."

Carmen had never felt this helpless in her whole life. She thought these things happened only in movies. She loved TV shows where CSI solved murder cases. Now she felt herself right in the middle of those movies and TV shows. Two dead bodies were lying on the ground in front of her. For a moment, she felt nauseous but then looked at their faces again. They looked as if they were sleeping. Carmen couldn't stop crying. She was only able to calm down after some time, but whenever she thought about the murders committed in front of her, her eyes welled up with tears. After some time, Carmen was able to stand up and go into the cabin. She took a shovel she found by chance, went out, approached Ron, and began to help him. Ron wiped the sweat off his brow.

"You don't have to do this."

"Why not? Is it because they aren't my family?"

Ron glared at Carmen but said nothing. They were both very tense. They finished digging the graves after a while then carried the corpses up to the pits. While doing this, Carmen's eyes filled with tears again. After lowering the bodies into the pits, Carmen stopped in front of their graves.

"I've known them for a very short time, but I liked them very much. I hope they rest in peace."

Ron spoke while covering them with soil, "Only when we slay the Soul Hunter, they'll be at peace."

Ron's voice stung as they covered them with soil together. They finished in the evening. An exhausted Ron went back into the cabin. After a few minutes, he came back with a large bag in his hand. He brought a bag for Carmen, too.

"We can't stay here any longer. We don't know if they'll come back or not."

Carmen looked at Ron as she took the bag.

"Where are we going?"

"Let's stay in the forest tonight. We'll figure something out later."

Carmen wanted to object, but she was too tired. They headed toward the forest together and approached a stream after a short walk. They found this site suitable to stay. They took some blankets out of their backpacks and laid them on the ground. While Ron lit a fire, Carmen took out some pieces of bread from the bag. They ate their bread together without saying a word. After some time, Carmen lay down on the blanket and tried to get some sleep. However, she couldn't do so after what she had witnessed. Whenever she closed her eyes, Mason and Ron's grandfather's faces passed before her eyes. She still couldn't believe that they were dead. She opened her eyes suddenly when the vision of their dead bodies lying on the ground came to mind.

Meanwhile, Ron was next to the stream, sharpening a branch he found on the ground with his pocketknife. He had a lot of things on his mind and was extremely upset with himself. He hated being helpless, and at that moment, he felt really helpless. Perhaps he could have gone there and drowned them all in the water, but that wasn't possible. He knew he didn't stand a chance by himself against the two most powerful men on Crictus and their many guards. It would be suicide to leave Anka behind all alone and throw himself in front of them. He couldn't put Anka's life in danger. Anka was more important than everything, even his family... his eyes filled with tears. He thought about his grandfather, who had raised him since he was born, and his brother whom he loved more than anything. Until that day, Ron had done many things to protect his brother from evil. He recalled how Mason came running home when their grandfather wasn't home. Mason looked very scared.

"They're chasing me," he said breathlessly. Ron was only twelve years old. Nevertheless, he picked up a shovel and tromped outside. Mason also went out, hiding behind his brother. There were two huge men standing in front of Ron.

"Give that kid to us! He let out my klaushes into the forest. Who's going to pay for them now?"

Ron hid his brother behind him and stepped forward bravely.

"He's very young. If you have a problem, settle it with me..."

The barely discernable smile on Ron's face disappeared as soon as it had appeared. The brother he had protected for so long was no longer alive. He hadn't been able to protect him enough. He began rubbing his pocketknife harder against the branch. There was an inconceivable rage inside him. He wanted to find the Soul Hunter and kill him. He wanted to avenge his family and many other families. A tear fell from his eyes. He had not cried in so long. He was making such a great effort to be strong that he had no time to show weakness.

"Aren't you asleep yet?"

It was Carmen. She got up from where she was lying and stood behind Ron. Ron replied, stopping his voice from trembling.

"No."

Carmen wistfully took a few steps closer to him.

"I'm sorry." Ron couldn't look at Carmen. He didn't want her to see him crying. "I shouldn't have come down so hard on you today. Their deaths were not your fault." Carmen's voice sounded sincere and apologetic. When she lay down to sleep, she thought about what happened and regretted shouting at Ron. "I had no right to yell at you like that. I was just very pissed off and sad, and... I took it out on you." Ron sniffed involuntarily. "Are you crying?"

There was surprise in Carmen's voice. She came a few steps closer and touched him on the shoulder. Ron quickly turned away from Carmen.

"No, I'm not crying."

As he was saying this, he wiped the tear from his eye. Carmen went and sat next to him and leaned her head on his shoulder. They were looking at the stream together. After a while, Ron put his arm around Carmen's shoulder. Carmen came closer to Ron. This was what they needed the most at that moment, compassion and not to be alone. It had been a very tough day for both of them. Ron felt better with Carmen's warmth. They both managed to regain composure at last and had calmed each other.

The two of them spent the following day in the forest just talking, without any sword practice or the like. They both needed to rest. Though still feeling blue, they supported each other and felt better than yesterday.

Before it got dark, they walked about to collect some firewood. When they finally returned to the camping area, Ron spoke.

"You can go ahead and light the fire. I'll bring some water from the stream."

Before Carmen could object, Ron had already reached the creek. Carmen looked at the firewood in distress. She stacked the firewood as she had seen in the movies, but she didn't know how to light it up. She wished she had carried a lighter with her. She took a furtive glance at Ron and saw that he was watching her mirthfully.

"You can't set that wood ablaze just by gazing at it."

"I was just trying my luck," said Carmen, partaking in his mockery.

Ron grinned and went over to Carmen. Squatting down, he started to talk, rubbing together two rocks he had picked up from the ground.

"If you do this and manage to light a piece of wood, you can light the blaze, but you have to be careful. The wood should be dry, so it can burn easily." Then he handed the rocks to Carmen. "Now you try."

Carmen took the rocks grudgingly. After trying a few times, she managed to produce a spark. When she succeeded, she looked happily at Ron. Ron looked at Carmen playfully.

"Do you want me to teach you another way?"

Carmen shrugged.

"If it's easier, why not?" Ron looked at the firewood with a gentle smile. He looked as if he was trying to focus. Carmen immediately used this opportunity. "You can't set that wood on fire just by gazing at it, Ron."

Her voice was clearly sarcastic. After Ron smiled and looked at Carmen, he moved his hands over the firewood.

"*Kati, sanim...*"*

(Fire, burn...)

The firewood suddenly burst into flames. Carmen's eyes almost popped out of her face.

"You said you didn't know how to cast a spell before?"

Ron shrugged.

"Because I didn't want my grandfather to find out. When I was a child, I used to study from the magic books he hid, but I could only keep a few of them in my mind."

Carmen suddenly got excited.

"Do you think I have a talent for magic, too?"

"I don't know. Even if your mom was able to cast spells, you wouldn't expect from someone who had the magic books banned to openly declare her talent."

Carmen looked at the fire despondently.

"I wish I was able to cast spells like you."

"Be careful what you wish for, magic is a dangerous craft."

Ron looked contemplative. Carmen grumbled faintly at Ron's words, and he chuckled at this. He found it funny that Carmen was fretting over the simplest things.

After talking for some time, they both went to sleep.

Toward morning, Ron heard someone cry. First, he thought he was dreaming. When he opened his eyes, he saw that it was only Carmen crying in her dream. As soon as Ron understood Carmen was weeping, he got up from where he was lying and went over to her.

"Carmen, wake up!" Ron was trying to calm Carmen down by stroking her hair. After a while, Carmen slowly opened her eyes. She continued to cry when she saw Ron in front of her. He hugged her as she straightened up a bit.

"Hey, it's okay, it's over now." He was trying to calm her down. Carmen was still under the influence of her dream.

"It was my all fault," she whispered. "It was my fault your family died."

"That's not true."

Ron hugged her more tightly. After a while, Carmen pulled back and gazed into Ron's eyes.

"Had I not been there, you could've rescued them and you wouldn't have to go through any of this." She bowed her head timidly. She seemed as if she was ashamed of herself. "I ruined your life."

Ron held and lifted Carmen's face. With his other hand, he wiped the tears off her cheeks. There was a sad smile on his face.

"This wasn't your fault. Had you not been there, I would've foolishly thrown myself in front of the Soul Hunter, then I would've died too." Carmen sniffed. Ron softly stroked Carmen's face. "You saved my life." Carmen looked at Ron, barely smiling.

"You're just saying that to make me feel better."

"No. It is the truth. You know me by now." Ron wiped the tears from her face. With Ron's touch, she gasped and looked into his eyes. But then, instantly she averted her gaze. She was overwhelmed with emotions. What she went through was too much for her. "Please, don't think like that again," Ron said. Carmen nodded and smiled faintly at him.

A few hours later, they went down to the city center to buy some supplies. Though Carmen had recovered, she wasn't feeling her best. Talking to Ron along the way made her feel better. As they headed into town, they saw people rushing toward the castle. They stopped and asked someone as they passed.

"King Edmund is going to address his citizens. He's summoned everyone into the castle courtyard."

Carmen and Ron looked at each other. Ron entered a shop to buy two cloaks with some of the money they were going to spend on food. Since Inca had seen them before, they couldn't take the risk of being recognized. Then they headed back to the castle after donning their cloaks. The courtyard of the castle had standing room only. As Ron decided that staying closer to the castle was too risky, they began to wait at the edge of the courtyard for the Soul Hunter to come out into the open and speak. There was too much noise as the crowd milled around loudly. The chatter was suddenly interrupted by the rumbling sound of a bugle. Now nobody made a sound. Everyone was just looking at the large balcony of the castle. When the guard on duty stopped blowing the horn, he announced that King Edmund would appear. The people suddenly bowed in reverence. Even though they disliked the situation, Ron and Carmen also bowed in order not to stand out from the crowd. It was repugnant for Ron to bow before a murderer who had killed his family a few days ago.

"Rise, my loyal people," Edmund said.

Carmen looked up. It was hard to endure bowing before such a disgusting man. Inca was standing right next to the Soul Hunter. Both their outfits were embroidered gaudily, as if to show that they were rich and noble. In fact, they were definitely not noble.

King Edmund cleared his throat and began to speak. His voice sounded as loud as the voice of a common king. Carmen made a grimace.

"My beloved people…" He slowly looked over his minions. "Someone amongst you spread a very unpleasant rumor a few days ago about the return of Anka." Muttering began to rise from the crowd. Edmund used his loud voice to silence his people. "Unfortunately, I was privy to that same gossip myself as well. Someone fooled all of you by declaring Anka's return. I can assure you, these ugly rumors are groundless, indeed."

Carmen and Ron glanced at each other. A large woman next to them grumbled.

"Why would anyone do such a thing?"

Carmen looked at Ron wearily.

The king continued his speech, "Don't you worry, my loyal subjects. The one who spread this gossip has been punished by me, personally."

Ron gritted his teeth and turned to Carmen.

"Come with me. We're going to teach him a lesson."

Carmen followed Ron without comprehending. Ron practically ran to the closest riverbank he knew. This was a river that came from distant mountains and flowed through the forest as it passed near the protective walls of the castle. Ron stopped when he came to the edge of the burbling river and gave Carmen a hopeful look.

"How about we piss that Soul Hunter off a bit?"

Carmen looked at Ron with a sly smile.

"I'd certainly like that."

"Then the only thing you need to do is to direct your energy to the sky, you know, the way you did when you pointed it at the tree while we were practicing. Then I'll raise the water up to the sky in the same way."

Carmen's eyes glowed.

"And so his lies will be exposed before his loyal subjects."

"Absolutely."

Carmen gleefully clapped her hands.

"Are you ready?" Ron said.

Carmen nodded as she raised her hands. During her training with Ron, she had nearly mastered full control of her Anka powers. She sent the light beams out of her hands into the air without any difficulty. At the same time, Ron hurled the water he pulled from the river into the air.

Edmund was still speaking in the castle's courtyard.

"There's nothing to worry about. Pay no heed to such horrible rumors. Anka hasn't returned and I will make sure she never does for that matter…"

A villager in the crowd suddenly pointed in a direction.

"Sie! *Anka ay miana!*" *

*Look! Anka has returned**

People in the courtyard, Edmund and Derick all turned their faces to the powerful beam of light that splits the sky. Water was revolving around and enveloping the light beam. Someone amongst the people pointed at the light beam.

"Rumors are true! She is back!"

When he said that, the courtyard sank into chaos. People were laughing, arguing, and yelling at the same time. The castle guards try to control the crowd.

Edmund, boiled with rage, glared at the light beam. Then he turned his back and walked to the castle exit to head toward the beam.

Just then, Anka and Ron wrapped up their show, pulled their cloaks up their heads, and mingled with the people behind some houses. Despite the guards' efforts to hold them, the crowd charged out of the courtyard and headed toward the spot where they thought they had seen the light. Carmen and Ron duly followed the crowd. After a while, Edmund emerged from the crowd with his protective guards.

"Where is she?" He pushed his way through the crowd angrily and went to the riverside. He turned furiously toward the crowd. "Did anyone see her?" No answer came from the crowd. Edmund glowered over the crowd in rage. "It won't be good for you if you hide her."

Silence fell over the crowd. Carmen and Ron were watching Edmund's frothing anger with immense pleasure. Edmund was absolutely immersed in his rage. Anka had made him look like a fool in front of his subjects. Worst of all, she was right here, somewhere amidst the crowd. He couldn't feel Anka because of the spirit of his brother standing next to him, but he knew she was somewhere out there. His eyes scanned the crowd, but he had no idea what Anka or her emerald looked like. All he wanted was to seek and destroy her for she had humiliated a king in front of his people. This was unacceptable.

"I know you're out there, you coward!"

Edmund was shouting at the crowd. Carmen had no intention of revealing herself, as she knew she had no chance against the Soul Hunter yet. Edmund listened to the crowd for a while longer. After an unbearable silence, he decided to force her out.

"You asked for it, little girl."

Then he grabbed a middle-aged, lanky man by the scruff of his collar and dragged him out. The man found himself cowering on the ground without being able to defend himself against his king.

"If you don't reveal yourself at once, this man will die!"

The cheerful smile on Carmen's face quickly faded. She looked at Ron in fear. He was fidgeting.

"Will he really kill him?" Carmen whispered.

"I don't know," said Ron whispered back. But he did know.

By now, Edmund was ballistic and wore a psychopathic smile on his face.

"Okay then. He will pay for your cowardness."

Just then, a voice was heard from the crowd. It was a young girl with long blond hair. She proceeded to the front of the crowd.

"Your Highness, I'm begging you. Please don't do this. Don't take my father from me."

The girl was down on her knees, pleading with Edmund. The king towered over the girl.

"Who do you serve?"

The girl answered without any compunction.

"Of course, yours, Your Majesty… You have no rival."

A big smile appeared on Edmund's face.

"No, Lilian! Don't pretend to side with this man just to save my soul." When he said that, the expression on Edmund's face disappeared as he gloated at Lilian.

"I'm so sorry, young lady, but it seems your father doesn't agree with you. Let me put it this way, those who support Anka deserve to die."

Lilian held her breath. Her eyes were filled with tears. But before she could object, her father started screaming. Lilian shrieked, too, as she tried to hold her father's body.

Carmen rested her head on Ron's chest and closed her ears. Her eyes were also tightly shut. Ron hugged Carmen. This time, he too couldn't bear to see what was happening. He turned his head the other way. After a while, the screaming ended. Carmen looked at Edmund in rage.

"That is what happens to Anka supporters!"

There was no sound coming from the people, just that of Lilian crying as she hugged her father's dead body. The anger inside Carmen was beyond words. She wanted to kill him right then and there. Yes, she really wanted this. She couldn't believe she was really considering such a thing, but she seriously wanted to kill this man. She looked at Ron.

"Get me out of here."

Ron agreed without hesitation since he saw guards starting to rush around the crowd. They were going to question anyone who was there. Ron was still hugging Carmen as they sneaked out through the empty streets. Carmen wanted to scream. She wanted to ask the people why they didn't stop the Soul Hunter even though she already knew the answer. They were scared… They needed a savior, a leader. Carmen finally understood her destiny. She wanted to stop that man with all her heart and ascend to her throne once again. She glanced at Ron. Yes… *She was adamant about stopping this disgusting murderer and ascending to the throne.*

7

Carmen and Ron were in deep sorrow when they reached their campsite. They had disgraced Edmund in front of everyone, like they wanted to do, but paid a heavy price in return. Carmen felt responsible for this death, just as she felt responsible for Ron's grandfather and brother's deaths. Perhaps, nobody would have to die if she revealed herself. But she knew well that Ron wouldn't allow such a thing.

Carmen removed her cloak in distress and sat down on the blanket she laid on the ground. They had also forgotten to buy food in the commotion, so they prepared a meal with what they had and ate it. They barely talked that day as they felt very depressed. Carmen prepared the meal when Ron went to collect some wood for the fire. After eating their dinner together, they watched the fire for a while without talking. Carmen was jabbing a long wooden stick in her hand into the fire and then drawing back. After some time, she decided to, at least, try to go to sleep. She thought that sleep would do her good, but she couldn't for the life of her fall asleep. Whenever she closed her eyes, she remembered the faces of the people slain by the Soul Hunter and then the cries of that girl, Lilian… She closed her eyes tightly. She didn't want to think about these things, but she couldn't avoid it. These deaths were too much for her. She felt as if everything she touched was ruined. She was ruining everything. *First Ron's family, and now this,* she thought. She felt awful. She couldn't hold back anymore and started to cry. She was crying silently as she didn't want Ron to hear. Ron was watching the flames when he heard Carmen crying quietly. He doused the fire with water and once the fire went out, he approached Carmen and caressed her head and hair. Carmen could not stop crying, but Ron's compassion was making her feel better.

"Please don't cry," Ron sounded sad.

"Was it my fault?"

"Soul Hunter is a ruthless horrible man. This is not on you." Ron wiped the tears from Carmen's face. "Try to get some sleep."

Carmen looked at Ron and nodded as if to say, 'all right.' He didn't want to leave Carmen alone that night. Ron had witnessed many people being killed before. In fact, he had killed some guards of the Soul Hunter to save his friends before, but he was aware of how all this was so new and hard on Carmen. He knew that she was strong enough to handle it, but he also knew that she needed time.

Ron slightly lifted the blanket on Carmen, lay down next to her, and embraced her. Then, he tucked her in. Carmen snuggled Ron and continued to weep quietly. Ron was stroking Carmen's hair. After a while, Carmen stopped crying and dozed off. Ron watched Carmen as she slept. A smile spread on his face for a moment as he admired Carmen's beauty.

He suddenly shook his thoughts off as he remembered that Carmen would be his queen one day.

He then put his head on the ground and closed his eyes.

When Carmen opened her eyes, she felt an arm on her. She turned slightly and looked. It was Ron. He seemed to be in a very deep slumber. Carmen giggled faintly. The giggling made Ron grunt and pull her over even closer. Carmen was contented and happy, but the sun was overhead, and they had to get up now.

"Ron…" He smacked his mouth. Carmen giggled. "Ron, it's time to get up." When Ron perceived Carmen's voice, he opened his eyes, and when he saw that he hugged her like a stingray, he pulled away his arm in embarrassment. Still sleepy, he looked around. "Hey, I thought you always woke up early." There was a smirk on Carmen's face.

"I must've been very tired," Ron said to brush it off.

In fact, he didn't remember sleeping so peacefully before. Lat night, he lay down next to Carmen to calm her. Apparently, Carmen had a calming effect on Ron as well.

Carmen didn't say anything about Ron's effort to brush it off. She only giggled. Hugging Ron while sleeping helped her relax. For a moment, she felt like she was at home in her warm bed.

Ron stood up with difficulty. He had slept longer than he had for a long time. He went to the stream and washed his face. Carmen straightened up. She was watching Ron with a smile on her face. When Ron turned back and looked at Carmen, he met her smile.

"What happened?"

"Nothing…" Carmen said, smiling.

Ron made a sour face without understanding. Then he went over to the cloth backpack and took enough money to buy a few things.

"I'm going to go and buy some stuff to eat. There's nothing left in the bag."

After a while, Ron took the road toward the city center. He enjoyed sleeping next to Carmen. Though, he was cursing himself inside. "You're such an idiot… Don't even think about it… She's your queen."

He reached the city after a long walk. He entered the first shop he found and bought some things to eat. He wanted to get back to Carmen without lingering much. He couldn't leave her alone for a long time. He watched the people around him while passing through the city on his way back. Everybody had already gone back to their daily lives.

When he returned to Carmen, he saw that she had folded the blankets on the ground and gathered some wood for the evening fire.

"I'm impressed," he said as he sat down and crossed his legs. Carmen sat right in front of him. Ron handed Carmen some of the food he had bought. Carmen started talking while she was taking the food Ron gave her.

"You know what? I was thinking about our next move toward the Soul Hunter and Inca." Ron sighed because Carmen's voice sounded more excited than it needed to be. Carmen continued to speak without losing her excitement. "I think we should break into the castle and possess the fire emerald."

Ron gave Carmen a look of disapproval.

"You aren't strong enough to confront the Soul Hunter yet."

"I'm not talking about confronting him, but we've got to act now. More people are dying even as we sit here."

Ron looked at Carmen. Since Carmen arrived on Crictus, it was the first time she had talked about taking action. Maybe he should use this opportunity, but he couldn't be sure if Carmen was ready.

"What we need is an army to march at the castle to take your throne back."

"Your grandfather said we should capture the fire emerald first. He said it will help our cause once I have two emeralds."

"We don't know if the emerald will find a host as soon as we get it."

"But shouldn't we at least try? You said it yourself; I am not strong enough to confront the Soul Hunter. With the power of two emeralds, I will be stronger. Anka has been gone for a long time. How will two of us convince a bunch of people to join our army? First, I need to be stronger and prove to people that I am worthy."

Ron hated to admit but she sounded wise.

"All right then, do you have a plan to get us into the castle?"

Carmen's excitement suddenly grew bigger.

"Yes, I've thought of something. When we were in the castle courtyard, I saw plenty of guards and maids. We won't be noticed if I disguise myself as a maid and you disguise yourself as a guard. Once we're inside, we can find the place where the emerald is held and take it."

Ron squinted.

"Okay, how are you planning to do all of this?"

The words sounded like mockery even though it was not Ron's intention. Carmen grumbled.

"You're not helping at all."

"All right, let's think it over together." Carmen straightened her back. She started to listen to Ron intently. "First of all, we have to find out how to get into the castle. Then, we have to find a maid outfit for you and a guard outfit for me. It looks difficult."

Carmen interrupted, "Isn't there anyone in the castle you may know? Someone who would be useful."

Ron mulled it over for a few moments. Klaus came to his mind. Klaus was an old friend of Ron's. Since Klaus's father was rich, he was on good terms with the Soul Hunter and he sent his son as a guard to the castle twice a week even though Klaus was not happy with this. His father was sending Klaus to the castle because he wanted his son to get a disciplined education, whereas Klaus hated the idea of fighting and being a warrior. He was not a great Soul Hunter supporter, but still, the decent relationship between his father and the Soul Hunter prevented him from hating the Soul Hunter.

Ron turned his nose up at the thought.

"In fact, there is someone, but I'm not sure if he'd like to help Anka or not."

"He's not going to know I'm Anka. We'll just say that we want to find work."

Ron started to realize that this idea could work. He narrowed his eyes again.

"Okay, let's say we get in. You should never encounter Edmund."

"Why?" Carmen made a sour face.

"Because he'll feel the presence of your soul." Carmen lifted her eyebrows. This could change the whole plan. "And Inca shouldn't see us either, because he's already seen us before."

Carmen sighed.

"Okay then. Neither of them should see us. Is there anything else we should look out for?"

Ron thought for a while.

"Of course, we shouldn't draw a lot of attention to ourselves either."

"That's easy," Carmen said, smiling.

"What about the room where the emerald is kept? How are you planning to find it?"

Carmen shrugged.

"By asking…" Ron frowned. Then, Carmen added. "Of course, without drawing attention…"

"Carmen…" Carmen stopped Ron.

"Look, I know the plan is… well, it's barely a plan. But I want to do this. I am ready." Ron studied her face. He could see her excitement. Carmen added.

"We will be careful. I promise." Ron still hadn't said anything.

"Oh, come on, Ron. We can't just sit here. I want to stop them. Or at least attempt. Please. I know I've been hesitant, but I know I can do this." Ron looked at Carmen for a while. He smiled slightly.

"I guess you *are* ready."

Carmen got excited again.

"So, are we going now or what?"

"Calm down. Not yet. First, we have to find jobs in the castle."

"Oh my God. We are actually going to do this!" Carmen said with an excited voice.

Ron added, "There's so many things that are bugging me. How am I going to protect you in the castle?"

"I can take care of myself."

Ron shook his head.

"Somehow, that doesn't put me at ease."

Carmen put her hand on Ron's knee.

"Just leave it to me."

Ron thought a little. Carmen's going to be queen in the future. He may not be with her all the time, and she's got to learn to protect herself. He thought, although this is risky, it may be a good opportunity. Ron held Carmen's hand.

"I trust you."

Carmen's eyes shone. Now she wanted to act and defeat the Soul Hunter as soon as possible. But first, she wanted to get the fire emerald out of that castle.

The idea sounded doable to Ron. One of the many things he worried about was that he had to leave Carmen alone. Despite this, he accepted the idea, because he wanted to go into action at least as much as Carmen. They had to start moving toward their goal at some point anyway. He wanted to give the Soul Hunter what he deserved and avenge his family as soon as possible.

For the rest of that day, Ron practiced sword fighting and one-on-one combat with Carmen. Carmen was better than before, but she still had no chance even against a weak guard. She needed more practice. On the other hand, though she was still making a lot of mistakes in assuming a position, she had started to perform her moves faster. Ron could easily reach her throat by dealing small, weak blows with his sword. When Carmen got bored of being defeated by Ron all the time, she would begin to grumble and hit faster. Ron loved her determination, but he couldn't help laughing when Carmen got angry every time. Her movements became stronger, but she started to make position faults more often. She couldn't manage both in any way.

At the end of the day, both were tired. After they ate dinner, they planned for the next day and then went to sleep. They were to go and talk with Klaus. Ron wasn't very hopeful about Klaus. Still, he thought that it was worth a shot. He was on good terms with Klaus. There had never been a conflict between them. Nevertheless, they weren't very close friends. They only greeted each other whenever their paths crossed. Ron was always getting in trouble while Klaus was a quiet boy. He never meddled in other people's business. Still, Ron thought that visiting Klaus the next day was a good idea since he had good intentions.

They went to visit Klaus the next day. Klaus' home was quite a distance from the castle. It was a colossal, magnificent house. Wealth was visible in every detail. Contrary to most houses made of wood in the city, this house was built from stone. It had a big and splendid door, a wide terrace, and a green garden. A housemaid opened the door. When Ron said they wanted to see Klaus, the woman kindly smiled and invited them in. The house was akin to a small palace with a rather high ceiling, several paintings hanging on the walls, and a very valuable embroidered carpet on the floor. Like the walls, the ceiling was also plastered with paintings. A large chandelier bejeweled with crystals hanging from the ceiling almost touched the floor. The interior of the house was quite gloomy. Even so, there was a strange beauty to the house.

While Carmen and Ron were waiting in the large entrance hall, Klaus started coming down the wide stairs. Klaus had short blond hair and was a well-dressed, charming young man. He wasn't so attractive, but he still had his own charisma.

"Ron! What a surprise!" Klaus came over to Ron with open arms, and hugged him in a friendly way, "Long time no see."

Klaus left Ron and looked at Carmen. Ron needed to make an introduction.

"Let me introduce you to… Carmen."

Carmen extended her hand. Klaus gently held and kissed Carmen's hand.

"Nice to meet you, m'lady."

Carmen just smiled softly in response to this strange flirtation.

"Nice to meet you too."

Feeling a bit perturbed by Klaus' sudden interest, Ron added, "We are to be wed."

Klaus stared at Ron in amazement. Carmen suddenly turned to Ron, floored with surprise.

"Congratulations. One day we should celebrate this."

"Yes, why not…" Carmen said, giving Ron a questioning look. She was smiling, trying to play along.

After a while, they ascended the stairs with Klaus and proceeded into the study room of Klaus's father. While Ron and Carmen were sitting on the two-seater sofa, Klaus pulled a chair and sat down in front of them.

"So, what brings you here?"

Ron got right to the crux of the matter, as he didn't want to stretch it out.

"We were wondering if you could arrange for us to work in the castle."

A great surprise appeared on Klaus' face.

"You... you want to work in the castle?"

"Yes," Ron said calmly.

"But you hate the Soul Hunter. And now you want to work for him?"

Ron shrugged, trying not to make him suspicious.

"I'm no longer among the rebels. After my grandfather and Mason died, I decided to start a new life." Ron looked at Carmen. "And now we need a place to work."

Carmen smiled and looked at Klaus.

"Yes, for our baby." Even Carmen couldn't believe what she was saying.

"Baby?" Klaus was astounded. Carmen had really messed things up. Fortunately, Ron saved the day.

"What she means is that we are planning to start a family, so we need to work and earn money. Don't we, my dear?"

Ron was warning Carmen with his tone. This time, Carmen merely nodded timidly. She decided not to speak again until the end of the talk.

"I see. I'm very sorry for your loss. I had no idea."

"It was sudden. An accident." Ron cleared his throat. "After their death, I needed to change my life entirely."

Klaus settled further into his chair.

"So, you're not a rebel anymore?"

"No, I'm not."

Klaus looked thoughtful. He was looking at Ron and Carmen in turns. It seemed as if he wouldn't agree to help if he saw the tiniest hesitation on their faces. After examining them for a long time, he took a deep breath.

"I can arrange something, I guess." Carmen could not stop herself from smiling. Klaus continued to speak. "However, I can't promise anything. I'll try to speak with the people in charge of hiring guards and maids. If you visit again in two days, I can give you the good or bad news."

Ron looked at Klaus thankfully.

"Thank you very much, Klaus. Thanks to you, we can start our family." Saying this, he hugged Carmen. Klaus looked at them, smiling.

A few minutes later, when they exited the house, Ron shot Carmen a mocking smile.

"A baby?"

Carmen glared at him.

"A marriage?"

Ron couldn't stop himself from laughing.

"What did you expect me to do? He was feasting on you with his eyes."

Carmen cheerily crossed her arms on her chest.

"So, were you jealous of him?"

"Of course not…" In fact, he was. Ron stopped. He thought of an excuse for a few seconds to convince Carmen. "Protecting you is my duty. I know how he gets with women. That's all."

Unconvinced, Carmen glanced at Ron.

"So what? Would you also be protecting me from the people I might be dating?"

Ron looked at Carmen in bewilderment.

"Did you like him?"

Carmen secretly wanted to see Ron's reaction. She shot a cross-look at Ron from the corner of her eye. He only looked surprised.

"I don't know, he is kinda nice…" She glanced at Ron again. When she saw the sadness that she hoped to find on Ron's face, she backed off. "But, no. I didn't like him." Ron remained reticent for a while. Noticing Ron's silence, Carmen took his arm. "Fine, my *fiancé*. I hope we'll get some good news in two days."

Ron smiled in response to Carmen's cheerful voice. They went back to their campsite in the forest together. Since it was still early, they decided that they could use some practice. This time, Ron focused on attack techniques. Until that night, he taught Carmen mostly defense. He thought it was now time to also teach her some attack techniques. Carmen was a fast learner. She was more beautiful, clever, and funnier than all the girls he had seen before. She had a subtle wit, a characteristic he usually didn't look for in the girls he went out with. No wonder why Anka had chosen her. Carmen made him feel better. However, he was constantly warning himself against feeling this way. Carmen was going to become a queen, who would rule the entire planet in the future. Ron's only duty was to protect her. If they had a relationship, this would inevitably catch the attention of their enemies and would pose a great danger to Carmen. An emerald could never put its Anka at risk. Showing weakness to the enemy would be Anka's end. He had also found out how brave Carmen was on the days they had spent together. If they got into a relationship and Ron found himself in danger, he knew that she would want to save Ron without thinking about Anka's soul, just like her mother. This meant putting Anka in jeopardy in yet another way.

Carmen lay down after they had finished practicing. She was exhausted. Carmen was watching Ron as he placed the swords into their scabbards. Ron prepared the dinner that night. Carmen washed their clothes in the lake. They were always sharing the tasks between them as they worked in harmony. After a long conversation around the campfire, they both laid out on their blankets. Carmen was watching the night sky, amongst the trees, the stars, and a red moon of Crictus she had just seen. The forest was bathed in a red hue from the reflection of the moon. Carmen remembered that the light of a white moon had reflected on her face when they were in Ron's cabin. She likened it to the Moon that revolved around the Earth, but this satellite reminded her more of the red planet Mars.

"How many moons does Crictus have?"

Ron looked at where Carmen was looking. The little crimson satellite hovered just overhead and brightened their environs.

"It has three."

"Three? Wow, Earth only has one." Carmen examined the red satellite. It looked like the Moon, but there were no craters on it. Instead, it seemed as if someone had drawn orange lines on it. Carmen spoke after a while. "I haven't seen the third one yet."

"The third is Jolast, the purple satellite... That's the farthest from Crictus. It's the slowest of the three and only gets close enough to be visible every few years or so."

Carmen giggled faintly. She liked the idea of a purple satellite. Carmen was learning new things every day. Ron had a major role in this. He was a good teacher. A teacher who protected her from everything... Ron was a great guardian. Over these past two weeks, Carmen learned she could trust him with her heart and soul and always felt like nobody could harm her while she was with Ron. On the other hand, she didn't want her life to depend on Ron's protection. There were many enemies out there, and Ron was only human. It would be foolish to pin all her hopes on Ron, which was why Carmen was trying to improve both her sword and her one-on-one combat skills as much as possible. She was committing everything Ron said to her memory and trying not to forget any of it. Sometimes, she thought that she might have become a scientist if she had shown interest in her lessons on Earth, the same way she was interested in what Ron had to say. But as it turns out, she was made for this.

Ron was very patient in teaching Carmen, and she admired his patience every time. Even if Carmen tried a lot, most moves Ron showed required physical strength, and indeed, Carmen was sort of a stranger when it came to sports. Still, Carmen was trying hard to do her best. She would be a queen if she could beat the Soul Hunter and Inca, of course. That's why she had to fight like a queen.

They both got up early the next morning. Ron was surprised that he didn't have to wake Carmen up for the first time. He usually had a tough time waking her up each morning in order to get her to go practicing. But this was not the case that day. When Ron woke up, he found she was not in her place. Ron leapt up in haste but found Carmen sitting, with breakfast already prepared. It was impossible not to be surprised.

"Wow, this must be the last day of our lives."

"Haha… Good morning to you, too."

Carmen said this like she was offended, but in fact, she wasn't. She usually was not an early riser, even if she went to bed early the night before. However, that morning was an exception. A disturbing dream had woken her up in which she saw somebody who woke up a man by pouring a bucket of water on him. The same person forced him to get to his feet, then tossed him amongst the other prisoners like a rag. Carmen was watching what was happening as if behind a curtain and everything seemed quite real. The man got in line with the other prisoners. Unlike the others, his body was more muscular, but it looked as if he had melted away over the years. He looked at least ten years older than he was. He had dark brown hair, hazel eyes that were almost green, and a scraggly beard covering most of his face. Sadness flowed from his eyes. One could easily fathom how much pain he had suffered throughout his life just by looking into his eyes. Carmen felt pity for this man. While he was in line with the other prisoners, a man approached him. It was obvious that he was an officer in charge. The officer told him that he had slacked off yesterday and smacked him with a whip in his hand. That's when Carmen awoke, startled.

"I'm sorry. Good morning to you, too. To what do we owe this honor?"

Meanwhile, Ron took his breakfast that Carmen handed him. In fact,

Carmen wanted to tell Ron about her dream, but she didn't want to bother him either. She didn't want to ruin Ron's cheerful morning. That's why she lightly mused and just shrugged.

"Nothing…"

Carmen changed the subject before Ron realized her languor. Her voice was artificially cheerful when she spoke, "So, what are we going to do today? We've got a long day ahead of us before we find out if we're going to be able to enter the castle or not."

"I want to get in some good practice today."

Ron didn't tell Carmen what he had on his mind. Instead, he went down to the city as soon as he finished his breakfast to buy two wooden training swords. Ron wanted Carmen to work with real swords first because he predicted that she could have difficulty switching from a wooden sword to a real one.

Ron came back to the camping site holding the two wooden swords in his hands. Seeing them, Carmen laughed.

"Is this the very special practice?"

Carmen stood up. Handing one of the swords to Carmen, Ron said, "Until now I always held myself back, but people you encounter in real life will strike you with all their might. We're going to work on this today."

Carmen complained about being physically inadequate. They took their positions. Carmen drew her sword. After sizing Carmen up for a while, Ron attacked with all his strength. Carmen stopped Ron's sword blow, but she couldn't resist its force and dropped her sword. She couldn't calculate that Ron would be so strong. Ron bent down and took the sword from the ground.

"Do you understand what I mean now?"

Carmen took the sword from Ron. Her voice sounded a little shaky.

"I can't counter such a hard blow."

"You can. Let's try again."

They practiced the entire day during which Carmen received a lot of blows. They were practicing like this for the first time, and Carmen felt terribly incompetent. It was as if she had suddenly forgotten everything she had learned. She was feeling down since she was so clumsy during the entire practice. She gave the sword to Ron, puffing.

"You'll get better over time. Don't worry."

"How can I not worry? I'm utterly useless. I couldn't stop even one of your strikes."

Ron was very gentle with her as usual.

"I think you were quite good."

"Yeah I bet."

Carmen stormed off and went to the stream. All her clothes and her face were wet with sweat. She leaned down to the stream and washed her face with cold water. The water soothed her a lot as she washed her face several times. Raising her head, she looked across the stream. She was petrified by what she saw. This was impossible. She closed and reopened her eyes. She wanted to be sure what she saw was real.

The woman she had seen in her dreams was standing in front of her, Juliet… The previous carrier of Anka's soul… Also, her mother she had never met before… she swallowed. Closing and opening her eyes made no difference. Juliet was still there, standing just across the stream and looking at Carmen. She was wearing a white and golden dress, just like in Carmen's dreams. Her brown hair was falling down from her shoulders. Her eyes were very dark like a deep bottomless well. There was compassion in her looks. It was as if she was finally looking at her daughter whom she couldn't hold and feast her eyes on when she was alive. Carmen was still having a hard time believing her eyes. The previous Anka had died sixteen years ago. But now she was standing in front of her. She was so real… Carmen stood up without taking her eyes off of her. Juliet's eyes were following her as Carmen moved. Carmen studied her. She was a young woman. She thought she must have looked like that when she died. How young had she died… She must have been in her late twenties. She looked very beautiful.

"Are you real?"

Carmen felt idiotic. Whoever was standing in front of her was probably not real. Even if she was, she couldn't be anything other than a ghost. Like a fool, she waited for a ghost to speak and stared at her.

"This is nonsense. You're not real."

Carmen patiently closed her eyes and opened them again. She thought she was going mad, but the woman was still there.

I'm real…

The voice echoed in Carmen's head. Carmen opened her eyes wide. It was impossible to think that what she was hearing was not real. Juliet's lips hadn't moved but it was her voice. Carmen was sure of it.

"You can speak!" There was an extraordinary surprise in her voice.

"Carmen?" This was Ron. Carmen quickly turned to Ron.

"Ron, Juliet's here!"

Carmen tugged at Ron's arm and showed him where Juliet was standing. But Juliet wasn't there anymore. Knitting his eyebrows in wonder, Ron was looking at where Carmen pointed. Since Carmen made herself look like crazy, she really felt bad.

"But… She was there." Her voice sounded whispery. After a moment, she turned to Ron. "Ron. I'm serious. I saw her. She spoke to me."

Ron looked at Carmen with compassion.

"I don't see her."

"I know but she was there. I know what I saw."

Ron looked again at where Carmen pointed. Then, he sighed and put his arms around Carmen's shoulders.

"C'mon, let's get some rest now."

Carmen was upset because Ron didn't believe her, but if she were in his place, she would do the same. As always, Ron showed patience to a person who said she had seen someone who had died sixteen years ago…

Carmen didn't see Juliet the rest of that day, but she couldn't get her appearance out of her mind. Ron didn't worry about Carmen. He knew that strange things could happen to a person who carries an immortal soul. That's why he didn't give this event much thought. They ate their dinner together. It was a dinner full of conversation followed by laughter as usual. In reality, they were both nervous, because their plan for entering the castle was serious and dangerous. Both were aware of this, and both inwardly hoped that Klaus's response would be negative. Still, they didn't mention any of this that evening. They wanted to keep their minds occupied.

Ron woke Carmen up in the morning. After getting ready together, they walked toward Klaus' house. They looked at each other nervously when they arrived at the door. It was Ron who knocked. It was the same maid who had opened the door two days ago. This time she took them right away to the study room of Klaus' father. Carmen and Ron sat down and began to wait. After they waited for a few minutes, Klaus came in.

"My friends, how are you?"

Ron smiled.

"Fine, De Gine*."

Thank you. *

Klaus smiled and sat on the chair opposite of them.

"Yes, about finding you a job…" Klaus settled into his chair. "I talked to the officers in the castle. They said that they wouldn't be able to find work for you."

There was silence. Carmen and Ron looked at each other. They were supposed to be upset, but they were neither sad nor happy. Klaus continued to speak.

"Fortunately, the Wensterdolph last name worked and I got you a job."

Ron looked at Klaus, smiling.

"That's great," said Ron but his face was telling another story. He continued.

"When do we start?"

"You can start tomorrow."

Just like Ron, Carmen tried to smile, but she was gripped by an abominable fear.

When they exited the house, they walked without talking. There were many thoughts in their minds. In fact, they were ecstatic that they could finally get into action, but they were still afraid. Carmen used to believe that spies and fugitives she saw in spy movies were only in the movies. Now she had to play the spy role herself by entering the castle, hiding, and then stealing a very precious emerald. She had no idea how she would manage to pull this off. It was frightening to even think about it. The most exciting thing in her life—in her previous life, that is—was to get carried away and get wasted at the annual, "Welcome Summer!" party. But now she was putting herself in imminent danger. She had only acted in a school play once in second grade, and she was quite a failure at that. She never tried acting after that. She didn't have a knack for acting. Now she had to make sure nobody noticed she was Anka and that she came from another world. And it was not the only thing she was worried about. It would be the first time she would be separated from Ron. Ever since she arrived on Crictus, she had been with him the entire time, and she had always trusted him to protect her. Now she had to take care of herself. This was scary. Until now, she had always trusted Ron. It was obvious that the days without him would be difficult for her. Moreover, there was this rule that neither the Soul Hunter nor Inca should see her, of course. Since Inca had seen them before, everything would come out and their plan would be ruined the moment he saw Carmen or Ron. On top of that, the Soul Hunter could feel Carmen's soul. This would also cause their plan to fail. That's why she had to be on her guard at all times.

Ron had his own reasons to be worried as well. He was only anxious about Carmen. He knew that she hadn't undertaken such endeavors before and that this would be the first time for her. Ron was generally a master at going undercover. Such things had gradually become routine. So, while it wasn't difficult for him to get to the castle for undercover duty, all of this was new for Carmen. It had been almost three weeks since she came to a planet she didn't even know existed. It was such a short time to accustom oneself. On the other hand, Ron thought that she wouldn't have suggested such a plan if she hadn't felt ready. It was his only consolation. He was worried that he wouldn't be able to protect her. This was his one and only duty and he didn't want to screw up. Unfortunately, the places where the guards and castle maids stayed were far away from each other, and he was less likely to meet up with her in the castle during the day, which gave him reason to be anxious. If and when Carmen encountered Inca or the Soul Hunter, he might not be able to protect her. Being unable to protect her meant that he failed, and an emerald could never fail.

They remained quiet as they walked to the camping site together. When they sat down, Ron was the first to speak.

"So, what do you think?"

Carmen was fidgeting with the grass on the ground. She looked stressed.

"This is going to be tough…" Carmen looked at Ron. Then, she shrugged. "I don't know. The most important thing I've ever done before was… Well, not much," she stopped and sighed.

Ron stood up and sat next to Carmen.

"We don't have to go through with this If you are not ready."

Carmen objected immediately.

"No, we definitely have to do this. This will be our only chance to take the emerald."

"But still, if you don't feel you're up for it, we don't need to do this."

Carmen thought for a moment. Ron watched Carmen to observe her gestures.

"We can try to build an army. I can reconnect with my rebel friends and maybe—"

"No. I'm ready. Only…" She wasn't looking at Ron. She didn't know what to say exactly. Fear, anxiety, and hesitation… But also, eagerness… she was confused. Ron tried to complete Carmen's words.

"… you're afraid."

"It's not only fear…"

Ron gently pulled Carmen toward himself. Carmen put her head onto Ron's chest.

"I understand. All of these are quite new for you but you're Anka. Being a queen is your destiny… The courage you are looking for is in you. Sooner or later, you're going to have to go into that castle and face them to take out the Soul Hunter."

Carmen sighed, worried, "I'm not strong enough to do that."

"Of course, you're strong. You're Anka."

Carmen moved away from Ron.

"No. I'm someone who's lived as an ordinary girl on Earth for sixteen years, and suddenly everyone expects me to go to another planet and rescue them, but I can't. I don't know how to fight, I don't know how to use a sword, and I don't know how to go undercover. I'm just not a strong person."

While saying this, Carmen's voice trembled, and her eyes filled with tears. Ron put his hands on Carmen's face. When Carmen closed her eyes, he caught and wiped away a tear as it dropped from her eye.

"Nobody expects you to be a perfect queen overnight, Carmen. You have plenty of time."

Carmen sniffed.

"No, you don't understand. Even you're telling me I am Anka. Now I know exactly what this represents. I was among the people. I saw what they truly need. They need a savior. They need their Anka and the Anka they expect is perfect and strong, but…" another tear drop fell from her eye, "that's not who I am."

Ron embraced Carmen. He held her tightly as she cried in his arms. Carmen's burden was too much for her. She was overwhelmed by her responsibilities. Ron wanted to get her out of this more than anything. After a while, he pushed her away a little and wiped the tears in her eyes.

"You're strong, Carmen. In fact, you're stronger than anyone I've ever met. You've experienced more pain than most people can endure in a lifetime. You had to leave your family and your home to come to a planet you never knew. You left everything behind for your people. Then, two people you cared about were killed in front of you, but you survived the pain of it. You tried to work harder and get stronger. That day, the day when the Soul Hunter killed that poor man, I saw your face. I saw how you looked at the Soul Hunter. I know how much you want to depose him. And you don't have to do it by yourself. I'll be with you all the time. We're going to do this together. I promise I will stand by your side no matter what and we are going to destroy that Soul Hunter, for your people. And tomorrow… We'll take the first step to depose him. We'll do this together." Carmen looked at Ron, smiling, and hugged him.

"Thank you for being with me, Ron."

Ron hugged her tightly.

8

The next morning, they took the road to the castle. Before they set out, they hid all their belongings at the campsite under a rock in a cave. They would come back to pick them up when they finished their mission. Carmen was taking deep breaths while walking together. Ron was trying to concentrate on other subjects to hide his stress. When they reached the castle, at last, they stopped in the courtyard. Ron looked at Carmen.

"Are we doing this?"

Carmen looked at the castle. She was full of fear, but she still wanted to do this. Ron's pep talk had worked.

"C'mon, let's do it."

They walked toward the castle together. The guard at the gate asked them why they were there. After they said they had come to work, the guard took them inside from one of the rear gates. A plump woman welcomed them inside.

"Welcome to the castle. Mr. Wensterdolph must have sent you."

The woman towered over them with her demeanor. In fact, she wasn't taller than Ron. Nevertheless, she was a portly woman.

"Yes, ma'am. We're here for work."

"Great. My name is Margaret. I'll be your supervisor."

She was looking at Carmen while saying this. Carmen smiled imperceptibly, but it was obvious that the woman was a pouter. There were deep wrinkles on her face. Her facial expression seemed as if she had never smiled in her entire life before.

"Let me show you around."

They followed Margaret as she gave them a brief tour of the castle. She showed some of the rooms, the kitchen, the area where the employees ate, and the place where they took their noon break. In addition, she also told them what they would do. When they finally came to the guard section, Margaret spoke.

"The attendant guard here will show you where you'll stay. Do you have any questions?"

Ron looked at Carmen.

"How will I be able to see my fiancée?"

"You can see her at breakfast, lunch, or dinner, but beyond these hours, both of you should be at your workstations. Remember, any intimacy in the castle is strictly prohibited. You can only be together on your off days."

Carmen blushed.

"Thank you," Ron said, and after smiling at Carmen, he proceeded to the guard section.

Carmen sighed after Ron. Margaret hurried off on her way. Carmen kept pace as she started to follow her. They went into the section where the maids were staying. Margaret showed Carmen her new room.

"From now on, this is your room… You'll be offered a better room if you don't slack off."

"Thank you, Margaret."

Margaret's face fell. She went out without saying anything and slammed the door hard. Carmen grimaced, not knowing what she had done wrong. After Margaret left, she glanced at the room. There was a wardrobe, an old carpet on the floor, and two beds instead of one in the room. Carmen realized that she would not be alone. She sat down on the bed with folded clothes. She picked up the clothes and sighed because there was no mirror around. It looked like this was going to be a very challenging process. She stood up and looked out of the window. There were iron bars on the window and the window was quite small. She was looking at the garden where they would take a break at noon. Carmen's room was in one of the buildings just next to the castle, just like Ron's room. Still, it was among the outer walls of the castle. Carmen sighed again. At that moment, she jumped as the door opened suddenly. A girl with piercing blue eyes and long straight blond hair entered the room. Carmen recognized her immediately. It was Lilian, the poor girl whose father was killed by the Soul Hunter. Carmen was looking in shock at Lilian who smiled slightly.

"You must be the new girl. I'm Lilian."

Carmen cleared her throat in astonishment.

"Carmen."

The girl knitted her brows.

"*Hmm*. That's a strange name, but cute. Where are you from?"

Carmen gulped. She didn't know anywhere on Crictus!

"I… I'm from here."

Lilian smiled.

"For a moment, I thought you were going to say you came from the Carnen Dynasty." She went and sat on her bed.

"No. How long have you been working here?" Carmen said this to keep Lilian from asking more questions.

"It's been almost a year now. I was saving money for my family." The smile on her face momentarily disappeared. She must have remembered her father. Carmen couldn't believe that the Soul Hunter murdered the father of one of his employees. But she didn't think the Soul Hunter knew his employees, or even looked at their faces. "Now I'm only saving for myself, I suppose."

Apparently, her father was the only person left from her family, and he was no longer here. Carmen spoke sorrowfully, "I'm sorry."

Lilian glanced at Carmen in surprise.

"So, you know." She stopped. She bowed her head unhappily. "Of course, you do. Everybody knows."

Carmen was blaming herself for Lilian's father's death. Ron said that it was unnecessary, but she could not help it. Now she was in front of the girl whose father was killed. She didn't know what to say. Carmen went over and sat next to Lilian.

"Of course, I can't console you, but I don't have a family either."

Lilian smiled unhappily.

"Were they killed in front of your eyes?" The regret inside Carmen gradually widened. She had a chance, but she couldn't save Lilian's father. Lilian looked down.

"I'm sorry. That was insensitive," said Lilian.

"I never met them."

Lilian lifted her head up and stared at Carmen.

"Oh, I apologize."

"It's all right."

Lilian laughed softly.

"If you don't get dressed soon, you'll be fired on your first day on the job."

Carmen stood up.

"You're right."

Thus, her first day at work began. Her maid dress was awful. She had to wear a long brown skirt that went up to her chest and made her look fat. She wore a long-sleeved top with a small V-neck that resembled a white shirt and some odd headgear. Even though Carmen was uncomfortable in this outfit, she started her job in the castle. Her first task was to scrub the floors. She couldn't believe that she was cleaning the floor for the sake of an emerald. When she was on Earth, she had never done any housework. In fact, she hated doing household chores. But she had to do this in order to find the emerald.

Fortunately, lunchtime came around quickly. She went to eat lunch with her new friend Lilian. This was also the only daytime opportunity she had to see Ron. Not everyone ate at the same time during the meal breaks. Half of the employees who continued to work went down to eat an hour later. She went down, hoping Ron was in the dining section. After she took her meal with her tray, she sat down with Lilian at a table in the garden. Next to them were the tables reserved for the guards. Carmen scanned the tables, hoping to see Ron. Lilian giggled.

"Some of the guards look handsome, don't they?"

"What?" Carmen looked at Lilian without comprehending. After a while, she understood what Lilian had said. "No, I'm only looking for a friend." She continued to look for Ron and when she saw him, she stood up happily. "I'll be right back," she said to Lilian and started to walk toward the only face she knew.

Ron smiled when he saw Carmen approaching him.

"Carmen…" His voice was cheerful.

"I'm really glad to see you." Saying this, she sat next to Ron. There was nobody else next to them.

"That dress looks good on you," Ron said, mockingly.

"Hey, don't mock me. It makes me look fat." Ron smiled. "Try to guess who I am sharing a room with?" Ron knew that Carmen didn't know anyone on Crictus. He knitted his eyebrows. "Lilian… The girl whose father was killed."

"That's unfortunate…"

"Why?" Carmen asked curiously.

"Because you blame yourself for what happened. Now you'll go on blaming yourself."

Carmen shrugged.

"Whatever. We should make a plan soon. I don't know how many more days I can keep scrubbing the floors."

"All right. Let's both try to find out where the emerald is and share what we found out at noon." Carmen agreed with this plan. Then, she went back to Lilian. She was not supposed to talk to a guard for so long. She was new at work and thanks to Lilian, she had learned how the other maids loved to gossip. When she returned to Lilian, Lilian smiled mischievously.

"Is that guard just your friend?"

"In fact, he is my fiancé."

When she said that, Carmen didn't look at Lilian. Lilian seemed to be surprised. Carmen and Ron had continued their lie about their relationship because they had told Klaus that they were engaged.

"You're really lucky. You two look great together."

Carmen swallowed her bite hard.

"What?"

For a moment, she forgot that she had to act. She stared at Lilian in astonishment. Lilian repeated, not understanding Carmen's reaction.

"I think you're a wonderful couple."

"Do you really think so?"

"Yes." Lilian giggled, without comprehending why Carmen had reacted in this way.

Carmen eyed Ron. There was nothing obvious between Ron and her. Still, she found him attractive, and she was definitely drawn to him. In any case, Ron was her protector. Any other kind of relationship sounded wrong to her. What Lilian had said confused Carmen. She had never thought about whether they looked good together or not.

For the rest of the day, Carmen swept the floors. When she was done, she did the dusting in one of the large halls inside the castle. Neither Inca nor the Soul Hunter were around. This worked for her. At the end of the day, she went to the dining area to eat her dinner. Meanwhile, Ron was tired of standing in front of the door of the royal dining room all day. After he turned over his watch to another guard to eat his dinner, he began to go down to the dining area. When he got there, he sat at an empty table. He glanced at the other tables and hoped to see Carmen, but she wasn't around. Just then, he heard a voice behind him.

"Are you looking for the maids?"

The voice startled Ron. He turned to the direction of the voice. It was a blond guy with a thick Paletan Talus accent. His eyes were dark brown, and a beard covered his face. The guy was about Ron's age, even though his beard made him appear older.

"No, I was looking for a friend."

The guard sat next to Ron.

"No need to be embarrassed. My name is Dean."

Ron shook Dean's hand.

"Ron."

Dean nodded to Ron.

"You're the newcomer, aren't you?"

"Yeah."

There was a roguish expression on Dean's face. He leaned toward Ron's ear and put his hand on Ron's shoulder.

"We need to find you a girl."

Ron had changed a lot since Carmen, or to be more precise, since the emerald came into his life. Ron would have accepted Dean's offer without hesitation before the emerald came into the picture, but now he had some serious responsibilities. Protecting the future queen was far more important than anything. Of course, there were other factors behind his kind refusal of Dean's offer. Still, one could say that the only reason was Carmen. As Dean was trying to persuade Ron, people quickly started to gather around them. Other guards whose watches were over, also came down to eat when they got hungry. Dean was popular with the other guards, which is why their table was suddenly surrounded.

"Hey, Harese, the newbie doesn't want us to hook him up with a girl. What do you say?"

As Dean said that, he gave Ron a rough smack on his back. He had a crooked smile on his face.

"We've got to object to this, my friend. You need a girl."

He walked over to Ron as he said this. He put his hand on Ron's shoulder.

"It's really not necessary, guys." Hanse was not listening to him. He pointed over to where the maids sat.

"How about that blonde sitting over there? She used to hang out with Dean but she's all right."

Laughter rose from the crowd. Ron shook his head. He was not enjoying this situation. Just then, Carmen appeared holding her bowl. She was moving gently and looking confused. Ron couldn't control his heart when he saw her.

"Hey, how about the one over there? She must be new…"

Everyone was looking at Carmen. Carmen found a suitable place and sat down.

"If you don't, I might," Dean said as he stared at Carmen with a smirk on his face.

Voices of approval rose from the crowd. Apparently, Carmen's noticeable beauty caught others' attention too. Ron didn't appreciate that the guards harbored such thoughts about Carmen.

"That's my fiancée."

The group of guards who were jostling around a second ago suddenly went stone quiet. Ron was looking at Carmen. This was all he could do to protect her for the time being.

"Sorry, man," Dean said. "Hey, why didn't you say you had such a fine fiancée before?"

Ron remained silent. He only smiled. Meanwhile, Carmen's eyes were searching for Ron. A big smile extended on her face when she saw Ron.

"Look at that. That's real love there," Dean said commenting on Carmen's smile.

Ron gasped for breath for a moment. Did Carmen love him? For a moment, he felt uneasy. Carmen wasn't supposed to like Ron. He had to prevent this somehow. This would put Carmen's life in danger. *Maybe I'm getting too close to her,* Ron said to himself. *Maybe she's misinterpreted my actions, my protection…* While Ron thought so, he also secretly wanted Carmen to misunderstand his actions. Still, he smiled at Carmen, suppressing his emotions. Carmen got up, smiling. After she said something to the other girls sitting at the table, Carmen started walking over to Ron and the other guards.

"Hey," Carmen said in a delicate and shy voice.

Ron jumped up.

"Sweetheart. I am so glad to see you."

He took a few steps toward Carmen and kissed her on the cheek. A pleasant redness spread on Carmen's cheeks. She gently cleared her throat.

"Can I talk to you for a bit?"

"Sure…" Ron said, and they went a little away from the crowd.

Once they were a little away, Ron stopped smiling.

"I told them you're my fiancée, and still they can't stop gaping. What kind of guys are they?"

His voice was angry. Carmen smiled slightly, enjoying Ron's jealousy.

"Don't worry. I have eyes only for my fiancé."

Ron was used to Carmen's improper jokes, so he responded with a smile.

"How was your first day?"

Carmen made a face.

"Awful. I wiped the floors all day and then did some dusting up. I've never done such things in my life before. I now see how hard it is. I feel so tired."

"What? You've never done this before?" Ron said ironically.

"Don't make fun of me. It was just a bad day."

Ron stopped laughing.

"All right, I'm sorry."

Carmen sighed.

"We need to learn where the emerald is as soon as possible, Ron."

"You're right. I'll try to see what the other guards know tomorrow."

"All right. And I'll sound out the girls."

Carmen looked at the table she had been sitting at. All the girls were looking at her.

"I have to go back now."

They said goodbye to each other and went back to their tables. Returning to their meals, they began to socialize with their new friends. Carmen didn't fail to look at Ron from time to time. When they caught each other's eye, they both looked away.

When it was time to go to bed, Carmen and Lilian retreated to their room. Carmen was so tired.

After putting on the nightgown that was rolled up on the bed, she lay down and pulled the blanket over her. The bed was hard. The pillow was stuffed with straw. For a moment, Carmen realized how much she missed her previous life. Since she came to Crictus, she had endured things she had never had to endure in her life before. She had slept in hard beds, slept in the forest, washed in the stream, watched a murder being committed in front of her eyes, buried a corpse, and now she had to clean the enemy's house. All this was really too much. A small part of her missed her old house, her family's warmth, her friends, even her school. Another part was happy to be on Crictus. Life here was hard and Carmen was a fugitive on Crictus. Nevertheless, a part of Carmen told her she belonged here. It was this feeling that kept Carmen on Crictus and made her endure it all. Another reason for staying on Crictus was that she saw how much its people needed Anka. It was her destiny to save them from the Soul Hunter. Carmen might have missed sleeping in a soft bed with her mother's good-night kiss, but she also knew she couldn't escape her fate.

She turned around in her bed and tried to settle in, but she found it impossible to get comfortable on such a hard bed. She turned her head toward Lilian's bed. Lilian's eyes were closed. When she looked at her, Carmen's thoughts went back to the day Lilian's father died. Her father's death was entirely Carmen's fault.

"Lilian, are you asleep?" Carmen said, whispering.

Lilian opened her eyes slowly.

"Not yet."

"I was just curious about something." Carmen sounded shaky. Lilian straightened up a little and began to listen to Carmen intently. Carmen also straightened up a little. "I was just wondering… Well… Did you ever hold Anka responsible for your father's death?"

Lilian was surprised at the question Carmen asked at this time of night.

"Of course, not. How can I be angry at an immortal soul? It's not my place to do that."

That was not the answer Carmen wanted to hear.

"C'mon. Anka won't hear you. Do you really feel that way?"

Lillian wavered. There was a hesitation in her looks.

"In fact…" She stopped. She was hesitant, but her hesitation disappeared within a second. "Actually yes, I am angry with her. Anka was there. She was somewhere in the crowd, and she saw everything that happened, but didn't even lift a finger."

Lilian sounded disappointed rather than furious. Carmen was feeling miserable. It was as if someone was applying pressure on her heart. She gulped. Lilian continued to speak.

"On the other hand, I understand her. Perhaps the Soul Hunter would catch Anka if she made an appearance. Many people have placed their hopes in Anka only. We have been miserable for so long… Almost everyone wants to see Soul Hunter's reign to end and the only one who can make this possible is Anka. That's why she needs to act wisely… Perhaps she could have prevented my father's death, but I'm not angry with her for not preventing it. She did what she had to do. We're at war and my father is just one of the victims who died. When the time comes, Anka will save all of us."

"You really believe that?"

"Well, yes. She must. She is our queen."

When she finished her words, she had a slight, sad smile on her shapely lips. There was the same sad expression on Carmen's face, too. Her conscience was clear now, but she still felt pressure on her. Everyone counted on her to defeat the Soul Hunter... She was happy that she could stop blaming herself at least.

Thank you, Lilian, she said silently to herself.

"Yes. She will save us and stop these deaths."

Thus, their conversation ended. Carmen fell asleep in peace for the first time in a while. Knowing that there were so many people supporting her made her feel strong.

The next day, she got to work early in the morning. This time she was scrubbing the floors in one of the big halls. Her arms were aching terribly. In the other corner of the room, Lilian was also cleaning the floors. The wicked witch, Margaret, was in charge of them and she was checking to see if they were doing their jobs well. That was what the maids called Margaret among themselves, *the wicked witch.* Margaret always yelled at people and was never satisfied with anything. Once on one of these days, Carmen started to get tired of Margaret's shouting. She could hardly stop herself from throwing the bucket full of water over her head.

"Scrub there again! Not a single stain should remain on the floor!"

Carmen gritted her teeth. *It's worth the emerald... It's worth the emerald...* She kept repeating these words to herself. She had to find a way to learn where the emerald was, grab it, and get out of this castle. Otherwise, she would reveal herself as Margaret's murderer.

The loud voice of one of the guards at the door interrupted Margaret's squeaking voice, "King Edmund and Prince Derick!"

Carmen was petrified. She didn't know what to do. If the Soul Hunter and Inca recognized her, everything would be ruined. This would be the end of everything. She tried to control her breathing and calm down. Margaret told Lilian and Carmen to get to their feet. To show respect, they had to bow down as the king and the prince passed the hall. Carmen's heart was beating in her throat. She was at a loss with fear. She wanted Ron to be with her more than anything at that moment, but unfortunately, this was impossible. Carmen stood up, and bent her head down, waiting for the Soul Hunter and Inca to enter. She felt exposed, out in the open. After a few seconds, the Soul Hunter and Inca came in when the wide, double door opened all the way. They were fervently arguing about something. Carmen glanced at them. She was almost going to faint from fear. "Don't faint." She ordered herself. She was pushing all her cells to keep calm and not to faint. Sweat drops appeared on her forehead. The Soul Hunter and Inca quickly passed in front of Carmen without noticing her. She held her breath and exhaled when the Soul Hunter and Inca sauntered out the door on the other side of the room. She could barely get a grip after a few deep breaths. Carmen felt huge relief. If Inca had recognized her, everything would have been different. But Inca didn't even waste his time looking at the maids, and it was highly difficult for them to perceive Anka was right under their noses in a maid's uniform.

The Soul Hunter could not feel Anka, either, because Inca's energy was camouflaging that of Anka. After Carmen took a few deep breaths, she returned to real life when Margaret barked out orders to continue her job.

She didn't want to tell Ron what had happened that day and worry him. If he heard this, he would say the emerald was not important and that they should leave the castle. As she knew for certain that Ron would say this, she didn't say anything. When she was so close to the Soul Hunter and Inca, she didn't want to lose her chance to play a trick on them.

Though she didn't see Ron either at lunch or at dinner, she kept inexplicably running into him in the castle. The castle was too big for two people to keep coming across upon one another, yet Ron and Carmen were constantly bumping into each other.

"I'm happy to see you," Carmen said as she put the bucket she was carrying down on the floor. Ron was standing guard in front of a double door.

"Me too. How's it going?"

Carmen thought about what had happened that day but decided that it would be better to remain silent. Also, she did not want to risk the guard on the other side of the door hearing them.

"Just the usual," Carmen said. Then continued, "How come we keep running into each other?"

After checking the guard standing next to him, Ron answered, whispering.

"Because we're connected to each other."

"How so?" Carmen said, without comprehending.

"Have you forgotten that some of Anka's power is within me. So, wherever we go, we feel each other. This increases our chances of meeting."

Carmen smiled.

"Wow, that's fascinating. Is this how you found me on Earth?" Carmen whispered.

Ron confirmed by nodding. It comforted Carmen to learn that Ron could always find her in some way.

"By the way, I couldn't find anything. Since I'm a newbie, I can't ask anyone about the emerald," Ron whispered.

"If we find anything, we'll let each other know right away. I keep running into you anyway," Carmen said as she winked at him and picked the bucket up from the floor.

At the end of the day, Carmen retreated to her room with Lilian. Lilian had been working in the castle for a long time and it was possible she knew where the emerald might be. However, Ron was right. Since they were new, asking questions about the emerald immediately would make them look suspicious. As it was, they had no information about the emerald on their second day in the castle.

Carmen was feeling very tired when she went to bed. The day's events shook her deeply and genuinely scared her to death. Still, she was happy just to see the end of the day. She fell asleep the moment her head hit the pillow. A tough day was waiting for her. Working in the castle wore her out. Carmen's only consolation was that this job would eventually come to an end.

The next day was no different from the previous two days. Once again, Carmen performed all the hard chores Margaret wanted and still couldn't please her. This time, Margaret made Carmen wash the windows. The castle windows reached practically up to the high ceilings. She nearly fell down a few times while trying to wipe the tops of the windows. She didn't neglect to curse Margaret every time. That day she encountered neither Inca nor the Soul Hunter. At the end of the day, she was so tired and hungry she almost threw herself into the dining area. She filled her plate with more food than she could possibly eat and sat down next to her new maid friends, who accepted Carmen right away. The plan she made with Ron included both making friends and then bringing up the matter of the emerald. If the others accepted them, the questions they asked wouldn't attract as much attention. Making friends was hard for Carmen and she had very few friends on Earth. She usually only had her close friends around. She had more close friends than she had acquaintances. However, it was worth trying to make friends to fulfill her mission.

After dinner, accompanied by a long conversation, she had to clean her plate and keep things clean, as everyone did. So, she got up and took her plate to the place where the dirty dishes were washed. While she was washing her plate, she heard a voice behind her.

"Can you wash my plate, too?"

Carmen looked back. There was a muscular guard standing before her. He was about Ron's age. He had blond hair and dark brown eyes. His unshaven beard made him look like a bum.

"Sure," Carmen said. She got embarrassed when she noticed she was staring at the guard and started to look at the plates again.

"I know you. You're Ron's fiancée. The newbie guard…"

Carmen looked at him again.

"Yes, I am."

"I'm Dean," the guard said with a flirtatious stance.

Carmen knitted her eyebrows. It seemed strange to Carmen that someone who just said he knew Ron was her fiancé was flirting with her.

"Carmen," she just said, her voice had a tone that didn't approve of Dean's flirting.

"So, Carmen, how long have you been engaged to Ron?"

Carmen cursed from inside. They had never talked to Ron about it. Of course, Carmen could lie, but if Ron had said anything about this subject, she would reveal their lies. She gulped. She was trying to keep her voice calm. She didn't understand why she got so excited every time she lied.

"It hasn't been long."

She wasn't looking at Dean. She was concentrating on washing the plate in her hand.

"*Hmm*… Well, how long have you known him?"

To get out of this situation quickly, Carmen quickly plunged the plate she was holding into water, pulled it out, and put it aside. As she turned around and took Dean's plate, she replied, "It's been a long time." Carmen wasn't able to hide the anxiety in her voice.

"Interesting," Dean said.

Carmen suddenly looked at Dean. She was nervous.

"Why is it so interesting?"

For a moment, she thought that Ron may have given him additional information about their relationship. Dean narrowed his eyes. On his face was the skepticism of a detective who had solved a great mystery. Carmen gulped unintentionally. Dean approached Carmen.

"You're not engaged."

Carmen's heart was about to stop. She was terrified that their secret would come out. She immediately became defensive.

"What makes you think that way? Of course, we are engaged."

The skeptical expression on Dean's face was replaced with a flirtatious expression.

"Can you give me an exact date of engagement?"

Carmen was frozen. She was very angry with herself since they hadn't determined such things with Ron before. And now she couldn't lie because she didn't know if the months were the same as the ones on Earth! She tried to get a grip. She thought of how she would have acted if someone in the world were hitting on her.

"Dean, right? It's not acceptable for you to interrogate me like that. And if Ron saw you flirting with me, he'd surely beat you up. Tell you what, let's make a deal. Don't bother me again and I won't tell Ron about this conversation." She stopped and gave Dean the plate she was holding. "Besides, you can wash your own plate next time."

As soon as she said this, she walked away from him. It was a miracle she was able to rid herself of Dean so fast. She was shocked at how she had found the strength in herself to get rid of him.

After this incident, Carmen managed to find Ron in a flash. She told him what had happened, and they quickly came up with a fake engagement date, a fake meeting date, and a fake future marriage date, so that they would not contradict each other. First, the run-in with the Soul Hunter and Inca and now this made Carmen realize how dangerous it was to walk around in the castle. So, they decided they should hurry up. Every extra moment they spent in the castle put them in more danger.

Carmen felt very tired as she started her fourth day in the castle. But here she didn't have the luxury of asking her mother for another ten minutes before getting out of bed. So, she got up, whining. That day Margaret had decided to make her work in the kitchen. Carmen's least favorite place in the house was the kitchen. She didn't even know how to crack an egg. Yet, she had no choice but to work in the kitchen. Margaret had already put her in the midst of a number of grumpy cooks. Carmen tried to do everything they asked of her all that day.

"Bring the salt…" "Get the knife…" "Clean off the counter…" "Stir the food…" Carmen was on the verge of going nuts.

The oldest and grumpiest of the cooks summoned Carmen. Carmen whimpered as she went over to the large woman. The woman placed the dish, which she had prepared in a giant pot, onto a silver plate and then placed it onto a silver tray. She placed matching forks and knives on the tray as well. After she was done, she put the tray in Carmen's hand.

"Take this to King Edmund's room."

Carmen's eyes nearly popped out of her head. She couldn't enter that room. If the Soul Hunter felt her soul, everything would be over.

"No," she said quickly.

The large woman put her hands around her waist.

"What do you mean *no*? You have to do whatever is asked of you."

Carmen automatically repeated his reaction.

"No."

The woman before her was about to run out of patience.

"If you don't take this tray into the king's room right now, I'll get you fired. The king will make all of us pay, if he doesn't find his food ready when he returns to the castle."

Carmen exhaled for a moment and realized that she was holding her breath all this time.

"Isn't the king in the castle?"

The woman was getting angry.

"Are you deaf? I just said no!"

Carmen left instantly in order not to annoy the woman any further. As the Soul Hunter was not in the castle, it wouldn't be any trouble to take his meal to his room. On the other hand, serving the Soul Hunter felt very odd to Carmen.

When she arrived at the Soul Hunter's door, the guards manning their post asked her why she was there.

"I brought the king's meal."

"The king's not here," one of the guards said.

"I know, but I have to prepare his meal before he arrives."

The guard opened the door and closed it behind Carmen. She took a glance at the room. It seemed almost as big as her house on Earth. There was a large double bed on the right side of the door. The top of the bed was flamboyantly decorated with tulle curtains and pillows. There was a set of comfortable sofas on the left side of the room and a very old fireplace just opposite the sofa set. There was a large dining table behind this sofa set. The table was almost as large as the room she had now. It was a wooden table, the legs of which were ornamented with golden inlays. There was a huge chandelier over the table. Raising her head, Carmen saw the ceiling embossed in more dazzling gold. All the hungry people on Earth could be fed with the gold in this room. There was a large desk to the far left of the room.

After Carmen looked around the room for a while, she remembered she had to hurry and thus she turned back to the dining table. She placed the plate unwillingly on the dining table. When she was done, instead of heading to the door, she turned to the king's desk. There were a lot of papers and maps on the table. Carmen leaned over and tried to read the writing but to no avail. She did not know the alphabet. Although her language was spoken on Crictus, the alphabet was completely different. Carmen stepped back, groaning, and started to walk toward the door. She would have to learn this alphabet in the future. I hope it's not difficult, she thought.

Carmen had just reached the door when it opened wide. Carmen was petrified. She could not move when she faced the cold eyes of the murderer who had killed her mother Juliet, Ron's grandfather, Mason, and Lilian's father. She held her breath. The Soul Hunter was standing right in front of her. Carmen was at a loss with fear. It was the first time she was this close to the Soul Hunter.

The Soul Hunter had a look of surprise on his face. He felt a great soul around him. He was used to this feeling due to Inca constantly walking around him, but this was different. Carmen's heart skipped a beat. They felt as if time had stopped. They were eyeing each other. Carmen knew she had to get out of this situation, but she could not move. She was scared to death.

She was finally able to speak.

"Meal…" Her voice trembled. She pulled herself together a little. "Well… I mean, I brought you your meal." Then, she added, "Majesty."

The Soul Hunter looked Carmen over. He nodded after a while. Carmen greeted him slightly with her head, passed by the king, and started quickly walking away from him down the hallway.

Meanwhile, Edmund was looking behind Carmen. Could what he felt be true? Could that girl really be Anka? Anka must be a sixteen-year-old girl, and the girl he met did not seem to be more than sixteen years old. But could Anka have dared to do this? At that moment, he was startled when a hand touched his shoulder.

"Edmund, what are you doing?"

He turned back in shock.

"Derick?" He looked at Derick and then the hallway where the girl disappeared. *I must have felt Derick's soul*, he said to himself.

"Are you okay?"

Edmund forced out a laugh.

"Of course, I am. Just a ridiculous feeling," he said, and they entered Edmund's room together.

By now, Carmen was running. Her hands were shaking as she was sweating profusely. She was running, looking back. Encountering the Soul Hunter had scared her to no end, and she was sure he understood she was Anka. She wanted to find Ron immediately. At that moment, Ron found her. While she was running, looking back, she ran into Ron and let out a piercing scream.

"Carmen, calm down. It's me."

When Carmen saw that the person she had run into was Ron, she hugged him.

"We have to get out of here. He knows…"

Ron held Carmen's hands, trying to calm her.

"Who knows? What happened?"

Carmen was gasping for breath.

"I… I went to his room… Then, he walked in… I didn't know he would come, and he saw me."

Ron was listening to Carmen seriously. Carmen was horrified. She had never been so scared in her life before.

"Are you sure he knew?"

"I don't know, Ron. It was so scary. We made eye contact and then I left."

Ron hugged Carmen.

"All right, I'll go that way to check, but an extraordinary situation is not declared unless the bells ring. You're safe for now."

Carmen's hands were still shaking.

"What if he understood?"

Ron held Carmen's chin and turned it toward himself. He looked into Carmen's eyes earnestly.

"Then I'll protect you at the cost of my life. You know this." Carmen nodded and then leaned her head against Ron's chest. Ron hugged her tightly. "So whatever you do, please don't go into his room again."

Carmen made an affirmative sound. When Carmen felt better, they parted. Carmen went to the buildings where the maids were staying. She knew that she could not work any longer that day. After taking a little tour around, Ron realized Carmen was safe and took a deep breath. He was very angry with himself since he had put Carmen's life in such great danger.

Carmen did not leave her room again that day, neither to eat nor anything else. She tried to pull herself together. She had never been more frightened in her life. She kept waiting to hear the bells ringing when she was in her room, but the bells never rang.

She felt better when she woke up in the morning, as nobody had tried to kill her in the last twenty-four hours. Since there were more maids in the castle than required, her absence was not noticed.

She got up in the morning and went back to work. Because of the fear she had experienced the other day, she told Margaret that she wanted to work in the maids' building. Surprisingly, Margaret agreed. Carmen folded sheets and cleaned rooms all day, and for the first time since her arrival at the castle, was happy to be working. Housekeeping kept her mind off of all this warfare. Forgetting her responsibilities even for a few hours made her feel better.

At lunch break, she sat next to her friend Lilian and the other maids. They all laughed and joked around. Some of them glanced at the guards. Carmen could see that it was getting even more dangerous to stay in the castle with each passing day. She did not know how long she could bear living under the same roof with the Soul Hunter and Inca without encountering them. That's why she decided to act quickly and joined the girls' conversation. They were just chit-chatting about guys. It was all they were doing all day long.

"Speaking of guys… Ron gave me a great engagement ring."

Giggles were heard among the girls.

"You're so lucky, Carmen."

Carmen was immersed in her role.

"What can I say? He knows what a girl wants. It's not difficult to guess," Carmen said. One of the girls spoke.

"Yeah, well, I wish I had someone like him."

"You will get there. But the important part is the jewelry. Make sure he knows what you want."

She was bringing the conversation to the point she wanted.

"A lot of guys have shitty taste, I'm telling you." This girl was one of the bitter ones.

"Really though… I was actually curious about something. I heard there was an emerald somewhere in the castle. It was the most precious emerald on Crictus. When I started working in the castle, I thought such a wonderful piece would be on display but I haven't seen anything yet." Carmen gave a legendary tone to her voice. The girls were all ears. One of them spoke.

"Are you talking about the fire emerald?"

The girls became quiet. Everyone was afraid of talking about Anka's fire emerald.

"Yes. I wish we had an opportunity to lay our eyes on it at least once. Who knows how beautiful it is."

The girls all went silent when talk of the emerald began, but one of them answered Carmen.

"We'll never have the chance. The emerald is guarded by heavy security measures in the room just below the belfry."

The room beneath the belfry… She repeated to herself several times.

"Oh, what a pity," Carmen said, pretending to look sad. She was screaming with joy inside. In fact, she was very curious about what security measures there were, but she did not push the matter any further because she did not want to draw attention.

Carmen could barely contain herself. She wanted to go quickly and give Ron the good news. While sitting with the girls, her eyes were looking for Ron. She suddenly jumped up when she saw him. Without even excusing herself, she almost ran to Ron.

"Carmen, do you feel better now?"

Ron had not seen Carmen after her encounter with the Soul Hunter. Carmen looked much better now.

"Yeah, I'm really fine," she said and held Ron by the arm to yank him away from the crowd.

"I know where the emerald is."

Ron started to share Carmen's joy, too.

"That's great. So, where is it?"

"In the room beneath the belfry."

"Wait here a sec," Ron said and left Carmen.

After a few minutes, he came back with a map of the castle in his hand. They went over to a quiet place and opened the map. There was only one room under the belfry. This room had only one entrance.

"It only has one door." Ron said. "This makes our job a lot harder."

Carmen chipped in.

"The girl who knew where the emerald was kept said that it was protected by extraordinary security measures. Do you think we can succeed?"

Ron thought for a little,

"I'm sure there are two guards in front of the door. These guards must be the first security measure. But if I can be one of these guards, that won't be very hard."

Carmen smiled. "Can you take a shift there?"

"I have to try," Ron said.

"What about the other things?"

Ron wrinkled his forehead.

"I don't know what's waiting for us behind the doors, but that's why we're here. We have to take the risk." Just then, their lunch hour was over. Everybody had to go back to work. "Our hours don't match at dinner, but we can talk tomorrow evening."

Carmen nodded. After saying farewell to one another, Carmen went back to tidying up the dormitories, and Ron went back to standing guard at the door of one of the huge halls inside the castle. They were both thrilled that they were one step closer to the emerald.

9

Carmen was so beat from the day she had that she went straight to bed right after dinner.

She started her sixth working day shortly after she got up in the morning. As she did every morning, Margaret gathered all the maids in the courtyard and assigned each of them workstations. When it was Carmen's turn, she found out that she was supposed to work in the kitchen. She objected immediately, but Margaret must have gotten out of the wrong side of the bed that day as she insisted that Carmen work in the kitchen. Carmen's last day in the kitchen last time had not gone well as she had encountered the Soul Hunter. She didn't want to have a repeat experience. That's why she pleaded with Margaret, who was quite the wicked witch, but to no avail. Now Carmen understood why the other girls gave her such a moniker.

In the end, Carmen had to cave, and she proceeded to the castle's kitchen. The kitchen was still boring, but at least the old, grumpy cook wasn't around. Instead, a charming woman was cooking. Her cheeks were unbelievably red, and she had an extremely pale complexion. Carmen thought about how it could be possible for a person to have such red cheeks without any makeup. Carmen was responsible for helping her in the kitchen and she gave Carmen the least tiring tasks throughout the day. Carmen thought it was better than working with that grumpy woman.

Lilian also came into the kitchen toward the evening. Carmen watched Lilian with her elbows propped up on the countertop and her face between her hands. After Lilian placed the Soul Hunter's meal onto the same silver plate Carmen had used the previous day, she took a little bottle from among the shelves behind. She opened the lid of the bottle and poured a little from it into the meal.

"What's that?" Carmen asked curiously.

"This is the king's sleeping potions… Apparently, he hasn't been sleeping well since Inca appeared. He can only sleep with this medicine."

A bolt of lightning struck Carmen's head. There was a curious expression on her face as she raised her head.

"Is it effective?"

Lilian shrugged.

"Enough to put the Soul Hunter to sleep." Then, she took the tray. "Excuse me," she said, as she went out to take the meal to the king.

After Lilian left the kitchen, Carmen first looked at the bottle and then looked around. The sleeping potion could be used in the plan. She looked around again. Everybody was busy with their own work. Carmen deftly took the bottle and hid it under the sleeve of her shirt. She went out of the kitchen, hoping nobody would notice. She was almost sprinting. She quickly went to her room. She had to hide the bottle in a safe place in the room before anyone noticed. However, it just was not Carmen's lucky day. Just as she turned into the last corridor to get out of the castle, she encountered Margaret's grim-looking face. She cursed inside, while mustering a fake smile on her face.

"What's this? Have you decided to run away from the castle?"

"N… No. I only…"

Carmen fumbled for an excuse. She bit her lip. The fear was swinging through her entire body.

"You only what?" the wicked witch said impatiently.

Carmen wished she could get rid of her.

"Lilian!" she said the first thing that came to her mind.

"What happened to Lilian?"

"*Hmm*… Her birthday is coming up and… I was going to the room to find a place to hide the present I made for her."

Margaret narrowed her eyes. She was trying to figure out whether Carmen was telling the truth. In feigning a smile, Carmen was also trying to hide her excitement.

"I don't want her to find her present before her birthday."

Margaret looked at Carmen for some time. She had the most hostile look a person could have. After an interminably long pause, she sighed gruffly.

"Have it your way."

Carmen breathed a sigh of relief. Before leaving, Margaret looked at Carmen, as if she was accusing her.

"You better not be slacking off!"

As soon as Margaret left, Carmen took a deep breath. She had just dodged a howitzer shell. She could have found a better excuse than Lilian's birthday, of course, but considering how bad she was at lying, it was a great victory for Carmen.

She quickly flew into her room, albeit more cautiously this time. She didn't see anyone this time. Entering the room, she closed the door behind her and took a deep breath. She opened her clothes cupboard and then stood up after hiding the little bottle under her clothes. She was proud of herself. Never in her life had she ever been involved in such exploits. Apart from the CSI series, even the TV programs and films with such plots weren't her cup of tea. However, she found herself smack dab in the middle of the action now. Never in her wildest imagination did she think her life would become like this. At that moment, she found herself smiling to herself as she sat by the cupboard. After hiding the bottle in a safe place, the next thing to do was to find Ron. But she needed to be careful not to be caught by Margaret again. Fortunately, Ron had said that they could easily feel and find each other since they were connected due to the relationship between Anka and the emerald. Carmen left her room and, trusting her instincts, she started to look for Ron. Ron said that they could see each other during the evening break, but Carmen didn't intend to wait for the break.

She entered the castle and quickly went to the upper floor. She just trusted her instincts. Pausing at the start of a hallway split into two for a few seconds, she took the corridor on the left. Passing by a few double doors, she turned right as a big smile emerged on her face. She approached Ron, smiling.

"Hey, these Anka instincts really work."

She had a crooked smile on her face. As usual, she could easily be snide, even about a serious subject.

Ron took an uneasy look around.

"Be quite... Someone might hear you."

Carmen shrugged.

"Where were you going?"

"I was patrolling in the castle. Why were you looking for me?"

Carmen's eyes glowed suddenly.

"You won't believe what I just snuck out of the kitchen." She was trying to keep her voice down. Ron glanced at Carmen with curious and skeptical eyes. Carmen continued to speak. "The Soul Hunter has been having trouble sleeping since Inca has been in the castle. Apparently, he's been using a sleeping potion so he could sleep better."

Ron crossed his arms on his chest.

"Did you steal his medicine?"

He lifted one of his eyebrows.

"Yes! Isn't it great?"

Ron smiled at this exaggerated reaction of Carmen.

"So, what are you planning to do with it? If they find out his medicine is missing, they'll search everywhere."

Carmen paused for a second. She hadn't thought about this. All her enthusiasm instantly disappeared. Still, she told Ron about her plan.

"I thought... I mean, if the medicine can put even the Soul Hunter to sleep, then it could easily put the guard who would be on station with you in front of the emerald room to sleep, too. I thought it would make things easier."

Ron looked thoughtful.

"That's a good idea, but you still have to put the bottle back. Can you do that after we take the amount we need?"

Carmen thought. She could put it back, but it might be difficult for her to find a bottle in which she could put the needed amount. Suddenly, Carmen's eyes glowed again.

"Or, I won't have to put it back right now. We can take care of this tomorrow afternoon. He won't need the potion until the evening anyway. No one will know that it's missing."

Ron mulled over the situation again. He was trying to come up with a clever plan. He shook off when he realized that he couldn't pull it off with a brief conversation.

"Let's talk about it in detail at dinner. We need a plan first, and I haven't talked to anyone about being a guard for the emerald room yet. I don't even know if they will give a shift to a newbie."

Carmen grumbled.

"Ron, time is running against us. I'm tired of worrying every day about whether I'll get caught by the Soul Hunter or Inca. I know it's been six days, but I don't know how much longer I can keep washing the floors. I want to get this over with as soon as we can."

"Okay, you're right. But we can't get the emerald without a plan. We'll talk at dinner."

Carmen gave Ron a reluctant nod. After saying goodbye to Carmen,

Ron continued patrolling the corridors. Carmen was disappointed after seeing Ron's reluctance in his plan. Even though she was in a funk, she still had to go back to work in the kitchen. Soon Margaret came to the kitchen for the evening check. When she saw Carmen there, a contented expression appeared on her face. After checking on the maids for a while, Margaret eventually exited the kitchen. Carmen dreaded Margaret's existence because she didn't like anything Carmen did.

Finally, when it was time for the evening break, Carmen breathed a sigh of relief. Now she would be able to see Ron and they could make a plan to sneak the emerald out of the castle. When Carmen went down to the large garden where they dined, the first thing she did was to look for Ron, but when she couldn't see him, she decided to eat quickly until he showed up.

Meanwhile, Ron was heading to the Waldorf's chamber, who was chief of the guards. He wanted to ask him for the shift in front of the emerald's room, but he didn't know how to do this without raising suspicion. As he arrived at the chamber door, he took a deep breath and knocked on the wooden door three times. He opened the door when he was permitted. The door was heavier than it looked. Upon entering, he found Waldorf sitting at his wooden table. There were stacks of paper on the table. A huge Devara head was hanging on the wall. Just below it, two swords were hanging diagonally on the wall. There was a large Srilan pelt on the floor. Ron wondered if it was Waldorf's hobby to collect dead animals. Waldorf grinned when he saw Ron examining the pelt on the floor.

"It leapt on me during a hunt on a snowy day about five years ago. That's when my sword pierced its heart." Ron smiled kindly. Waldorf looked at the pelt on the floor serenely as if he was looking at an old friend. "That's the price of trying to hunt the hunter."

He remained quiet for a few seconds. Then, he suddenly looked at Ron as if he remembered Ron was there. Waldorf was a middle-aged, bulky man. He was strong and the best among the guards. That was what made him a leader. He was also organizing all the shifts. Waldorf's dark brown hair had started to turn grey, as was his beard stubble. The lines on Waldorf's face were very deep and he had the look of someone who had seen it all. The wrinkles next to his eyes and the deep creases on his forehead seemed to be specially placed to remind him what kind of difficulties he faced during his life.

He stared at Ron with his dark brown eyes.

"Yes? What can I do for you?"

Ron gently cleared his throat.

"I wanted to know where I'll be working tomorrow."

"I was assigning guard just now. Let me have a look at it." Waldorf reached for the papers on the table and easily found what he was looking for in that mess. "Your name?"

"Ron, sir."

"*Hmm*, you'll be guarding the door of the third dining hall tomorrow morning and patrolling the castle in the evening."

Waldorf raised his head from the papers and looked at Ron. Ron had to find an excuse and switch his post with the emerald room, but he couldn't think of anything. He gulped. Waldorf was waiting for Ron to say something, but he had become tongue-tied. Finally, he was able to speak.

"All right. Thank you."

After he said that, he practically ran for the exit. It would attract attention if he asked Waldorf for a shift at the emerald room on his sixth day at work. He had to find another way. He quickly dashed to his room. He took the map of the castle from the room and went straight to the dining hall. It was fortuitous that all the guards got a map of the castle.

Upon arriving at the dining hall, he first looked about for Carmen. She was dining with the other maids. After a while, she also noticed Ron. Ron went to get something to eat and sat on a table in a remote corner. Carmen was with him a few seconds later.

"Where were you?"

Ron unhappily took a bite of the bread in front of him.

"Don't ask." Carmen fidgeted uneasily. When Ron finished the bite in his mouth, he spoke, "I went to request to stand a shift at the emerald room…"

Carmen interrupted Ron without waiting. She was suddenly excited.

"And…? So, what happened?"

"Carmen, calm down. What happened was… I couldn't even ask."

Carmen looked at Ron with disappointment.

"Why not?"

"Because if you've been a guard here for only six days, you're not going to get to guard the most important room in the castle."

Carmen's shoulders fell.

"What will we do then?"

"We've got to find another way."

Saying this, he sighed. Carmen looked impatiently at the map Ron had put on the table.

"Are we doing this tomorrow?"

Ron paused.

"I don't know. You're right. The more time we spend in the castle, the more risk for you to get recognized. Every day you're not recognized is sheer luck and I already regret leaving you alone. Besides, I want to get out of here as soon as possible, too. It's tough for me to protect the castle of my family's murderer." For a moment, Ron remembered his brother Mason and his grandfather, whom he regarded as his father. There was visible pain on his face. He didn't want to look weak near Carmen. He shrugged slightly and continued, "But that said, entering the emerald room probably won't be easy. We don't even know what we're up against, and I don't want to put you in danger. One wrong move, even a minor setback in the plan would be enough to give us away. Then, you'd be in great danger. It'd be really difficult for us to escape, and then we'll only see the emerald in our dreams. Of course, that is, if we're lucky enough to survive."

Carmen grumbled. Ron's pessimism was depressing.

"In any case, we're here to face this risk, Ron. It doesn't matter if it happens tomorrow or two weeks later. We're still going to have the same problems. There's no way of knowing what's waiting there for us, even if we have to wait a couple of weeks."

Ron sighed.

"You're right."

"Am I?"

Carmen didn't think Ron would give in so quickly. While she had prepared herself to make a long speech, this happened rather quickly.

"Aren't you?" Ron said in doubt.

Carmen immediately replied, afraid that Ron would give up, "I'm absolutely right."

Ron laughed at Carmen's reaction. After quickly chewing the bite in his mouth, he wiped away the crumbs from his hands and opened the map onto the table. After looking around a bit to see if anyone was around, they focused on the plan.

"All right, so here's the emerald room," he said, pointing at the emerald room.

Carmen studied the map carefully, but all she saw was a large sheet of paper with a bunch of confusing lines on it. But she pretended that she understood. Ron went on.

"Unfortunately, there is no way to find out what kind of dangers awaits us in there but we know the first obstacle. The guards will be at their posts until the shift changes to the next guards."

Carmen looked at Ron thoughtfully.

"I have a plan. It's a bit vague but hear me out. We're just gonna lie to them." Ron looked at Carmen expressionlessly. "Tell them your shift is for that room. I'll come out when you manage to replace someone."

"And we can carry out your plan of knocking them out."

Carmen continued, "I'll come around with soup in my hand. We'll somehow have the guard drink the soup and when he goes unconscious, we get in. But after that…" Carmen had a bit of despair on her face. Other than that, she was feeling very pumped up for acting criminally.

"We're just going to have to wing it after that."

Carmen smiled. The plan was deficient in every respect. It had a beginning, but it lacked a conclusion. Moreover, they could easily come up with ten reasons why even the beginning of their plan would not work. Under normal circumstances, Ron would never carry out a plan without having everything safe and sound. This was always the case when he was a rebel. But now he couldn't come up with a solid plan even if he wanted to, because nobody in the castle knew what was in store in the room where the emerald was kept. Perhaps the emerald wasn't even there. But it was too late to think about all that now. The plan had been hatched, and Carmen looked very eager to go along with it. Ron wasn't even sure if she could sleep with all the excitement tonight. In a sense, it was good to see that she was raring to go. Carmen was acting like a brave queen fighting for her kingdom, but on the other hand, Ron was angry with himself for dragging her into such a dangerous situation. He wasn't sure whether Carmen could handle such an action-packed scheme. It had been almost a month since she arrived at Crictus, and in that month Carmen had changed considerably. Her experience had changed her. Nevertheless, the girl standing before Ron was just a sixteen-year-old kid who had spent all her life in a town on Earth and learned what adventure was from spaghetti westerns. What was Ron dragging her into?

At dinner, they put as much detail as they could into the plan. They would execute the plan at noon. Half of the guards would be at lunch at that time. They figured they wouldn't have to deal with the other half either because their plan was to get the emerald quietly and leave the castle.

After dinner, Carmen retreated to her room. Working hours were over and she knew that she needed to gather her wits for tomorrow. But, as Ron predicted, she was so excited that she didn't know how she would fall asleep that night. After wearing the nightgown that made her body itch, she went to bed.

"It was a very exhausting day today," Lilian said as she went into her bed.

"Yes, exceedingly."

"I hope Margaret will give us easier tasks tomorrow." With that, Lilian blew out the candle next to her. The room turned dark instantly. Now, the only light in the room was coming through the window, emanating from the strange planet.

"Good night, Carmen."

"Good night." After a few minutes of silence, Carmen spoke.

"Lilian?"

"Yes?"

"When's your birthday?" Lilian looked at Carmen in curiosity.

"It was about two weeks ago. Why?"

Carmen shrugged. She wished she could have thought of a better excuse than Lilian's birthday when she ran into Margaret.

"Just asking. By the way, if Margaret asks about your birthday, can you tell her it's next week?"

Lilian looked at Carmen in surprise.

"Sure, but why?" While Carmen was trying to come up a new excuse, Lilian spoke, "I'm sure you had a good reason to lie to her."

Carmen smiled. A minute later, Carmen broke the silence again.

"Lilian?"

"Yes, Carmen?"

"I'm sorry to constantly bother you, but I want you to know…" Carmen stopped and looked at Lilian. "You're a good friend. Thanks for everything."

Lilian was more surprised now.

"Thank you. You're a very good friend, too." She stopped for a moment and made a face. "You're talking like we won't be seeing each other again."

Yes, Carmen may possibly never see her again. If something went wrong in the plan at noon tomorrow, she could get caught and killed. Even worse, her soul would be eaten by the Soul Hunter. Carmen was startled when she recalled their worst-case scenario. At any rate, she wasn't going to be staying in the castle any longer if the plan worked. This was her last day in the castle. She wanted to say goodbye to her friend when she had the chance.

Carmen merely smiled.

"Good night, Lilian." Then, she closed her eyes. But she couldn't fall asleep no matter how hard she tried. Thousands of possibilities were crossing her mind. She had already come up with many scenarios in her head, all of which ended in disaster. She opened her eyes and tried to escape from her evil thoughts. But she was so excited that she felt like she was in a TV show. She closed her eyes again.

All right, Carmen. Try to think of good things. Everything will be fine tomorrow, and you'll leave this castle with the emerald. Nothing bad's going to happen. Carmen was trying to comfort herself. She eventually collapsed from exhaustion later at night and fell into a deep slumber.

She dreamed of that man again. The man with the dark brown hair, a beard, greenish hazel eyes... Carmen was watching everything again behind a smoke screen. The man was awake, and his eyes were staring at the same point on the wall. Carmen pitied him. She went over to him a little closer. The subtle light seeping through the small, iron-barred window lit up one side of the man's face. As always, his countenance bore great sorrow. The shadows on his face couldn't hide the dark circles under his eyes. The man was suddenly startled out of his wits. Carmen thought it was because of her at first, but then a guard came in. The man gave the guard a hostile look.

"What?" Carmen couldn't believe her ears. It was as if the voice came from nearby... It was hard to believe it was just a dream.

"King Edmund sent you this." Carmen suddenly felt as if she had been slapped on her face. King Edmund? What did the Soul Hunter have to do with this man? Carmen started observing what was happening more intently. The guard handed the man a piece of paper. The man opened the paper and took a look at it. Carmen approached the man and tried to see what was written on the paper but stopped when she saw the writing. It was written in Critian script. Carmen muttered to herself.

And suddenly she was out of her dream. She opened her eyes. She was in the maid's room in the castle. It was a very peculiar dream. Carmen remembered the dream down to the most infinitesimal detail and for the first time she felt as if she was no longer able to control her dreams and viewed these dreams as a third party. She wondered, what this man could have to do with the Soul Hunter. Was he real, or part of her imagination? This whole dream thing confused her greatly, but she would have to deal with it later. Today was the big day.

Carmen quickly got out of bed. She was feeling very anxious, and she could barely conceal her excitement. Lilian got up from the bed as well. After they both made up their beds and got dressed, Lilian headed to the door, but when she realized Carmen was not heading to the door, she turned to Carmen.

"Aren't you coming?"

"You go ahead. I've got one last thing to do." Lilian shrugged lightly and closed the door behind her. As soon as Lilian left, Carmen opened her clothes cupboard and took out the small bottle. After putting it in her apron pocket, she shut the cupboard and went to breakfast to join her friend.

She took her breakfast and then sat with Lilian at a table. Her eyes roved for Ron while she ate. When she finally saw Ron, he was walking over toward her. Carmen looked at him with joy.

"Good morning, ladies," Ron said kindly to Carmen and Lilian.

Lilian greeted him with a smile.

"Good morning, Ron," Carmen said. His eyes were beaming brightly. Carmen looked at Lilian after some time. "Can you excuse us for a second?"

"Sure thing, I've already finished my meal."

Lilian smiled and got up from the table. Ron immediately sat down in her seat. As soon as Lilian left, an immense anxiety spread over Carmen's face.

"I don't think I'll be able to survive this stress until noon."

"Just take it easy. Everything will be fine."

Ron was trying to calm Carmen as usual, but that didn't work because he was as tense as Carmen. Nevertheless, unlike Carmen, he was concealing his feelings very well.

Carmen took a deep breath.

"All right. I'll take it nice and easy." She closed her eyes and opened them a few seconds later.

Ron laughed softly.

"The first group of guards goes on break when the bell rings once at noon."

Carmen continued, "And we'll be beneath the belfry just at that moment."

"Yes, precisely," Ron confirmed.

"I hope everything will work out okay."

"It will. Trust me." Ron stood up after saying this. Just as he was leaving, he looked at the breakfast in front of Carmen. "You should eat something. You'll need your strength."

Carmen picked at her food reluctantly. She was so nervous that she hadn't even touched it, mulling over all that might happen.

When Ron left, she ate as much as she could. After leaving her tray, she went to the courtyard where Margaret would be handing out the work assignments. Margaret was reading the names on the papers she was holding and telling the maids where they would be working that day. When it was her turn, Carmen bit her lip. She was hoping to be assigned to the kitchen that day. She bit her lip so hard that she almost drew blood.

"Carmen, second floor…"

Carmen murmured a curse. She was tired of having morning fights with the old witch. But this time it was more serious. It was not personal. She had to work in the kitchen. After Margaret read all the names, everyone rushed to their posts. Carmen approached Margaret timidly.

Margaret looked at her cross-eyed.

"What is it this time?"

Carmen gulped.

"Can I change my assignment?"

Margaret looked at Carmen more harshly than ever.

"You've been causing nothing but trouble ever since you arrived. No, you may not change your assignment. You're going to work on the second floor."

Carmen continued to speak without caring, "But you said it yourself yesterday. More help is needed in the kitchen."

Margaret raised an eyebrow.

"Do you want to work in the kitchen?"

"Yes."

Margaret looked over at Carmen curiously.

"Whenever I gave you a kitchen duty, you objected."

"Yes, but I like it now."

There was great eagerness in Carmen's voice. She was praying Margaret wouldn't notice. Margaret looked at Carmen carefully. Then, she turned her eyes away.

"Well, then go and work in the kitchen and just leave me alone."

Carmen was filled with joy.

"Thank you, thank you…" she said and threw her arms around Margaret's neck.

Margaret was confounded as she hugged Carmen. Carmen started running toward the kitchen immediately. Margaret stared behind Carmen. Carmen's behavior made no sense to her at all.

Carmen quickly went to the kitchen. She had done it! All she had to do now was to go to the room where the emerald was kept with two bowls when she heard the bell ringing.

That was all she had to do, but she was still very nervous. She had never done such a dangerous thing in her life before. There was not even an amusement park in her town back on her world, so she was not familiar with this heady thrill. So, this was over the top for Carmen. While she was on Earth, her only entertainment was going out to the local bowling alley with her friends on Sunday night. Carmen was always looking for new thrills, but her life had always been pretty mundane where she lived. Now she was angry with herself because she had looked for more excitement. Bowling would have been exciting enough for her right now. Unfortunately, she was no longer even on Earth. Here she was, on another planet, hiding in the castle of the murderer who wanted her dead and she was about to steal the thing he cared the most about. Indeed, it was quite natural that she was nervous. Carmen was counting the minutes while she was in the kitchen, but it felt as if time had come to a standstill. On the one hand, Carmen wanted time to stop, because she was scared. On the other hand, she wanted to take the emerald and leave the castle. Her heart couldn't bear this tension anymore.

Finally, the sun had reached its zenith overhead. There was very little time left before the meeting beneath the belfry. Carmen felt like her heart was about to implode from excitement. She got to work shortly before meeting Ron. She began to cook the simplest soup recipe that she had learned from her mother. Of course, she had to improvise since the food was different here than on Earth. After making the soup, she put it in two bowls and put the bowls on a tray. Just then, the sound from behind her startled her.

"What are you doing there?"

Carmen turned back. It was the troublemaker chief cook in front of her. The unpleasant woman was staring at Carmen.

"Nothing..." Carmen stuttered.

The woman raised an eyebrow and looked at the tray behind Carmen.

"Where's that tray going?"

Carmen was never good at lying, but she had to lie.

"I... I was... I was taking it to Margaret." Carmen swallowed hard.

"Both bowls?"

Carmen was looking at the woman, dumbfounded.

"No..." The woman was now very suspicious.

Carmen knew she had to come up with an excuse fast.

"I... I'm taking the other one to the guard chief."

"Did they ask you to make soup?"

Carmen nodded desperately. The woman looked at Carmen for a little longer. Then, she added, "Well then, take them quickly and come back. I have a few other things for you to do."

Carmen nodded hurriedly and quickly took the tray. As soon as she took the tray, she went out of the kitchen. She left the tray on the first table she saw and took the sleeping medicine out of her apron's pocket. She poured it all into the soup on the left. Then, she picked up the tray. It was time. She started to walk toward the belfry.

Meanwhile, Ron had vacated his duty station and began walking toward the belfry, as well. Arriving at the belfry, he quickly walked downstairs. As he climbed down the narrow stairwell, the soft light coming from below illuminated the walls. There was a big door below. There were two guards and a pair of torches at the door. The guards were startled when they saw Ron descending.

"What are you doing here? It's forbidden to be here..."

Keeping his calm, Ron went to the guards who were holding their swords.

"Waldorf sent me here." He looked at the guard on the right. "He wanted us to change places."

The guard knitted his eyebrows.

"You're new here. Waldorf doesn't assign newbies to the bell tower."

Ron continued to speak without stepping back, "Why don't you take it up with Waldorf? I'm sure, he'll kindly listen to you."

The threatening attitude in Ron's voice caused the guard to get stressed. The guard hesitantly gave Ron a dressing down from head to toe. The guards had always feared Waldorf. No one would dare stand up to him. Although Ron was new in the castle, he knew the impression Waldorf had made on the guards. After all, he was a guard, too.

"Well then, I will go and ask him myself."

"Suit yourself. You'll be at the throne hall entrance. I was told our King needed a trustworthy guard by his side."

Ron was anxious but didn't show it.

"Throne hall? The King?"

"They couldn't assign a newbie to protect the King now, could they?" Ron nodded.

After the guard gave him another look over, he bumped slightly into Ron's shoulder and began climbing the stairs. Ron took his place at the door of the room where the emerald was being kept. Now all he had to do was to wait. But he knew they must hurry. He had just sent the other guard to the throne hall, which was on the opposite side of the castle, but this still limited their time. Even though Ron didn't show it, he was very nervous. His apprehension increased as he knew he was putting Carmen's life at risk. He couldn't stop thinking about what would happen if the tiniest thing went wrong. He breathed heavily. He needed to calm himself down so he could protect Carmen.

As Ron was struggling with his thoughts, the walls trembled as the bell rang out. The time had come. After the bell rang once more, the castle became silent again. Ron took a deep breath. They were soon going to start their mission. The light reflecting from the torches onto the stairs flickered just then. Ron and the guard next to him snapped to attention. Someone was coming down. A few minutes later, Carmen appeared with a tray at the top of the stairs. Ron understood the time had come. He gulped with difficulty. Carmen was having a hard time holding the tray in her hands because she was nervous, too. Carmen smiled faintly as she descended down to the step before the landing. The guard next to Ron pushed slightly forward.

"Hold it right there! You're not allowed down here…"

Carmen stopped suddenly and glimpsed Ron. Then, she turned to the guard. Ron looked calm, despite the storms breaking within his heart.

"Well, I… I brought you food."

The guard knitted his eyebrows.

"Why?"

Carmen took a deep breath. She had to come up with a good, juicy lie. She repeated to herself quietly. *You can do this…*

"Your chief wants you to continue your shift here in the afternoon, too. So, I was told to bring you food."

Ron gave Carmen an admirable look. For a moment, he was afraid Carmen might spoil everything, but she was doing great. Carmen was at least as surprised as Ron at the words that came out of her mouth. It made her happy to see that she could spin a good lie.

The guard sighed slightly and turned to Ron.

"You see how they treat us."

Ron laughed softly.

"At least they think to feed our bellies," Ron said.

Carmen went down the last step of the stairs and went to the guard. The guard reached out to the soup on the right. Carmen suddenly remembered that the sleeping medicine was in the one on the left.

"No!" she said and pulled the tray back. The guard looked at Carmen in surprise.

"Well… This one's hotter…" Carmen said, whispering with a crooked smile.

She was angry at herself because she had almost exposed them. The guard shrugged and took the other soup. Carmen went to Ron to give him the other soup. Ron looked at Carmen as he took the soup and nodded. Carmen shook her head slightly and began climbing up the stairs. She was going up very slowly. Because she didn't know when the guard would faint.

The guard had already started drinking his soup.

"*Hmm*, delicious soup," he said as he sipped spoonful of the soup in quick succession.

Ron pretended to drink his soup but didn't. He was watching the guard. The guard was just taking his sixth sip when he swallowed hard. He blinked and shook his head. Ron was looking at the guard suspiciously. The guard dropped the soup from his hand and held onto the wall. Suddenly, he was gasping. He soon collapsed to the ground. Ron was looking at the guard in surprise. He had not expected the potion to act so quickly.

"Carmen…" he whispered toward the stairs.

Footsteps were heard from the stairs. After a while, Carmen went back down.

"Has he fainted?" she asked anxiously.

"Yes. How much did you put in the soup?"

Carmen shot Ron a guilty look.

"All of it…"

"Carmen!"

"What? You see how quickly it worked?"

Ron sighed.

"Whatever. Let's get this over and done," he said and looked at the door.

There was an iron chain at the door. There was also a lock at the end of the chain.

"How are we going to unlock this?" Carmen sounded perturbed.

Ron leaned toward the guard and gently searched him, but there was no key on him. Then, he looked at the door. He had to break the lock somehow. He reached his hand over to the soup on the floor and started to cut the iron by using the soup broth like a razor blade. He controlled the water by fervently moving his hands up and down. After a while, the lock was broken. An ordinary person could never break this lock, but this was no problem for the water emerald and Anka. Carmen looked at Ron excitedly.

"Wow! Pretty clever."

Ron smiled softly and cracked open the door. Carmen was about to go in when Ron stopped her.

"Let me go first."

Carmen nodded. Ron carefully pried open the door and entered. Carmen was right behind him. They went in together. The room was round with stone masonry walls and a high ceiling. Torches were hung on various parts of the walls of the room. There were no windows. There were only two small holes in the ceiling. A stone platform was standing in the center of the room. Upon it was a blood-red emerald displayed in all its glory. When Carmen saw the emerald, she was stunned. The emerald looked gorgeous. It was the largest jewel Carmen had ever seen. While Ron and

Carmen were looking at the emerald, Carmen heard something hissing from the left. When she looked in that direction, she almost couldn't stop herself from screaming. There was a large lizard with the face of a snake and the mane of a lion in front of her. The creature stared at Carmen with its terrifying red eyes as it hissed and slithered toward her. At that very moment, King Edmund raised his head from his desk in his room in the castle. There was something that made him uneasy.

In the room of the emerald: "Ron!" Carmen said anxiously, keeping her eye on the creature. She was clinging to Ron's arm. Ron looked where Carmen was looking. Just then, the creature lunged. Carmen would do the best thing she knew and send her energy to it, but Ron drew her aside.

"No, Carmen! Don't!"

Carmen looked fearfully at Ron. Carmen's energy missed the creature and hit the wall.

"What are you doing? Let's kill it."

"No, Carmen. It is a Barelan."

The creature was attacking again as it rapidly headed toward Carmen. While the creature was about to lunge again, Ron drew Carmen aside again.

King Edmund suddenly stood up in his room. Something was wrong.

"Guard!" he screamed.

A second later, the door opened, and a guard entered.

"Go and check on the emerald. Immediately!"

The guard nodded slightly and responded with certainty.

"Yes, sir."

As soon as he said this, he exited the room.

Meanwhile, back in the emerald chamber:

"These animals are faithful to their owners and have some kind of telepathic bond with them. They sense the fear of their adversaries and direct this fear to their owner. So, if you kill it, its owner is going to know about it. As it was left here, its owner has to be the Soul Hunter…" Ron said.

"Then, what are we going to do?" Carmen was looking at the creature in desperation. The creature was preparing to lunge again. Carmen couldn't stop looking at the creature's eyes. Its red eyes were so freaky… Ron held Carmen by her arms and shook her.

"Focus on me, Carmen, and let's both relax. Look at me, take a deep breath." Carmen took a deep breath. "I know it's difficult but, try to calm down. It won't harm us unless you show you're scared."

Carmen took a deep breath and tried to block the fear from her mind. She opened her eyes and stared into Ron's eyes. Ron smiled gently. He held Carmen's hand. Carmen took a deep breath again and looked at the Barelan. It was hard to hide her fear, but she had no choice. She was looking at the creature without any emotions. It was more difficult than she thought. While doing this, she was squeezing Ron's hand with all her might. After some time, the creature stopped hissing at them, dropped the attack position and moved to a more comfortable position, but it was still staring at Carmen's face as if looking for a sign of fear.

"That's it. It's calming down," Ron said.

Carmen laughed softly. After a while, the creature stopped completely. It turned its back and returned to its corner, pretending to be bothered by something.

Sitting in his room, Edmund felt that the Barelan was calming down. *It was probably nothing*, he thought and went back to his work at the desk.

Meanwhile, in the belfry, when the creature went to the other end of the room, Carmen took a breath and looked at Ron.

"I can't believe I did it…"

Ron sighed.

"Still, we don't have much time. The Soul Hunter should have already felt the Barelan's distemper," Carmen continued.

"Let's get the emerald and get out of here."

Together they approached the emerald. While Carmen was about to take the emerald from its pedestal, Ron grabbed her hand.

"Wait."

"What's the problem now?" Carmen said in distress.

"Look."

Carmen looked at what Ron was pointing at. It was a barely visible thin wire attached to the ends of the pedestal on which the emerald was placed. Carmen followed the wire with her eyes. It went up to the ceiling of the room and its end was not visible.

"Where does this wire connect to?"

"My guess is it's connected to the bell. It probably triggers the bell if the emerald is moved," Ron said.

Carmen sighed in frustration.

"We need to find a solution and quick." Carmen knitted her eyebrows.

She had an idea. She leaned over and looked at the place where the emerald sat. It seemed like a special setting for the pointed end of the emerald. Carmen lifted her head and looked at Ron.

"Give me your cap." Ron gave his cap to Carmen without compunction. Carmen looked at the tip of the cap. It was pointed. It could work. She walked straight to the door. Half of Ron's soup was on the floor. She picked up the bowl, and poured the soup into the cap, and then went right back to Ron.

"What are you doing?"

"The end of the cap and the emerald housing look similar. If we can replace the emerald with the cap, the bell won't go off." Ron looked at Carmen in awe.

"I'm impressed."

Carmen smiled but after a second, she pulled herself together.

"C'mon. Let's do this."

Carmen told Ron to hold the wires gently, which he did as Carmen approached the emerald. She had to replace it in under a second. She counted to three in her head. One... Two... Three... She replaced the emerald with the cap. Ron cautiously released the wires. Carmen took a deep breath. It had worked! The cap served as the emerald.

"We did it," Ron enthusiastically.

Carmen looked at the blood-red emerald in her hand. It was very beautiful, and it was now where it belonged. She remembered they had to leave now, so she put it in her apron pocket and turned to Ron.

"C'mon. Let's get out of here now."

Ron and Carmen had managed to nab the emerald. Now the only thing they needed to do was to find a way out. The most difficult part was just about to start. Ron turned to Carmen.

"Now we'll get out of the castle slowly and very quietly. No one will notice the absence of the emerald."

They walked toward the door together, then they quickly climbed up the stairs. As they were about to enter the corridor, they encountered a guard. It was the one Edmund had sent. The guard looked at Ron and Carmen suspiciously. Ron saluted the guard and managed to pass by him with Carmen. Without looking back, they walked into another corridor. They were walking very slowly not to attract any attention.

"Do you think they suspect anything?"

When Ron was about to answer, the guard's voice was heard.

"You two! Stop!"

"Well there's your answer!" Ron said, quickly looking behind. "Run!"

As soon as Carmen heard the command, she began running. After Ron yanked up the carpet where the guard was standing, he caught up with Carmen. The guard fell flat on his butt.

"We have to go down! To the stairs!" Carmen shouted.

They were about to reach the stairs when the ringing of the bell resonated throughout the castle. The cap full of soup they replaced with the emerald gave them only so much time.

Ron stopped Carmen.

"Damn! We can't head down. They'll close the gates."

"So now what?" Carmen asked in fear.

Just then, three guards appeared at the end of the corridor.

"Here they are! Catch them!"

Ron started to pull Carmen by her arm.

"Follow me!"

Ron and Carmen made a run for it. They tried to take every turn and disappear without a trace. When they turned into another corridor, four more guards appeared. Ron braked suddenly and turned into another corridor. Now there were seven guards in hot pursuit of them. As he ran, Ron spotted a vase in the corridor, broke away from Carmen, and smashed the vase onto the floor. The water in the vase spilled on the floor. With one swift move, Ron transformed the water into ice.

"Get 'em!"

The voices coming from behind were getting closer. Ron grabbed Carmen's hand again and they kept running. After a while, falls and shouts were heard behind them.

"We have to get out of here!" Ron was thinking through the castle's plan, but he had no idea how they could get out. They couldn't go down; it was too late. How would they go out if they went up? He abruptly decided.

"From here!" he said as he made a sudden turn. Just then, five guards appeared in front of them.

"No, not from here!" he said, and they turned into another corridor. Just then, Lilian appeared in front of them while they were running in the corridor.

"Carmen? What are you doing?"

Lilian couldn't believe her eyes. Carmen stopped as soon as she saw her.

"Lilian, they're behind us! Distract them!"

Ron drew Carmen closer.

"C'mon, Carmen. We don't have much time!"

Lilian stared back in surprise. The guards chasing them were approaching quickly. Lilian suddenly made up her mind.

"They went that away!" she said as she pointed the guards in the wrong direction. Without any hesitation, the guards continued down the way the girl showed them.

The chase was still ongoing in the castle.

"Where are we headed?"

"If we reach the terrace, we can get out from the way to the cellar. I'm sure they didn't lock it down," Ron said.

They were both running out of stamina and were forced to slow down. All the guards in the castle received orders to capture them. As Ron was walking fast, he stopped when he came to a fork. As he tried to figure out which way to go, he saw guards running toward them from the left.

"I think we gotta go this way," he said as he yanked Carmen to the right. They were running at top speed again.

"There it is!" Ron said as he pointed toward the door that led to the terrace. They had to reach the door opening to the cellar on the opposite side of the terrace. Just then, someone cut them off. It was Dean. He pointed his sword at Ron.

"Get out of our way!" Ron said threateningly. Dean looked at Carmen, then at Ron. Carmen was looking at Dean in fear. The guards' voices were heard behind them. They were advancing toward the corridor, bellowing.

"Ron! They are approaching."

Dean looked at both of them hesitantly. Then, he lowered his sword with an indecisive expression on his face.

"Go on, get out of here quickly."

Carmen and Ron looked at Dean, not believing their eyes. They smiled.

"Move it!"

With Dean's second command, Ron grabbed Carmen's arm, pushed the door open, and went out onto the terrace. But the view before him was not what he expected. There were at least six men facing him. They attacked them with vengeance. Ron desperately shoved Carmen aside and drew his sword. He was fighting off the men who swarmed him with all his might.

"Go on, Carmen!"

"No, I won't go without you!"

Ron tossed a guard who lunged for him onto the men behind him and looked at Carmen.

"Go on! Get out of here! I'll slow them down!" he yelled at her.

10

Carmen felt trapped. She didn't want to leave Ron. If she did, they'd kill him. But she knew that he was right. If she stayed there, they both would die, and the important thing was to keep Anka's soul alive. She moved forward but hated herself for it. She started running on the terrace.

"She's getting away!" somebody shouted.

Carmen looked behind to see two men running behind her. Looking in front of her, she saw there were two other men as well. She was caught in a trap. They were all armed and they all wanted to kill Carmen. She was overwhelmed with fear and was barely able to escape an assault from an attacker in front of him. This made her pull herself together. *Remember who you are!* This was not her voice. The voice inside her… It was her mother's. The previous carrier of Anka's soul! She was right. She had to remember who she was. She was Anka and she had unique powers. At that moment she regained her wits and repelled the men with her powers. The other guards who saw this all took a step back. They were all surprised when they understood that she was Anka. At that very moment, a strong energy force passed near Carmen. Carmen looked in the direction from which the force came. It was Inca. Ron had jumped over Inca and knocked him down, which is why Inca's energy had missed Carmen.

Ron ran to Carmen with all his might.

"What are you waiting for, idiots! Catch them!"

The guards looked at each other hesitantly. The idea of attacking Anka was troubling them.

"What are you waiting for!"

The guards finally recouped after hearing Inca. They started sauntering toward Carmen and Ron again. Ron pulled Carmen to the railings.

"Climb up the railings!"

While he said this, he was also trying to ward off the sword blows while climbing to the railings himself.

"What! It's too high!"

Ron grasped Carmen's hand after pushing the last man back.

"We jump on three."

Carmen looked down. There was a white knuckler of a river below. She knew she had no choice but to jump. She was never afraid of heights before, but this was just too high. She held Ron's hand tightly.

"One!"

Carmen screamed and found herself in the raging waters a few seconds later. She thought she would hit the water hard because they had jumped from a quite lofty height, but Ron had softened the water beforehand. They swam up to the surface together.

"You said we'd jump on three!" Carmen said as she tried to regain her breath.

"There wasn't any time…" Ron said with a grin.

Carmen laughed. Just then, they heard a sound.

"Take aimmm!"

Carmen looked up.

"Ron! Arrows!"

Ron raised the water with a single motion of his hand before the arrows reached the water. There was a wall of water above them. The arrows shot from the castle wall got stuck into the wall one by one, and lost velocity as they fell into the water.

"Swim to the shore!"

This time Carmen immediately did what Ron said. After a while, Ron also swam to the riverbank. Carmen checked to see if the emerald was still in her apron. It was.

"C'mon, run!"

And so, they started to run into the depths of the forest.

ANKA'S CASTLE

Edmund entered the terrace with edgy, quick steps. His brother Derick was standing in front of a line of soldiers. He looked at Derick with rage.

"Where are they?"

Derick could barely look at his elder brother.

"They got away… " he whispered. Derick spoke suddenly just as Edmund opened his mouth, "But I sent a search team after them. They're looking for them all over the forest and in Zirkus."

Edmund was blinded by anger. He was so angry that he didn't know what to say.

"You..." he lunged at Derick. Derick had to take a few steps backward. "How could you let them run away! And with my emerald, on top of that!"

"I..."

Edmund interrupted Derick's word.

"You've seen Anka before. Why is it you didn't recognize her! How could you have made such a huge mistake!"

Derick had seen his brother angry before, but this time was different. He had never seen him so furious.

"I... I wasn't paying attention to the maids. I couldn't recognize her."

"You did one hell of a fine job there! Thanks to you, they escaped!"

Derick glanced at the guards. It was happening again. He was being humiliated in front of everyone, even though he was no longer an ordinary person. He was Inca. He shouldn't allow this. He glared at Edmund.

"You can't yell at me in front of the guards..." he said in a whisper.

Edmund raised his head as if looking at Derick from above.

"I am your king. I can damn well do whatever I want," Edmund barked.

Derick knitted his brows. He took a step forward and came closer to Edmund.

"Yes, you're just an ordinary king, and I am the mighty Inca, the rightful heir to the Crictus throne," Derick poked his finger at Edmund's chest. "I don't think you'd want to piss off one of the oldest spirits on Crictus, *brother*..."

Edmund was surprised by Derick's reaction. He was not expecting such a response from him. Regardless, he did not let his surprise show.

Derick pulled his hand back after giving his brother one final furious look.

Edmund spoke, "Look at what you're doing instead of owning your mistake. It's your fault she escaped, so you better fix it." Edmund took a few steps back and stood in front of the soldiers. After sizing them up, he turned to Derick. "Bring her to me. You can use all the guards and archers. I give you all my authority."

Derick stared at Edmund in surprise. Edmund approached Derick and whispered in his ear from the top of his shoulder, "Whatever you do, bring her to me, so her soul shall be mine forever..."

Then he vacated the terrace with his two guards.

THE FOREST

Carmen and Ron were still running into the depths of the forest. After a while, Carmen held onto a tree, gasping for breath.

"Can't we… Just stop… For a while?" she said breathlessly.

"They're still coming after us, we can't stop."

"Do you have any idea how hard it is to run with this wet skirt? It must weigh hundred pounds."

Ron grinned and approached Carmen. He made a simple move, and the water in Carmen's clothing suddenly dissipated into the air. After a while, the water fell to the ground. Carmen looked at Ron in surprise.

"How! Why didn't you do this before?"

Ron shrugged.

"Well, you didn't complain before."

Carmen smiled and leaned against the tree. There was a cheerful expression on her face.

"I can't believe we did it." Ron started to walk to set her in motion.

"If we stay here any longer, everything we've done will be for naught. I'm sure they've sent the whole army after us."

They set out once more and came to the rock where they had hidden their clothes before going to work at the castle. They changed their clothes there. Carmen put the emerald in her bag and hung it on her back. They hid their maid and guard clothes again under the same rock. Carmen talked after she was all dressed.

"I wouldn't think I'd miss these clothes." Ron finished up and put his bag on his back. Carmen sighed as she continued, "Well, what are we going to do now?"

Ron looked far away.

"We have to get away from here. Maybe we should leave Zirkus, but right now we're far from the city borders." Ron pulled out a map from his backpack, unfolded it on the ground, and studied it for a while. "We have to go to a place where they wouldn't even think of looking for us," he said as Carmen leaned toward the map.

"I don't think there's such a place. He'll be looking for us everywhere.

The Soul Hunter is not someone who'd leave his job to chance."

Ron looked at the map a little more.

"He may be thinking we'd be heading out of Zirkus. So, my suggestion is to remain within Zirkus city limits, but not to be seen very close to the castle."

"So where are we going?" Carmen asked curiously.

Ron spoke as he folded the map and put it back in his bag, "Let's go east. It's worth trying at least."

So, their journey to the east began. Ron's goal was to stay within the boundaries in order to surprise the Soul Hunter, but he was unsure if his plan was good. If he chose to go to the other end of Crictus, there would be a high risk of getting caught while they passed through the other cities along the way, but at least they would be away from the Soul Hunter. Ron's plan was to remain close to the Soul Hunter. He hoped he was making the right decision for Carmen's sake. He sighed and continued walking as he flashed Carmen a fake smile.

ANKA'S CASTLE

Derick and his guards hurried toward Edmund's room. The hall guards swung open the double doors when they saw Derick coming. Derick entered the room to find Edmund playing a one-on-one game of chess with himself. Finally taking notice of his brother who entered the room, Edmund spoke without looking up.

"I'm assuming you brought good news, right brother?" he said, moving his bishop forward.

Derick replied instantly, "All kingdoms were alerted. They are required to capture Anka and the emerald wherever they see them."

Edmund spoke blithely while playing his game, "So, you mean you couldn't find them yet? You know, they still may be in Zirkus."

Derick answered, "I looked under every nook, rock, and cranny, but there's no trace of them. I'm sure they're beyond the Zirkus limits."

"No," Edmund said while taking the pawn in front of the king with his white knight. "They couldn't have crossed the borders so quickly. They're still here somewhere." Edmund took the white knight with his black rook. Derick was ready to object.

"We're still searching. I'm personally taking care of this issue."

Edmund finally threatened the black king with the white bishop. The king had no place to escape.

"*Checkmate...*" he said in a whisper and then looked at his brother. He stood up slowly and then paced back and forth in front of his brother.

"It's been two weeks, brother. And you... You come here and tell me you've got nothing to show for it."

Derick gulped faintly.

"Finding them isn't that easy," as he went on the defensive.

Edmund grinned.

"Indeed. Did you manage to find the rebels in the forest?"

"We have captured many but no sign on Anka yet." Edmund seemed deep in thoughts.

"She will assemble an army eventually, if we don't capture her first." Then, he walked past his brother and reached the window. He continued to speak while looking out the window. "I'm taking you off this search. This is a serious assignment, and you don't seem to be taking it seriously enough."

"You can't do this. I can find them. Just give me a little more time."

"There's no time left," Edmund said sternly and looked at his brother again. "Anka's discovering herself and getting stronger day by day. I can't let this go on any further."

"Edmund, just give me one last chance. I'll find them."

Edmund looked over at his brother. He didn't believe he could do it, but after all, he was Inca. He sighed. "All right, but this is your last chance, do not make a mistake."

Derick took a deep breath.

"Don't worry, I will be successful."

"I hope so..." Edmund said sarcastically.

THE FOREST

Ron looked around. After a long trek, they arrived at a burbling creek. The sky was almost dark, and the sun had now turned orange. Ron turned to Carmen.

"We can spend the night here."

Carmen suddenly tossed her bag on the ground, as if she had been waiting for that for a long time.

"For a moment there, I thought you'd never say that."

Ron kept talking without paying attention to Carmen.

"All right, we have to divide up the tasks again. You can spread the blankets and start preparing a meal. I'm off to gather up some wood."

Carmen accepted without objection. She was unable to walk any further as they had been walking nonstop for about four hours.

Once Ron left her to gather wood, Carmen opened their bags and laid out the blankets. After that was done, she took out the loaf of bread and something that resembled salami they had bought from the last village they passed through. When Carmen was done with this, she walked down to the bank of the sparkling stream to fill their flask with icy cold water. Setting the flask aside, she then dipped her hands in the water. It was very relaxing. Carmen took a few sips and then she splashed some water on her face. It was then when she heard that voice again.

Carmen...

Carmen was scared out of her wits. The voice echoed inside her head. Carmen couldn't lift her head out of fear. She did not want to hallucinate again. She knew this voice as the one she heard in her dreams almost every night when she was on Earth. Carmen took her eyes off her reflection in the water and slowly looked toward the opposite bank. There she was. Her mother...

Her mother's ghost was standing on the water. She was wearing the same white and gold dress again. It looked as if rays of orange sunlight were passing through her. Juliet seemed translucent. Carmen looked her in the eye. Her eyes were not looking affectionately this time. There was a different meaning in her eyes. They looked as if... as if they were pleading for help.

Carmen poured more water into her palms and dashed it on her face to be sure of what she was seeing. When she looked up again, her mother was still there. Carmen got up quickly.

"I guess you won't be playing your disappearing act?"

Juliet was looking at her silently. Carmen had never looked this long at a person who looked so much like her. Juliet moved her lips faintly, but no sound was heard. Carmen fidgeted.

"Do you want to say something to me?"

Juliet was silent.

"Carmen?"

It was Ron. He was standing behind Carmen. Carmen didn't turn her head this time. Her eyes were glued on Juliet. Without understanding, Ron looked at where Carmen was looking, but couldn't see anything. Juliet was staring back and forth between Ron and Carmen.

Save!

The voice reverberated in Carmen's head. She was not expecting this.

"Save who?"

Ron looked at Carmen in shock.

"Who are you talking to?"

Carmen gestured for him to be quiet. Carmen repeated her question.

"Who or what do we have to save?"

Juliet looked at Carmen imploringly. Carmen was trying to make sense of what Juliet said.

Save!

The voice repeated itself. Carmen asked impatiently this time, "Who do you want me to save?"

Juliet's silence was annoying. All she said was "Save!" Juliet looked at Carmen for a while and then turned her back slowly.

Carmen shouted in haste, "Wait! You can't go. Who do we have to save?"

Juliet disappeared into the sunlight. Carmen turned to Ron in anger.

"You saw her too, didn't you?" She was pointing to the stream.

Ron stared at Carmen as if to say he was sorry.

"I didn't see anything."

Carmen lowered her arm as if she had given up.

"I can't believe this."

She quickly passed Ron and sat down on one of the blankets lying on the ground. Ron followed her and sat on the opposite blanket.

"Did you see Juliet?"

"Yes, and it was very annoying."

"Did she say something to you?"

"Yes. She told me to save something or someone, but she left without telling who or what we must save." Ron looked thoughtful. Carmen continued to speak, "Do you know what it means?"

Ron looked at Carmen thoughtfully. He was trying to think what it meant, but nothing came to his mind.

"I've got no idea."

Carmen sighed.

"Wonderful. My birth mother was really helpful there."

Ron ignored Carmen's angry attitude and talked.

"Perhaps she's talking about someone in the castle. But I don't think so."

What Ron said brought Lilian to Carmen's mind at first. She wondered if she needed help. But even if she needed help, they could never go back to the castle. Even Carmen wouldn't act so carelessly.

"I don't think so, either…" Carmen said and lie on the blanket. "Frankly, I don't care. I've asked her four times whom or what I was supposed to save. It's her fault that she didn't answer at all."

Ron was still thoughtful.

"Maybe she'll come calling again."

Carmen grimaced. Yes, it was a strange experience to see her mother who she had never met before, but it still did not change the fact that she was a ghost. Carmen suddenly discovered something strange. Ron said her mother was the previous carrier of Anka's soul. When her mother died, Anka entered her. Carmen leaped up suddenly.

"Wait a minute. If Anka's soul is inside me, how do I see my mother's soul?"

Ron smiled.

"Because when Anka enters someone's body, it integrates with that person's soul. When the Soul Hunter wanted to capture Anka, the soul of your mother must have been released from her body. Then, Anka's soul entered your body."

Carmen knitted her eyebrows.

"Then, when Anka comes out of somebody, the body has a chance to survive."

Ron shook his head.

"No. Since Anka is integrated with the soul of the carrier, in the absence of Anka, the soul can hold onto the body only very briefly."

"Wow. How can you know so much?" Carmen said in astonishment.

Ron shrugged.

"I used to read my grandfather's books when I was a kid. I learned it all from them."

Carmen smiled. Ron lifted his head up and looked toward the setting sun.

"Let's start the fire. The sun's going down…" Ron said.

Carmen spoke suddenly, "This time I'll make it."

Carmen looked around and found two stones on the ground. She clanked the stones together several times toward the leaves under the pieces of wood. She had a few unsuccessful attempts but didn't give up. Finally, when Carmen managed to ignite one of the leaves, she looked at Ron with joy.

"Congratulations…" Ron said, impressed.

They sat together by the fire and the sky around them got darker as they ate.

"We should discuss where we are heading. We are going in circles."

"Actually, we are going to a secret rebel base. We are near. But I am not sure if we will find anyone there. Anka was gone for so long, the rebels eventually spread out to different corners of Crictus." Carmen glanced at him and asked.

"You were a rebel right before you became an emerald."

"Yes, but we were weak, and the last attack killed most of my friends." Ron said. Carmen didn't know what to say.

"I'm sorry for your loss." Ron returned her words with a faint smile.

"We will find a way to gather an army. Let's try to find the rebel base, if they are still there." Carmen sighed, hopelessly. They finished their meal by the fire while having a conversation. They were both very tired. They both fell asleep after talking for a while.

They travelled the next couple of days as they discussed. Unfortunately, as Ron predicted, the rebel base was vacant. Ron didn't want to linger around that area, so they kept moving. It was hard to move around with the search parties all around the forest. But Ron grew up in these woods and he knew his way around. They found a creek where they could rest for the day. The next day, Carmen was awakened to the sound of Ron gathering up their gear. She looked at Ron with sleepy eyes.

"What are you doing?" Carmen said, rubbing her eyes.

"I'm getting ready. We've got to get moving. You know we can't stay in a place too long."

Carmen threw herself to the ground as if giving up. She was still rubbing her eyes.

"Do we have to go? Changing places all the time is so tiring," Carmen implored.

Ron paid no heed to Carmen's whining when he answered.

"Yes, Carmen, but we still have to move. Hunters might be after us."

He finished packing his own bag. He turned to Carmen's bag to get her into gear. Carmen turned face down where she was and started watching Ron.

Carmen sighed.

"Please Ron. We're both tired of constantly changing places. It's so nice here…" Carmen pointed to the burbling creek. "The stream is also beautiful." She was begging Ron to stay. Ron gave her a pensive look. Carmen stood up quickly and walked to him. She spoke, with her hands in a begging gesture. "Please, please, please… Just for a day…"

Ron examined Carmen's face for a while. One day would do no harm since they haven't seen a search party for a few days.

"Okay, just one day…"

Carmen couldn't contain her ecstasy and hugged Ron. Ron hugged her back in surprise.

"Thank you."

After letting him go, Carmen wiped the smile off her face as she cleared her throat slightly.

"Now I'm going back to enjoy some sleep."

Then, she turned around and went back to sleep on her ground bed. Ron laughed at her from behind. Carmen really knew how to entertain Ron. Some of her exaggerated gestures in the face of events warmed his heart. In some cases, she remained calmer than she should have. Sometimes she seemed to take nothing seriously. But Ron had seen her in the struggle for the emerald in the castle. Yes, Carmen seemed a bit scared, but that did not take anything away from her determination. Ron knew how determined Carmen could be when she wanted. He looked at Carmen lying on the blanket on the ground and smiled. She was going to be a very fine queen in the future.

Carmen fell asleep the moment she closed her eyes. She suddenly found herself in that unsettling dungeon. Light that drifted through the bars was hitting a man's face. It was the same man again. There was great sorrow on his face. Another man approached him. He wore a ragged outfit like the one this man wore. He looked filthy. The man had dark skin. The dark-skinned man came over and sat next to the other.

"Are you thinking about them again?"

His voice still sounded very realistic to Carmen. The sadness on the man's face grew.

"I can never get them out of my mind."

The dark-skinned man approached the other man's ear.

"Both Anka and Inca are back. All hell is going to break loose soon. One of them will certainly be ascending the throne and be sure they won't be leaving that Soul Hunter alive."

The man smiled softly. There was pain in his smile.

"I hope it happens as you say, my friend."

Carmen opened her eyes after a long slumber. Huge trees were dancing in the wind over her. Only after she had blinked a few times did she remember where she was. She was awake. Her dream felt so real that it would take the testimony of a thousand witnesses to convince her it was merely a dream. She straightened up a little and stretched out thoroughly. Then, she turned her head toward the stream and saw Ron. He was bathing in the stream. Carmen turned her head in case he was naked.

"Ron? Are you wearing anything?"

"Yes?"

Carmen stood up and walked to the stream.

"It was a very uncomfortable sleep. Maybe we should stay in a hotel instead."

Ron was coming out of the water as he frowned.

"Stay where?"

As Ron stepped out of the water, Carmen looked at Ron's body involuntarily. She hadn't realized before how muscular his body was. A moment later, she realized Ron was asking her a question. She tore her eyes away from Ron's body and cleared her throat.

"*Hmm*, a hotel... Anyway, never mind. It was just a joke." Ron got out of the water and dried his body with the blanket he was lying on. "You know what? It'd be better if we were running away on Earth. There are a lot of technological tools out there. And I always wanted to pretend as if I were on CSI."

Ron glanced at Carmen after wiping his hair with the blanket.

"Pretend to do what?" There was an expression on his face showing that he understood nothing.

Carmen smiled.

"You don't know what CSI is, do you?" Ron shook his head. Carmen spoke as if she had gained a victory, "See, you don't know some things either."

Ron laughed at what Carmen said, too.

"C'mon, let's eat something then practice our sword combat."

Carmen didn't say "No" to his offer. She had realized when they were in the castle that she needed to improve her skills. They hadn't practiced their sword fighting in quite some time.

After a meal that was not nutritious at all, they both picked up their swords. Because Carmen hadn't held a sword in a long time, it felt a little heavy to her. Still, she knew that she would soon get used to the sword as it had been made specifically for her.

They stood facing each other. Both took the 'ready' position. Both seemed cautious. Of course, compared to Ron's experience and composure, Carmen looked like a novice. But she could still pose a threat to someone who did not know how to wield a sword. Ron was peering at Carmen, trying to find a weakness in her. Carmen was watching his movements carefully. Meanwhile, she did not forget to pay attention to her own movements. When Ron came forward, Carmen was able to lift her sword at the very last instant. Ron's blow was very harsh and nearly made Carmen tumble. At the last moment, Carmen managed to maintain her balance by pivoting her left foot. While she was trying to stay balanced, Ron lunged at her again. This time, he was striking with his sword repeatedly. They were all very strong blows. Carmen could barely defend herself. He stepped back reluctantly and was constantly charging at Carmen.

"Hey, slow down. You're pushing me too hard!"

Ron struck a few more blows without paying her any heed.

"Try to use your environment to fight against me," Ron said.

Carmen didn't understand what this meant. Just then, her foot made contact with the tree behind her. Carmen bent down and Ron's sword got stuck in the tree as he swung his sword in a controlled but stern manner. Taking advantage of this, Carmen thrust her sword against Ron's neck.

"Aha, now I get what you mean." Carmen was laughing and panting.

Ron smiled as he pulled his sword from the tree.

"You need to be more agile. Don't wait for your enemy to attack."

The sword came out of the tree with a hard tug. In taking positions again, it was Carmen who attacked first this time. She was trying to apply all the techniques she knew. Ron had noticed this.

"Use only the technique that works for you. Using all of them at once doesn't make you the winner."

Meanwhile, Carmen delivered a blow to Ron with all her might. Even though Ron thwarted Carmen's blow with his sword at the last second, he nearly lost his balance. He was not expecting this move from Carmen. He smiled softly. Ron enjoyed seeing her make progress.

"Yes, there you go..." he said while blocking another parry from Carmen.

Ron slightly lost his balance with her last move. Seeing that, Ron attacked. Two swords clashed in the air. Carmen had to pivot backward again. In recalling what Ron said, she could use her environment to her advantage. Taking a quick look around her, she saw the tree behind her. She could try the same move again. And she tried. But this time Ron's sword didn't get stuck in the tree. Nevertheless, this gave Carmen the chance to excel. Carmen charged toward Ron's back. As soon as Ron saw this, he swung his sword back and rushed toward Carmen with all his might. With the impact from the sword, Carmen fell to the ground. She targeted Ron's feet with her sword. This blow wouldn't hurt, but Ron lost his balance. He also fell down to the ground. Ron sprang upon Carmen with his body. Carmen's sword fell a little forward. The fight was over. They were both lying on the ground, panting. Ron threw his weight onto Carmen. He had a sword in his hand. They were a mere breath apart from each other.

"I beat you..." Ron said with a smile.

Carmen was smiling, too. Ron was gasping as he examined Carmen's face. He had never been this close to her before. It was such a captivating feeling. The scent of her skin was attracting him like a moth through a flame. Carmen was also struggling with the same feelings. Not bothered with being under Ron's weight, she was just admiring the beauty of Ron's face. Ron's gaze fell on Carmen's lips. Carmen held her breath. But when Ron realized how long they had been like that, he cleared his throat and moved his body away from Carmen. Ron stood up. The smile on his face disappeared and was replaced by seriousness.

"I gotta go and change my clothes."

Carmen straightened up as she nodded slightly. She was still breathing irregularly. Ron moved away so suddenly that all Carmen could do was to watch him walk away. Was such a thing possible? Carmen never felt like this before. Being that close to him was an incredible feeling. She thought he was both impressive and a handsome guy when she first saw him. But, she also couldn't possibly imagine such a thing, especially considering how protective Ron was of her… Ron was her teacher and protector. Standing there with these feelings, she wondered if anything more than a friendship was possible…

Carmen finally decided to get to her feet. Ron never liked to display his feelings. Even when he lost his family, he tried not to show his sorrow to Carmen. It was very difficult to understand his feelings. She knew the most important thing for Ron was Carmen's safety. So, Carmen decided to leave Ron alone for a while. If there was 'something else' between them, it would come to the surface sooner or later.

Meanwhile, Ron removed his clothes and tossed them aside. He was not supposed to make such mistakes. It would make him weak. All he was supposed to do was protect Carmen. That was his only purpose in life and having feelings for her would put his task at risk. He kicked the first stone he saw. The stone bounced off a tree far away and fell to the ground. Ron bent down into the water and splashed some of the cold liquid on his face. He looked at the stream after repeating this process a few more times. The creek was still except for the tiny waves Ron created with his hands. He stared at his reflection for a while. He was mad at himself. He could never let this happen again. As he watched his reflection in the water, he managed to calm himself down by breathing deeply. Now he was calmer. But he was suddenly taken aback when his reflection in the water disappeared. He looked at the water in shock and frowned slightly. The water became cloudy. Soon, he began to see reflections of other people in the water. Ron peered carefully into the water cautiously. The cloudiness of the water gradually decreased as the reflection in the water cleared. It was Carmen. She was running away from something. Ron shuddered when he saw what she was running away from was Inca. Inca smote Carmen with a mighty blow and Carmen fell to the ground. Inca kept going. He approached Carmen and continued to surge his energy into her with all his might.

Carmen was screaming. Ron looked at the water, not believing his eyes. His eyes wide open, he was left breathless. Beads of sweat cropped up on his forehead. He continued to watch the reflection. Carmen was still screaming. After a while, her screams stopped. Carmen was dead. Ron punched the water.

"No!"

The reflection disappeared with Ron's smack on the surface, and it returned to its previous state. Ron couldn't believe what he saw. He was totally aghast. In a rage, he felt his eyes well up with tears. His heart was beating madly as he turned back. He saw Carmen coming toward him from just beyond their camping area. She smiled at Ron at first, but then stopped smiling when she saw the horrified look on Ron's face. She understood something was terribly amiss. She hurried toward Ron.

"Ron, are you okay?" Her voice was worried.

Ron was not able to get over what he had just seen. He raised his hand and touched Carmen's face. Carmen was examining Ron's movements. Ron looked absolutely awful. Ron swiftly pulled Carmen toward himself. He embraced her. He needed to feel that she was still alive. What would he do without her? Carmen embraced him too. She didn't understand what had happened, but still realized that Ron needed help. She caressed Ron's hair with her hand. Ron hugged her for a long time. This calmed him down a bit. But when Carmen pulled herself back a little more, Ron let her go. Carmen examined Ron's face carefully.

"What happened? Why are you acting like this?"

Ron tried to weigh the thoughts in his head. The reflection passed before his eyes again. Carmen's dead body was lying on the ground. He pushed the images away from his head. He stared at Carmen.

"I saw you die…"

Carmen was petrified.

Ron continued to speak, "And I wasn't even there."

11

Carmen sat down at the foot of the tree and leaned her back against it. Was she really going to die? She couldn't make any sense of Ron's words. They were terrifying words, but could they be true?

"What do you mean you saw me die?" Ron sat next to Carmen. He looked thoughtful. He was having trouble getting over the reflection.

"Do you remember that my grandfather said we had powers besides the elements? He said the water emerald could see the future in the water." Ron paused. He gulped before speaking. What he was going to say was difficult.

"When I just looked in the water, I saw you escaping from Inca. What's more, you got caught and…" He paused. "And he…" Ron couldn't continue. Carmen's lifeless body swam before his eyes. Carmen cut in before he could go on.

"Look, Ron, look at me."

She was trying to get Ron's attention. Ron gazed at Carmen as she held his hand and squeezed it.

"What you saw may not be absolutely for sure. I think seeing me die is an opportunity to prevent this. Don't you think?"

Surprised that Carmen spoke so calmly, Ron kept his surprise to himself. Instead, he just nodded his head. Carmen could have been right. Thanks to this ability, he could save Carmen's life.

When Carmen saw the pain in Ron's eyes, she reached out and hugged him.

"Everything's going to be all right," Carmen said. Ron nodded, although he wasn't quite convinced.

He answered, smelling Carmen's hair, "I hope so, Carmen…"

ANKA'S CASTLE

Meanwhile, things were chaotic at the castle. Having no news from Anka and the emerald kept adding to the tension in the castle. From the throne room, Edmund watched as the soldiers mustered into the courtyard, while his brother Derick paced up and down in front of them, chewing them out for their abject failure as he went. Edmund sighed. He had given him all the authority in the world and had absolutely nothing to show for it. The plan he had in mind took shape. It was brilliant and his brother wasn't needed in this plan. If it worked, he could both eliminate Anka and retake the fire emerald. He might even have two emeralds. Edmund summoned in his door guard loudly. The guard came the moment he heard the voice.

"Yes, sir."

"Have my brother and the head maid brought in here."

As soon as the guard received his orders, he saluted and backpaddled out the door. Edmund resumed looking out the window. It wasn't long before he saw the guard standing beside his brother. Edmund turned around and examined an oil painting hanging in a corner of the room. This picture was made when he was younger. Edmund examined his painting. He was an unattractive man, but he had the nobility to rule. He was ready to do anything for his throne.

He looked at the door when he heard the knock.

"Come in."

His brother came in. Even the splendor of his soul was making Edmund ravenous. Every time he saw him, he had to stop himself. He was always repeating himself. *Not yet. You can't have his soul yet, but you will enjoy this privilege soon enough…*

When his brother entered, the guards closed the door behind him.

"You wanted to see me." There was an expression of discontent on his face. He wasn't happy that Edmund summoned him into his gracious presence every time.

"Yes, my brother. Tell me, have you found any trace?"

Derick gulped.

"No, but we are very close…"

Edmund interrupted him.

"Getting close doesn't take us forward," Edmund said sternly. Derick remained reticent. "I'm dismissing you from this duty, Derick."

"No, you can't do this!" Derick immediately objected.

"This is my final decision," Edmund said.

"So, who will look for them? You can't find anyone more competent than me in this castle. I am Inca. It is my duty to find Anka. Nobody else can perform this duty."

Edmund laughed at Derick's passion. Derick found this smile strange.

"Nobody will be looking for her, brother."

Derick looked at Edmund in astonishment.

"What?" Was all he could say.

Edmund walked to Derick and put his hand on his brother's shoulder.

"Nobody will be looking for her, because she'll be coming to us of her own accord."

"Did you find another whisper stone?"

Edmund laughed.

"No, brother."

There was a knock on the door just then. Margaret entered. The head maid…

"You asked for me, sire?" Margaret said delicately. Compared to her portly size, her voice created a contrast. She was looking at the floor, not at the king. Like everyone else, she was dreadfully afraid of the king.

"Come in. I shall ask something special from you."

"Anything for you, sire," Margaret said.

Derick was listening curiously.

"I want you to bring me some of the clothes Anka wore."

Derick knitted his brows. He didn't understand what was going through his brother's mind. Margaret spoke in a shy, cowardly manner.

"But sire, a lot of time has passed. We washed those clothes."

"Not important. Bring me one of the garments she wore or anything that belonged to her. Make sure you bring it."

Margaret nodded.

"Of course, Your Majesty."

Margaret then made her exit out of the chamber.

Derick shot Edmund a curious look. He was still frowning.

"What are you going to do with her clothes?"

Edmund turned to Derick. His brows were still knitted.

"There's something I want you to do as well. I want you to find me an Abron."

Derick suddenly stared at Edmund in surprise. Why didn't he think of this before?

"Where can I find an Abron? Those birds are on the verge of

extinction."

The Abron was a kind of messenger bird. It would search and find whatever it smelled. Edmund spoke, "You'll find a way," he squeezed his brother's shoulder slightly while he said this. "I trust you."

These words pleased Derick to no end. He now had a new opportunity to prove himself honorable and this time he would not fail. He would find an Abron at all cost.

"I won't disappoint you," Derick said and left the room.

After Derick left the room, Edmund called in the guard again. He asked the guard to summon the scribe. The man was brought to the king's presence a few minutes later. He was a skinny old man. His white beard almost reached his shoulders, and he had a slight hunched back. As he entered, he could barely bow before his king.

"You called me, Your Majesty," the man said with the cracked voice of old age.

"Yes…" Edmund said. "I want you to write something for me."

"Of course, sir."

Then, he put some of the papers he had squeezed under his arm on the board he had brought with him. After arranging the papers, he removed his pen from his pocket. He looked at his King. Edmund began to dictate with his powerful voice:

Noble soul Anka…

THE FOREST

Carmen had begun to prepare the dinner. Ron was in deep thoughts that all he could do was sit and watch. Carmen had to gather the wood as well. Because Carmen did all the work, the meal was a little late. It was completely dark by then. Carmen had to light the fire on her own too. At dinner, there was some canned food they usually ate. Carmen was not able to pin down the flavor of this food. Maybe it was peas or okra… It had a very different taste. At any rate, she wouldn't touch this food if it were the last thing on Earth to eat. She missed the food on Earth so much. Or she would even go for a Klaush right about now.

Carmen gave Ron his share after she finished her meal. Ron took the meal unwillingly.

"Perhaps we need to spice up the food we've been eating lately," Carmen said.

Ron was playing with his food.

"We haven't got much money left. In fact, we're almost out of money. We must spend it carefully. This is the cheapest meal."

Carmen sighed. Ron took a small bite from his meal. Then, grimacing in disgust, he tossed it aside. Carmen was watching Ron anxiously. Realizing he was under surveillance, Ron looked at Carmen.

"I'm fine," he said matter-of-factly.

Carmen put her plate down.

"You don't look fine."

Ron slightly shrugged.

"I just can't get that image out of my mind. Your... your lifeless body..."

Ron bowed his head. Carmen crawled up to Ron.

"Please don't do this to yourself. We can't know that what you saw is going to really happen."

Ron looked at Carmen suddenly.

"Don't you understand? I can't lose you!"

Ron's voice sounded harsh. Carmen spoke without paying any heed to Ron's tone.

"You won't lose me."

Ron laughed nervously but didn't say anything. He wasn't looking at Carmen. He spoke after a short silence.

"How can you know that?"

Carmen tucked her hair behind her ear and got even closer to Ron. She held Ron's hand.

"I know because I trust you. I know you'll protect me from all danger, and I know how much you value me."

Ron glanced at Carmen. A second later, he turned his head again. He was feeling guilty. He felt like he couldn't protect and save Carmen. That's why he was ashamed.

"I couldn't protect you in that reflection. I let you down. Maybe..." Ron paused. What he was going to say was hard for him. "Maybe the emerald chose the wrong person."

Carmen approached Ron a little more. She held his arm and pulled him to herself. She was embracing Ron's arm.

"Do not ever say that. I trust you and this will never change. The reflection you saw doesn't mean anything. You will be there for me."

After a long pause, Ron looked at Carmen for the first time. Carmen stood so close to him that the scent of her skin was making him dizzy. They were only a breath's distance apart. Ron spoke, examining Carmen's face.

"What if I can't?" he stopped. He continued to examine Carmen's face. Her upturned nose, cheekbones, pink lips, those inviting hazel eyes… his heart ached. He touched Carmen's face. He pushed back a few strands of hair touching her face. "What if I lose you?"

Carmen didn't speak. Ron leaned his forehead on Carmen's forehead. This little contact brought them closer. Carmen felt as if her heart would skip a beat. She was breathing heavily. Being so close to him… It was intoxicating.

Ron continued to speak, "I can't even imagine losing you." His voice sounded like a whisper. They were so close to each other that Carmen heard him easily. Carmen gulped faintly.

"Then don't imagine…" Carmen whispered.

Her voice trembled with excitement. She could feel Ron's breath on her face and the sound of her own heart. For a moment, Carmen brought her face closer to Ron. She pressed her lips onto his lips and planted a hesitant kiss. Just as she was about to draw back, Ron's lips found her lips again. Ron pulled Carmen in and kissed her passionately. He moved his hand over Carmen's face. He ran his fingers across Carmen's cheekbones. Carmen's skin was warm. Then, his fingers dropped from Carmen's neck to her shoulders. He pulled her to himself a little more. He was kissing her as if he'd never let her go. A moment later, the voice in his head spoke, *What do you think you are doing! She's your queen. You can only be her protector. You are not supposed to have any other feelings for her!*

Ron was suddenly horrified. He pushed Carmen a little away from himself. Their lips were no longer touching each other. They were both breathless. When Ron pulled away, Carmen longed for the same feeling, as if something had been taken from her. She moved toward him again craving his touch, but Ron stopped her. He gulped and opened his eyes and glanced at Carmen. What he saw in Carmen's eyes alarmed him even more. It was passion, it was love. This couldn't be possible. It shouldn't be. Ron softly stroked Carmen's face and spoke, "It's late. Let's go to bed now."

Carmen was still under the influence of the kiss. She wanted more but obeyed Ron by nodding her head. Ron let Carmen's arm go and moved away a bit. Then, he looked at her.

"Good night."

"You too..." Carmen said.

Ron pointed at the blanket on the other side of the fire with his head.

"Would you like me to sleep there?"

Carmen had forgotten she was sitting on Ron's blanket... When she realized where she was sitting, she suddenly stood up.

"No, I..." she gulped. "I'll go back to my place."

Ron shook his head. Carmen went back to her blanket and sat down. Ron had already lied down. Carmen was watching Ron. This time she was watching him not anxiously but both with amazement and curiosity. Ron smiled softly as he noticed Carmen's gaze. Carmen responded to him, too. Then, Ron turned his head to the other side. Carmen was still looking at him. Her heart still hadn't fully returned to its regular beating. It was the first time she had experienced such a thing in her life. She slowly laid her head on the blanket and continued to gaze at him through the fire. After a while, she dozed off while watching him.

When Carmen opened her eyes the next morning, Ron was getting ready to go. Carmen realized that he had gotten up early again. She lifted her head from the blanket and began watching him. With his back turned to her, Ron was packing his bag. He picked up the blanket on the ground, folded it, and placed it in the bag. When he was done, he turned around and came eye-to-eye with her as he was about to drop the bag on the ground. Carmen was surprised when she saw Ron's face. His eyes were red.

"You're awake."

Ron's voice was cold. Carmen straightened up a little.

"Yeah, but it seems that you couldn't sleep well."

Ron averted his glance from Carmen.

"We've been here for two nights. Somebody had to keep watch," he said and got back to work. This time he turned to Carmen's bag. He was not looking at Carmen and his voice was very cold.

"Is everything all right?" Carmen said doubtfully.

"Yeah, sure," Ron spoke with a fake smile.

Carmen got up, went to the stream, and washed her face. It was obvious that Ron had a problem, but she couldn't figure out what it was. After washing her face, she opened Ron's bag and took out a piece of bread. When she opened his bag, Ron looked at Carmen. Carmen spoke just as she was going to toss the bread in her mouth.

"We're not going right now, are we?" There was some doubt in her voice.

"Actually, I thought of leaving right away. In the reflection I saw, you were dying in a forested area. So, we can't travel in the forest anymore."

Carmen perceived the coldness and uneasiness in Ron's voice, so she wanted to lighten the atmosphere a bit.

"But you didn't mention there was a stream in the reflection?" Carmen said and pointed at the stream. "If we stay next to the stream, the reflection will not come true," Carmen said in her sweetest voice.

Ron looked at Carmen harshly.

"My duty is to keep you alive. Let me do my job."

Carmen froze. She was not expecting such a tense reaction. Suddenly, the smile on her face disappeared. Ron moved his hand nervously over his hair and put the bag on the ground. He took a few steps toward Carmen.

"I'm sorry. I didn't mean that. It's just that… I'm a little nervous now. Because of the reflection…"

Carmen nodded, but she was overwhelmed. After taking a deep breath, Ron went back to what he was doing. Carmen approached Ron. She didn't want to ask this question, but she had to. She took a deep breath.

"Are you sure there's nothing else going on?"

Her voice sounded very weak. Ron stopped for a moment. Yes. There was another problem. He shouldn't have kissed Carmen last night. Now he had to tell her that he couldn't be with her, but he had no idea how to do that. So yes, there was a problem, and it was a huge problem. He took another deep breath and spoke.

"No, everything's fine."

Ron continued to fold Carmen's blanket. Carmen came one step closer to Ron. Meanwhile, Ron folded the blanket and even placed it in Carmen's bag.

"Well, why don't you repeat that while looking into my eyes?"

Ron zipped up the bag, turned around, and handed it to Carmen. He looked into Carmen's eyes.

"There's absolutely no problem whatsoever."

Though not totally convinced, Carmen nodded anyway. Ron walked past Carmen and picked his bag up from the ground. Using his powers, he extracted some water from the stream and washed out the camping area. Just so nobody would see any signs that they had been there.

"Let's go now. There used to be another rebel camp a day walk from here. Even if they are not there anymore, we can leave a mark in case one of them passes by there." Ron said and they set off together.

It was going to be a very long trek, and they had been walking for only about an hour. That hour seemed like a year to Carmen. Every time she had tried to talk to Ron, he replied evasively, killing the conversation. After a while, Carmen also gave up her attempts at talking. Their journey used to be fun with Ron, but today was different. It upset her that this had to happen right after they had kissed. A lot of things passed through her mind. Ron said the problem was the reflection he had seen, but Carmen knew it was something else.

After a three-hour walk, Carmen spoke.

"Can we take a rest now? We've been walking nonstop for three hours," Carmen said, slowing down.

Ron looked around. Pointing toward the left, she added, "The sound of water is coming from over there. We can take a break there."

Thus, they headed that way. Indeed, there was a fast-flowing river in that direction. It was thin and curvy. Ron filled his flask with water and handed it to Carmen. After taking a drink, Carmen put her bag on the ground and sat next to it. They were walking at a fast clip and Carmen was pooped. After Ron put his bag on the ground, he sat down, like Carmen had.

"We can't stay here more than fifteen minutes. We must keep moving."

Carmen nodded to Ron. Meanwhile, she was watching Ron, who was digging into the ground in distress with a couple of stones he had found. Although Carmen didn't want to discuss the matter, she knew she had to get it out in the open because she couldn't stop thinking about what was bothering Ron. She spoke after taking a deep breath.

"Ron, I'm not good at talking about such things, but… I think we need to talk."

Ron looked up at Carmen.

"About what?" He acted like he was unaware of what had happened.

"About what happened last night…" Carmen was feeling embarrassed. Ron studied Carmen's face as if he still hadn't understood. Carmen finally couldn't bear it. "Do you have to make me say this?"

Ron sighed and put down the stone he was holding.

"Of course not. I'm sorry." Ron hesitated and looked at Carmen. "I only…"

Silence.

"You only what?"

Ron gulped. He was dreading having this conversation. Again, he averted his gaze.

"I wish we didn't have to talk about this."

Ron bit his lip. How was he going to say that to her?

"Why would you say that? Was it really that awful for you?" Carmen asked, disappointed.

Ron stood up, came up to Carmen, and bent over.

"No, Carmen. I just… I just want you to know that…" Ron's voice sounded very serious. This seriousness frightened Carmen a bit. "I will never, ever leave you alone. And I will protect you from all danger at the expense of my life. I promise you."

Carmen was just stunned and confused. She was able to smile only after some time. Ron's voice was stern, like he was swearing allegiance to his queen.

"I already know that," Carmen finally said.

Ron gulped.

"Good…" After saying this, he took a deep breath and continued talking. "Then, I want you to listen to what I have to say now."

Carmen listened to Ron with complete rapture. She hadn't seen Ron so serious for a long time.

"What happened last night…" he closed his eyes, "was a mistake." Ron interrupted while Carmen was about to object. "Please listen to me until I finish my words." Carmen closed her mouth. Ron continued, "As I said, what happened last night was a mistake, because…" Ron paused. He bowed his head. His heart was beating madly. He didn't want to tell her a lie, but it was for her own good. This was the best way to protect her.

"Because what?" Carmen's heart was also beating madly. It was as if she was in a nightmare. She was wondering what Ron would say. Ron looked at Carmen.

"Because I don't have that kind of feelings for you."

Carmen was petrified. She couldn't believe what she heard. This time,

Ron was looking at Carmen without taking his eyes away. He was trying to be convincing, and he succeeded. Carmen shook her head. She knitted her eyebrows.

"But you kissed me back." There was despair in her voice, despair, and shock.

"I know, that was a mistake. I should have never responded to you." Carmen had a hard time believing what she had heard. "I'm sorry…"

There was sadness in Ron's voice. He was sorry that he couldn't tell her the truth. He reached for Carmen when he said this. He touched her shoulder trying to console her. Carmen was startled by Ron's touch and jumped up instantly.

"You mean… are you telling me now… you took advantage of me?" Carmen covered her eyes with her hand. She couldn't believe what was happening. Ron stood up, too.

"I am really sorry, Carmen. In that moment I—"

Carmen laughed nervously.

"You're sorry?" "Really?" Carmen suddenly became serious. "I trusted you."

"You can still trust me…"

"No!" Carmen interrupted Ron. She angrily wiped away the tears that were pooling in her eyes and took a few steps toward Ron. "Last night was important to me, Ron. I…" Carmen had a hard time saying this. "I'd never kissed anyone before and…" Now she had a harder time keeping her tears. "And more than that, it was with you. I never felt…" Just then she stopped herself from saying more.

Ron was looking at Carmen in anguish. He was tormented. *I love you too, Carmen! I wish there was a way…* But he kept his thoughts to himself. He was just watching Carmen, her desperation… He wished he could tell her the truth, but no. He had to be strong. *Love is weakness! It is an opportunity for enemies who wanted to ambush them!*

"How can you expect me to trust you now!"

Ron bowed his head. He couldn't find anything to say. All he could do was to apologize.

"I would never dream of hurting you. You have to believe me." Ron only wanted to console her, but he could not.

"I was thinking about what you said yesterday. Maybe you were right." Ron looked into Carmen's eyes. There was fury in her eyes. *This is good,* he thought. "Perhaps the emerald did chose the wrong person."

Ron's eyes widened, but he remained reticent. What he said in sorrow yesterday was now pouring furiously from Carmen's mouth. He couldn't be mad at her. Whatever she said was right. He had hurt Carmen. He too was hurt, but Carmen didn't and shouldn't know this. Carmen started to walk, not knowing what to do with her anger.

"Where are you going?" Ron called after her.

Carmen kept walking without answering. Ron ran after her and stopped her. As Carmen tried to escape from him, Ron saw her face. She was crying. Carmen, Anka, his queen, the only being he had sworn to protect was crying because of something he had caused. Ron couldn't stand it. He embraced her. Carmen resisted at first. She refused to hug him. But she finally gave up. She had nobody else except him. She had only him on this gigantic planet she was a foreigner to. She was furious with him, and she was embarrassed, but she needed someone to console her. Ron hugged Carmen as if he wanted to absorb her pain. He felt helpless while Carmen was crying in his arms. Since the death of his family, this was perhaps the first time he felt terrible. He had witnessed many deaths, joined wars, and passed through so many hurdles. But this was worse than all of that. The only person he valued and could value in his life was crying in his arms because of him. Ron could barely stop his tears. He reminded himself again.

Love is weakness. Stay away from love!

12

Carmen was sitting beside a tree, watching the fast-flowing river, as the sun was about to set. The landscape looked great when the sky was painted in crimson tones. Ordinarily, Carmen would be enjoying the view, but not even the scenery could cheer her up today. She felt like she had been used and thrown aside, and what was worse, by the first person she ever fell in love with. By the only person she could trust on a planet she did not know… By her friend, companion, protector… She was furious with him. She had never been more embarrassed in her life before. How could he do that to her? Carmen trusted him without any compunction. The similarity of men throughout the universe annoyed her. *It doesn't matter if they are from Earth or Crictus, men are all the same*, she thought. Carmen was full of rage again. She tried to block these things out of her mind and began viewing the landscape.

"Dinner's ready."

It was Ron. They had not walked much longer when Carmen got upset, so they had to make camp in that place. It was he who had done all the chores. Carmen had been stewing in her fury in the same spot since the morning. She turned down Ron's every effort to speak.

Carmen got up and took the meal from Ron's hand without looking at him. Then, she went and sat on her blanket. Ron sighed and sat down on the blanket on the ground opposite Carmen.

"Aren't you ever going to talk to me?"

Carmen spoke without looking at him.

"I'm eating." Her voice was harsh.

Ron sighed once again.

"I'm planning to go to Zirkus tomorrow. The last place they will be looking for us is around the castle. We still have to be extremely cautious."

Carmen just nodded. Ron watched Carmen for a while.

"Carmen, I'm begging you, say something."

Carmen stared at Ron, whom she had not looked at for a long time.

"Say what?"

"You are acting like I don't even exist. I know what I did was wrong, but I didn't mean to."

Carmen put her food on the ground and glanced at Ron.

"Look, I won't do anything to anyone if they don't deserve it, Ron. I'm not like you."

Ron was petrified. Carmen stood up after saying this.

"Where are you going?"

Carmen stopped in distress and turned to Ron.

"I don't have to explain you anything."

Carmen started to walk next to the river. Staying near Ron was doing her no good. If someone dissed her like this on Earth, she would probably never talk to them again, at least for a long time. But the situation here was different. Carmen was like a fugitive on Crictus because she had stolen a very precious emerald from the castle, and she was the real heir to the throne. On top of everything, she didn't have anywhere to go, and she did not know anyone on this planet. Carmen felt as if she was imprisoned. For the first time in a long while, she missed Earth. She even missed that little town of hers. Her family, her friends… But Ron said it would be risky to go back because Anka's soul would be imprisoned on Earth forever if she died there. Supposedly, Anka could only enter the body of a person from Crictus and other nonsense. Perhaps she should go back. For a while… At least to hide. She wouldn't have to see Ron, either. But even to go back to Earth, she would have to ask Ron's help because even if she traveled once, she didn't know how to travel between worlds on her own yet. She was furious with Ron. She had never thought she'd think that about Ron one day. She loved Ron dearly, in every sense of the word. But being with him now only made her feel upset and reminded her of the same shame she felt that moment he rejected her.

After a long walk, when she realized that it was getting dark, Carmen decided to return. When she came back, Ron was sitting by the campfire, poking at the wood with a stick. When he saw Carmen, he dropped the stick and leapt to his feet.

"Carmen, I was worried about you."

Carmen came over with a mocking attitude and sat down by the fire.

"Don't worry, I didn't run away."

Ron sat down again. Carmen sat cross-legged; she was upset. She placed her hand under her chin and just started to observe her surroundings. The only thing she did not do was to look at Ron. She did not even look at Ron once. But when Ron smiled softly, Carmen glimpsed at him.

"What?" Carmen's voice was calm.

Ron shook his head.

"You're being childish." Carmen stood upright. She gave Ron an inquisitive look. Ron felt as if he had to explain. "You're ignoring me, not even looking at me…"

Carmen crossed her arms.

"What do you want me to do?"

Ron spoke, "Yell at me, say what you want. Release your anger. Just don't keep quiet." Ron's voice was soft, compassionate. He continued to speak. "If you repress your anger, it'll keep growing. We'll never be apart. I'll protect you until my last drop of blood. I'll never leave you. You can't stay mad at me forever."

Ron was right. They would never be apart. There was a matrimonial bond between them. This was exactly what that nonsense *"until death do us part"* meant. Carmen had to stand beside him for the rest of her life. Sooner or later, she had to forgive him, but not just yet. She needed more time as her emotions were still very fresh.

"Don't tell me what to do, Ron. It's my job, remember?"

Ron looked at Carmen in surprise. It was the first time that Carmen had used her authority as Anka against Ron. Carmen was right. Even though Ron knew his main mission, he almost forgot how important Carmen was and what great things she would achieve. The person whose heart he broke this morning was the ruler of the planet Crictus. She was a queen and the carrier of a noble soul. Ron bowed his head.

"You're right. I'm sorry."

Ron's reaction surprised Carmen, but she didn't show it. Carmen wanted to hurt him only because she was hurt as well. But for the first time, she was using her powers against Ron. Carmen asked herself for a moment what she was doing. What she said in anger in the morning suddenly came to mind. *Perhaps the emerald really did choose the wrong person…*

Had she gone too far? But this still could not replace the pain inside Carmen.

She decided to think about it later. After wishing Ron a good night, she curled up on top of her blanket and fell asleep.

She dreamt of the same man again in the morning. Seeing this man in her dream almost every day had started to bother her. The man was sleeping under the light seeping through the iron bars. His roommates, more like cellmates, had also drowsed off. Strange fly-like creatures were zigzagging over half-eaten bread on the ground. Carmen felt pity for the men there. What a miserable life it must be languishing in such conditions. Approaching the man behind a smoke screen, Carmen was examining his face. Her dream felt so real. Could she touch him? Just then, he opened his eyes when he heard voices coming from outside. Carmen backpaddled a few steps and looked at the iron door.

A guard opened the door, looked at him, and said, "You've got a visitor."

The man muttered obscenities under his breath as he straightened up, "I have no family."

The guard grinned.

"I didn't say he was a relative." Then, he became serious. "Move."

The man could barely stand up. He walked past the guard, giving him a disdainful look. They started to walk down the narrow corridor together with Carmen following quickly in tow. Escorted by two guards, the man was taken through narrow corridors and grimy places with iron bars and brought in front of a staircase. They went up the stairs and arrived in front of a large door. There were two more guards at the door. The guards holding the man by the arms dragged him in. The man shut his eyes at first because of the glare inside. It was the first time he had been this close to the sun in a long time. At the end of the room, a large man in a cape was waiting, his back turned to them. As the back doors closed, the man turned to face them.

"My dearest friend."

With both arms wide open, the man looked at the man in the guards' arms. Both Carmen and the man looked at him in bewilderment. Carmen felt a chill down her spine. It was the Soul Hunter before her. Carmen stared at him in surprise and horror. What was he doing in her dream?

"Edmund."

The man glared as if he recognized the Soul Hunter. There was hatred in his gaze. The Soul Hunter was grinning.

"Were you expecting someone else?" He took a few steps forward. The wrinkles on his face became more visible in the sun. "Were you waiting for your wife, or perhaps your daughter?"

The man struggled desperately between the guards.

"You bastard!"

The Soul Hunter laughed at his effort. Then, he paused for a moment. He took his eyes off the man and then directed his gaze at Carmen. Carmen was suddenly horrified. Nobody had noticed her until now. How could the Soul Hunter see her?

Carmen opened her eyes in fear. Her fear had woken her up from the dream. The Soul Hunter scared her. Ron gave Carmen a worried look as he went over to her.

"Hey, you all right? Is everything okay?"

Carmen spoke without looking at Ron.

"I'm fine. It was just a dream…" she said.

It was a very humdrum time for the next couple of hours. They got ready without a single word to each other and set off. After three or four hours of hiking, they checked the hidden rebel camp. But as predicted, it was empty. Ron was starting to feel desperate. Soon he will have to find a lead. They needed to start assembling an army as soon as possible. After they walked for couple more hours in silence, they found a lake and Ron deemed it suitable to bivouac there. They were just a few hours away from the castle and getting any closer would be dangerous.

After settling in along the lakeshore, Carmen leaned against a tree and sat down. Walking all day in silence was not her idea of a fun day. Carmen was still bored to death until Ron threw a wooden sword in front of her. Carmen raised her head and looked at Ron.

"We need to practice."

"Now? We've been walking all day."

Ron pressed, "Your enemies don't care if you're tired or depressed."

Carmen glared at Ron.

"All right, let's fight then," She grabbed the wooden sword off the ground and stood up.

They stood facing each other and started to circle one another. Carmen was the first to pounce. Ron attacked after easily blocking Carmen's move. After a few blows, Carmen started to get in close proximity to Ron. She was fighting with her anger. Her blows were very powerful, but anger would cause people to make mistakes. This continued for a while. Carmen was striking Ron with all her might. Having finally caught Carmen's weak spot, Ron destroyed Carmen's balance. Carmen's sword dropped to the ground as she fell. Ron could catch Carmen before she hit the deck. Carmen suddenly found herself in Ron's arms. It was a familiar feeling.

"Don't let your anger control you and never show your adversary your weaknesses."

Carmen escaped Ron's arms and took the sword back into her hand. Ron continued, "The Soul Hunter killed your mother. He almost killed you. He killed my brother, my grandfather and another innocent person in front of your eyes. The hatred you feel for him must incite you. But you should never let hatred get the best of you. You must fight with your mind, not with your heart."

Carmen hated to admit it, but Ron was a very good teacher. Still, she attacked Ron with a quick move, ignoring him. This time she was more careful. But her blows were still very strong. Ron, who survived Carmen's strong blow at the last moment, caught Carmen's weak spot again. Taking advantage of her incorrect grip on her sword, he dealt a strong powerful blow to the sword. Carmen's sword flew from her hand. Ron then pointed his sword at Carmen's neck.

"You're still fighting with your anger."

Carmen responded breathlessly, "Weren't you the one who said to release my anger yesterday?"

Ron lowered his sword.

"Yeah, but not during the fight."

Carmen raised her hands.

"As you wish…" she said mockingly, as she turned around and walked away.

They were both quiet as it started to get dark. Carmen was lying down and watching the dancing tree branches, while Ron was carving a branch with the knife in his hand. As she gazed at the sky, Carmen saw a bird circling overhead. She called out to Ron nonchalantly.

"Hey, do birds hunt humans on Crictus?"

Ron quit what he was doing and looked at Carmen.

"No, not even if they're big. Why do you ask?"

Carmen pointed at the bird with her index finger. Meanwhile, the bird started its descent. Ron stood up as Carmen straightened up. Ron extended his hand skywards. Ron spoke as the bird came and perched on his arm.

"This is an Abron. A messenger bird."

Carmen looked at the bird in bewilderment. The bird's eyes were extremely white and scary. It had bright red and white feathers and a long tail. A small piece of paper was rolled up and tied around the bird's leg. The bird had a small piece of cloth in its beak. While Ron was untying the rope on the bird's foot, Carmen got closer to the bird. Just as she was about to pluck the piece of cloth from the bird's beak, the bird ate it.

"These birds eat clothes. They find the owner from the scent of the garment that is put into their beaks. When they find the owner of the scent, they eat the cloth as a reward." Ron had finished untying the rope.

"What happens if they can't find the owner?"

"They starve to death," Ron said calmly.

"The animals here are really interesting," Carmen said. While Ron was spreading out his blanket, Carmen approached Ron anxiously. The message was written in Crictus script which she couldn't understand. As Ron read the paper, his face fell.

"Can you translate it?"

Ron sighed and started to read the paper:

Noble soul Anka,

I wish I had met a noble soul like you under better circumstances. I would love to reach a compromise with you, even though I don't approve of you entering my castle secretly and stealing a valuable item of mine.

I want to make a trade with you. I have something that you value very much. If you agree to return my emerald, in return I offer you former King Richard, that is, your own father. If you accept my offer, I invite you to come to the place specified below on the specified date.

With kind regards to the Noble soul,

KING Edmund

Both Ron and Carmen were suddenly petrified. Nobody had ever told Carmen about her father. She didn't even know that he was alive. Ron read the paper again quietly. Then, he crumpled it up and threw it on the ground.

Carmen suddenly gathered her wits and hurriedly picked the wad of paper off the ground.

"What are you doing? The place and date are written on it."

"We're not going there, Carmen."

Ron sat down. Carmen glanced at Ron with questioning eyes.

"But why not?"

"Don't you see? It's an obvious trap… for all these years, no one heard from the former King Richard. When the castle was captured, the Soul Hunter killed him."

"How can you know that? Maybe it's true. Maybe my father is alive."

Ron sighed.

"Carmen… your father is not alive."

"You can't know that."

"Even if he were alive, why does the Soul Hunter want to trade him for the emerald? He won't have any gain from having the fire emerald back. He wants you."

Carmen knew Ron was right, but this was her father. Her father she had never seen before. If it was true or if he needed help… Suddenly, everything in Carmen's head fell into place. Her mother had asked her to save someone. It was her father that she had to save. He was alive!

"My father's alive…" Carmen said in a whisper.

"What?"

Carmen turned to Ron.

"Juliet told me to save someone. The person she meant was my father." Carmen's eyes were beaming. Ron glanced at Carmen, not understanding. "My mom asked me to save my dad!" Carmen explained.

Ron stood up and came in front of Carmen.

"Even so, I can't put your life in danger. He is not an honorable man. He is a murderer. He is trying to pull you into a trap." He tried to take the paper from Carmen as he said this. Carmen pulled the paper away. "Carmen, give me the paper."

Ron sounded serious. Carmen objected.

"This may be our only chance to save my father."

"Carmen, the paper!"

Carmen took a few steps back as Ron walked over to her.

"If you found out your father was alive after a long time, wouldn't you try to save him?"

"If it meant putting your life in danger, never."

Carmen hid the paper behind her back. Ron was still asking for the paper with his hand outstretched.

"Since when have you started thinking about me so much?" Carmen said, sarcastically.

"What do you mean by that? I *always* think about you."

Carmen took a few steps toward Ron. She spoke as she looked at him as if she were challenging him.

"If you thought of me so much—" Carmen said and stopped speaking. Ron knew whatever Carmen would say would hurt him, so Carmen chose to keep quiet. He was grateful to her for that.

"Carmen, please. Don't act like this."

Carmen showed the paper in her hand to Ron.

"I'll keep this paper and we'll sit down and really think about going there."

There was certainty in Carmen's voice. It was as if she was ordering Ron. But he was having nothing of the sort.

"No, Carmen! We're not going there. There's nothing to discuss."

Ron turned back. He was angry. Carmen walked over to him.

"You can't make this decision…"

Ron suddenly turned toward Carmen and interrupted her.

"Of course, I can! My sole duty is to protect you, and this is far too dangerous!" He laughed nervously. "Do you really think I'd let you go to them? That's suicide," Ron was shouting.

"It's my father we're talking about here!"

"Yeah, *your father* who we're not even sure whether he's alive or not!" Ron said, moving his hands angrily.

Carmen spoke, trying to control her nerves, "We have a chance to save my father, Ron. We both have powers. You're a good fighter. We can defeat them."

Ron moved his hand in his hair.

"You're still not making sense. We can't defeat them. We don't know how many of them there will be." He spread his hands. "Moreover, we don't know whether your father will be there or not." Ron showed a point in the forest with his index finger. "This man is a liar… how can you even consider trusting him! He is the murderer of your family!"

Carmen darted forward.

"He's also the murderer of your family! Aren't you the one who wants to face him and get revenge?"

Ron stopped. Carmen was right. He hated that man who murdered his family in front of his eyes. Yes, there was a fire for revenge burning inside him. Even still, he couldn't let this change his decision. Ron took a deep breath.

"I won't do anything that would put you in danger." He approached Carmen, getting closer until there was a tiny space between them. Then, he grabbed her arms. "My only duty is to protect you. You're the most important being on this planet and none of my desires can outweigh you. And that goes for killing the Soul Hunter as well." He left Carmen and took a few steps back. "We will continue seeking rebel camps. If we can manage to find one, the rest will follow. I don't care how much you hate me, we're not going there, period."

Ron turned and sat down. Carmen didn't have the energy to object. Ron was a good speaker, and it was hard to debate him. Carmen also sat down. In her heart, she knew he was right. It was a mad thought to even consider going there. But she was intrigued. She wanted to see if her father was alive or not.

Ron said the conversation was over, but for Carmen, it still wasn't. Carmen folded up the paper and put it in her pocket.

ANKA'S CASTLE

Edmund and Derick were walking in the castle garden. A few servants and guards passing by bowed and greeted them upon seeing them.

"I hope your plan will work, Edmund."

Edmund had a slight grin on his face.

"That stupid girl is just like her mother. She cares too much for her family." His grin grew. "They'll eventually both meet the same fate. I'm going to kill her just like I killed her mother."

Derick interrupted, "And you'll eat her soul too."

Edmund smirked. "Exactly, brother."

They continued to walk together as Derick spoke after a brief pause.

"Do you really think Anka is foolish enough to fall into this trap?"

Edmund answered, "The girl is only sixteen years old and naive. It's been just a few months since she arrived on Crictus. I don't think she's experienced such traps where she came from. So yes, she's naive enough to fall into our trap."

"What about the water emerald? Judging by his fighting ability, he's not new to these things."

Edmund passed in front of his brother and stopped him.

"Still, he's also very young and not experienced like me or you. Of course, he'll have his doubts. I'm sure Anka will be suspicious too. But I know she's ready to do anything for her father." Edmund's smile grew. "Anka will come to our feet quite willingly all right, and I'll kill her without batting an eye…"

Dean overheard this conversation while the king and the prince walked pass him. He waited until they walked away. Then he swiftly moved and went straight to guards' hall. There he found Geir, another guard he had known for the last five years. He knew he could trust him. Dean sat next to Geir.

"We need to talk. About Anka." This drew Geir's attention.

"She might need our help soon, if she survives what is coming for her. We should be prepared." Dean whispered. Geir nodded, and they dived into a deep discussion.

THE FOREST

The tension between Carmen and Ron did not cease and desist, but rather grew even more intense. After Ron dropped the subject, Carmen had never opened it, but something was still bothering Ron. His insides were churning with turmoil. Neither had spoken since the matter was dropped. Ron was preparing the fire while also rummaging through his bag. He apportioned a tin of canned food he removed from the bag on two leaves.

"This is our last remaining food." After rummaging in the bag once more, he took out three coins from the bag. "And this is the last of our coins…" Ron said.

Carmen sighed anxiously, "So, what are we gonna do?"

Ron shrugged. "I'll find a way."

Carmen took the leaf Ron offered and tasted the food on it. It was really atrocious.

"Why am I not upset this is the end of the food."

Ron spoke, ignoring what Carmen said, "I'll go early tomorrow and buy some new food with our last money. Perhaps I can get someone to loan me some money."

Carmen only nodded. She had a lot going through her mind at that moment. For one, she had to find a way to reach her father. Her mother wanted this. Carmen was sure of it.

Carmen managed to keep the paper from Ron, but she had a problem. She couldn't read the script on it. It was written in the strange alphabet of Crictus. Carmen had to learn the place and time first. As she couldn't ask Ron, she tried to drum up another option.

They both went to bed early that evening as they still weren't talking to one another. Carmen had a dreamless night, for a change. With the first light of the morning, she woke up to the sound of Ron rustling through his bag. Carmen straightened up slightly and looked at him.

"Are you going to the city?"

Ron pulled the three coins out of the bag and stuffed them in his pocket.

"Yes, I'll be back in a few hours. You stay put here."

As he said this, Ron removed his cloak from the bag, donned it, and set off on his way shortly afterwards. Carmen stared at him as he left, then as soon as Ron walked away some distance, she jumped up, opened her own bag, and took out her cloak. There was no way she could afford to leave the emerald in the forest. After donning her cloak, she flipped her bag onto her back and headed off in the same direction as Ron. It wasn't long before she caught up with him. She continued following him, keeping a safe distance between them. Ron was leading her straight into the city. Carmen etched marks on trees with stones she found on the ground in order to find her way back as they went. She did not want to experience any trouble getting back. Carmen continued to track Ron. It was the first time she had done such a thing in her life. So, she was excited but also proud of herself. Somehow, she could sense this planet was turning her into a more mature person.

For a moment, Carmen got a little too close for comfort as she followed Ron. She got nervous the instant a branch snapped under her foot and hid immediately behind a tree. Hearing the sound, Ron looked back, but couldn't see anyone. Standing breathlessly behind the trunk, Carmen looked furtively at Ron from where she was hiding. Meanwhile, Ron turned around and kept going. This time, Carmen continued to follow him more cautiously. When they finally reached the city, Carmen put up her hood. Ron was going in a different direction. As she had very little time before he returned to the campsite, she had to act fast. She was looking into the shops, trying to find someone to read the paper she had. But there was another problem. The paper bore a royal seal, which meant no commoners were supposed to see it. So, entering the first shop she encountered, Carmen asked for a piece of paper and a pen. After taking these implements, she tried copying the strange script at the bottom of the paper. Her writing was not perfect, but she did a pretty decent job with the letters. She looked at her work. A moment later, she remembered she had to hurry and get out. All she had to do now was to make someone read the address on the paper.

She entered another shop. This was a fabric shop offering a wide assortment of cloth inside. All of them looked like felt and almost all were gray. The shopkeeper was an old, grey-haired man whose head looked like a pumpkin having a bad hair day. He was a large man whose neck was practically invisible because of his jowl. His eyes looked like they were tinged with mascara. If one saw only his eyes, he could pass for a very young man.

The man raised his head as Carmen entered. Though she lowered her hood, she still had a suspicious aura about her. It was clear she was doing something secret. Though she felt rather nervous about conducting something akin to a covert operation behind his back for the first time, Ron was still the only one on this planet whom she trusted. Of course, this disturbed her, but the crux of the matter was that she wanted to save her father more than anything else.

"How can I help you, little miss?" the man said, knitting his brows.

"I…" She reached inside her bag and took out the piece of paper from it. "I thought you could read this for me." The man leaned over and glanced at the text handed by Carmen.

"Why? Are you illiterate?" The man raised an eyebrow and looked at Carmen.

"I'm most certainly not!" Carmen shouted with sudden excitement.

The man studied Carmen with a curious glance.

"Then, why do you want me to read it?"

Carmen glanced at the paper as if she were giving up. She was nothing but a little ignorant girl on this planet. She didn't even know how to read.

She looked at the man timidly.

"All right, so I don't know how to read. Could you still read this for me, please?"

The man took the paper Carmen was insistently handing to him. After looking a little bit, he turned his gaze back to Carmen.

"I think there's an address and a date written here."

"Yes, I know that. But where and when?" Carmen said impatiently.

The man looked back at the paper.

"Lake Owlana. Eight o'clock in the morning… But I'm not sure of the date. It's badly written."

Carmen looked at the man, pleading. Her time was running out.

"Please I need that information."

The man shook his head. After looking a little longer, he spoke.

"I think it is written the 21st of the month, but I don't think it will be that day."

"Why's that?" Carmen asked curiously.

The man knitted his eyebrows.

"Are you sure you're from here?"

Carmen gave the man a distressed look.

"I'm just a voyager," Carmen said with a nervous grin.

"That day is Anka Day. It's not been celebrated since the Soul Hunter claimed the throne, and nobody goes out except those who work in the fields and similar places. Since it's forbidden to celebrate, nothing entertaining is allowed on that day."

Carmen looked at the old man in surprise.

"Well, that's interesting…"

The man handed the paper back to Carmen.

"I think you'd better ask someone else for the date. If you can find someone who can read that scrawl."

Carmen headed toward the shop door, ignoring what the man had said, "Thank you." She stopped just as she was going out. "One more thing… How can I find Lake Owlana?"

The man smiled in disbelief.

"You really don't know this area, do you? It's the famous lake in the forest at the end of the river flowing next to the castle."

Carmen smiled gently at the man.

"Thank you so much."

After Carmen left the shop, she donned her hood once more. She had to get back immediately. She didn't feel the need to ask anyone else about the date because she was certain the Soul Hunter had picked that day specifically. Besides, her handwriting was very good.

As she struggled with these thoughts, Carmen changed direction. Just as she turned around a corner, she panicked when she spotted Ron coming toward her. She recognized him from his cloak. She immediately turned around and started walking briskly. She turned into the first street she saw and waited there until Ron passed. Immediately after Ron passed, she went into the forest to go back down the path she had come from. Fortunately, she had thought to leave signs on the trees. Otherwise, she could never have found her way back. On her way back, she didn't forget to erase the traces. She hustled back to the campsite, removed her cloak immediately, and shoved it into her bag. As she sat down, she jumped with a sound that came from behind her.

"I'm back."

It was Ron. He was surprised when he saw Carmen's reaction.

"It's only me."

Carmen took her hand to her heart and answered Ron.

"I was caught off guard," Carmen said, smiling.

She had gotten back just in time. Ron put what he had brought on the ground and took off his cloak.

"So, what did you buy?"

"Just some snacks," Ron said.

After sitting down, he showed her what he had brought. Carmen grimaced when she saw Ron had bought canned food again. Fortunately, there were other things.

"Ron, what's the date today?"

"It's the 16th. Why?" Ron asked suspiciously.

Fine, this means five more days, Carmen thought. Then, she shrugged.

"Nothing, I only asked because of my birthday." Though still a bit skeptical, Ron seemed convinced.

"Are the months here the same as on the Earth?"

Ron looked inquisitively at Carmen again.

"Yes."

Carmen spoke in her most adorable way as she realized Ron thought something was up.

"All right, I'll let you know when it is my birthday."

Ron shook his head. He couldn't make any sense of this conversation. Ron spoke as he placed the food he bought in his bag.

"What did you do while I was away?"

Although Carmen didn't relish lying to Ron, she told him she slept since she had no other choice. Ron would easily believe this because he knew how much Carmen enjoyed sleeping.

So, they both sat there until evening. The tension remained palpable, as Carmen was still mad at him. Still, she was determined not to let Ron sense anything out of the ordinary so her plan wouldn't unravel. She had to get there and see her father with her own eyes. And she had only five days to meet her father.

ANKA'S CASTLE

Derick was wiping down his sword in his chamber. Ever since Edmund dismissed him from the task of finding Anka, he had nothing else to do. He started to feel worthless again. It had been like that before he became Inca. He stayed in his room all day long and *did not get in their way*. This was a term Edmund always used for him. *Getting in their way!* It was frustrating for him to be back where he had started, despite having all sorts of powers and possibilities invested upon him now. He deserved more. He... He deserved to be king. He was Inca. The great, invincible, immortal soul of Inca was inside him. Being stuck in his room was an insult to Inca.

Derick got up and headed straight for the throne hall. When he came to the throne hall, one of the guards at the door spoke, "The king is not here right now, Prince Derick."

Derick spoke in his sternest voice, "Open the doors, this is my throne hall too."

The guards hesitated for a moment, but this did not prevent them from opening the doors. Derick entered the hall, and the doors closed behind him.

The hall was silent. There was not a sound to be heard. A magnificent throne was standing in front of Derick. That splendid throne with meticulously gold inlays engraved on its legs... His dream was planted squarely in front of him. He began to walk slowly over to the throne. His footsteps echoed in the room. He touched the throne gingerly. It belonged to him. Derick glanced around lightly. Taking a deep breath, he sat on the throne, and moved his hands over its arms. He closed his eyes and started to imagine a place without Anka, the emerald or Edmund. It was like a wonderful dream. The nice part of this was that he could actually pull it off. All he needed was a wise plan. Unfortunately, he knew that he wasn't very successful at planning. At any rate, this wouldn't prevent him from asking for the throne. Treacherous plans had already started to invade his mind.

Just then, he heard footsteps approaching behind the door. Derick opened his eyes with the sound. He stood up in a hurry. The door guards told Edmund his brother was inside.

As he felt the power of Inca while he approached the room, Edmund was not overly surprised. He gestured to them with his hand to open the door. Derick was standing next to the throne when the doors opened wide and he entered the hall, spreading his hands.

"My dear brother, pray tell, what are you doing here?"

Derick tried to answer nonchalantly, "I was taking a stroll through the castle as I was bored in my room. This hall was my last stop."

Edmund passed by his brother and sat on his throne. Derick could have killed him right then and there. *First things first...* he thought.

"Why are you here?"

Edmund had a pleasant expression on his face.

"My plan is working like clockwork. I came here to take a break from the rush."

Derick asked curiously, "How can you be so sure your plan is working?"

The smile on Edmund's face grew.

"Because the Abron flew back without the cloth in its beak. It succeeded in getting our message to Anka. Which also proves, she is not too far."

"Still, we can't be sure of that. What if she doesn't take the bait?" Derick said reticently. Deep down, he was afraid of Edmund.

Edmund straightened up slightly from his throne and put his hand on his brother's shoulder.

"Sometimes you have to take risks, brother. And trust me, she'll come. That girl's a complete idiot." Though he wasn't convinced, Derick smiled anyways. Edmund understood his uneasiness. So, he continued talking, "Free your mind of such thoughts. Trust me."

Edmund could've been right. Derick had never seen Edmund miscue with anything before. He always had solid plans. Derick's smile was real this time.

Edmund stood up.

"You know what? Let's have a celebration. And you should organize the celebration. What do you say?"

Derick would be happy every time Edmund gave him a duty, but this time he wanted him to plan an event. He was making him run an errand. Derick stood upright. He would no longer allow Edmund to push him around. He was chosen to be king.

"Tell you what, why don't you have your servants plan the celebration, Edmund. How about giving me a real task?"

Edmund was surprised at his brother's response.

"But I thought you'd like to plan a celebration."

Derick took a deep breath. It was difficult to challenge his brother without annoying him.

"Like I said, I want a real mission."

Edmund was trying to fathom Derick's mood. He had seen him rebel many times after he had become Inca, but this time there was a difference, one he couldn't comprehend…

"Then, there's a lot of paperwork in my study room waiting for you," Edmund said unperturbed.

Derick suddenly reverted back to his normal self. Edmund knew this facial expression well. Derick was an easy person to control. Give him something which will create the illusion that he is important, and he will serve you, no questions asked. That is why Edmund didn't consider his brother a threat. He didn't have what it took to be a king, and he never would. Edmund had been concocting treacherous plans for a long time. He might be carrying the same blood as his brother, but that didn't mean he had any fondness for him. His brother had always been a parasite for him, a shame he had to carry on his back… Edmund knew he was always superior to his brother. Their parents had also been Soul Hunters, their two other brothers as well… But Derick had no such talent. He never had. When Edmund and his brothers were kids, they used to all poke fun of him, making jokes like their mother had found him in a swamp and brought him home. Now, his awkward brother was the only family member who survived. It wasn't fair.

Suppressing his thoughts, Edmund smiled at his brother.

"All right, I'll go to the study room then," Derick said as he exited the hall.

Edmund leaned on his throne and watched his brother go. He had an arrogant smirk on his face. He loved how everything was going according to plan.

THE FOREST

Only two days remained until the meeting. Carmen was getting more and more hyped up as the days passed. That's because she was going to see her father. She had no intention to reveal herself since that would have been a suicide like Ron described it. Needless to say, she was aware how dangerous this was, but still thought it would be worth it for her father.

When they woke up that morning, Carmen told Ron she wanted to get in some sword practice. Ron wasn't expecting such a request from Carmen, as she usually preferred to sit idly in a corner. Ron accepted Carmen's offer on the spot. It was hard to find her this eager. The only reason Carmen wanted this training was to prepare herself for the Soul Hunter and Inca, *just in case*. Of course, she could not make incredible progress within two days, but she could pick up a couple more moves.

Ron was even more astounded when Carmen wanted to do one-on-one combat after their sword practice was over. He knew that something was up, but he couldn't figure it out.

"Are you sure you're all right today?" Ron asked suspiciously.

"Of course. Why are you asking?" Carmen said quickly, trying to parry him.

Ron shrugged.

"Nothing... I normally have a hard time even getting you to do some sword practice and here you are now, asking for both trainings," Carmen looked at Ron mischievously.

"I'm trying to listen to your words and improve myself, that's all."

Carmen spoke persuasively. Ron nodded, though he wasn't entirely convinced. There was definitely a shift in Carmen. For the first time since they kissed, she was so friendly to Ron. Ron was suspicious because he knew how stubborn Carmen could be. *Anyhow, it'll soon come to light*, Ron thought.

They both got very tired after the one-on-one combat. Carmen threw herself to the ground. She was out of breath. The two successive training sessions had exhausted her. She did not remember exercising this intensely before. Ron sat somewhere opposite Carmen after washing his face with water.

"You fought well today."

Carmen responded breathlessly.

"You're right. I tortured my body well today. Unfortunately, I'm sure it's going to torture me tomorrow in return," Carmen said, grimacing.

Ron laughed at Carmen's joke. Then, he stopped after a while. He looked at Carmen. By kissing her, he had screwed up. Now, for the first time, he felt that he could be with her as before. He loved Carmen very much as a protector, as a best friend, and as more than friends. He was devoted to her from the heart. He wanted to be with her like how they were before more than anything.

Carmen saw that Ron had been staring at her.

"What?"

Ron smiled slightly and shrugged.

"Nothing…"

Carmen also laughed lightly, and they both leaned back and rested for a while. Carmen didn't get up almost until the sun went down. She even dozed off for a while. Only after he prepared the dinner and the fire, Ron could convince her to get up. Muttering to herself, Carmen got up and sat down for dinner with Ron. There was that strange, canned food again for dinner. Carmen made a face. If, one day, she became queen, she had to ban this canned food.

They were both silent during the meal. There was no sound other than the sound of tree leaves rustling in the warm wind. After Carmen finished half her food, she put it down.

"Aren't you going to eat any more?" It was Ron who broke the silence.

Carmen held her stomach.

"If I eat any more, I'm gonna throw up. How can you eat this?"

Ron smiled and took another bite of his food. As Carmen made a retching sound, Ron burst into laughter. Carmen accompanied him, too.

After a while, when both stopped, Ron looked at Carmen as he had in the morning.

"What now?" Carmen asked.

"I missed talking to you," Ron continued to talk as he played with his food. "It's good to see that we can be friends again," he said, as he smiled at Carmen. Carmen bowed her head down shyly. She was still not ready to go back to how it was before, but she was pretending to be close to him so that he wouldn't doubt her. She didn't like lying to him, but there was nothing else she could do. She merely smiled. Ron spoke:

"I should've never..." he stopped to take a breath, "... kissed you. I didn't want to risk our friendship."

Carmen shrugged.

"What's happened has happened."

There was sorrow on Ron's face. He was looking at Carmen with longing.

"It's really good to know that you can forgive me..." Ron got up and approached Carmen. He took Carmen's hands in his palm. Carmen's heart skipped a beat with this little touch. "You aren't just the person I have to protect, but also my best friend and my family. I never wanted to break your heart. You can forgive me, can't you?"

Carmen didn't know what to say. Ron was so sincere... his eyes shining in the light of the fire were showing all his emotions. Carmen could see how much Ron loved her. But only as a friend, as a companion... She felt a twitch in her heart. Carmen shook her head slightly. Ron let go of Carmen's hand and hugged her. He hugged her tightly as if he'd never leave her. Carmen also hugged him tightly. Suddenly, the pain in Carmen's heart invaded her body. Her eyes began to well up. When her eyes began to well up, she let go of Ron a little. Ron did the same and they parted. At that moment, both were struggling with complex emotions. Although Carmen was unaware of Ron's feelings, she knew she could still trust Ron. He would be always there for her. Carmen even thought about telling Ron about her plan. But Ron would never allow such a thing. So, she just kept quiet.

When the morning came, Carmen's whole body writhed in pain because of the extra practice she had put in the day before. She didn't get up until noon, using this as an excuse. When she finally got up, she realized she was starving. She got a bite to eat. Then, she threw herself back onto her blanket on the ground. Tomorrow was the big day and Carmen was very excited even if she didn't show it at all. Her plan was simple. Toward the morning, she would set off after making sure Ron was deep asleep. She knew where to go. She was only going to peek but if she was revealed, she would have to negotiate with the Soul Hunter. Carmen was nervous but the key to her success was keeping it quiet and not being seen by anyone. King's men were searching for them in the forest ever since they left the castle with the fire emerald. Carmen thought going to the meeting point was not that different from hiding in the forest. She had plenty of practice already. Now all she had to do was to get some sleep since she needed to reduce her muscle pain and also because she was going to make a night journey. So, she tried to sleep almost until the evening. She had a hard time sleeping because of her excitement. Ron tried to wake her up several times during the day to no avail. Carmen had no intention of waking up. Carmen was pretending to be asleep just to get Ron mad and she so enjoyed it very much.

After she had ignored Ron's efforts to wake her up all day, she got up toward the evening. She felt really rested. Her pain had almost disappeared, with just a little in her leg muscles. This could cause a bit of a problem while she walked.

Ron had to prepare dinner alone again, but he had no complaints. It was like the price of his sin against Carmen. He was aware that regardless of whatever he did, it wouldn't be enough to make her forget his rejection, but it was still worth a try.

"Hey, how about getting up and eating something now?"

Carmen got up in an instant. She did not neglect to moan a bit in pain when she got up.

"I'm always ready to eat." She was very happy to see there was no canned food today. There was something like bread and salami in the meal. "Please tell me we don't have any more canned food left."

Ron shook his head.

"Nope, we still have a few cans."

"Can't we hunt in the forest? By 'we,' I mean you."

"In this season, we would have to go deep in the forest to hunt, and I know there are search parties and other dangers there."

"There are search parties here too. And what other dangers?"

"You know, predators. There are not searching around the city enough, so for now, we are safer here. But we still must keep moving."

Carmen sighed and took a bite out of her meal as they ate together. Unlike the past few days, they were talking to each other again. Carmen was making jokes though not as much as before. Ron enjoyed seeing her as she once was. He knew she would slowly return to normal.

After it got quite dark, Carmen feinted a yawn. Ron looked at her in surprise.

"Don't tell me you're sleepy again," Carmen shrugged. "You already slept the entire day," Ron continued.

"What can I do? I must've got really tired yesterday."

Carmen was getting ready to go to sleep as Ron spoke.

"Well then, you get your rest. We're leaving here tomorrow."

Carmen lifted her head up.

"Where are we going?"

There was a note of concern in her voice. Ron got up early on the day of departure to tidy up.

"Like I mentioned, we have to keep moving. Let's get a little further from the castle to the West I'm afraid they'll start searching near the city before too long."

Carmen didn't know how to convince him to stay, but they had to stay put there.

"Can't we just stay here one more day?"

"We've stayed here long enough, Carmen."

Carmen straightened up.

"One more day. It won't change anything."

"You increase our risk of getting caught."

Carmen objected.

"You're wrong. It's harder for them to find us if we stay here."

Ron knitted his brows.

"How's that?"

"I heard it when I was still on Earth. If you run under the rain, you'll get wetter." Ron stared at Carmen, not comprehending. Carmen felt the need to explain. "What I mean is, if we don't change places constantly, it'll be better for us. I'm not saying we should always stay in the same place, but at least we can change places once a week."

Ron got confused. She could be right. One more day wouldn't really hurt, would it?

"Well, fine then. Just half a day more…"

Carmen glanced at Ron, surprised that she was able to convince him.

"All right. Great then…"

Carmen smiled at Ron, too. Then, she put her head down.

"Good night, Ron."

"Good night, Carmen."

A little after Carmen fell asleep, Ron put out the fire and went to sleep. Carmen was just resting her eyes as she had slept all day. She had to stay awake, anyway, because if she fell behind her plan, everything would be ruined.

So, hours passed. Carmen decided that it was time to leave, as the sky turned from dark blue to light blue. She got up and tiptoed over toward Ron. The emerald was in his bag. When Edmund's note came, Ron had asked Carmen to keep the emerald himself. Carmen had agreed so as not to have Ron suspect anything. She opened Ron's bag very slowly and picked out the blood-red emerald. Just as she was closing the bag, Ron turned toward her. Carmen froze where she was. Ron had turned in his sleep, but that was enough for Carmen to have a heart attack. Carmen stood up carefully after taking a deep breath. After removing other items from her bag, she placed the emerald inside. She took her cloak with her. She might need it to disguise herself. She then took all the items she removed from her bag and stashed them under her blanket. Finally, she took her sword and tied it to her waist with a fabric. Just in case.

She looked at Ron one last time.

"I'll be right back, Ron," she said by herself and headed out into the forest.

OWLANA RIVER

Carmen had been walking for about half an hour. She was keeping her tempo slow as her legs were still aching from the training two days ago. Moreover, she had still time. She did not know the exact time. If she were on Earth, she'd just look on her cellphone. She missed technology a lot… Now she had to predict the time according to the rise of the sun. It was probably something like seven thirty a.m. As long as she continued to walk like this, she'd be there at exactly eight, as written in the letter. She got excited when she thought she'd be seeing her father half an hour later. Carmen kept walking.

Meanwhile, Ron had opened his eyes as he usually woke up early in the morning. He straightened up and yawned. After a while, he got up to wash his face in the stream and glanced at Carmen's blanket. He stopped just as he was going to the stream. He looked back at where she was lying, thinking he couldn't see Carmen in her bed. Carmen wasn't really there. He gazed around in surprise. He could not see Carmen around. *Maybe she went to gather some wood?* he thought and splashed cold water on his face. Then, he came back and started taking out the food for breakfast from his bag. While doing this, he gazed upon the lump that was apparent under Carmen's blanket. Curiously, he lifted the blanket. Under the blanket were things that Carmen usually kept in her bag. He knitted his eyebrows. He suspiciously looked around. Carmen's bag was not there. Suddenly, his whole body quivered with panic. He quickly got up and grabbed his own bag. He dug into his bag with panic and fear. Finally, he dumped everything onto the blanket, rummaging through its contents. The emerald was gone! Ron's eyes got bigger. This could not be happening! She could not have gone to the meeting! He jumped up. He tried to remember the date and time on the paper. But he hadn't told her, had he? How could Carmen have learned it? He had thousands of questions in his mind. Perhaps she just went for a walk. But why did she just take her cloak and the emerald with her? He had to check the meeting place. He tried to recall what was written on the paper. He remembered the site, Owlana River... It was the place where Carmen's mother, the previous Anka, Juliet was killed. His hair stood on end. So, when was this meeting? What if Carmen had already met them... The reflection he saw on the water came to his mind. He was completely stunned. He had to get there immediately. He would have to go there at all costs. So, he started to run as fast as he could, hurriedly and frantically.

The sun was now slightly above eye level. Carmen knew that it was getting close to eight. Now she had to pick up the pace a bit. She approached the castle but did not know how to find the river. She stopped for a moment and listened around. She heard the sound of water in the distance. She decided to head in that direction. After walking for a while, she realized she was on the right track. There was a river in the distance. She then slowed her pace. Hiding behind the trees, she started to walk toward the river. Meanwhile, she was looking up into the trees in case there were hidden archers in them just as Ron had previously taught her. As she got closer, she started to see a number of people. She immediately recognized two of them, the Soul Hunter and Inca… There were four guards beside them. When she pulled her head a little further from behind the tree, she saw a man tied to the tree. His mouth was gagged shut and there was a hopeless expression on his face. Carmen gasped for air when she saw the man. She was looking at the man in shock. She had seen him before. He was the man she saw in her dreams! Now the man's eyes made more sense. How similar his eyes were to hers. The man she had seen in prison in her dreams was her birthfather! A moment later, she remembered what Ron's grandfather had said. "*Anka can see events that happened in her dreams,*" he had said. Now everything fell into place. In her dreams she had been seeing her father and her mother's soul wanted her to save her father. She was absolutely sure of that now. She put aside her surprise and took a deep breath. She saw what she needed to see, and now it was time for a journey back to Ron. Being this close to them was too dangerous for her soul. She glanced at the man again, at her father… Her heart ached to leave him there. For a split second she considered confronting them. She put her hand inside the bag and held the emerald. Was it worth it? After having survived all the dangers for the emerald was it worth risking her life, or more precisely to risk Anka's soul inside her, against a monster like the Soul Hunter? Carmen knew the answer as she looked at her father. She took her hand out of the bag. She had to do the right thing. She could only help her father by staying alive and dethroning the Soul Hunter once and for all. At least now she knew he was alive and that needed to be enough for now.

She sighed and turned around but she paused abruptly. She didn't expect to meet cold black eyes behind her. Two large, masked guards were standing just behind her, looking at her a few steps away. Carmen glimpsed at them, trying not to show her fear. One of them pointed forward with the sword in his hand.

"Come ahead, Anka." She was caught. Carmen knew she had no other choice. She was trapped and would have to face her enemies. *Don't show your weaknesses to your enemy…* So, she turned toward the Soul Hunter and Inca with slow steps and walked confidently to confront her enemies. While she walked, all she could think of was the reflection Ron saw on the water.

13

Edmund, who saw Anka walking slowly toward them, raised his head. She came without her guardian emerald. This pleased him. He turned slightly to his brother as if to say *I told you*. Derick watched Anka as she approached with confidence. Carmen was staring directly into their eyes. In reality, her heart was beating madly, but there was only one way to win this war, being a real Anka and standing your ground! She walked until she reached a distance she found suitable. Then, she stopped. Her hand was on her sword, as if she could fight back as soon as she saw a threat. Carmen had been practicing sword combat all this time, but she had never thought of harming someone. Still, there was nothing wrong with showing some teeth.

Meanwhile, when Richard saw a girl fearlessly coming through the trees, the despair in his eyes was replaced with love. This girl looked so much like Juliet. He didn't remember what he himself looked like, as he hadn't looked in a mirror for many years. So, he couldn't see any similarities between himself and the girl, but Juliet… It was as if Juliet was walking before him. Those eyebrows, those eyes, those lips… They were all quite familiar. His heart ached. He was seeing his daughter for the first time in sixteen years. His daughter who he could not hold in his arms once, could not smell even once… How much she had grown up and he had missed everything. Her first words, her first step, the first time she said, "Father" … What was her name? He felt a glow of longing. He felt his eyes filling with tears. But besides longing, his fear also grew. She should not be here. This was a trap. She should never have come here. He wished he could do something, but his hands and feet were tied. He just looked at her, with longing and fear. When he made eye contact with his daughter a moment later, his heart began to beat faster than before.

When he saw the brief eye contact between Carmen and her father, the Soul Hunter grinned. Then, he spoke, "I'm so pleased you decided to come, Anka."

When the Soul Hunter spoke, Carmen turned her attention to her enemy. There was a determined expression on her face, but this could not prevent her whole body from shaking. They weren't supposed to see her hand trembling. So, she reached for her bag and then spoke.

"I'm here to make a trade." Even her voice almost trembled. *"Pull yourself together!"* she commanded herself. Now was not the time for weakness.

While waiting for the Soul Hunter's response, she took a furtive glance at her father again. The Soul Hunter also caught this eye contact.

"You recognized him, didn't you?" Carmen glared at the Soul Hunter. "I know you visit him in your dreams. I felt you once." Soul Hunter said.

Carmen remembered the last dream when she saw her dad. How scared she was when the Soul Hunter looked directly at her. Carmen gulped faintly. The Soul Hunter was able to feel the power of Anka's soul even during astral projection.

The Soul Hunter continued to speak.

"I would also like to congratulate you for your time at the castle." He took a step forward and continued, "You were brave and daring enough to enter my chamber." He continued, pointing at the bag with his head, "And, of course, brave enough to steal the emerald from me…"

Carmen's fear was growing. She had encountered the Soul Hunter on her way out of his room at the castle, and now he recognized her. This was getting scarier by the minute. At that moment, she wanted to turn away and escape, but she couldn't. It was too late to go back. On some level, she always knew she shouldn't have come here. But just like that, she had and now she was deeply regretting it. Still, her father was here, and she was sure he was her father.

As the Soul Hunter stepped toward her, all the muscles in her body were ready to turn and run away. Carmen knew that she had to stand still as she fought the instinct to escape. She barely suppressed her instinct to step back and looked straight into the eyes of the Soul Hunter.

"I only took what belongs to me."

Though the Soul Hunter was surprised Carmen didn't step back, he didn't reveal it. It was obvious the girl was demonstrating great effort. Even though she was trying to hide it, there was nothing but a frightened little sixteen-year-old girl in front of him. She couldn't be a threat to him. He was an experienced, wise man. No matter how strong her soul was, she was only a weak girl. He could defeat her.

Carmen continued to speak.

"Let's get on with the trade already," she said.

It wasn't just that she was afraid and wanted to get away from there immediately, but she also wanted to reunite with her father as soon as possible. The Soul Hunter nodded. He made a sign to one of his men to untie Richard. Meanwhile, Carmen took a deep breath and took the blood-red emerald out of her bag. One of the Soul Hunter's men brought Richard to the center. Carmen didn't know what to do. She could only get the hint from what she had seen in the movies, but nothing came to her mind. Finally, she spoke, "Send him first."

Inca had taken a step forward and clenched his fists as the Soul Hunter's grin grew. It was as if he could attack Carmen at any time. Carmen didn't miss this move. Her heart was beating madly.

"As you wish," the Soul Hunter said pleasantly.

It was very annoying that this man looked so pleased in such a situation. Carmen felt more stressed.

The Soul Hunter's man pushed Richard forward. Richard staggered and almost fell to the ground. Carmen leapt forward to catch her father before he fell. Richard looked at his daughter and shook his head. When Carmen removed the binding from her father's mouth, her father spoke quietly, *"Run..."*

It took a while for Carmen to understand what her father had said. She was standing next to her father when all of a sudden they were surrounded by countless men that appeared out of nowhere in the forest. Taking advantage of her momentary distraction, a group of men hiding behind suddenly stood right by Anka, their swords pulled out. Carmen was petrified when she saw the swords pointed at her and her father. She knew the soul hunter wouldn't do a trade and knew this was a trap but still she couldn't hide her panic. What was she going to do? She looked at the Soul Hunter in fear. There was no point in hiding her fear anymore. She was trapped like a fool. Sixteen-year-old, immature fool! She knew this was going to happen! She should have listened to Ron. It was too late now, and she had to get a grip immediately. Carmen stood up slowly. She guessed the men around her would not kill her. Otherwise, The Soul Hunter wanted her soul.

"Look at you, just like your mother, you came to me voluntarily. Now you will share the same fate as your mother. You will die right where she did."

Carmen's eyes got bigger. Was her mother killed here? Carmen gulped. She wasn't supposed to die. At least not today. She could almost feel the uneasy, powerful soul inside her. She spoke, paying attention to the swords around her.

"My mother came here for me…"

Inca interrupted her.

"Indeed, and you came for your father. The same stupid courage."

Carmen glanced at Inca. She was paying attention to him for the first time. How passively he was standing next to the Soul Hunter. *Maybe,* she thought. *Maybe she had to use this.* Carmen remembered how calm she could be in most situations. This was no different. It was true that one of the swords around her could kill her in seconds, but if she was the old Carmen, she could still find a way to make fun of the situation. She was smart enough to turn the situation around. She turned to Inca.

"And who are you? His clown or his puppet?"

There was a reckless expression on her face. She crossed her hands on her chest, hiding her fear. The Soul Hunter knitted his brows. Inca angrily stepped forward.

"How dare you talk to me this way! I am Inca."

Carmen shrugged and continued to speak, "Yeah right.

Sorry, didn't see you there for a second. You were the incompetent guy who couldn't even kill me on Earth, right? Or was that someone else? You have such a common face."

Inca clenched his fists even more. Carmen released her hands. She had to trigger him more. She was scared to death, but she had no other choice.

"I think you're the pathetic one, am I wrong? The pathetic, cowardly brother. Nothing but a puppet…" Carmen released a short laughter. "To be honest, I didn't even realize you were here until you opened your mouth." Inca gritted his teeth.

"Shut your mouth, girl!"

"Derick!" Edmund nervously warned his brother. Carmen continued.

"Tell me, does that ever work for you? Next to your brother, I assume no one would ever listen to what you say. My emerald told me before Inca chose you, you were a nobody. The cowardly brother with no soul-hunting powers. I wonder why an immortal soul like Inca has chosen such an unworthy body."

"He chose me because I AM WOTHY, you little brat!"

"Derick, restrain yourself!" Derick ignored Edmund's words and took a step forward.

"I am the mighty soul Inca! And I—"

Carmen laughed, cutting his little speech and then she pinned her gaze upon Derick and smirked. "All right, *mighty spirit*. Why don't you finish what you started? I am standing right here, aren't I? Oh, do you need permission from your brother? Or, are you *scared*?"

Edmund saw his brother's look right then. He was going to ruin everything. He shouted in fear. He should've had Anka caught before his brother attacked Anka, otherwise everything would be messed up.

"Guards. Catch her!" No sooner did the Soul Hunter say this than Inca sent his energy. Before the guards understood the command, Inca had already aimed his energy at Carmen. Carmen was just about to raise her hands to stop the incoming energy when a wall of water appeared in front of her, and her hands remained motionless in the air. Everybody stared in surprise. It was Ron. He managed to hinder the energy coming at Carmen. He was a sweaty mess. He had come all the way, running at top speed to arrive just in time. Everyone came to their senses as the wall of water came crashing down. Ron shouted at Carmen.

"Anka, run!"

When Carmen heard the order, she shoved the emerald back in her bag and moved.

"Catch them!" the Soul Hunter said to his men.

As his men followed Carmen, a sword hit Carmen's leg. Carmen shouted in pain. With a moment of pause, another guard came in front of her. Carmen escaped his sword blow at the last moment with a swift counter move, but the sword cut her arm. Carmen shouted again, holding her arm. Meanwhile, Inca headed toward Carmen but Ron intercepted him.

"You and I have some unfinished business," Ron said.

Inca aimed a beam of energy at him with all his fury.

Richard got up from the ground with all his strength during this chaos. Her daughter needed him. Though his hands were tied, he still managed to leap on the men attacking Carmen with the bulk of his large body, taking out three of them in the process. Meanwhile, Carmen grabbed one of the swords that fell to the ground and charged the other man. It was very difficult for her.

"Run, now!"

She looked at where the warning came from. It was her father. He had freed himself from the rope tied around his hands and he was punching a guard. She looked around. The Soul Hunter was coming for her. She had to make tracks fast.

"Run!"

It was Ron. He was barely able to stop Inca. Carmen started running as fast as she could into the forest without a second thought with the Soul Hunter and countless guards on her tail. She ran and ran. She didn't know how long she had been running, but she did so without stopping or looking back. She was under the impression there weren't as many guards behind her now. She kept hiding as she fled so they would lose sight of her. After running for a long time, she paused for a moment to look behind her. She did not see the root on the ground, tripped over it and fell to the ground. At that moment she felt a terrible pain in her foot. Her ankle was sprained. But she couldn't stop. She had to keep moving forward. She clumsily picked up the emerald that had tumbled out of her bag when she fell and stood up with difficulty. She tried to run but she couldn't. Her ankle hurt too much. She tried to move forward by limping and grabbing on to the trees in her path. She was about to cry out from the pain. In a rage, she pushed back the hair sticking to her sweaty forehead. She tried to force herself to go a little further, but she couldn't. She leaned against a tree, gasping for air. She looked from behind the tree to see whether anyone was coming. She saw the Soul Hunter a little behind. She didn't dodge him yet! Out of breath, she hid behind the tree again. Her heart throbbed as if it was about to pop out of her chest, as she tried to catch her breath without being heard. Just then, the Soul Hunter stopped. He was feeling her soul's presence. She was so close. Old and aching all over, he was exhausted from running. But he was not going to give up while Anka was so close.

"I know you're here somewhere! You can't hide from me! I can feel you!" he shouted.

Carmen looked around with fear. She had to get out of there. Right at that moment, she was able to avoid a sword blow aimed at her face by leaning forward at the last instant. The sword stuck into the tree for a short time, but the Soul Hunter was too strong, and he yanked it out without any difficulty. While trying to overcome the shock of the near miss of the sword, Carmen took her weapon in her hand and started to counter the Soul Hunter's blows as she backpaddled, but it was difficult to fend him off as he was striking her with all his might. A moment later, Carmen felt a different kind of pain than the one in her ankle. This pain was so different from any other pain she had experienced before. She was… Fading… The Soul Hunter was trying to suck out her soul! She shouted in agony. She couldn't allow this. At the last moment she aimed her energy with her hand at him. The pain in Carmen's body disappeared as the Soul Hunter staggered backwards. She had to run! She forgot the pain in her ankle and started running. Though the pain was agonizing, she had no other choice but to run with her last remaining strength. She saw a road ahead. A cart pulled by some type of beast of burden was trudging along the road. There was hay in the cart. This was her ticket to freedom. She kept running without looking back. The Soul Hunter was older than her and she had to take advantage of this. This time she couldn't look behind her. She ran with her last vestiges of strength! She reached the road and launched herself into the hay with all her might. She was able to catch the cart at the last second. The pain in her ankle spread throughout her whole body. She blacked out as soon as she threw herself onto the hay and the last things she saw were leafy tree branches on both sides of the narrow road, swaying in the sky.

OWLANA RIVER

Seeing that Anka was running toward the forest, Inca made a move to follow her, but encountered Ron's attack instead. Ron could barely ward off Inca's fierce counterattack. He looked at the direction Carmen went and noticed most of the guards and the Soul Hunter were chasing her! He had to avert them somehow but was expending all his effort in fiercely repelling Inca's energy. Knowing Ron would go after Anka, Inca kept his energy beam focused on Ron. By now, Ron was beginning to wilt in the face of this beam and could only hide behind his water shield. He had to employ another tactic, as he couldn't withstand it much longer in the defensive position. He looked behind him and saw the river. Then he looked at his other side and noticed Richard had gotten busy pummeling the guards. After all these years, he was still impressively strong.

Ron looked back at the river behind him once more. After repelling Inca's move, he directed all his power to the river. The river water suddenly swelled up to transform into a tsunami wave. As Ron moved his hand slightly toward Inca, the water towered over Inca, whose eyes opened wide with fear, as hadn't the time to run out of its path. The tremendous water formation came crashing down on Inca, knocking him unconscious. Richard's yell was heard as Ron was reconverting the water. He swung his sword as hard as he could, plunging it in the heart of the guard fighting with Richard. The guard screeched as he fell to the ground. Ron took the sword from the slain guard's hand and attacked one of the few remaining guards. The guard was an agile swordsman, but Ron took him to task. In blocking the guard's blow, Ron riposted toward the guard. The guard retreated at the last minute but couldn't prevent his uniform from being torn. The angry guard attacked Ron with rage. Ron saw the imbalance in the guard's move and pounced on him. Upon stumbling in the exact way Ron had wished, he then took this opportunity to plunge his sword into the man's heart. The guard fell to the ground. Meanwhile, Richard had taken out the other guards. There were so many of them that it was not possible to fight them all. Ron focused on drawing water from the river. The river's water erupted into the sky and swallowed all the guards. While they were not all dead, it would take them some time to get up. They had to leave But Richard had something else in his mind. He glared at Inca who was sprawled out. He wasn't dead, but he was unconscious. He clenched his sword tightly in his hand and began to saunter toward him. When Ron realized what Richard wanted to do, he jumped in front of him.

"What are you doing?"

Richard pointed at Inca lying on the ground with the tip of his sword drenched in blood.

"I have to make this bastard pay for what he did." The anger in his voice was incredible.

"Kill him, and the spirit of Inca enters another body. Perhaps a stronger host." Ron turned around and looked at Inca lying on the ground. "It's better for us if Inca stays in his body."

Richard lowered his sword slightly. The water emerald could be right. He remembered how quickly his daughter had gotten under Inca's skin. Inca was an easy mark.

"It's better for Inca to remain with the Soul Hunter. It's best to let the Soul Hunter take his soul whenever he wants."

Richard approved of what Ron said. He gazed around and saw the guards were getting up.

Then he glanced at Ron in haste.

"My daughter! The Soul Hunter went after her."

"Carmen," said Ron. Richard nodded and taken it in. *Carmen*... that was her name.

Ron had no intention of waiting. They started to run to the forest without further talk. Ron was running at top speed. He had to find her at any cost. Just then he heard a scream, and his heart seemed to skip a beat. He was petrified. Gasping for breath, his whole body wracked with fear. The sound stopped after a bit. He glanced at Richard. He had also had desperation and fear on his face. What if it was Carmen who was screaming?

Ron walked hesitantly in the direction of the voice. He glimpsed at where the voice was heard from behind a tree. A guard was pleading with the Soul Hunter on the ground. Another one was lying lifeless on the ground. Ron sighed a deep breath of relief. He was glad to see it wasn't Carmen. But where was she?

He started listening to the Soul Hunter intently.

The guard was begging. "I beg you, my lord, forgive me! Spare my life. I'll never make such a mistake again."

"You're right, because, guess what, there's not going to be any next time!" the Soul Hunter said.

He was breathing angrily. A tear dropped from the guard's eye. As the Soul Hunter raised his hand, the guard began screaming. Suddenly, images of Ron's grandfather and brother appeared in front of his eyes. How the Soul Hunter had killed them... Merciless... Without even batting an eye... In a rage, he turned his head away as he couldn't lose control now. After taking a deep breath, he motioned to Richard with a nod of his head. Together they walked quietly away. Rather than fighting the Soul Hunter and his men or killing Inca now, Ron's priority was to find Carmen. But he had no idea where she had gone. At least he now knew Carmen had somehow escaped the Soul Hunter. But where was she? Where had she escaped? Where could she have gone alone on a planet she didn't know? Besides, she didn't even know how to read or write. He sighed. He had to find her at all cost. Carmen had attempted to do such a thing because of him. He was cursing at himself. He was unable to protect her and now he had no idea where she might be on this vast planet.

ANKA'S CASTLE

The shouts heard within the castle walls terrified everyone. The Soul Hunter was terrorizing the castle. He was so angry to have missed Anka that he took the soul of whomever dared to come within visual range. The castle servants were now scurrying about for places to hide whenever they encountered him. The Soul Hunter's rage did not abate in the slightest. It was all because of his brother, Derick… He hated his guts. His brother was making his life miserable. He was constantly thwarting him as if he were a burden he always bore on his back. As he paced back and forth in the throne hall, he was trying to rid himself of this anger. Even the soul of the guard lying on the floor, whose soul he had just sucked out, could not put him in a better mood. He nervously kicked the corpse. The only thing he had on his mind was that he had lost Anka because of his brother. He could really kill him. He could have his soul forever and become more powerful. "No, not yet," he stopped himself. Inca was his bait. He was like a mighty slave who was unaware of his strength, and he could use him for everything. He had to use his brother wisely. Still, he wanted to kill him and have his soul, the great Inca… He wanted to make his brother pay for all he had to live through because of him.

He stopped his pacing with a knock on the door and sat nervously on the throne, straightening his back for posture's sake.

"Come in," he commanded.

The double doors opened wide. Derick came in timidly. Even seeing his brother was enough to fuel his anger.

"Did you find anything?"

Derick swallowed and looked at the corpse on the ground. His brother had really lost control these past few days. He was becoming more and more cruel every day. He looked in Edmund's eyes.

"No, we're still searching the forest."

Edmund got up nervously and went to his brother in a few steps. Derick stood tensely.

Edmund spoke, "Anka was injured and was limping while she fled. She couldn't have gone far. I'm sure she's hiding out there. And you're standing in front of me, still talking incompetently!" Edmund's furious voice echoed.

"You bloody amateur!" Edmund shouted as if he was cursing. Derick didn't know what to do about Edmund's rage. It was clear the only thing protecting him at that moment was Inca's soul. Otherwise, Edmund would've already killed him.

Derick gulped and averted his eyes from Edmund.

"I'm trying to do my…"

"Are you telling me this is the *best* you can do?" Edmund interrupted Derick. Then, he continued, "You know what the best thing you can do is, Derick! Just stay out of my way! You can't do any of the tasks I give you properly! You've always been a disgrace," Edmund continued glowering at Derick. "I can see that even having a mighty soul like Inca couldn't change that."

Derick glared at Edmund. He had always been subjected to the same insults throughout his life, but nobody could say anything to the soul inside him. He was filled with rage. He poked Edmund's chest with his index finger.

"Now you listen to me, you Soul Hunter rubbish. I put up with you and our brothers long enough. You always treated me like I was nobody, but I've had enough! Contrary to what you believe, I'm not nobody, I'm everything! You've got no right to talk to me like that! I am the absolute power! Let me tell you something else, you know that throne you sit on? It's my right, not yours!" He pointed at the throne. He took a step back and continued. "So, it's me who should be barking the orders around here, not you! But I still put up with you! Now apologize to me right this instant!"

Derick's voice reverberated off the walls. Edmund was looking at his brother in shock. His brother was yelling at him for the first time. It was the first time that he had dared to do such a thing. He knew he had an eye on the throne, but saying this out loud…

Edmund suppressed his anger a little. He had to pivot to calm his brother. Edmund still needed his help to defeat Anka once and for all. Even though he didn't like to admit it, they were stronger together against Anka.

He took a deep breath and began to speak.

"You fool. This throne…" He turned and showed the throne, "belongs to both of us, to our family. This castle and all of Crictus belong to our family that you hate so much. I earned this throne when I defeated the strongest spirit on Crictus! I granted this life to our family long before Inca has chosen you!"

"I am sick of being ordering me around."

Edmund responded quickly, "I don't order you around. I always give you the highest duties. I gave you the task to find Anka. Find her and bring her to me so that I can take her soul forever. So that our family can rule all of Crictus together."

Edmund's words calmed Derick a little. Edmund continued, "I do everything in the name of both of us and our family. The only thing that can prevent us from ruling Crictus is Anka. We couldn't capture her. If you had controlled your anger at that particular moment, we would've been sitting comfortably on the throne right now," Edmund continued to speak by touching his brother's shoulder. "Now I'm giving you the opportunity to compensate for your mistake." He whispered into his brother's ear, "Go and bring her to me…"

What Edmund said made sense to Derick. He didn't know if Edmund really thought that way, but he was right about one thing. Anka was the only obstacle before him. As soon as Edmund destroyed Anka, he would kill Edmund and be the sole owner of the throne.

He nodded in affirmation to Edmund and left the throne hall. When he went to his chamber, he summoned Chief Guard Waldorf. Waldorf entered Derick's chamber a few minutes later.

"You summoned me, my lord."

Derick spoke with determination, "Expedite the searches in the region where Anka disappeared. I also want all the villages in that area searched. All houses will be raided one by one. Find Anka wherever she is and bring her to me. If necessary, the whole army will be tasked for this mission. Is that clear?" Waldorf spoke, bowing to Derick respectfully, "As you command, my prince."

Derick stopped Waldorf before he left.

"And from now on, everyone will address me as the king!"

Waldorf looked at Derick in surprise, but he managed to hide his surprise.

"As you wish my king…" he said and left the room.

A smile spread across Derick's face. Now he was feeling closer to the throne. The throne would be his very soon!

SOMEWHERE IN CRICTUS

Carmen opened her eyes in great pain. She had a throbbing headache and moaned as she touched her head. She was badly battered. She remembered for a moment what had transpired. The guards and the Soul Hunter who were chasing after her... She had jumped behind a cart and then... What happened next? She suddenly lifted her head and scanned about her. Where was she? She was in a room she had never seen before. The bed she was lying in was resting against the right wall of the room. She saw the door a little further away. There was a large cabinet right across from the bed. Next to the bed was a coffee table, and next to that was a chair. The carpet on the floor made the room cozy, but right now Carmen was not able to warm to it at all. Whose room was this? Could she have been caught? *No, it can't be...* she thought. If she had been caught, they would've already killed her. Or were they waiting for the Soul Hunter to arrive? Suddenly she remembered Ron and her father... She had left them behind. Were they alive? Her heart began to beat uncontrollably. She had risked their lives. What if something had happened to them? What if they couldn't fight off Inca and the guards? Carmen felt some tightness in her chest. She couldn't lose them. She had to find them immediately. So, come what may, she had to get out of here as soon as possible.

She saw the bandage on her left arm as she straightened up a bit on the bed. Someone must have dressed it. Then she lifted the blanket that was on top of her. There was a similar bandage wrapped around her right ankle. She remembered she had sprained her ankle. But no force could keep her here. She had to find Ron as soon as possible. She had to get out of here.

She touched her feet to the floor. Just as she was getting up, she sat back with great pain. Her ankle ached much more than she thought. She took a deep breath and tried again. This time, she tried to head toward the door by balancing on her left foot, but the pain on her left arm threw her balance off. As she couldn't find a place to hold on to, she collapsed back onto the bed in incredible pain. She heard voices coming from outside the door. She hurriedly tried to regain her former position in the bed. Covering herself, she turned her face to the wall. Her pulse rate shot up when she heard the door opening. Her eyes were open. All she wanted was for the people behind the door to think that she was still asleep. She began listening intently to them. Two people entered the room.

"She's still sleeping."

It was a male voice. From his tone, she assumed he was young. An old woman's voice was heard behind him.

"We have to wake her up now. It's been days since she last ate something."

The young one spoke, "She's sick. Let her sleep. And so, what if she hasn't eaten? It's none of our business. She's not our responsibility."

"You brought her here, Maha, so do what I say and make her eat this."

The young boy scoffed.

"I didn't bring her. She jumped into my cart."

The sound of the door closing was heard. Carmen perked her ears up. There wasn't a sound in the room. She wished she hadn't turned her back to the door. From the conversation she understood she wasn't in any danger, but she couldn't take anything for granted.

She listened behind her back in discomfort. Was the boy gone? Or was he standing extraordinarily quiet in the room? Both options were unsettling. Carmen tried to regulate her breath. She closed her eyes. She had to find out what was behind her. Unfortunately, she didn't account for her arm as she rolled over to the other side. She involuntarily grimaced as her left arm was pressed under her body. If there was someone inside, that person knew now Carmen was awake. She opened one eye first and saw a young boy with a know-it-all, bored attitude sitting on a chair across from her with his hands clasped. Then, she opened her other eye.

"Good morning stranger," the boy said.

Carmen straightened up with trepidation. She was still grimacing as her arm ached as she sat up. She studied the boy for a while. He had sandy hair, hazel eyes, high cheekbones and a wide forehead. With the stubble on his face, he seemed as if he was trying to prove he wasn't very young, but he looked not much older than Carmen. When he realized Carmen was scrutinizing him, the boy grinned.

"I think you've swallowed your tongue."

Carmen raised her hand just as the boy was propping himself up in his chair. The boy stayed where he was.

"Who are you and where am I?"

This time, the boy gave her a bitter smile.

"First of all, who are you, and what were you doing in my cart?"

Carmen persisted with her smart disregardful attitude.

"I asked first."

Uneasy because she felt unarmed and defenseless, Carmen couldn't show her feelings without knowing who that boy is. So, she preferred to act clever. The boy smirked in anger.

"Well, I don't want you to be here either, but Mother believes you are a special guest. Sent by the mighty Phoenix." He especially emphasized "a special guest." He paused and showed her the food. "And she doesn't want me to leave the room before you finish this meal. So…" he said, and Carmen recoiled as he reached for the meal. The boy didn't finish what he was saying.

"Is this how you treat someone who is trying to help you?"

"How do I know you're helping me?"

The boy was even more infuriated.

"Are you blind? Can't you see the bandages?" The boy knitted his eyebrows. "Well, how did you get hurt anyway?"

Carmen bowed her head down.

"I was practicing sword fighting with a friend."

"It's obvious you can't tell a lie."

Carmen glared at the boy again. He was truly annoying.

"All right, fine, I wasn't sword training with my friend. I was running away from somebody."

The boy straightened up.

"I see." He crossed his arms. "So, you're a thief, are you?" Carmen responded quickly.

"I'm not a thief," she said chagrined.

"So, what were you running away from that made you end up like this?"

Carmen bowed her head down. She couldn't tell him; she couldn't tell anyone. She wished Ron was there. She looked at the boy again.

"It's none of your business."

The boy took the soup from the tray.

"Then, thief—"

"I'm not a thief."

"Whatever, eat your food as soon as possible so I can go about *my* business."

Carmen pushed the soup with her hand.

"I have no time to eat. I have to go."

She wanted to go and find Ron immediately. The boy stood up, looking frustrated.

"You can't go anywhere in this condition."

"I can," Carmen said stubbornly as she threw off her bedsheets. Then she gingerly lowered her feet to the ground. The boy grumbled wearily.

"Have it your way…"

Carmen looked at her feet. She could do it. She first put her weight on her left leg and tried to stand up like that, but when she lost her balance, she put her weight on her right foot. She lowered herself back down on the bed in pain. The boy was getting a big kick out of watching her. Carmen tried once again nervously but to no avail. Indeed, she was unable to walk right now. She hated giving up, but she would be incapable of moving without gathering at least a bit of her strength. She breathed heavily and heaved her legs back onto the bed. The boy came and sat on the chair next to her and took the soup in his hand.

"I told you," he said with a know-it-all attitude.

Showing displeasure with his snippy attitude, Carmen furiously grabbed the soup from the boy who was trying to feed her.

"I can do it myself."

The boy stood up immediately.

"As usual, have it your way."

Meanwhile, Carmen noticed her left hand was not very strong. She could barely hold the soup bowl. The boy looked at Carmen just as he was going out of the door. He sighed and closed the door to go back to Carmen and took the soup from her.

"Did anyone ever tell you that you're stubborn and arrogant?"

Carmen objected again.

"I said I could eat by myself…"

She had to shut up with the spoon that was shoved into her mouth.

As he was saying, "I don't like to do this either, thief, but…" Carmen interrupted him.

"I'm not a…" Another spoonful of soup was shoved in her mouth.

"Yes, I get it, you're not a thief," he said, looking bored and continued with the sentence he had not finished. "You need to eat something. I don't know who did this to you, but someone beat you up pretty badly."

Carmen was about to say something but thought the better of it. She did not want the spoon to be shoved in her mouth again. She quietly slurped the soup from the spoon. Then she remembered her bag. The emerald! She pushed the soup back and looked around.

"Where is my bag?"

The boy glanced at Carmen, knitting his eyebrows. Carmen realized she was too panicked, and she calmed herself.

"I hung it into the cupboard."

"All right, thanks," said Carmen as she continued to sip the soup from the spoon.

The boy knitted his eyebrows again.

"You are very mysterious, stranger."

"Carmen." Carmen corrected.

"And I am…" Carmen interrupted.

"Maha, isn't it?"

The boy smiled.

"No, you can call me Matthew. Maha is my name in the old language. My family usually calls me that."

Carmen nodded. Perhaps this boy was not so annoying after all.

After Carmen finished her meal, Matthew left her alone to rest. Though she was terribly fatigued, Carmen couldn't sleep. She could only think of Ron and her father. What had happened to them? All sorts of things came to Carmen's mind. She could never forgive herself for having dragged Ron there. She sighed and closed her eyes. She wished there was a way to reach them. Carmen wished she had her cellphone with her. She wished mobile phones could be used on this planet, too. She missed Earth very much. She missed the convenient possessions on Earth, and she even missed her town. At least nobody tried to kill her there and she had a warm home she could call her own. Unfortunately, such opportunities were not available here. Still, she liked Crictus and felt an affinity here in a way she had yet to understand. But she wished she could find a way to reach Ron and her father. Ron had previously told her that they could easily find each other because of the bond between them. So why wasn't Ron coming to rescue her? Couldn't he find her yet? Or was he… Carmen opened her eyes in fear. He couldn't be dead. *The damned ankle…* she thought. She had to get better and leave here as soon as she could and find Ron. But she couldn't just sit here doing nothing until then. She suddenly recalled what Ron's grandfather had told her. As she had seen her father in her dreams, when she slept now, she might see Ron as well. But how was she going to do that? She didn't know how to use this power. She hadn't consciously gone to her father in her dreams.

Carmen sighed again and decided that she should sleep, leaving her thoughts aside. All she could do was to rest, recuperate, and find Ron later.

THE FOREST

Ron slashed the bushes angrily. He took the thin branches that fell to the ground and went back the way he came. He had enough kindling now to light a fire. They had moved around all day. He was trying to find Carmen through the bond between them, but he couldn't manage. He didn't know the reason. Perhaps Carmen… But no. He knew the Soul Hunter couldn't reach her. That was also the only reason he was alive. If the Soul Hunter had caught her soul, Ron's emerald energy would fade away and kill him immediately. So, where was she?

He arrived at their campsite with these thoughts. Carmen's father, Richard was sitting on the ground. Ron came and tossed all he had gathered on the ground. Neither of them was speaking because they were downhearted. Camping was Richard's idea. It got dark now, and they had been looking for Carmen for days. After trying very hard, Richard finally persuaded Ron to take a little rest. Ron would have preferred to search for her without stopping.

After starting the fire, he sat down next to it, feeling totally dejected. He wrapped his hands around his knees and took a deep breath. He was trying to eliminate the distress inside him.

"We can resume looking for her early in the morning," Richard said.

"Of course…" Ron replied sadly. He still couldn't believe he'd lost Anka. He had one purpose in life and that was to protect Carmen, a.k.a., Anka. But he had failed. And now he couldn't reach her.

"Perhaps tomorrow you'll sense where she is."

Ron sighed.

"I don't know. It had worked before. When I went to find her on Earth and in the castle… But now I can't make it happen."

Richard thoughtfully moved his hand over his bushy beard.

"Do you think there is a specific reason why that's so?"

Ron shrugged.

"It's probably because we're too far from one another. The connection loses its strength at very long distances." He stopped and took his eyes off the fire. He looked at Richard. "Even so, if the bond is used on both ends, we can find each other again." He looked thoughtfully at the fire again. "But why isn't she coming toward us? Why can't I feel her yet?"

Thoughts came to Ron's mind. The moment he kissed Carmen, how she got mad at him… Was she not coming back because she was still angry with him? Carmen went alone to save her father because of her stubbornness. *Why not?* he thought. But if so, how could he find Carmen again? He felt incredibly desperate. He missed her a lot already. He wanted to see her, to smell her, to kiss her…

Richard's voice interrupted his thoughts.

"We'll find her, emerald. We'll find her, sooner or later."

Richard's determined voice brought Ron back to his senses to an extent. Of course they would find her. He just didn't know how to go about doing so just yet. Ron responded with a mere smile.

Richard got up and touched Ron's shoulder.

"Get some rest. I'm going to scout around. I'm sure the Soul Hunter ordered the forest to be searched."

Ron nodded. Even so, he sat with his hands wrapped around his knees for a while. It wasn't long before he lowered his head onto the blanket on the ground. He was exhausted, but he couldn't sleep. How could he sleep without her? He gazed into the fire. The crackling of slightly wet wood burning was like a sad melody. He sighed. "Where are you, Carmen?" he said to himself and closed his eyes again.

Meanwhile, Richard was out on reconnaissance. It seemed like nobody was around. The disappearance of his daughter occupied his mind. They had to find her. He couldn't lose his daughter again just after finding her and without fulfilling his yearning for her…

He returned exhausted after a short walk to find Ron sleeping. He too had to sleep, as they were supposed to try and find Carmen tomorrow, which meant plenty of hours on their feet. He then put his head down onto the blanket on the ground and closed his eyes.

14

ANKA'S CASTLE

Derick was examining several documents in his chamber when he ordered whoever was knocking on the door to enter. Waldorf came in.

"Did you find anything?"

"Unfortunately not, sir. We're expended our search."

Derick knitted his brows. He put down the documents he was holding and suddenly got to his feet.

"Didn't I demand you to find her immediately!"

Derick had raised his voice. Waldorf softly cleared his throat.

"Your Majesty, there are at least twenty villages in the area you ordered us to search."

Derick angrily walked over to Waldorf.

"I don't care. I ordered you to assign all the castle guards and the army if you must! There's no task more important than finding Anka!"

Even though Waldorf was taller than Derick, he felt he was being crushed under Inca's authority.

"Sir, then the castle will be left unprotected."

"The only force threatening the castle is Anka… And it's your duty to eliminate that threat. Is that clear?"

Waldorf straightened his back and bowed with respect before Inca.

"Your every wish is my command, Inca," he said as he exited the room.

Derick liked the way Waldorf treated him. He sat back at his desk with confidence. He thought Waldorf wouldn't fail. Nonetheless, he wouldn't be leaving anything to chance this time. He had to learn to use Inca powers somehow. He stood up calmly. He had brought several books about Inca and Anka's soul down from the castle library. He didn't have the opportunity to examine them before. He picked up one of them and started glancing over the pages. In truth, he wasn't sure what he was looking for. All he knew about Inca was that it could control energy and could walk into Anka's dreams with a special magic. He already knew how to control energy. But he had never been able to visit Anka. He leafed through the pages in the hope of finding something. He wished he knew exactly what he was looking for.

While browsing through the pages, several lines caught his attention. There was some information about dream walking in these lines. Derick read more carefully. According to the book, Inca could enter Anka's dreams. This was what he was looking for! However, as he read through, he learned losing his health could be the price for using such a great power. Derick took his eyes away from the book. If he succeeded, maybe he could see where Anka was, or maybe he could pull her somewhere. Both options were very desirable. He grinned involuntarily. Now all he had to do was to learn how to do this.

KATABLANA VILLAGE

Carmen suddenly found herself behind a smoke screen. This was very familiar. Yes, it was like the one when she saw her father in her dreams. She had done it! She didn't know how, but she had. She was looking at everything in her periphery from behind this smoke screen. She was in the forest. She saw a fire a bit further up the way. She quickly walked in that direction. An incredible happiness spread inside her when she saw Ron by the fire.

"Ron!" Carmen shouted joyfully. She went to him as if to hug him, but when she tried to touch him, her hand passed over Ron's shoulder. She pulled her hand back in fear. She was there, but Ron couldn't see her, hear her, or feel her. She sighed. Desperate, he was watching the fire with empty eyes, but at least he was still alive. She looked around but couldn't see her father. She was filled with fear again. Where was he? Maybe Ron could hear her if she tried?

"Ron, can you hear me?" Ron was still staring blankly at the fire.

"Please hear me," Carmen said in a pleading tone.

Ron put his head on the blanket. He was still watching the fire. Carmen desperately looked at him. She missed him so much. She wished she could talk to him and tell him where she was and what condition she was in. Though she didn't know where she was, at least she could give him a few clues. Carmen sat down beside Ron and was watching him.

"Where are you Carmen?" Ron said desperately to himself and closed his eyes.

Carmen felt the worry gnawing inside her.

"I'm right here Ron. I wish you could see me…"

When she woke up in the morning, she was under the influence of her dream. She had managed to get in touch with Ron, but one-way communication was of no use. At least she was sure he was safe and sound. Her father… she couldn't see him. She would never forgive herself if anything happened to him. But she didn't think they would hurt him. After all, they thought her father was her weakness. Carmen frowned. It was really true. She still wanted to save her father very much. Where could he be… She had to recover and set off immediately.

After a while, Matthew's mother entered with a bowl of soup. She was a short chubby woman. She had hazel eyes just like Matthew and chestnut colored hair. She approached Carmen with a big smile on her round face. Behind the woman, Matthew was standing at the door with his know-it-all face again.

"Seklony pu tuy," said Matthew's mother in a most compassionate tone.

Stunned Carmen placed a smile on her face. She was speaking Crictian. What should Carmen say? What did the woman ask? What did she say? What could be said in the morning? How are you today? Good morning? Carmen cleared her throat.

"I'm fine. Thank you."

Matthew started laughing while the woman looked blankly at Carmen. Carmen suddenly blushed. She had said something wrong. Matthew continued to laugh and spoke, "Don't you speak our language? Where are you from?"

Carmen protested immediately, but her embarrassment was clearly evident.

"Of course I do."

Matthew crossed his arms on his chest and looked at Carmen.

"You don't say? Then what did my mother just say?"

Carmen gulped. Matthew and his mother were looking at Carmen. She felt like she was trapped. Why was he right every time she locked horns with Matthew? She had no idea what his mother had said.

"I…" Suddenly she came to herself. "Look, I don't have to prove anything to you."

Matthew turned to his mother after Carmen said that, "*Hat meri, to Anka Suanae ke torini.*"

He glanced at Carmen while he said that with a faint grin.

"I told my mom you don't speak our language. If you did, you would've responded. Anyways…" he said, as he shrugged, straightening up from the door he leaned against to go out. He was exiting when he said, "By the way, for your information, *Seklony pu tuy* means 'good morning, my dear'…" Then he shut the door behind him.

Carmen looked at the door angrily. Matthew's mother came over and sat on the chair next to Carmen. She had her customary smile on her face. Apparently, she didn't worry about Carmen not speaking their language. The woman fed Carmen and dressed her wounds. Carmen looked incredulously at the wound on her arm. She hadn't realized it was so deep before. Once Matthew's mother finished what she was doing, she left Carmen alone in the room.

Carmen dangled her feet from the bed as soon as she left. She had to get walking again. Of course, there couldn't be much difference with her feet in one day, but she still had to try anyway. She first stepped down with her left foot. Then she stepped on her right foot. She felt a slight pain. She was still not strong enough to stand. She looked at her ankle in distress. Just then the door opened. Carmen hurriedly pulled her feet back up onto the bed, as if she were doing something forbidden. It was Matthew who came in.

"Haven't you ever heard of knocking?" Matthew responded arrogantly.

"Sorry, that's how we do things on Crictus." Carmen gulped involuntarily. Did Matthew understand something? It would be difficult for him to grasp that she was not from this planet, but still Carmen felt suspicious.

"Really, why is it you can't speak our language? I thought everyone knew this language. Even thieves…" Matthew headed to the wardrobe. This time Carmen pretended not to notice he called her a thief.

"I come from far lands."

Matthew pulled his head out of the wardrobe and glanced at Carmen.

"Where do you come from? Carnen Talus islands? Or Etanus?"

Great, Carmen thought. This boy was overly curious. Unfortunately for Carmen, she didn't know any place on Crictus! She couldn't tell Matthew the truth yet. She did not know him and therefore she couldn't trust him.

"From so far away…" She tried to slide over.

Meanwhile, Matthew took some clothes from the wardrobe.

"*Hmm*, so, you're stubborn as well as mysterious."

Carmen looked at Matthew shyly. Matthew grinned slightly and walked out of the room.

A few days had passed. Carmen didn't see either Ron or her father in her dreams. Her ankle was a little better now. At least when she woke up and tried to stand up, it was less painful than the day before. She still couldn't walk, but she would be able to do so in a few days, she hoped. Apart from that, she was bored of sitting in bed all day. Carmen would have nobody to talk to if Matthew hadn't occasionally come in and annoyed her. Matthew was often busy with the farm work outside. But whenever he was bored, he visited Carmen and teased her, and he took great pleasure in doing this. That day, he saw several soldiers loitering around the houses while he was plowing the land on the farm. When he noticed they were barbarically raiding neighboring houses, Matthew wiped the sweat from his brow, dropped his fork on the ground and ran quickly back into the house.

"*Vasa tai Maha?*" his mother asked.

(What is happening Matthew?) *

Matthew smiled at his concerned mother.

"I don't know, but I'm sure there's nothing to worry about. We've nothing to hide from them." Matthew's father came out from the room inside.

"Take your mother inside. And go check on our guest, Maha. I'll take care of the soldiers," said his father.

Matthew nodded to his father as he quickly began climbing up the narrow staircase.

Meanwhile, Carmen was lying on her bed, unaware of what was happening. She was humming a song because she was bored. Her voice was not beautiful, and she could never sing but humming never harmed anyone. Suddenly, she stopped her song when Matthew abruptly entered the room.

"Knock on the door!"

Matthew grinned again.

"I don't want to bother you, but soldiers are searching the houses. They might come here and look, too."

"What!" Carmen said as she leapt in fear. Soldiers! They were coming for her. Matthew grimaced, unable to make sense of Carmen's behavior.

"Don't worry, just a few barbaric soldiers will be entering the house."

"No they can't! You have to hide me!" Then she tossed the sheets aside and put her feet down. Her heart was beating madly. Matthew knitted his eyebrows.

"Why?"

A panicky Carmen put her hand on her forehead. She didn't know what to do.

"Because they're looking for me! You've gotta help me." She stood up on her one good leg.

Matthew stared at Carmen suspiciously.

"Why would they be looking for you? What did you do?"

Just then, they heard a noise from downstairs. They were in the house. Carmen stared fearfully at the door. She couldn't go anywhere on one leg. She desperately clutched Matthew.

"Please Matthew! They'll kill me! You have to hide me!"

"What have you done!" He was holding Carmen by her shoulders so she wouldn't fall. Now he was afraid, too.

"I promise, I'll tell you everything. But please, I am begging you. Hide me!"

Matthew examined Carmen's frightened, pleading face staring at him. Footsteps were approaching. Carmen's heart skipped a beat. Matthew stared at the door one last time.

The footsteps were so close. And then the door opened wide.

THE FOREST

Ron and Richard had been walking for a long time. The sun was so hot that day, they had no energy left to walk from all their sweating. As he trudged along, Ron could feel his despair of not finding Carmen grow with every step. Where did she go? What was she doing? Nothing... Not being able to hear from her was distressing him very much. He suddenly stopped.

Richard noticed that Ron had stopped only after taking a few steps. He turned and eyed Ron.

"Why did you stop?"

"Why are we walking anyway?" he asked, his arms were wide open. "It's so pointless," he added, pressing his hand in his forehead as if he was trying to stop a bad headache.

Richard approached Ron.

"We'll find her."

Ron took a few steps back and crouched down. He felt very helpless without Carmen. He would supposedly make her queen and have her take the throne. He couldn't even manage to keep hold of her. He stood up from the ground angrily and landed a heavy punch on the first tree that appeared in front of him. He wasn't satisfied and kept punching.

"Ron! Ron!" Richard was trying to stop him.

"I don't deserve it! I don't deserve the emerald!"

Richard pulled Ron away from the tree with all his strength and turned him to face himself. Ron suddenly regained his wits with a strong slap to his face.

"Pull yourself together!"

Ron held his cheek. Richard's hand was extremely strong, and his slap had knocked him to his senses.

"If you continue acting like that, yes, you don't deserve the emerald. So now get your act together and let's find a way to bring her back to us."

Ron's hand was still on his face as he glared at Richard, who angrily threw his backpack under a tree. He was embarrassed. Richard was right. He shouldn't have acted like this.

Richard went to sit under a tree. After removing his flask, he drank some water and poured some of it into his hand to wash his face. Meanwhile, Ron sat under the tree near him. Richard handed his flask to Ron who politely turned it away. Richard looked at the flask.

"I'm sorry. I shouldn't have smacked you," said Richard.

"We're both nervous."

"You're right."

"And meandering about only makes us feel more hopeless and purposeless," said Ron.

Richard looked at Ron.

"So, what's your plan?"

Ron turned his head to the trees. He was looking at a distance.

"Maybe we should go back to Zirkus," he said unwillingly.

"We can't just walk into the city. They're searching for both of us." He stopped. "Do you feel that Carmen might be there?"

Ron grimaced.

"No, I don't feel anything. Only if…" He stopped. He was entertaining a stupid, irresponsible thought. But it was perhaps the only way to find Carmen. It still wasn't worth it. He changed his mind.

"Only if?" Richard asked.

"Naw, forget about it, it's not important."

Richard looked at Ron with questioning eyes. Ron looked down.

"Only if Carmen gets caught, I'd feel her while she's being taken to Zirkus. That's because if she gets caught, they'll bring her to the Soul Hunter in Zirkus. But this is stupid. I mean, waiting for her to get caught."

Richard spoke, "Or maybe she'll get to Zirkus before she gets caught. Isn't Zirkus the only place she knows around here?" Ron leaned his head on the tree.

"That's the problem… she doesn't know any place yet."

Richard straightened up.

"If my daughter's like her mother, she'll use her head and come to Zirkus. Despite the possibility of getting caught… We'll be there to save her. Yeah, so, it's smart for us to head to Zirkus."

Ron stood up.

"No, It's not."

Richard stood up and put a hand on Ron's shoulder.

"I know, even the thought of her being in danger drives you mad. Trust me, I know. I don't like it either, but I think it's best we go to Zirkus. At least, there's the chance Carmen will go there."

Ron looked at Richard, as if giving up.

"I miss her a lot."

"I know."

Ron closed his eyes. Ron was still not feeling comfortable but returning to Zirkus seemed better than walking around desperately. He opened his eyes again.

"Let's head back to Zirkus."

So, they started to walk toward Zirkus. They were not too far anyway. They had been walking in circles, as they didn't even know which way Carmen might have gone. Going back was not a problem for them. They reached the city a day later but opted not to enter the city. Instead, they went to Ron's old cabin, which had not been visited in nearly a month and a half. It would not attract anyone's attention since it was in an isolated spot next to the forest. They just had to be careful not to burn any candles or make loud noises. The cabin appeared after a long walk. Old memories rushed into his mind when Ron saw the cabin. As they got up close to the cabin, he saw two small mounds right out in front. He paused momentarily. The Soul Hunter appeared before his eyes. The last breaths of his brother and grandfather. He shut his eyes, took a deep breath, and continued walking. When they arrived in front of the house, Ron glanced at the graves. Then ignoring them, he walked past and opened the creaky wooden door. Everything was as before. Only all the furniture was covered in dust because it had not been handled in a long time. The old table, pots and pans… This was where Ron spent his childhood, and he had many memories here. And it was sad to see this place now, all dusty and abandoned. Suddenly, he was furious again. He would depose the murderer of his brother and grandfather from that castle. Forever…

Richard rescued him from his thoughts.

"Nice cottage."

Ron sighed.

"Yes, it is."

In the evening, they had dinner in dim light. They couldn't risk anyone seeing inside. While eating their meal, Ron broke the silence first.

"Had you seen Carmen before?"

Richard looked at Ron.

"Yes." Suddenly, his eyes were fixed at a distance. "The day she was born, I was patiently waiting at the door of the maternity ward for my wife to give birth. All of a sudden, my wife's screams stopped, and I heard a cry. I could not resist and ventured inside with the fire emerald. I first saw my wife bleeding in bed. Then a maid approached me. I saw her at that moment. She was wet and bundled up in swaddling. Her eyes were just like her mother's. The woman wanted to hand me my daughter…" Richard swallowed. He was having difficulty talking as his eyes filled with tears. "I glanced at my baby and the maid. I said, 'Later…'" His gentle laugh was nervous and sad. His voice sounded like a whisper. "But that 'later' never came."

Richard turned his gaze to Ron, who had paused to take a sip of water from a copper cup.

"I'm really sorry."

Richard smiled.

"It's not important. The fire emerald did the best thing by sending her to Earth. Neither Carmen nor Anka would have survived if the emerald hadn't done that."

Ron also smiled. Then, he stopped smiling.

"That bastard snuffed out the lives of many people's loved ones. He's going to pay for his sins."

"I deeply hope so," said Richard and he raised his glass. Ron accompanied him.

KATABLANA VILLAGE

Carmen held her breath as the door swung open. Two uniformed, armed soldiers entered. Their swords were in their scabbards, with the soldiers' hands on their hilts.

"How about knocking first?" Matthew said in his usual mocking tone.

"We enter however we want," said the soldier in the front.

Matthew asked as the soldiers entered, "What are you looking for?"

"A young girl. She's a brunette, of medium height with an injured foot."

Mathew smiled. One of the soldiers was already standing in front of the cupboard. Carmen put her hand to her heart. She was scared out of her wits.

"The girl you're looking for is in the cupboard," he pointed to the cupboard.

Suddenly, everyone in the room, including Carmen, froze. She put her hand over her mouth. She almost shouted, "What…" She couldn't believe Matthew had betrayed her. Should she have gone out? What would she do? Was she going to try to make a run for it with her crippled leg? She couldn't surrender…

The soldier looked suspiciously at the cupboard, then at Matthew. Matthew challenged the soldier and pointed at the cupboard again with his head.

"C'mon. I'm telling the truth." The soldier put his hands on the handles of the cupboard. Carmen held her breath inside and shut her eyes tightly. She knew the man was very close. Her heart was beating madly. The soldier suddenly lowered his hands nervously and walked over to Matthew.

"Who do you think you are, playing games with us like that!" he said and pushed Matthew. Matthew hit his back to the wall. The soldier spat on the floor and then a soldier from downstairs shouted.

"It's clear down here!"

After the soldier in front of Matthew gave him a foul look, he barked an order to the other soldier and they both went downstairs.

Carmen couldn't believe what she had just heard. She thought her end was near, but she had miraculously survived. She exhaled her breath that she had kept pent up for a long time. The doors of the cupboard swung open. It was Matthew.

"What do you think you're doing! They could've opened the doors! I can't believe you! You risked my life!" She was whispering so that they wouldn't hear. Meanwhile, she was hitting Matthew while walking on one foot. Matthew chuckled as if he was enjoying it. When Carmen stopped, he sat on the bed and gloated.

"But nothing happened, and they didn't open it, did they?"

"But they could have!"

Matthew looked at Carmen lightheartedly.

"Relax. They're gone now."

"Yeah, meanwhile, I went on a little mental trip to the netherworld."

Matthew laughed. Carmen had no intention of laughing. All her nerves were frayed. Why was she always dancing with death? The moment she was caught, they would've taken her to the Soul Hunter, which would've meant instant death. She limped back to the cupboard and yanked her bag off the hanger it was hanging from.

"I can't stay here anymore. It's just not safe enough."

"Where are you going with a limp like that? Besides, I think you owe me an explanation!" Matthew straightened up.

While Carmen was huffing and rummaging inside her bag, the emerald slipped out of her hand and fell to the floor. Matthew looked at the blood-red emerald, petrified. Carmen hastily picked the emerald up and put it in her bag. Matthew stood up; his eyes as wide as saucers.

"Give it to me."

Carmen hid the bag behind her. Matthew wasn't supposed to see that.

"No," she said hurriedly.

"Carmen!" He walked over to Carmen, reached out, and took the bag from her hand.

"No. Matthew, please, I can explain," said Carmen, pleading.

She was limping and jumping, trying to get her bag from Matthew. Matthew kept her away from the bag with no difficulty and removed the red emerald from the bag. Carmen retreated, giving up. There was a hopeless, pleading expression on her face. Matthew showed the emerald to Carmen.

"Is this your explanation?" He was furious. Just as Carmen was about to defend herself, he continued, "You know what this is, right? The fire emerald!"

"Matthew, please listen to me."

"Why would I listen to a thief?"

"I'm not a thief."

"Then, what is this?" He walked over to Carmen. Then he stopped. The apprehension on his face was replaced by seriousness. "I get it now. The soldiers are searching for you because you stole the emerald from the castle. That's why you were so scared of the soldiers…" He stopped. He continued to speak, pointing to Carmen's arm. "Which explains your injuries."

"Nothing's like what you think. Okay, it looks like that, but it's not. Please, you must believe me. Give the emerald back to me, please…" Carmen was almost begging.

Matthew moved the emerald a little further away from her.

"Why should I believe a thief who doesn't tell me anything?"

Carmen took a step toward Matthew.

"Because you have to believe me. I am… I can't tell you, but really there's an explanation. Now please give it back to me."

He took a step back. There was rage on his face. He was angry because he thought Carmen was lying and he had helped a thief.

"If you don't explain yourself in three seconds, I'm calling back the soldiers, thief!" He was holding the emerald in his hand, and he was losing his patience.

"I'm telling you for the last time. I'm not a thief."

Carmen shouted as Matthew headed to the door.

"Because it already belongs to me!"

Matthew stopped. Carmen's heart was beating in her mouth. Matthew turned around and glanced at Carmen. Carmen was staring at him with a look of defeat. She had to tell the truth. Matthew started laughing abruptly after examining Carmen a little. Carmen was confused. Matthew was chortling, holding his belly. After a while, his laughter ceased. He took a step toward Carmen and said, "So what? Are you trying to tell me you're Anka?"

His voice sounded mocking. Carmen crossed her arms on her chest and shrugged.

"Is it that hard to believe?"

She looked annoyed. It irritated her to no end that Matthew didn't believe her. Matthew walked toward Carmen again indignantly.

"Tell me the truth, Carmen."

"I am telling the truth. But it seems like the truth is hilarious to you."

"Then why isn't the water emerald with you?" Matthew asked.

"Because I foolishly went on my own to meet the Soul Hunter to see if my birth father was still alive. Ron didn't want to go there, and he was right. Then I got caught, and they attacked me. Then I escaped from there and jumped into your cart. I got injured and left Ron and my father behind. And I have no idea where they are right now. Because I know nothing about Crictus, I don't know where I can find them, and I have no idea where to start looking," Carmen said all this so fast that Matthew was listening to her with his mouth open. Carmen looked desperately at Matthew.

"Do you believe me now?"

Matthew straightened up and closed his open mouth.

"I…" He didn't know what to say. Nobody could lie so fast. Besides, she had even said the name of the emerald. But she still could be lying. "Could you show me your powers if I wanted to see them?"

Carmen clapped her hands as she saw that she was close to persuading him.

"Yes, yes, sure. But first, we have to be sure the guards are really gone."

Matthew believed her when he saw Carmen's excitement and certainty.

"You are Anka."

Carmen raised an eyebrow.

"Thanks, I didn't know that."

Matthew closed the door of the room with seriousness and surprise on his face.

"But…" He was confused. He looked at the emerald in his hand. Then he looked at Carmen. Anka was standing before him. A queen. And he was holding the heart of her protector in his hand. He smiled suddenly. This could be his way out. This was the key to getting off the farm and reaching a lofty position. Maybe being an emerald… He looked again at the cold emerald in his hand. *Why not,* he thought.

Meanwhile, Carmen was watching Matthew's facial expression change. After a while, Matthew glanced at Carmen again.

"You won't inform the soldiers about me, will you?"

Matthew bowed exaggeratedly to the ground.

"Never, Your Majesty. I serve only you."

She responded by laughing at Matthew's funny attitude. They smiled. Carmen's smile was gone quickly. "Nobody can know about this. I can't trust anyone."

There was concern in Carmen's face. Matthew bowed again. This time he bowed respectfully.

"Don't worry, your secret is safe with me, my queen."

Carmen struck Matthew's shoulder as a joke.

"Stop that."

They both smiled again.

ANKA'S CASTLE

Inca didn't venture out of his room the entire day. Not to eat nor for anything else. He also didn't let anyone enter. He was totally engrossed with reading the book of spells that was lying on his desk. In fact, he was constantly reading the same page, the same lines. He repeated the same words in a whisper:

Skluy man, tuy mas… Skluy man, tuy mas… Skluy man, tuy mas… Skluy man, tuy mas… *

(The inside of you is the inside of me. *)

He had tried to enter Anka's dreams all day. He repeated the same words without pause until the evening.

"The inside of you is the inside of me." Meanwhile, he was holding a piece of cloth from a dress of Anka's that was identical to the one they had stuffed in Abron's beak. Inca started to swing to and fro after a while. He shut his eyes as he repeated the same words. His attitude hadn't changed since the morning. He concentrated on using all his energy to focus on the fabric in his hand. After a while, the fabric started to warm up. Without losing his concentration, he continued to utter the words as he swung to and fro. It wasn't long before he found himself in a lit passageway with darkness at the end. He continued to repeat the words louder and with more conviction. As he evoked the words, the darkness began to move toward him. As the words sped up, so did the darkness, which eventually enveloped Inca.

Carmen was looking at Inca in surprise. Inca had an expression of victory on his face. He was laughing.

"Now in my dreams... That's just terrific," said a disgruntled Carmen. Derick focused on Anka. "Can't I be left in peace at least while I'm sleeping?"

", You won't be able to sleep comfortably until you die, until my brother eats your soul," Derick said in a disgusting voice.

Carmen was even more surprised. How real her dream felt! She knitted his eyebrows.

"Interesting. So realistic..." Carmen suddenly paused. She was aware this was a dream. She was aware she was sleeping, but she felt awake. She stared at Inca. Could it be real? She knew nothing about Crictus. Could people enter each other's dreams here? Or was this just a feature unique to Inca and Anka? Or perhaps this was just her imagination. Then she remembered what Ron's grandfather told her. Could Inca be dreamwalking?

She looked at Inca suspiciously.

"Are you real?"

Inca laughed.

"What do you think? You are just a child, aren't you?" Carmen couldn't believe what was happening. "Now tell me where you are so I can end your misery. Of course, if you dare!" Inca said.

Carmen crossed her arms over her chest.

"I'm not afraid of you." Carmen's face was furious. She remembered her father for a moment. "I will find out where you're holding my father and after getting him back, I'll track you down. I'm certainly not afraid of you, Inca." Inca didn't know it then but she was actually trying to convince herself rather than him that she was not scared and she was capable of beating him.

Inca was surprised but did not show it. Anka's father, Richard, had disappeared in Lake Owlana. This meant that Anka thought he had her father. Inca challenged Carmen without showing his surprise.

"I put your father into his old hole. Just like in the old days. They welcomed him there more than ever," he said with a grin. Then, "You and your emerald can never get him out of there." Then he raised his voice and felt a jolt. As if his whole body was shaking. He felt dizzy. Carmen opened her eyes before she could understand what had happened. She was awake. She straightened out of bed. It was dark. The light of a planet was entering through the window. It was a very strange dream.

Meanwhile, Derick coughed with a shake and fell down from the table. His lungs were burning. He was suffering from a massive coughing fit. He barely heard his guards as they ran inside. He had a splitting headache.

"Leave me alone!" he shouted.

He was coughing while shouting. He covered his mouth with his hand. There was blood on his hand. Just as he was wiping his mouth, he noticed blood coming from his nostrils too. It started to get dark. His shouts got hoarse. The healers who entered quickly carried him to his bed and immediately started to administer aid. Inca recalled what was written in the book: *Such a powerful spell may cause Inca to lose his health.*

KATABLANA VILLAGE

Carmen was sitting in bed, thinking about her dream. Had she really seen Inca, or was it just a dream? It was hard to understand. She wrinkled her forehead. She thought about Inca's words:

I put your father back in his old hole. Just like the old days. They welcomed him there more than ever.

She remembered how cruelly her father was treated in her dreams. Was he subjected to worse treatment now? She had to get him out of there. Desperately, she laid her head on the pillow. Without Ron, she couldn't take such a risk. She couldn't repeat the same mistake. But it was her father in question. Carmen sighed. It was best to wait until the morning. She had felt safer ever since Matthew learned she was Anka. She trusted Matthew for no reason. If Ron were with her now, he would tell her not to trust anyone. She smiled slightly. Her sad smile ended with a look out of the window. Now she had longing in her face. She missed Ron so much…

She drifted asleep the moment she closed her eyes.

When she woke up the next morning, the first thing she did was to stand up. Even though she still limped, her ankle was much better than before. Just as Carmen stood up, there was a knock at the door. Carmen looked up in surprise.

"Yes?" The door opened and Matthew came in. Carmen smiled. "Did you remember to knock on doors when you learned I was Anka?" Then she crossed her arms over her chest. Matthew looked embarrassed, grinning.

"The future queen is before me, after all," Carmen smiled. There was a sadness hidden in her smile. She was so far from being a queen… Matthew pointed at her foot and spoke without noticing Carmen's facial expression. "I think your ankle is better today."

"Yes. I'm able to stand up now. I think I should be able to walk in a few days." Then, she added, "And don't worry, I'll leave here in a couple of days." Then she went and sat on the bed.

Matthew sat down next to her, frowning.

"Where will you go? I thought you didn't know anywhere here."

Carmen shrugged.

"Well, I don't. But I hope to find my way somehow. A GPS would have helped a lot but… I just need to figure out how to find Ron, no matter what."

Matt knitted his eyebrows.

"GPS?"

Carmen smiled softly. It was odd that people on Crictus were unaware of technology.

"Never mind."

"So, you're going to wander about by yourself on a planet you don't know to try to find your emerald?" Matthew's tone was humiliating.

Carmen shrugged.

"Yes."

Matthew straightened his back. He had an ambitious expression on his face.

"How about I come with you too?"

"I can't ask you to do anything like this. You have a life here." Matthew objected.

"You call this a life? Gather crops from dawn to dusk, work like a porter, find a market to sell crops." He stopped. There was a frustrated expression on his face. "This is not the life for me."

"What do you want to do then?" said Carmen.

Matthew jumped up and went to open the wardrobe. He took Carmen's bag from inside.

"This is what I want," he said, holding the blood-red fire emerald. He continued to speak excitedly. "To go on an adventure every day, to fight for you, to protect you..." He looked at the emerald with longing. "To be an emerald..."

Carmen stood up and came near Mathew.

"Matthew, this is not an easy life. Trust me."

"I don't care if it's hard. I want to fight. I know how to use a sword very well and I'm ready to do anything to protect you. I can be your emerald."

Matthew's voice was more excited than ever. But Carmen hesitated.

"I want you to be my emerald, too. I trust you." She looked at the emerald. "Besides, having an emerald would be great right now. But Ron told me that when the emerald finds its owner, it will shine and get warm." Carmen apologized with her eyes. "It's cold and dull right now."

Matthew glanced at the emerald again. The emerald in his hand was cold. It looked dead.

"If this was something in my power, I'd happily make you a fire emerald, but the emerald chooses its own owner."

"I don't get it. Why doesn't it choose me?"

Carmen looked as sad as Matthew.

"I don't know. I am new to this too," Carmen said. Then, she put a little smile on her face and spoke, "But if you want to be my guard, then I'd love for you to come with me."

Matthew looked at Carmen, revitalized. As he bowed down before Carmen, he said, "It's an honor for me to serve you, my queen."

Carmen smiled.

"Stop that," she said, hitting him playfully.

Matthew laughed as he straightened.

"All right, now that I'm your official guard, where do we go first?"

Carmen made a face. She remembered her dream. Inca's words... She took a deep breath.

"I had a dream last night." Matthew also became serious at once. Carmen continued to speak, "I saw Inca in my dream. I think he dreamwalked. I am almost sure." She paused for a brief second and continued. "He still thinks I'm with the emerald."

Matthew interrupted.

"Then that's a good thing."

"There's something else..." said Carmen, embarrassed. Matthew glimpsed at her with questioning eyes. "They threw my father back in his old prison and there is a pretty good chance that they're torturing him."

Matthew crossed his arms over his chest.

"Do you know which prison it is?"

Carmen lifted one eyebrow and looked at Matthew.

"Are you kidding me? I know nowhere."

Matthew had forgotten for a moment Carmen didn't know this planet.

"Apologies. Well... Where could they be keeping him?"

"What do you think?" said Carmen.

Matthew looked thoughtful. Where could they be hiding a former king, who was thought to be dead all this time? Suddenly, he remembered Crictus' highest security prison.

"I think I have a guess."

"Yes?" Carmen said impatiently.

Matthew spoke with uncertainty, "Yaskla Gusav. It's the highest security prison in Zirkus. It's a great place to imprison a king."

"So, you think they're keeping my father there?"

Matthew shrugged.

"Why not, they could be."

Carmen mulled over the situation. Meanwhile, Matthew continued to speak, "But it won't be easy getting your father out of there. Security measures are extremely strict..."

"Wait, wait." Carmen silenced him. "I can't take the risk of being caught going there. Especially without Ron."

"I thought you wanted to save your father?" said Matthew in a questioning way.

Carmen curled her lip in distress.

"Yes but…"

"I can protect you."

Matthew looked very brave. But Carmen still was not convinced.

"This is very risky, and trying to do such a thing without finding Ron first…"

Matthew insisted.

"Look, you said it yourself. The only way to save your father is for both of us to go there and get him out. We can handle this with your Anka powers and my sword." He stopped and showed the emerald he was still holding. "And maybe the emerald will pick me on the way."

Carmen smiled slightly. Matthew's courage and enthusiasm were astonishing and endearing. But Carmen still couldn't decide.

"Um… I'm not sure."

Carmen had a lot on her mind. Matthew was right. The only way to save her father was to do this without Ron. But there would be thousands of guards there. It was almost impossible for just the two of them to ward off that many people. During the rest of the conversation, when she told Matthew about this, Matthew told her that after they neutralized two guards, they would steal their uniforms and enter in disguise. He said the guards there wore masks to remain unidentified. The plan could fail in many ways, particularly as Carmen was a wanted fugitive everywhere… And she didn't feel safe because she was about to undertake an endeavor without Ron's knowledge. Had Ron been with her, he would have come up with the most rational solution. Instead, she was left with a farmer who was recklessly eager to fight. She didn't know why, but for some reason she trusted Matthew. Matthew's excitement also got Carmen pumped up. It sounded as if they could do anything. Carmen felt as if they could just go out to the castle and beat the Soul Hunter and Inca there and then.

Despite Matthew's effort to rally her, Carmen still wasn't up for going there. Finding Ron was her foremost priority. With Ron by her side, she could build an army to march on the castle and take what was rightfully hers. That's how she could help her father. Matthew was obligated to accept this. They would set off whenever Carmen's ankle was strong enough to support her.

After talking to Matthew, Carmen lay down on the bed to rest her foot. Now all she had to do was wait for her ankle to heal…

Edmund was sitting at his desk in the royal chamber, examining documents in front of him, signing the necessary ones, and reviewing contracts. Just then, there was a knock on his door. He yelled "Enter" without raising his head. Chief Guard Waldorf entered. He bowed in reverence and then spoke.

"My Lord, as you ordered, fifteen hundred guards have set out to suppress the rebellion at Danen Talus."

Edmund answered without raising his head from his desk.

"I ordered two thousand guards." He directed his dark, frightening eyes at the chief guard standing in front of him, who was shaking in his boots. "Are you questioning my orders?"

Waldorf began to sweat profusely.

"Of course not, sir, your Highness, but…"

"But what?"

Edmund's coarse tone boomed in Waldorf's ears. Waldorf swallowed.

"Prince Derick said he would set off by taking over five hundred men with him. I sent my fifteen hundred men to Danen Talus so as not to leave the castle unguarded."

Edmund knitted his eyebrows. It was an insult his brother was acting against him! It was a greater insult that the man before him hadn't listened to him. Edmund stood up, slowly but angrily. A chill passed through Waldorf's body. He knew what a brutal man like the Soul Hunter could do.

"Did the prince tell you where they would be going?"

"I have no information, your highness," Waldorf said with a whimper.

Edmund laughed in anger. His laughter made Waldorf uneasy, he had goosebumps. Edmund approached Waldorf after he stopped laughing.

"You disregarded my orders, you took orders from the prince, and you don't even know why you disobeyed my orders. Is that correct?"

Waldorf swallowed hard. He would very much like to stop the sweat pouring from his forehead at that moment.

"Sir, I think it was something to do with Anka."

Edmund took one step back. Waldorf was slightly relaxed.

"Anka?"

"Yes, your majesty."

Edmund wanted to find out what his brother was up to. But no matter what he was doing, he had defied his orders. He had to be punished. Only in this way could he protect his kingdom.

Edmund stroked his beard, which was beginning to weigh down on his face. He was growing a beard because it concealed at least some of the wrinkles on his face.

"Guard!" he shouted toward the door. The guard who came in first bowed in reverence and then waited for his orders. "Go and bring me the prince."

The guard bowed then backpaddled immediately. When Waldorf cleared his throat, Edmund looked back at him.

"There is one more thing you should know, your majesty."

"What's that?"

Waldorf spoke after plucking up his courage.

"Prince Derick has commanded us to address him as king."

Edmund was shocked. He gaped at Waldorf.

Derick had to be stopped immediately...

In another chamber, Derick was making his final preparations. He would set off that evening. Inside, the servants were packing some items. Upon hearing a knock on the door, Derick commanded whomever it was to enter.

The guard who entered first saluted then said, "King Edmund summons you, my prince."

Derick stared harshly at the guard. The guard was stunned and spoke again, "King Edmund summons you, my king."

The servants in the room looked at each other furtively. It was unheard of for two kings to be residing in the same castle. Derick was delighted.

"Tell him if he wants to see me, he has to come here himself."

The guard looked at Derick, not knowing what to do.

"But my Lord..."

Derick looked at him harshly again.

"Are you defying my orders?" Derick walked over to the frightened guard. "Just because I can't eat your soul doesn't mean I can't order you to be beheaded." The guard was standing expressionless. Derick stepped back and spoke, "Now go and do as I say."

After saluting, the guard backpaddled hastily out of the room. When

Derick turned around again, the servants who had been watching him quickly went back to doing their tasks.

In the Royal Chamber, Edmund went mad when he heard Derick's insult. As soon as he caught the guard, he sucked out his soul. Waldorf watched the terrifying scene with fear, averting his gaze when he saw the king turning toward him. Edmund had gone ballistic. But he had to calm down. He couldn't kill him just yet, not yet… After he calmed down a bit, he beckoned Waldorf tersely. A terrified Waldorf approached Edmund.

"Go and find out what he's after, and don't you dare come back without an answer."

Edmund was practically hissing. Waldorf saw this as an opportunity to escape. He nodded and double-timed it out of the chamber, taking a deep breath as soon as he completed his exit. Living this close to death every day in this castle had begun to become very tiring for a man his age.

Waldorf went to Inca without delay. He asked Derick the question King Edmund wanted him to pose. Derick smiled.

"Tell him I'll be back soon with a gift for him."

Waldorf was not pleased with the reply he received and did not want to go back to Edmund and annoy him, since dissatisfying information might cost his life. Unfortunately, he had no other choice.

When Edmund summoned him in, he bowed respectfully.

"Yes? What did he say?" Edmund asked impertinently.

"He asked me to inform you that he will be returning with a gift for you soon, my lord."

Edmund squinted his eyes and stared at the trembling old man before him. Waldorf had told him that Derick was dealing with something to do with Anka. So, his useless brother had finally found the trail of Anka.

"That will be all," he said.

Waldorf relaxed and went out. If he managed to stay alive in Edmund's realm, he would definitely retire as soon as he had an opportunity.

Edmund was rather pleased in his chamber. Very soon his brother would bring him Anka, and after he hunted her soul, it would be his brother's turn next. Then he would be the one and only king. He would be the strongest person alive on Crictus. He smiled pleasantly and glanced at the corpse lying on the floor.

"Guards! Toss this out to the Baleran."

KATABLANA VILLAGE / TWO DAYS LATER

Carmen was loading provisions that would last them a few days behind a beast of burden that resembled a horse. She paused for a moment and asked herself what she was doing. She was aware she had embarked on a very hazardous task while they were searching for Ron in the forest. On the other hand, she knew that she had to do something. She couldn't ascend to the throne by sitting around doing nothing. She was supposedly going to rule Crictus, but the only time she got near the throne thus far was when she swept the corridor floor leading to the throne room. At this rate, she might as well be a zillion miles away from becoming a queen. She was still thinking about Matthew's offer to rescue her father, but she didn't want to put her life in jeopardy again. Even if she managed to save her father, that wouldn't bring her any closer to the throne. Yes, the priority had to be finding Ron. She missed him so much. A voice coming from behind her jolted her back to reality.

"Yeah, I think we're ready, aren't we Hahim?" Matthew said, stroking Edram tenderly. He seemed to have a good bond with Edram. Edram nodded slightly his head as if he understood. At least it looked like that from afar.

Carmen turned to him.

"We will be passing near Yaskla Gusav. You can tell me if you change your mind." Carmen didn't pay much heed to what Matthew said.

Matthew glanced at Carmen.

"Don't worry. Everything's going to be fine."

Carmen smiled at him. She wished it could be as simple as he claimed.

"Did you say goodbye to your family?"

Matthew took a step back. His face looked weary.

"Yes, but my mother didn't take it very well."

Matthew's parents emerged from the house just then. It was time to leave. His mother, whose eyes were swollen from crying, came up to Carmen and embraced her. Carmen reciprocated in kind.

"Take care of yourself. May Phoenix protect you." Carmen smiled.

"You take care of yourselves, too."

She let the woman go. While Matthew's mother threw herself her son's neck, his father touched Carmen's shoulder.

"Safe travels."

Carmen looked gratefully at the man.

"Thank you." Meanwhile, Matthew had hardly escaped from his mother's arms. "I'm grateful for everything you did for me," said Carmen.

"You're always welcome here. This is your home now, too," said Matthew's father. Carmen guessed that Matthew's mother was trying to say the same things from the words she murmured, although she could barely speak from all her crying.

"We've got to go now," Matthew said.

Together, they mounted the horse-like creature. Matthew gazed at his home for one last time, the home he might never come back to. He had chosen to embark on a perilous journey and there was no turning back. Anything could happen to him while he was with Anka. But he was sure he wouldn't be staying in that pit forever to spend his life as a farmer. He would become a great man, maybe a commander, maybe a king... Anything and everything was possible when he was with Anka. He looked at his home for the last time, the abode where he spent all his years... *At last. I'm free,* he thought. He had never imagined in his wildest dreams that leaving would be so easy. And for one last time, he looked at his mother and father whom he would miss very much. One day, after he had done great things, he would make his family very proud if he could come back here. With that thought, he smiled at them. He waved farewell to them and his home for the last time. Then they galloped away and disappeared into the forest.

Carmen was very uncomfortable atop the horse-like creature because her feet came right down to the beast's nostrils. The animals of Crictus were *different* to say the least. After a long ride on the animal's back, they took a break by a river. Carmen threw herself off the animal to the ground. Her legs were in pain. She had never ridden a horse on Earth and now she understood how difficult it was.

She bent down gingerly then sat on the ground as she held her waist. Matthew looked at her and laughed.

"What, you've never ridden an Edram before?"

"Do I look like I have?" she scolded Matthew. The pain was excruciating.

Matthew laughed.

"No, not at all. Though, it is amusing to watch."

Then Carmen smiled too. Matthew was in a cheerful mood.

"Do we still have a long way before we get there?"

Matthew looked away for a moment.

"Yes, because unfortunately, we can't use the shortcut."

Carmen leaned against the tree behind her.

"Why can't we use that road?"

Matthew sat cross-legged on the floor.

"Because it's dangerous. Wild animals roam around that road."

"I remember Ron telling me about predators, but we hadn't encountered many animals on the way."

"Are you nuts? There are countless predators on Crictus. The reason why you haven't encountered them is probably because the emerald knows the animals' habitat. They generally wander around in their own habitat in the summer months, but if they can't find food during the winter, they can be seen anytime, anywhere."

Carmen felt a chill. The Baleran had come to her mind for a moment. Soul Hunter's *pet*... She'd never forget those eyes that froze her blood.

Carmen and Matthew set off again after resting for a while and eating their meal. Carmen wasn't fond of Edram. It didn't look cute with its skin like an elephant's, deep black eyes, clawlike feet, a long snout and nostrils in its body. It even had a spooky side. Thank goodness it was tame. It shook a lot when she was on it, but after a while Carmen got used to it. Of course, she knew that she would not get used to the pain in her legs when she got off the animal.

Days of riding on the back of the Edram got Carmen pretty tired. That day, when it got dark, they decided to camp in a suitable spot. According to Matthew, they were now in close proximity to both Zirkus and Yaskla Gusav Prison. Though she wasn't thrilled about staying near the prison, Carmen didn't appear to object. So, they spent the night there.

RON'S CABIN

Many days ago, Ron rose early in the morning. As was the case for the past several days, he wasn't able to get a good night's sleep. All he could do was think of Carmen. Was she well, where was she, why wasn't she coming? But today he woke up with a different feeling. As if... As if she was here. This strange feeling made him want to look for her under every rock, nook, and cranny. Of course, this wasn't a strange feeling. He could do it every day without getting bored, but today it was different. Could it be hope? He believed he could find her. *Maybe she got closer,* he thought. Just the thought made him smile. He missed Carmen so much he couldn't find the words to describe his feelings. He loved her smile, the way she looked and smelled, how she talked, and sometimes even her improper jokes. Though he had known her for a very brief period of time, his loyalty to her was very strong and he couldn't even recall life before her. He could neither think of a life without Carmen nor did he want to think of such a thing. She was as crucial to him as gravity. Maybe this feeling was a result of being an emerald, he did not know, but this infinite loyalty occasionally frightened him. He was frightened because he was afraid to lose her every second of every day. Just as he did now, he felt empty without her. But this day was different. He could feel the inner strength to find and reunite with her today.

After Richard woke up, they had some food to gain their strength. He spoke after taking a spoonful of food.

"I want to look for Carmen today."

Richard lifted his eyebrows.

"Are you feeling something?" Ron shrugged. Richard stroked his newly trimmed beard, sprinkled with white. "Fine, let's look for her. We set off in half an hour."

Ron nodded. He didn't understand the reason for the excitement in him, but he sensed that he would find her soon enough.

A few hours later, they snuck out of the cabin and hit the road. Ron turned around to look at the graves of his grandfather and his brother Mason for the last time. Maybe after everything was done, after he took his revenge, he could organize a ceremony for them. He glanced at them with grief for the last time as they set off. They started talking about their usual topic, which was, of course, state affairs. Richard missed the good old days. The throne was his daughter's right, and he was ready to do anything to get her back on the throne. It was very comforting to know his daughter had a knowledgeable, intelligent emerald like Ron. Because no matter what, he knew very well he could trust Ron with his daughter. When they lost Carmen, he witnessed how Ron fell apart. The emerald bond was strong.

After walking for a good amount of time, Ron stopped abruptly.

"What happened? Why did you stop?" Richard said.

Bliss spread over Ron's face.

"We've been walking for hours."

Richard glanced at Ron, not comprehending what he meant.

"Yes?"

Ron kept smiling.

"Don't you understand? We're heading to her."

For the first time, Richard had hope.

"Are you sure?"

Rather than replying, Ron continued to walk more briskly. *We're so close*, he thought.

Indeed, she was close.

YASKLA GUSAV PRISON

Inca was in the command room of the prison. He was steadily beating the floor with his foot out of nervousness. He was so close to nabbing Anka and was feeling the stress of it to boot. Everything would go as planned. Anka would fall for his trap and come to the prison, that is, to his feet, of her own accord. At least he hoped that would be the case. After that, he would take Anka to the presence of his *beloved* brother in order to neutralize her and suck out her soul. As soon as his brother destroyed Anka's soul forever, boom!

Suddenly, with the knock on the door, he stood up anxiously.

"Come in!" he said sternly.

The incoming guard was one of those he posted.

"Any news from Anka?"

"We haven't received any news yet, sir, but your task force is hidden at all the positions you wanted. We'll be notified as they approach the prison."

"Good…" said Derick with a disgusting smile. Then he sat down calmly and crossed his hands on the table. "I definitely want to be notified."

"Of course my king," the guard bowed in reverence.

"This time, I won't leave this to chance. I want you to assign all your men to this task. You'll have two powerful opponents facing you in the form of the water emerald and Anka. Don't underestimate them."

A slight smirk appeared on the guard's face.

"No need to worry, sir. I'm posting my strongest and best-trained men. They won't even know what hit them."

Derick grinned. He waved away the guard. The guard bowed and headed to the door to leave the room. Derick called out before he left.

"Commander!"

The guard turned and looked at his king.

"Remember I want to hold an emerald in my hand."

The man grinned. He bowed again and went out of the door.

THE FOREST

The only reason Carmen woke up yawning just past noon was that the trees could not block the glare from her eyes as the sun rose over the hill. After stretching out thoroughly, she went down to the bank of the river and washed her face nonchalantly. Then she turned and glanced around. Matthew was still sleeping like a log. She looked at the river and then at Matthew again. She took the flask and dipped it in the river. As soon as it was full, Carmen went over and woke up Matthew.

"Wow, we really got some shuteye there," said Matthew.

Carmen looked up at the sky and was suddenly worried. Normally Ron would wake her up early in the morning. This time, she had to wake Matthew up.

"I think we should get going. We'll find Ron quicker if we move."

"You're right. We're also near the prison. They may be patrolling around here." Just when Matthew said this, Carmen knew sleeping here had been a huge mistake. Ron would have never let her take the risk of sleeping near a prison.

They packed their stuff together and loaded up the Edram. Carmen took the fire emerald and sword, which she always carried with her. Matthew took his sword and their flasks in case they got thirsty. Just being close to the prison made her nervous. She felt the need to braid her hair in case of combat. Matthew had taken this road in case Carmen changed her mind, but Carmen's fear and the lesson she had learned earlier stopped her from taking risks.

A little later, they were all packed and ready to set off. They had just started walking when Matthew stopped Carmen.

"Carmen?" Carmen looked back.

"Yes?"

"We're going this way."

Matthew was pointing in the opposite direction. Carmen was surprised as she gazed in the direction Matthew was pointing, and then the way ahead of them. Every cell in her body pressed for her to proceed. It was strange. She had never experienced such a feeling before. So, she didn't know what to make of it. Hesitation overcame her.

"But this road seems more accurate?" said Carmen.

"If we go that way, we'd be heading toward downtown Zirkus. You don't want to be there," said Matthew and pointed the other way. Carmen looked reluctantly at Matthew. Matthew went near Carmen.

"Trust me. I'm trying to keep you safe, my queen."

Carmen nodded in a delicate manner. Matthew held Carmen's hand.

"Then we'll go this way."

Carmen glanced at the road behind her one final time then she decided to listen to Matthew. Together they headed down the road Matthew pointed out.

Carmen didn't understand why she wanted to go that way. Little did she know, her instincts were correct. Ron and her father whom she thought was in prison were in that direction, but now she was headed in the exact opposite way, toward a trap.

Carmen was scanning her surroundings as they walked. Matthew seemed like he had no fear of being caught. Carmen sighed. She could not rid herself of her anxiety but kept on walking, nevertheless.

Meanwhile, a trained guard wearing camouflage was observing them in a nearby tree. He examined the girl. She fit the description. It was her all right, it was Anka. He took both hands to his mouth and whistled. A very realistic bird sound echoed in the forest. The guard listened intently for a response, and it wasn't long before a reciprocating bird sound was heard.

The mission was just now getting underway.

15

YASKLA GUSAV PRISON

News spread like wildfire in the prison, and everybody was put on alert. The guard who entered command room was breathless. Inca knew right then it was time. His prediction was right, Anka was going to try to save her father, who had disappeared into the forest that day. Now Inca had reached the point where everything was about to come to a conclusion. As he quickly stomped out of his room, he knew he couldn't afford to miss this scene.

Oblivious to what was going on, Carmen and Matthew were walking through the trees. Matthew stared at Carmen and smiled.

"We're really close to Yaskla Gusav now. Are you sure you don't want to change your mind?"

"So, you intend to have me killed as well as yourself?" Carmen smiled.

"I'm just saying that your father is here and so are we. If you want, I'm here for you." Carmen laughed slightly at him, but this time she didn't want to walk into a trap.

"No, Matthew. I need to ascend the throne first." Matthew shrugged. Just then, Carmen saw the contours of a structure rising skywards amongst the trees to her right. She found it strange to see Yaskla Gusav. She knew what the interior looked like from her dreams. She shuddered when she imagined her father was there.

"We'll go this way." Carmen, who regained her wits when Matthew said that, saw that he was taking a route away from prison. She was a little relieved. As they were walking, Carmen suddenly turned her back. There was no one behind them, but there was something making her uneasy. *This is very natural*, she thought. Especially, considering the things she had been through ever since she had left her ordinary life behind. But there was something else. Maybe an animal was passing. Carmen gently gripped her sword hilt. When Matthew noticed Carmen's move, he paused. Carmen knitted her brows.

"Matthew…"

They both stopped. Carmen listened to the forest intently. There was no sound except for a few birds' chirping and the rustle of leaves. But she was still not convinced. Something was wrong. Her anxiety increased.

"I think we have a problem," she said.

A few dozen men watching from behind the trees had closed in on them. When they realized they had stopped walking, they also stopped. They almost didn't even breathe. All the men were looking at their commander, who had been observing Anka's movements for some time. It was only a matter of time before he signaled his men.

THE FOREST

They were on the road for many days. That day, Ron was overly excited. They got up with the first daylight and they had been walking ever since. Ron was walking more briskly today. Having picked up the pace, he was still cautious. He didn't want to make the mistake of going in the wrong direction. He knew Carmen was out there nearby. He could feel it in his bones.

Richard had a hard time keeping up with Ron's pace. No longer as strong as they once were, Richard's bones were challenging him. He was stuck in that hole for many years. He was sure all his bones would've crumbled away like dust in the last sixteen years if they didn't make him work in the mines. In retrospect, he was glad to have served hard labor in the mines. At least it kept him fit. He couldn't keep pace with Ron, but at least he was trying to. The worst part was that he couldn't ask him to slow down. He knew very well that Ron wouldn't stop at any cost or slow down even a bit if he knew Carmen was at the end of the road. He got to know Ron well while they were together. He glanced at Ron, who had incredible determination in his eyes. Had a mountain come before him, he would've pierced it and continued to move steadily forward. Richard made no sound. He took a deep breath and stretched out his steps in an effort to catch up to Ron. After all, his daughter was worth it.

YAKLA GUSAV PRISON

Carmen looked over her shoulder. Her hand was still around her sword. Matthew scanned around, too.

"I don't think there's anyone. You're worried for nothing," said Matthew.

Carmen turned her head toward him but just then her eyes wide open in fear.

"Matthew! Behind you!" As she brandished her sword with incredible speed.

The two men pounced on Matthew with all their might. Matthew found himself on the ground before he knew what hit him. He was struggling with the two men while trying not to lose the Edram's rope. When he realized this was impossible, he released the animal. He didn't want it to get hurt. Fearing for Matthew, Carmen tried to reach to help, but a rope tripped her to the ground. A rope, which had a heavy weight on the end, wound itself around her feet. Panicked, she tried to wrangle free of the rope. When she saw a dozen men lunging at her, she realized she had no time and severed the rope with her sword. Just as she was about to get back up on her feet, somebody grabbed her by her foot. She screamed bitterly and swung her sword toward the man, who shrieked in pain. Carmen stood up with difficulty.

"Run, Carmen!" Matthew screamed at the top of his lungs. Now she was standing and fighting off three men who were swinging their swords at her. A fourth man would soon join them. In an effort to get rid of the men around her and help Matthew she rushed over toward him, but two men appeared before her. Two more suddenly appeared behind her. Carmen was swinging her sword unconsciously in fear. She had forgotten all the techniques she learned. "Remember!" she forced her brain, but there was just no time for it. She felt a man grabbing her by the hair. As soon as she turned back, she launched the man into a tree with her Anka energy she beamed out of her free hand. Meanwhile, Carmen wasn't able to prevent another guard from grabbing her from behind. She was swinging her sword like mad. She kicked another man advancing toward her in the stomach with all her might. Unfortunately, her kick didn't have the desired impact, as he was able to pull himself together immediately. Just then, another man was trying to pin down Carmen's arms. Carmen swung her hand holding the sword at him, but she couldn't get rid of the guy holding her from her backside. She gathered all her might, and this time she directed her Anka power not to her hands, but to her entire body. The man released Carmen with a weak scream. This move in turn caused the other men around her to fall back. Seizing the moment to escape, Carmen tried to run but came face to face with someone's sword.

"I want her alive!"

She knew this voice. She didn't need to look behind her. Carmen fought against the man's sword as another sword moved toward her. Carmen pulled away with an agility that surprised even her, as she thrust her sword into the man's stomach. The man screamed and fell backward. Carmen glanced at the man gasping. For a moment, the time slowed down around her. She saw blood dripping from her weapon. The bright redness made everything even more real. She felt like she was suffocating. But just then, a few guards took this pause as an opportunity to jump on her. This act brought Carmen into her senses, and she brandished her sword at them without knowing what to do.

"Carmen!" shouted Matthew as he struggled with the other men. He suddenly broke free and jumped on the men rushing toward Carmen.

"Run!"

Carmen heard this and started running with trembling feet. She was inexperienced but fast. With a swift move, she passed the guards. All of a sudden, a hand grabbed her from behind. Carmen turned back with a sudden move and deftly knocked the man's sword down with an instinctive move. With a quick step, she got him to lose his balance while performing one of the moves Ron taught her. The men fell down. Carmen whipped her sword up against the man's jugular vein. As she was about to make her move, she suddenly came eye-to-eye with him. Carmen was breathless, her hands trembling madly. Sweat dripping from her forehead clumped in her hair. Her heart was beating at light speed, but for a moment all the mess around her disappeared. Only the man's frightened eyes remained; deep, fearful, intensely blue... The man's life was at the tip of Carmen's bloody sword. Death was so close. She gulped and she felt her whole body stiffen. She couldn't do it. She couldn't end the life of another creature. Even if it was in self-defense, she didn't have the heart. Her eyes filled with tears. The man took advantage of this by swiftly kicking Carmen's leg. Carmen screeched and looked around as if she had awakened from a dream. She could move her body again. Suddenly, five men jumped on her. Carmen was screaming, trying to free herself from the arms of sweaty, strong men. One was trying to take her sword away while another was wringing her throat. Suddenly, she saw Matthew. He was in the same situation. *It shouldn't be like this!* She thought. She mustered all her power and screamed. With her scream, the men restraining her fell sideways. Carmen felt the power flowing through all her veins. Instead of blood, pure power was rushing through her veins and was radiating through her body. She seemed invincible then.

"Anka!"

The voice brought Carmen back to reality. It was Inca, watching the entire battle with a disgusting smirk on his face... Carmen looked over to where Inca was pointing. A noose had been swung over Matthew's neck, and a man was holding it in place with both hands. His sword was no longer in his hands, and the two men were restraining Matthew by the arms. Matthew was still struggling madly, but to no avail. Inca raised his hand. When the man squeezed Matthew's neck with the rope, Matthew was left gagging for a moment.

"No! Don't!" Carmen took a step forward, panting in fear. Inca's hand stopped her. Carmen's eyes were fearful as she kept gazing between Matthew and Inca. Meanwhile, the guards, who were finally able to get to their feet up, surrounded Anka. Although Carmen was on guard, her hand trembled so much that the sword could fall from her hand at any moment.

"Leave him alone!"

"Surrender!"

Carmen glared at Inca in rage.

"Don't, Carmen! Don't surrender!"

Matthew cried. Carmen gulped. Her eyes were filled with tears.

"Promise you'll let him go."

Carmen's voice was calmer now, but she was still breathless. Her hands were still trembling, and her legs were about to let her down because of the adrenaline rush.

"What are you talking about! You can't surrender! Carmen, look at me!"

The guard behind Matthew cut him off with a punch.

"Shut up!" he shouted as he hit Matthew again.

This time, Carmen addressed Inca with a more determined voice.

"I'll surrender, but you'll let him go."

Inca stepped forward.

"You're in no position to negotiate."

Carmen glanced around her. He was right. She was surrounded by at least twenty men. Moreover, Matthew could not endure the rope around his throat for much longer. Still, she had put Matthew's life at risk. He was her responsibility. Carmen pointed her sword at herself. Inca was watching her closely.

"I said let him go!"

Carmen shouted unexpectedly. Her voice was full of fury.

"Lower your sword, Anka," Inca said in a threatening voice.

"You need me alive. Promise on Inca you will let him go, or I will kill myself and release Anka's spirit!" Carmen responded in a surprisingly threatening and steady voice. She wasn't panting as much anymore.

"No, please!"

Matthew was pleading with her. Carmen didn't even look at him. Inca scaled her up and down.

"You don't have it in you." Carmen glared and spoke.

"Try me." A moment that felt like forever has passed. Carmen pressed the sword into her throat even harder. She could feel the sharp edge eager to cut through her fragile skin.

"Promise!" She yelled.

Inca looked at Matthew. Then, he turned to Carmen.

"Brother's promise."

Carmen gulped. She was desperate as she looked at Matthew one last time. There was nothing more she could do. She had failed. She tossed the heavy sword from her trembling hand onto the ground. The guards grabbed her by the arms as soon as the sword hit the ground. She could still feel the tension of her sword on her neck. And just like that, she became a captive for the first time in her life. The guards tied her hands tightly behind her back. Carmen's tears were ready to rush out, but she knew she couldn't effort to show weakness. Not now. Matthew was shouting as he struggled.

"No! Leave her! Carmen, what did you do!"

Then suddenly, he crumpled to the ground with a blow to his head.

"No!" Carmen said, trying to move forward but she was immobilized.

Inca approached Carmen.

"As you can see, I didn't kill him," Derick said.

Carmen was breathing fire. Meanwhile, a guard presented Carmen's bag to Inca. Carmen held her breath. Inca opened the bag and placed the blood-red emerald between his hands. He burst into laughter.

"I was going to say that you were being foolish coming here without the emerald, but it looks like you actually brought an emerald with you."

"Don't touch it," Carmen said angrily. There was nothing she could do.

"This is no longer your concern. You no longer need the emerald," said Derick.

Carmen gulped. Her pent-up anger was growing. Derick summoned a guard.

"Take this and destroy it."

The guard's eyes were shining as he took the emerald. He was proud to be assigned a task with this importance. He nodded to Inca and moved away quickly. Carmen glared at Derick.

"What can I say, sister? Sacrificing your life for a stupid mortal soul was absolutely pathetic, to say the least." As he kept talking in a humiliating tone, he pointed at Matthew lying unconscious on the ground. Then he clasped his hands behind him. "Looks like you've reached the end of your journey. I feel sorry for you." He turned around and glanced back at Carmen as he was just leaving. "No, actually. I would be lying if I say I'm not enjoying this."

"You disgust me!" yelled Carmen. Inca grinned and turned to the man beside him. "Put her in the cart immediately. We're heading to the castle. I have a gift to present to my brother."

Everything was going as Inca planned. Now he had Anka captured. The water emerald didn't cause any problems, and he had just ordered the destruction of the fire emerald. The only thing left to do now was to transport Anka to the castle and present her to his brother. After that, everything would be over. Anka would be forever lost.

And he would be the one and only sovereign!

NEAR YASKLA GUSAV PRISON

Ron was walking fast, and Richard was out of breath a few steps behind him. They had been walking for days and he no longer had the strength left to walk. He wiped the sweat off his brow with the back of his hand. The sun was burning hot. After a few more steps, he couldn't endure walking any longer and held onto a tree. When he looked around for the first time, he remembered he had seen this road before. He knitted his eyebrows slightly. How did he know this road? He opened his eyes wide. This couldn't be happening!

"Ron!" The urgency in Richard's voice was hard to ignore. Ron turned back inquisitively. Richard started to speak as he walked up to Ron. "I know this road."

Ron looked in front of him and then back at Richard.

"Where does it lead to?" he asked.

"Yaskla Gusav."

Ron's heart started beating faster. Was Carmen caught? Or was she...

He shrugged and pulled himself together and started to run as he turned around. His heart was beating madly. He'd never let anything happen to her. He was running as fast as he could. He reached for his sword as he ran. He was ready to kill anything that came between him and Carmen. He saw someone lying on the ground a little ahead. He went up to him and then looked ahead. The prison was over there. Just as he was about to continue moving, something on the ground caught his attention. He leaned down and took the crumpled canvas bag. It was empty. He knew this bag. It was his mother's bag he had lent to Carmen. Carmen was just here. And something bad had happened to her. He scanned around in horror. Just then Richard caught up with Ron. Ron spotted the young man who was regaining consciousness on the ground. He was furious as he grabbed the young man by his collar and lifted him to his feet. Matthew looked at him in surprise, wondering what was going on.

"Tell me! Where is Anka? What did you do with her?"

Matthew didn't know what to say to the young man who stood, full of sound and fury, before him. As he was just about to reply, Ron smashed him into a tree. He then brandished his sword.

"Wait, wait!" Matthew cried with fear. The sword pinned against his throat was not a joke.

"Tell me! Where is she?" Ron bellowed angrily.

"They took her. Inca is taking her to the castle. I couldn't stop them."

Ron was still glaring at Matthew. Richard slowly touched Ron's shoulder.

"He says he was helping Carmen. Let him go, Ron."

Matthew's fear suddenly turned into astonishment.

"Ron? You're the emerald."

Ron started to calm down. He let Matthew go.

"Yes, I'm the water emerald."

Matthew spoke as he tidied himself up.

"Carmen mentioned you. And you…" he said, glancing at Richard. Then a spark ignited in his head.

"It can't be…" he said in a whisper, staring at the man in surprise.

"You're her father."

Suddenly, a feeling of remorse filled Matthew.

"You're supposed to be in prison! Carmen and I were discussing breaking into the prison to rescue you! But you're here." He was pointing at Richard with his index finger. Ron glanced at Matthew suddenly. The anger in his eyes came back.

"What did you say?" He was about to charge at Matthew. "Did you bring her here? Did you put her in the middle of such danger!"

Matthew fell back without knowing what to do. The boy in front of him was perhaps younger than himself, but his authority was greater.

"I was just trying to help her."

"Help her? Do you call this help? They're taking her to the castle!" Ron stopped. They were taking away his life's purpose, his Anka, to the castle. To be presented to the Soul Hunter… To destroy Anka forever… He was petrified. Carmen was about to die. He had to act, right now!

He pinned his gaze on Richard.

"We've got to get to the castle now," he said worriedly.

"We'll never catch them on foot."

As soon as Richard said this, Matthew spoke.

"Maybe an Edram might help."

Ron reluctantly glanced at Matthew. Although he didn't want to accept the help of someone who jeopardized Carmen for naught, he had no other choice. He was in the midst of a crisis and had to reach Carmen before it was too late. Entering the castle was suicide, but he didn't care. Anka was more important than anything.

When Matthew realized Ron was convinced, he put his hand to his mouth and emitted a high-pitched whistle. A little later, Hahim came at them at a gallop. Although Matthew was proud of himself and his Edram, he soon realized that expecting a compliment from the emerald was an expression of futility.

The three of them leaped onto Hahim and hit the road. Not only were they worried sick, but they also knew that time was of the essence.

BURNING ROCK

Grasping the fire emerald firmly in his hands, the guard was just assigned a very honorable task. He had noticed the jealous looks on his colleagues' faces when Inca gave him the emerald. He looked at the emerald, smiling. It was nearly time. He thought the best way to completely destroy the emerald was to toss it into a volcano and melt it. That way, nobody would ever access it ever again. Once the Soul Hunter destroyed Anka and made her history, there would be no need for the emerald anyway, but nonetheless, it was still an honor to carry out this task no matter what the cost.

He was riding his Edram at breakneck speed toward the nearby Burning Rock, located just above the farmlands, a short distance from Owlana Lake that flowed behind the castle. After ditching the emerald, he planned to ride over to the castle to receive his reward. A big smile spread on his face. He wondered what it might be. Could it be a large sack of gold, perchance? Who knows what he would do with it!

After a while, he arrived at Burning Rock. Intimidating as it was exciting, this spot was a natural wonder that sat in the middle of flower meadows and natural beauty. It featured a terrifying great chasm, ready to roar like hell, as it emitted burning steam and lava. He dismounted from his Edram and proceeded cautiously over toward the burning cauldron, shielding his face from the heat with one hand as he went. He stopped when he arrived at the outer lip of the volcano. Beads of sweat had already begun cropping up on his forehead. He held up his hand and looked at the *warm, shining* emerald one last time.

EN ROUTE TO ANKA'S CASTLE
BURNING WAY

It was a bumpy ride inside the carriage. Carmen sitting behind the wooden carriage while glowering at the guards. Then she studied her surroundings. There had to be a way to escape from here. It could not end like this. She was going to her death, and she had nobody to blame but herself. She was scared, yet she couldn't show her fear. She was breathing deeply and trying to comfort herself, but it was impossible. She closed her eyes. "Now you're in your warm bed at home. You were very impressed by the movie you watched last night, and this is all a dream. Soon the alarm will go off and you'll wake up. You'll get ready and go to school as you do every day. And from now on you'll study very hard. You'll become an even better person and listen to your mother and father. Now breathe deeply, count to three and open your eyes on your bed. One... Everything's fine." Two... You're not imprisoned. This is only a dream. Three..."

Carmen opened her eyes slowly. She was about to cry. No, she was still on Crictus. She was captured and her mortal enemy Inca was sitting across from her. Her eyes were wet as she averted her gaze from Inca. Her heart was beating madly. She tried to wriggle her hands, but the ties were too tight. Even if she jumped from the cart she would be caught immediately.

"What's that? Are you going to cry now?" Inca said, grinning.

Carmen closed her eyes and took a deep breath. She was trying to calm down. After a while, she looked resolutely at Inca. Although it was tough maintaining the determination in her look, she must have managed because Inca's grin disappeared.

"I'd be sorry for myself if I were you. You have just sacrificed your immortal soul for a mortal."

"You can't understand such things, Inca. You don't have a heart," said Carmen firmly. Her voice was almost trembling. She shouldn't show him that she was scared. She had to be strong.

Inca smiled.

"Look, where your *good* heart brought you. It was foolish to come here," Inca said, leaning toward Carmen.

Carmen glared at him, breathing fire. She was not going to reveal that it was never her intention to break into the prison. She just stared at him. The distance between them was so minute that she could smell Inca's putrid stench. Inca leaned back a little.

"And you know something? Your father wasn't even there."

Carmen knitted her eyebrows.

"No, you're lying."

"We lost track of your father during the Owlana River Incident."

Carmen was shocked. Inca had tried to set her up. This meant that she would've never succeeded in saving her father even if she were able to breach the prison. She was proud of her decision not to go in, but it didn't matter anymore since she was captured in the mere vicinity of the prison.

Derick continued enjoying the astonishment of Carmen. "You tried to ambush me," said Carmen, pushing herself forward in anger. Unfortunately, her range of motion was limited as her hands were bound. Inca grinned.

"Tired? Look around you. Thanks to you, my plan is working wonderfully…" he leaned back.

"That's what you think! The Soul Hunter will never let you sit on the throne," Carmen raised her voice.

Inca suddenly became serious.

"That throne is my right, little girl, and I won't let anyone get in my way. Neither you nor my brother." He patted his messy hair with one hand. Then he went on. "As soon as Edmund destroys your soul, I'll finish him off. When he takes your soul, I'll take advantage of the brief moment he's vulnerable and take his life. And then the throne will be mine."

Carmen's anger was replaced by surprise.

"You would kill your *own* brother? This is very…"

"primitive?" Derick suggested.

"I was going to say 'cruel' and 'soulless.' How can you kill a person you grew up with? Your own blood?"

Inca was still serious.

"You've got no idea what I've lived through. You've got no idea what it means to be the only powerless child of a family full of Soul Hunters, and what it means to be humiliated and excluded by everyone, every single day." Inca's voice sounded resentful. He went on, "I was hoping to get back at him one day, and that day has finally arrived." Cheerful now, he had a disgusting expression of pleasure on his face, pleasure he took from death. Carmen grimaced. "Very soon, I'll wipe him off this planet and become its only ruler... Besides, killing my brother won't be different than what our immortal souls have been trying to achieve for centuries. You think you are better than me, but you aren't. We are the same, you and me."

"You and the Soul hunter are a disease to this planet." Derick laughed while Carmen was glaring at him

"There is nothing you can do now little girl. You should have stayed on Earth, where you belonged."

As soon as Derick said this, Carmen started screaming. Her heart was burning. Her eyes darkened suddenly. She saw a boy, a blonde boy. As he fell into the lava, she saw the blood-red emerald shining on his chest. The pain intensified; the pain caused by the emerald when it replaced a heart... His body, skin, face, eyes, veins... They were all being scorched. Carmen screamed and suddenly found herself in the lava. The pain was unbearable. For a second later, the image disappeared. Carmen's vision slowly reverted back to normal. She looked around and at her body in a hurry. She had felt her whole body had been burning, but now everything felt normal. Her body was fine. She had the wind knocked out of her. Her pulse hadn't yet slowed back down to its normal rate. Her skin was relieved by a gentle breeze. Only a few seconds later, when she noticed Inca staring at her in terror did she understand what had happened. She had experienced this pain before. As the water emerald settled into Ron's heart, she felt all the pain he had experienced, the drowning and then the pain... Now she felt her whole body was burning. Carmen laughed after her breathing returned to normal. A tear dropped from her eye, perhaps from pain or maybe from hope...

Derick looked at Carmen in rage.

"This isn't going to change anything! He will never catch up in time and save you! It's too late for everything now! It's all over!"

Carmen wiped the smile off her face and looked at Inca with a determined expression.

"You are wrong, Inca. I belong here, I always have. You think this is the end but you're wrong about this too. My emeralds are coming for you. You better be ready." She felt strong for the first time since she left Ron. Inca didn't respond to her, but she knew she managed to frighten him, at least a little bit. However, there was something he was right about. She was galloping to her death, and it was really too late for everything. Still, an absurd hope flared up inside her. She remembered the words her mother always told her: *There is always hope.*

BURNING ROCK

Jonathan was a twenty-four-year-old, tall, dexterous warrior. He was born during a battle fought against the Soul Hunters and had spent his life in wars. A rebel like himself, his father taught him to hold a sword since the day Jonathan started walking. His father did his best to give Jonathan the proper training. And so, Jonathan became a mighty insurgent by the age of fourteen. He grew up with hatred for Inca and the Soul Hunter. For three years, he had been in charge of locating Inca sect lodges outside of Zirkus and organizing attacks on them. But when he learned of Anka's return, he decided to return to Zirkus a couple of weeks ago. Rebels weakened over the years and most of them were driven away from the capital. When he proposed the idea, rebels were reluctant to join his quest. But he was ready to do his best to help restore her to her rightful throne. Thus, he left his rebel base and got on his Edram. But finding Anka was comparable to seeking a needle in a haystack. Consequently, he began keeping tabs on the castle affairs. Inca's departure from the castle a few days ago caught his attention. He tracked him from afar and arrived at Yaskla Gusav. He had all the entrances under surveillance. He saw a guard dashing out from one of the rear gates at Yaskla Gusav. A smile spread over his face when he noticed a shining object in the guard's hand. He finally had a clue. The guard was holding the crimson emerald in his hand. This was Anka's emerald. The guard exited the gate on his Edram and rode off at full speed. Jonathan followed him on his steed. Although Jonathan followed the guard in close proximity, he wasn't noticed. The guard was heading toward burning rock. He was curious about what he was going to do there.

The guard dismounted from his Edram. Jonathan left his steed at a safe distance away and continued to follow him on foot. The guard was walking cautiously toward the mouth of the volcano. Jonathan immediately understood what was about to happen. He was going to destroy the emerald! He couldn't allow this. He quickly approached the guard, who raised the emerald without hesitation and looked at it one last time.

The guard felt his hand getting warmer as he looked at the fire emerald.

Of course, it must be because he was standing next to the volcano, he thought, but something was amiss. His eyes were locked onto the emerald just as he was about to heave it into the lava. The emerald was shining. He looked at it in surprise.

"Hey you!"

He was startled by a voice from behind and glanced back. The moment he turned his head, a hard fist slammed into his face. The man staggered and threw himself to the side. But he dropped the emerald at the edge of the volcano. He came eye-to-eye with a tall boy in front of him. Then they both lunged toward the emerald simultaneously. Just as the guard was about to grab the emerald, Jonathan tried kicking him on the ground this time, but the guard pulled him to the ground by grabbing his foot. They were both rolling on the ground. Jonathan was trying to take him under, but the guard was stronger than he thought. He picked up a rock that had struck his hand as he was rolling on the ground and threw it at Jonathan's head. Jonathan screamed in pain. But he had no intention of letting go of the shining emerald, which he barely held with one hand.

When the guard saw Jonathan hadn't released the emerald, he smashed him hard with a rock. The guard then snatched the emerald as Jonathan pulled his hand back reflexively. He stood up unsteadily and headed for the volcano. Jonathan immediately stood up after him. He wasn't about to let the guard destroy the emerald. As the guard was about to throw the emerald into the volcano, Jonathan leapt on him and the fight ensued again. Jonathan grasped the man's throat. While gasping for air, the guard managed to pummel a gashing blow to Jonathan's eyebrow with his free hand. Jonathan took a step to the right, dragged the guard along as he went. He glanced beside him. They both saw the boiling lava was just inches away from them. Jonathan grabbed onto the emerald the guard was holding in his left hand. The guard desperately wanted to push Jonathan into the lava, as he knew he had no other options to survive. He punched Jonathan strongly with his right hand. Jonathan was stunned. He lost his balance when he slipped into a hole, holding onto the emerald with his right hand. The only thing keeping him from falling into the lava was the emerald, which was held by the guard. The guard looked into Jonathan's frightened eyes, grinned slightly then released the emerald. As Jonathan fell into the lava with the emerald in his hand, he felt his whole body slowly burning. He screamed as he brought the emerald to the level of his heart. The emerald emitted a bright red light and was very warm. Just meters away from the lava, the emerald touched his chest as he lost consciousness from the heat. Just then, his eyes opened wide. An excruciating pain wracked his entire body. As the red light ascended into the sky, his entire body was aflame. He then fell into the lava, his skin burnt to a crisp. A horrific pain spread from his heart to his entire body. Carmen was feeling this pain simultaneously.

Then… The pain suddenly disappeared. Jonathan opened his eyes. There was molten liquid all around him. Though it was scalding, it didn't hurt as he raised his hands. It was almost peaceful now. He heaved himself to the surface with all his might.

The guard had lost his balance and rolled to the ground from the dazzling red light rising over him. Horrified, he fixed his gaze at the light in disbelief.

"This can't be happening…" he muttered. The light disappeared as quickly as it appeared. The guard listened around for a few seconds. His body was shaking terribly. Curiously, he stood up slowly. What had just happened? He had just taken a slow cautious step toward the lip of the volcano when he found himself on the ground again with lava splashing up toward him. When he saw the boy in the lava, he almost bowled over. Jonathan was standing godlike on the lava and looking skyward. Suddenly, he turned his gaze to the guard on the ground. The man swallowed hard, petrified with fear. He tried backpaddling like a crab but had to stop when he bumped into a rock formation. Controlling the lava flow, Jonathan went down to the man's side. He was naked as his clothes had burned off in the lava. He stood in front of the man, grabbed him by the collar and heaved him up. The man was on the verge of crying, as he looked terrified at Jonathan.

"Where's Anka?"

"I… I… I…"

This time, Jonathan's voice boomed.

"I asked you where she is!"

Tears were running down his eyes.

"In-ca took h-her to the ca-castle…"

Jonathan was looking furiously at the man.

"You just tried to kill me, didn't you?"

The man was looking at Jonathan without knowing what to say. He couldn't even speak from fear, and his crying got worse.

"I-I am so-sorry. Please fo-forgive me."

Jonathan smiled.

"Of course…" he said and put him out of his misery with a fireball he created in his hand. The man's scream hung in the air as Jonathan dropped the man to the ground. He then restored the lava. He realized he had to reach the castle immediately. He glanced at the clothes of the corpse under his feet in disgust. To him, wearing a guard's outfit was a putrid idea, but he had no other choice.

He quickly put on the man's clothes and ran back to his Edram. He was the fire emerald now! His purpose in coming to life was to protect Anka. Even though he strangely felt like this even before he became an emerald, he was now the official guardian of Anka. He leapt onto his Edram and set off at a galloping pace to save Anka.

ANKA'S CASTLE

The guards holding Carmen by both arms were practically dragging her on the floor as they sauntered through the castle corridors. Inca was in front, followed by Carmen and the two guards gripping her, then many guards taking up the rear. Carmen was struggling desperately, but both guards were very strong. She could not even move because her hands were bound securely. She was trying to force her tears back. Here she was, at the castle… Ron pointed to this castle on the day she first came to Crictus and said that it would belong to her when they were done. Now, as he said, everything was about to end. But there was something wrong. She hadn't come here to seize the castle as he had said. She was walking to her doom with two guards' vise-gripping her arms. Her heart pounded madly. She looked about helplessly, but nobody was around to help her. This was how she would be shuffling off this mortal coil. The Soul Hunter… When she confronted the Soul Hunter in the forest, she felt that her soul was being sucked out. She remembered that pain. Her eyes got moist. No, she wasn't supposed to cry. She was strong. *Strong? I'm a just little girl,* she thought. *A girl who's about to die.*

Several guards appeared in front of them as they turned around a sharp corner in the corridor. The guards stood in silence before Inca. Inca walked past them briskly. Carmen glanced at the guards and came eye-to-eye with one of them. It was Dean! The shock in their eyes was mutual. Dean was looking at her in surprise. Carmen beseeched him for help with her eyes as they suddenly walked past the guards. Dumbfounded, Dean was startled by his friend poking him.

"Did you see that? They caught Anka." He whispered.

"It's time. Alert the others." When Dean's friend was about to leave. Dean grabbed his arm and whispered.

"Subtly. No one can know." His friend nodded.

Dean stared after Anka for a brief moment. They were taking her to the presence of the Soul Hunter. The soul of Anka would be no more. Anka, the immortal soul, would die not to be reborn again. He could not be a spectator to this. He took a deep breath and followed Anka silently.

Meanwhile, Inca had already reached the doors of the throne hall.

"Finally," he said to himself. He shoved open the double doors with his hands without waiting for the guards. Inca and everyone behind him walked into the middle of the hall. It was deserted. Inca turned back angrily. He hoped to find his brother here, to no avail. Carmen could barely stand on her feet as she squirmed. The guards had difficulty holding her. Inca glanced at Anka and then turned to the guards.

"Guard!" A young guard approached him. "Go and find my brother right now! Tell him I've brought Anka!"

The guard went out after nodding.

The guards holding Carmen dumped her right in the center of the hall, directly in front of the throne. Carmen collapsed to her knees. She was breathing heavily. Carmen raised her head slightly off the ground. The throne was in front of her; it was splendid, with exaggerated golden inlaid legs, and it mocked her. The throne assumed a dark aura with light seeping through the two frosted windows behind. There it is, Carmen thought. The reason for her very existence was standing in front of her. Fearlessly displaying its glory, it taunted her as if it was staring pitifully at Carmen. Carmen recalled her thoughts from a few weeks ago when the closest she had been to the throne was while she cleaned the corridor leading to the throne hall. Though she was a mere couple of steps from it, it had never seemed so far away. *Isn't it ironic?* she thought. The throne was still gaping sarcastically at her. Nobody in the room was talking. Carmen stared defiantly at the throne. It was supposed to be mine, but it was too late now, she said. Hope, hope... Where are you? She was looking for a grain of hope in herself, but there wasn't any. Soon the door would open, the Soul Hunter would enter, and she... Carmen shut her eyes to block her tears. She didn't want to die. She was breathing heavily. The only sound in the hall was the sound of her breathing. The last breaths of a dying person... Carmen opened her eyes. She had to remain calm. She focused her eyes on a single point on the floor. She was trying to calm down. It couldn't end like this. She shouldn't be dying like this. So many people trusted her... *How stupid have I been,* she thought. She should never have left Ron. But it was too late to think about this now. She then thought about Ron. She would never see him again. Not just Ron, she would never see anything else again. She felt her heart aching. As she closed her eyes, a teardrop rolled softly down her cheek. She was going to die in just a little while. This was really happening. Her mother, her father, her friends on Earth, Earth, Crictus, trees, nature, and animals... All of that would cease to exist for her. She closed her eyes tightly. She couldn't stop crying. She could no longer hold back her tears. Inca approached her and stopped.

"Look at almighty Anka weeping! There's no use in crying!" He spit out these words. Carmen shot Inca a glare. She absolutely loathed him. The fear in her heart turned into fury.

"I hope he kills you," Carmen said in disgust. Inca grinned but said nothing. He was taking delight in Anka's anger. Inca walked to the back of the room. Carmen turned her head back to the throne. The throne was still mocking her.

Inca was becoming increasingly impatient inside the throne hall.

"Why isn't he here yet!" he shouted nervously.

"He'll be here shortly, sir," said a guard.

Inca stared harshly at him and breathed nervously.

They were all unaware of the incident that had occurred just outside the room. Inca had summoned a guard to call King Edmund. The guard left the throne hall and began to walk quickly toward the king's chamber. Turning the corridor, he was startled when somebody tapped him on the shoulder from behind.

"Hey, what's going on in there?" It was Dean.

"I don't have time for this," the guard snapped.

Dean jumped in front of him swiftly. The guard was forced to stop.

"Where are you off to?"

The guard sighed and looked impatiently at Dean.

"I have to summon King Edmund to the throne room. Get out of my way."

Dean quickly seized the guard trying to pass him by the throat. He pulled the knife from his waist and brought it up to the guard's throat in one swift move.

"You're not going anywhere."

The guard was more confused than angry. He was holding Dean's hand, which was holding the knife to his throat. He had not expected that move.

"What do you think you're doing? This is treason!"

Dean grinned with his usual dirty smile.

"Oh yeah? Says who?" As he said this, he quickly pulled his knife away and struck the guard in the head with the knife handle. The guard collapsed to the floor and was knocked unconscious when Dean hit him once more. Dean put his knife back in its hilt with a grin, satisfied with his work, and started dragging the guard from his armpits. He dropped him in the first room he found. He left the room after binding his hands, feet, and mouth.

At least this will buy Anka some time, he thought and headed for the corridor opening to the throne hall in case another guard was sent.

ANKA'S CASTLE

They dismounted from the Edram. The river was a little further behind the castle. Guards were posted on the walls of the castle. Everything seemed calm. All three hunched down in order to go unnoticed as they headed toward the rear of the castle. Richard was leading the way. He came up to a point in the castle wall that had a door with an iron fence. They knew they couldn't enter through the front gate to save Anka. So they had planned to enter via the secret escape route, which was known only by the royal family.

"Here it is," said Richard. Then, he went on. "This place was built by the first rulers. You're lucky I'm with you. It's a bit confusing inside, but I still remember my way around." He paused to recall his years in the prison. He took his hand to his chin and beard out of habit. He was unable to trim them while in prison. He had forgotten he shaved in Ron's cabin. Shaving his beard was an indication he had left those years behind. Of course, if they couldn't save Anka, he might have to go back there, but that was something he didn't want to think about now. He was going to save his daughter.

Matthew moved forward with a swift move and pushed the door.

"It's locked!" he said, frustrated. Ron went ahead.

"No worries, I'll take care of that."

He used the water he had poured from his flask by controlling it like a buzzsaw with his hand. The chain of the lock snapped in just a couple of movements. Ron pushed the door forward. It was dark inside. He grabbed the torch hung on the wall. He muttered something and the torch lit up. Matthew looked at Richard and then at Ron in turn in astonishment.

"You used magic, that's forbidden."

Ron's glare made Matthew gulp.

He didn't say anything and just took a step forward. Ron stopped him.

"You're not going any further. It's too dangerous for you. You'll get in the way."

"If you don't mind, I can fight, too. I can't let you leave me behind here. I want to help save Anka, too."

Ron couldn't help but notice Matthew's determination. Realizing he wouldn't be able to stop him, he said, "Okay then, but if you run into trouble, you are on your own."

They started to walk down a narrow passage. Richard led them, as he knew the way. The path was very narrow, but every five meters or so they came to a junction. As they moved forward, the sunlight disappeared from behind them. It was airless inside and illuminated only by the torch in Richard's hand. The path sloped upwards. The walls were slightly damp. As they passed a junction, Matthew said, "This place is no different than a labyrinth."

Richard spoke without looking at them, "This place was designed as an alternate escape route in case of attack. It's impossible not to get lost if you don't know the way."

"What, there's only a single exit in the place?" asked Ron.

"No, actually, there are five. This is the easiest one to find. The others are more hidden."

They went quiet again as they proceeded a little further. As the path narrowed, it was getting hard to breathe as they moved forward. After walking for a while, they saw something squirming ahead of them. Richard halted suddenly.

"There's someone there…" he whispered.

Ron knitted his brows. He doused the fire in Richard's hand with the water in his flask. He tensed up when he noticed a weak light coming from in front of them when he expected it to be pitch black. There was someone there for sure. Ron went in front of Richard and led the way with caution, keeping the water in his hand ready. In the meantime, Richard and Matthew pulled their swords. The light in front of them was getting closer. It came from the other branch of the junction in front of them. Ron turned back and looked at the others. After signaling them to wait, he came to the side of the path very slowly. He took a deep breath. He launched on the path, ready in an attack stance with the water in his hand, and suddenly froze. The person in front of him was staring at Ron, just as stunned. Ron looked over at the boy from head to toe. He was wearing a guard's uniform. But then, looking at his hand, he felt a chill. The boy was holding fire in his hand! The fire emerald was in front of him!

Jonathan also looked incredulously at the boy in front of him. When he saw water hanging in the air, he took a step back and lowered his hand.

"You should be the water emerald."

Ron also lowered his hand and the water down.

"Yes, and how are you the fire emerald?"

Matthew and Richard were astounded, looking at the fire emerald standing next to Ron. Matthew was also looking at the fire emerald, but he was enraged. That is because the fire emerald had not chosen him but the boy in front of him.

"Long story," Jonathan said, and went ahead of him.

"Can we keep going now? Anka may still be alive, but her time is running out."

Ron was still staring at the fire emerald in shock. What had happened that he was here? And what was with the guard's uniform? But now was not the time to find out. He was right. Anka had little time left. They couldn't waste time. They knew that she was still alive because Anka was the source of their powers, and if she died, the powers of the emeralds in their hearts would also fade. This meant that they'd also die instantly.

Ron pushed these thoughts away from his head. *We'll save her. We're more powerful now, and most importantly, she is more powerful now* he thought. After nodding at the emerald, he started following him.

"Who made this man the leader?" Matthew fretted, but this was not a good time for fussing.

They had Richard lead again and continued walking with Jonathan's fire.

After a short walk, they came across a wall. Richard touched the wall with both hands.

"Oh no! They put up a wall here!" There was despair in his voice.

"Are you sure this is the place?" Ron said.

"Yes I'm absolutely sure. It was here," he said, touching the wall with his fingertips.

"Is there another way?" Ron said.

"There is, but it'll take us a long time to get there."

Ron looked desperately at the wall. They had to pass behind it. They had to succeed at all costs. While Ron stepped forward with water in his hand, Jonathan stopped him.

"Allow me," he said.

Richard retreated as Jonathan stood against the wall and inhaled. Then he put both hands on the wall. The spots he put his hands on began to melt. After a while, the whole wall had disintegrated onto the ground and a passage was opened. Jonathan stood in front of them. All three had hope and courage on their faces.

"Let's go and save her," Ron said.

Richard took the lead again, followed by Jonathan, Ron, and finally Matthew. The latter looked astonished as he walked over the melted hot stones.

A little later a door appeared before them. Richard stopped in front of the door.

"Here we go!" He turned and looked at those behind him. "For Anka."

Ron drew his sword. The others nodded.

"We'll go in without anyone noticing us, without drawing attention. We will quietly kill everyone we encounter. If we run into a problem, the fire emerald and I'll go save Carmen while the two of you distract the guards. Any questions?" Then he looked at them all one by one. Richard grasped his sword tightly. They said, "Let's move" and quietly pushed the door.

THE THRONE HALL

Inca was a nervous wreck by now, anxiously pacing inside the hall, frenetically. Why hadn't he come? Somewhere, something had gone wrong. He stopped in front of Carmen, who was breathing deeply. He looked at her with disgust. This whole thing should've come to an end by now. He turned his head to the other side and saw the throne in front of him. A faint smile appeared on his face. *Very soon,* he thought. Then he turned sharply to the guards.

"Guard!"

The first guard in line stepped forward and gave a salute.

"I want you to take three men with you and go, get my brother." He glanced at Anka, standing on her knees on the ground. "It seems like there are those in the castle who don't want Anka to perish."

The guard called out two other men.

"Yes, sir," he said and they walked over to the door of the hall.

Carmen heard the sound of the door opening and closing from behind. Her heart was pounding, and she was still breathing heavily. When Inca leaned in front of her, she turned her gaze at him with hatred.

"My brother will be here soon. Are you ready?"

Carmen clenched her teeth and fists. She was thinking about the possibilities. It wouldn't change anything if she launched on him.

"Rot in hell…" she said in a whisper.

When he heard that, Inca laughed and stood up. Carmen glowered at him. When she first came to Crictus, she thought this sibling war was meaningless, but now she thought it was justified. Such a person had to be stopped. She moved her hands. It didn't work. She still had time. She could still escape from here. It wasn't over yet. Carmen scanned around. Torches on the walls… They were useless. Magic… She didn't even know if she had a talent for casting a spell. She moved her eyes around the room again. The throne… The mocking throne… It wouldn't work for the escape plan. She turned her head to the left, and her eyes fixed at a point. A double door stood there. It was as if this door existed just to save Carmen. She didn't know if it was locked, but maybe she could break it using her energy. Her hands were tied but… She looked at the other side. There was another door there. At that moment she heard the door behind her open. Carmen held her breath. The room became silent. Footsteps and then words from Inca's mouth.

"My dear brother. Let me present you your gift, Anka…"

16

OUTSIDE THE THRONE HALL

Dean noticed the three guards exiting the hall but couldn't do anything to deter them. The men had quickly passed in front of him. A little later, the Soul Hunter would come down the same way, and the era of Anka would be over forever. He had to do something. He felt desperate. Where was Ron? Why had he left Anka alone? Perhaps he should barge in with the guards he gathered but would it work? Against the Soul Hunter, and Inca, did they stand a chance? *It's worth trying,* he thought. But if they failed... Then the Soul Hunter would suck up all their souls, one by one. Dean was undecided. He couldn't make up his mind. He began to descend slowly. He had to gather his wits and didn't want to encounter the Soul Hunter in the process. He quickened his steps. He felt like he would be free of having to make a choice and be rid of his dilemma once he left Anka upstairs. He proceeded into the corridor once he reached the landing two floors below. Inca's chamber was in this corridor. He was just about to pass in front of the chamber, when he noticed there weren't any guards posted. Something was terribly amiss. He pulled his sword out of its hilt and listened around him. He heard a slight moaning. Dean pointed his sword forward.

"Hark, who goes there?" Nobody came out. He took a few steps forward. He called out toward the other end of the corridor.

"I know you're there. Show yourself." Somebody appeared from the other end of the corridor. Dean was staring at him.

"Hello, friend." It was Ron. "You probably won't kill me, will you?" he continued. Dean couldn't believe his eyes. The solution stood before him now. He could help him save Anka. Dean lowered his sword.

"Thank Phoenix you are here!"

Ron approached and patted his shoulder amicably.

"Pleased to see you too."

"Anka's in the throne room. She's in trouble, Ron."

"I know, that's why we're here." Then Jonathan and the others appeared behind him. There was blood on their swords.

"I hope you didn't kill my man. They are on our side. Come on, I'll show you the way, but we must get a move on. We've got to get there before the Soul Hunter gets into the room."

Ron nodded in consent. And they moved toward the stairs. Dean went up to the corridor first and checked out the situation.

Before he reached the stairs, he saw four guards heading toward them. Dean moved toward them.

"Where are you headed?"

"Waldorf sent us on patrol," one of them said, then all four of them walked past him.

Dean drew his sword. As he followed them, Ron and Jonathan launched on them. All four guards tried to draw their swords in shock, but Jonathan acted first, as he sent his fire over them. One of the guards screamed when his uniform started burning. He stopped screaming when Ron stabbed him in the heart. But in the adjacent corridor, the guards at the door had heard the scream. They looked at each other.

"Go and check it out," one said to the other.

Meanwhile, Dean had jumped on one of the guards.

"What are you doing?" "This is treason..." He couldn't finish his sentence as Dean had already slit his throat.

"Again, says who?" he asked as the man collapsed, covered in blood.

Richard and Matthew took care of the remaining two guards in short order. After Ron put out the burning man's flame with water, he dispersed the smoke with his hand and then turned to Jonathan. He smacked his shoulder hard.

"What the hell are you doing! Do you want to give away our location!"

Jonathan glared at Ron angrily.

"It was reflexive. Can we go now? We're running out of time!"

Ron knew they didn't have time to fight.

When they all turned back to keep walking, they saw a guard at the end of the corridor staring at them. The guard took his hand to his waist, pulled up his horn, and blew on it as hard as he could. Just then another Geir came behind him and hit him in the head. Dean nodded at his friend.

But it was too late. Everyone who heard the horn started blowing their own horns on the other sides of the castle. Shortly, the entire castle was shaking with the raucous sound of these horns. Dean yelled at Geir.

"Gather everyone to the throne room." Geir nodded and disappeared into the corridor. Meanwhile, Ron pointed to the stairs.

"Hurry up! We don't have much time!"

THE THRONE HALL

"So you finally did it…" Edmund said with a smile. He looked at his brother, who had an expression of victory on his face, and then at the girl sitting on the floor on her knees with her hands tied.

"I told you."

Edmund laughed softly. He started to walk over toward Anka, with his hands behind his back. He stopped just shy of Anka. Meanwhile, Inca had moved to his left side. He stood a little behind Edmund. Carmen raised her head slightly. Her eyes met his. Her murderer's eyes… She looked at him angrily, but in truth, she was terrified of him. The first time she had looked into his eyes, she was coming out of his chamber, and they'd run into each other. She remembered her fear then and she was even more afraid now. She was breathing heavily. She didn't know how much longer she could hold back her tears. She wanted to cry out sobbing. She wanted to be home. She didn't want to die.

A slight smile appeared on Edmund's face.

"You resemble so much of your mother."

Carmen could feel her heart ache. Her mother's murderer was now going to be her own murderer. She closed her eyes and bent her head down. She was ordering herself not to cry.

"You know, I took you in my arms before your mother could."

Carmen swallowed hard and raised her gaze.

"It'll be sad to kill you." Inca was laughing, mercilessly. Edmund took a step toward Carmen. Here it was. She was going to die. Her heart was about to leap out of her chest.

"Stop! Please stop!" Edmund stopped. Carmen looked into his eyes and then at Inca's eyes in turn. She began to speak, her gaze stuck with Inca, "He told me about his plans on the way. He told me everything!" Carmen was raising her voice. Inca's face was now serious. She turned to Edmund. "He told me with great relish how he was conspiring to kill you!"

Inca frowned and approached Edmund in one quick step.

"Don't listen to this nonsense. Finish her off now."

Edmund glanced at his brother sideways. When Anka spoke, he turned to her again.

"There you go! He wants me dead immediately." And she looked at Inca again. "Because he can kill you then. When you are vulnerable." She turned her glance at Edmund again. "After you take my soul, he's going to kill you the moment you let down your guard!"

"Enough! Shut up already!" Derick said. There was an expression on Edmund's face he couldn't comprehend. No expression could be fathomed from his gaze other than the slight knitting of his eyebrows. "Don't you get it? She's trying to create a rift between us. She thinks she can escape death this way. Finish her off! Now!"

Carmen studied Edmund's face, who kept staring back at her. She thought the longer she delayed her death the better. It seemed inevitable, but it was worth trying.

"Do you really think you can sit on the throne together? There's only one throne there!" she said, gesturing to the throne with her head. "Crictus can have only one ruler!"

As she said this, they heard the raucous sound of horns blowing simultaneously. The windows of the castle trembled as if they were about to break. Carmen looked around without understanding what was happening.

"It looks like you've dragged your friends after you," exclaimed Edmund.

Warmth spread inside Carmen. He was here. Ron! He had come here to save her.

"You see, they're here in the castle! She's trying to buy time. Finish her off now!" Inca said.

Ron and the others were in the castle, but could they get here in time? Carmen wasn't sure, but at least she finally had a glimpse of hope.

THE CASTLE

Ron swung his sword with all his might. A muffled scream echoed in the corridor. Meanwhile, he turned around when he felt heat coming from behind. Jonathan was turning everything into hell. Two men were flaying about in flames.

"More guards incoming!" Matthew shrieked. His eyebrow was bleeding. Matthew was helping Richard while he fought off five men. Ron brandished his sword in the face of the loud rallying charge that came from behind. As he swung his sword at the man before him, he cut his throat with water in his hand. The man collapsed as Ron turned to Jonathan.

"We've got to keep moving forward!"

Jonathan glanced at Ron after killing the man whose throat he was holding.

"How! They're coming from everywhere! It's impossible to move!"

"You go! We'll keep them busy!" It was Dean speaking.

There were twenty men coming from behind. Just as many guards were coming from the front side and the lower floor. Among those guards, some of them were Anka supporters but Ron still knew it was suicide to leave them here. He had no choice but to leave. Anka's life came first. Ron caught Jonathan's gaze. They nodded to each other in agreement. Jonathan took the lead. They were running, setting the corridor on fire as they went. The men before them fled the moment they saw the fire.

"Upstairs! The throne hall is upstairs!" Ron said.

The two of them charged rapidly up the stairs together. Ron was sweating profusely due to the heat Jonathan was creating. When he noticed the guards behind him, he used the water in his hand as a whip to push them back down. They kept going.

We're so close, Carmen! Hang in there... he thought. They reached the upper floor.

Jonathan asked Ron as fire shot from his hand, "Which way?"

Ron showed the way. Working at the castle as a guard came in handy. They proceeded quickly to the door of the throne hall.

THE THRONE HALL

"If you kill me, he'll kill you!"

"Shut your mouth!" Inca shouted.

Carmen was still trying her luck.

"He always hated you! Now if you kill me, you're giving him the chance to kill you! You will be vulnerable. He is only waiting for an opportunity to take your life!"

Inca walked in front of Edmund.

"Don't listen to her. She's trying to set you against me. We'll share this throne. You're my blood."

Carmen laughed angrily.

"Do you really believe this nonsense? He wants the throne for himself. Don't you see!"

"Enough! Shut up!" Derick said, he turned back and slapped Carmen.

Carmen screamed and lost her balance as she fell to the floor. Two guards grabbed her up by the arms to her knees again. Carmen could no longer hold back her tears. Edmund touched his brother's shoulder calmly.

"Calm down, Derick."

Derick turned toward him.

"Do you think I believe in my brother or our common enemy? I don't get why you're so bent out of shape."

Inca grinned slightly.

"You're right. I should not. Only… the horns…"

"I'm sure our guards can handle an emerald."

"Two," Inca corrected.

Edmund knitted his eyebrows.

"There are two now," Derick explained. Edmund nodded vaguely. There was no need to fight anymore because soon he would take the soul of both his brother and Anka. But he couldn't decide upon which one first. They were both there. He knew Anka had told him the truth, but on the other hand, the emeralds were in the castle. He closed his eyes. He took a deep breath and made his decision.

"Derick back off, there's no need to lose any more time."

Inca was delighted and took a few steps back.

Carmen was breathing heavily. She had come to the end of the line. She was going to die soon. Would it hurt? What was it like to die? But she didn't want to die. She tried to move her hands. It was impossible to escape. She glanced at Edmund. His eyes were determined. She closed her eyes shut. *Calm down Carmen,* she thought. *Think of your mother and father. Your friends, Earth, Crictus. Think of all of them for one last time. They all will disappear very soon. Ron… I love him. I love Earth and also Crictus. I love my family and my friends. No, it can't be like this. I love life.*

A tear brushed her cheek. Soon everything would be over. Her chest was heaving. She was afraid. And suddenly...

Scream! She heard a scream. But there was no pain. She opened her eyes in fear. She fixed her gaze at the scene before her. The Soul Hunter Edmund was sucking out the soul of his own brother, Inca Derick. Inca was screaming. Derick was helpless, struggling. He attempted to raise his hand but couldn't resist the power of the Soul Hunter. He was sucking the life out of Derick. After a while, Derick's body fell to the ground, but the screaming did not stop, it got shriller instead. The black silhouette of Inca was hanging in the air and screaming. It looked like a terrifying wisp of smoke. The Soul Hunter was drawing it to himself.

At that instant, Carmen screamed with the sound of an explosion from behind. She fell on the ground. She looked back to see the door had disintegrated and lit up in flames. She smiled when she saw Ron emerging from the flames. She had never been happier in her life. The explosion had distracted the Soul Hunter. Sucking out an immortal soul like Inca was already very difficult, but the disturbance made him unable to control his actions. The soul screamed and began to circle around the room. He hovered over Carmen who was lying on the floor. Carmen screamed when she saw Inca's real face. But the soul quickly flew over Carmen and hovered outside. The Soul Hunter was staring behind Inca. He had lost it.

"No!" he shrieked. He looked at his brother's dead body lying on the floor. Then, he turned to Carmen.

Meanwhile, Ron had passed over the dead and wounded guards on the floor and approached Carmen. He held her face.

"Carmen, are you okay?" Carmen shook her head. Ron untied her hands. While he helped her to her feet, they both stared at the Soul Hunter.

"You! You've ruined everything! I lost Inca because of you. You are going to pay for this!" Then he swung his sword at Carmen. Ron intervened just in time but was having a tough time holding back his attack.

"Go, Carmen. Go!"

Carmen retreated. She turned toward the gates, but it was in flames. There was no exit. Someone inside the flames was keeping anyone outside from coming in. *He must be the emerald,* she thought. It was impossible to get out from there. She looked at the door on her right. Just as she was heading for the door, someone grabbed her foot. Meanwhile, Ron was swinging his sword against the Soul Hunter, but he had never fought with such a strong man before. The Soul Hunter was evading all his moves and countering with stronger ones. Ron had a hard time running away from him.

The man plunged the knife he was holding into Carmen's leg. Carmen screamed in agony, pulling her foot away. The man then stood up and took a sword he found on the ground. He walked over and swung his sword at her. Carmen threw the man back with her energy. The man flew on the other side of the hall. Carmen instinctively studied her hands. The power in her was heightened because of the fire emerald. Carmen smiled to herself for just a second before the doors she was headed toward swung open. Countless guards were rushing in. Hearing the guards in the throne hall, Ron struck the Soul Hunter's face with water and immediately rushed to Carmen. The Soul Hunter screamed in agony. Ron jumped out in front of Carmen and began fighting the guards. The Soul Hunter touched his bleeding face then his eyes spotted Carmen. When Carmen saw the Soul Hunter glaring at her, she stepped back in fear, but she had nowhere to flee. Maybe she could try the door behind her. Her hand holding the sword was shaking terribly and her foot was bleeding. The Soul Hunter charged her with his all might. Bellowing, he brandished his sword onto Carmen. While Carmen was trying to block the blow, her sword dropped from her hand. The Soul Hunter cackled as he went on the rampage again. Carmen retreated with fear and started to limp away. She had to find a sword. As she ran toward the corner of the room, she whipped around and smashed the Soul Hunter with her energy beam. The Soul Hunter retreated. Using this opportunity, Carmen picked up a sword off the ground only to find the Soul Hunter had come over next to her and was striking heavy blows. Carmen could do nothing but try to escape. The Soul Hunter screamed and brought his sword down in the middle of Carmen's sword. Carmen thought her sword was going to snap in half. She just wasn't strong enough to stop him. They were standing in a breath away from one another when Carmen suddenly felt the agonizing pain in her body. She started screaming. Her soul was being sucked out. She moved her sword to one hand while beaming her energy to the Soul Hunter with the other. The pain stopped, but the Soul Hunter was still coming at her. Carmen turned back and saw there was a door behind her. She blew up the door using her energy. Carmen entered the room as the wood shattered all around. This was a meeting room, with stone walls, a long table in the center, a crystal chandelier overhead, a giant fireplace in one corner, and two large windows at the end of the room. Apart from this, there were some sculptures around the edges. The most spectacular sculpture was that of the Soul Hunter himself and was seated right between two windows. Carmen went under the table the moment she entered the room. The Soul Hunter leapt onto the table and began to plunge his sword into the table at random. Carmen was screaming as she tried to protect her head. Just as she was trying to get from beneath the table, a blow hit her arm. She screamed in pain. She emerged from beneath the table on one side. But she couldn't get rid of the Soul Hunter. The Soul Hunter then slammed her to the wall and Carmen shouted as she struck her head. The Soul Hunter commenced squeezing Carmen's throat, rendering her breathless. And then the pain… her soul was being sucked out again.

While Ron fought with the guards in the next room, the guards under Dean's command were fighting for Anka. This was encouraging but there were still too many of the Soul Hunter's men to fight off. Ron leaned over and plunged his sword into the belly of a guard jumping in front of him. Jonathan was fighting the guards with him. Countless guards were still rushing in. Matthew and Richard were also trying to fight off guards in the doorway. Ron scanned around. Carmen wasn't there but neither was the Soul Hunter. His eyes roamed for Carmen and noticed the door was in flames. Then he looked at another door just across from him. That door was smashed in. He heard Carmen scream from inside the room. His eyes opened wide in fear. She was dying. He ran to the room at the utmost speed. At the end of the room, the Soul Hunter had Carmen trapped between himself and the wall and was sucking out her soul. Carmen's sword fell limply to her side. Ron quickly ran over to the table and jumped on the Soul Hunter's back. Carmen collapsed gasping as the Soul Hunter tried furiously to throw Ron off from his back. Carmen's eyes darkened for a moment. Then she began to regain her wits. Ron fell to the ground in agony when the Soul Hunter slammed his back with Ron on it against the wall. Carmen picked the sword up in her shaky hands again when she saw Ron was in deep trouble. Just as the Soul Hunter was about to plunge his sword into Ron, Carmen came from behind and swung her sword at the Soul Hunter. The Soul Hunter writhed in pain from the blow she dealt to his groin and turned his back. While Carmen wanted to keep on hitting him with her sword, the Soul Hunter slammed her onto the wall with his shoulder.

Thinking her arm was dislocated for a moment, Carmen managed to push back the Soul Hunter with an energy beam, thus not giving him the chance to trap her against the wall. Her whole body still trembled with fear, which caused her to emit a weak energy beam. The moment the Soul Hunter rebounded from the energy blast, he snatched her by the hair and smashed her to the ground. Carmen screamed, but it was cut off abruptly when her head struck the foot of the Soul Hunter sculpture sitting between the two panes of glass. Carmen remained motionless on the ground with the impact of the crash. Meanwhile, Ron got to his feet. He had seen the Soul Hunter tossing Carmen to and fro and like a rag. Carmen was lying on the ground as if she was dead. Ron's anger grew suddenly. He attacked the Soul Hunter with all the water he had.

"Leave her alone!"

The Soul Hunter turned to Ron, stunned. He walked fast and furiously toward him.

"You won't be able to cause me any more trouble!" he said and plunged his sword in Ron's shoulder as he bent down at the last minute. Ron screamed. He was trying to push him away with his sword, but to no avail. Ron almost dropped his sword when the Soul Hunter veered his weapon fiercely against him. The Soul Hunter grabbed his chance to sucker punch Ron. Ron found himself near the wall. After grappling Ron from the back with both hands, he tossed him to the ground with all his might.

Carmen whimpered and touched her head. She opened her eyes slightly. When she saw blood on her hand, she remembered for a moment where she was. Her head ached very much. Not only her head, but her entire body. Carmen straightened up in pain. She held her breath when she saw the Soul Hunter throwing Ron down to the ground. This was a deadly move. The Soul Hunter grabbed the sword he laid down then leaned over Ron's head. He was about to remove his emerald heart!

"No!" cried Carmen, and she rose with a force she could not grasp. She shot a beam of energy at the Soul Hunter's back. The Soul Hunter groaned and turned toward her.

Carmen pushed the Soul Hunter with all her strength again without allowing him to approach her. The Soul Hunter found himself at the wall. Carmen smashed him again with a full energy beam. The Soul Hunter couldn't get anywhere near her. This led him to distract Carmen by throwing a switchblade he pulled out from his waist at her. The Soul Hunter then grabbed her by the shoulders and plastered her onto the window. A struggle ensued. Meanwhile, Ron was slowly regaining his wits. The Soul Hunter smacked Carmen's head hard twice against the window. The window cracked slightly as Carmen screamed in agony. Just then, she felt the pain of her soul being sucked out again. It was not like any other pain. She couldn't allow this. She mustered her energy and beamed it at the Soul Hunter. Carmen pulled away the window with a swift move and hit Soul Hunter with all her energy. The Soul Hunter clung onto the glass behind him. Carmen had to use this opportunity well. The Soul Hunter had tried to kill her, he murdered her mother, Ron's family, and numerous other people. Carmen aimed her energy at the window behind the Soul Hunter. The glass shattered into smithereens and spilled onto the floor. The Soul Hunter's foot fell into the void. For the first time, he looked fearfully at Carmen. He was trying to maintain his balance by gripping the edges of the window. Carmen came eye-to-eye with the Soul Hunter. She hesitated! Why! The Soul Hunter sensed this hesitancy and launched onto Carmen. Carmen then pushed away the Soul Hunter with her energy, just as he was about to catch her. As the Soul Hunter was on the verge of falling out the window, he clutched Carmen's arms. He was pulling her down with him! Carmen screamed.

"If I go, you'll die too!"

Carmen was so close to death. She couldn't free herself from his grasp, but she couldn't hold onto him either. They were both on the verge of falling from the window. Carmen could see the bottom. It was like falling from a seven-story building. At that moment, she got ahold of herself as two hands gripped her from behind.

"I have you!" It was Ron.

"No!" the Soul Hunter shouted.

"Push him, Carmen!"

Carmen felt her soul being sucked out again. She screamed. Then she rid herself of the pain by directing an energy beam at the Soul Hunter. The Soul Hunter had to release his hands in pain and began falling. He soon crashed on the ground. Carmen had seen the moment of his falling. She had watched as the Soul Hunter stared at her as he descended to his death. Ron pulled Carmen back inside and embraced her. Carmen's whole body was shaking. Her hands were cold and sweating and she was breathing erratically. Carmen raised her head and looked at Ron, who was hugging her. Then she started crying. She was sobbing and screaming. Ron hugged her even tighter.

"All right. It's all gone. Calm down. It's all over. He is gone. We did it. You did it," he said, kissing Carmen's head. Carmen was sobbing convulsively. She couldn't stop herself. It was over. It was really all over. She embraced Ron tightly as she inhaled his scent. She had thought she would never see him again and thought it was all over for her. She had survived. She couldn't believe it. She was crying with joy, but at the same time she was crying for the terrible moments they had to experience. After a while, her sobbing subsided.

"That's it. Calm down…" Ron said and pulled her slightly away. "Do you feel better?" Carmen merely nodded, as she was still unable to speak. "Let's get you up."

Ron helped Carmen stand up. Carmen was holding onto Ron because her feet trembled, and her body ached. She had bleedings and bruising that needed attendance. They walked slowly to the throne hall. It resembled a battlefield with many corpses on the floor, but the battle was over. Jonathan was checking if the bodies on the ground were dead. Carmen knew him from her vision. Ron looked at Carmen.

"I want to introduce you to someone."

Jonathan smiled when he saw Carmen. He approached and when he came in front of Carmen, he knelt in reverence.

"My name is Jonathan. I promise to serve you as long as I shall live, Great Anka," said Jonathan as he got to his feet.

Carmen let go of Ron.

"Jonathan," she whispered. She glanced at him, the blond boy in a guard's uniform. She threw herself in Jonathan's arms. She hugged him as if she had seen someone whom she loved so much but had not seen in a long time. "You can't imagine how happy I am to see you."

Jonathan hesitantly glanced at Ron as Carmen hugged him. He acted like he didn't know what he was doing. After Carmen let go of Jonathan, Ron held her again. She was unable to stand on her own. Jonathan had found this hug very warm and had never imagined Anka would be someone like her. Ron turned to Jonathan.

"The Soul Hunter has fallen. They may still be fighting in other parts of the castle. We have to ring the bell."

Jonathan left the room after nodding to Ron.

Carmen turned to Ron.

"Where's my father?"

"Look who's here?"

Carmen turned to the mocking voice. Carmen stumbled and embraced him.

"Matthew!"

After Matthew hugged her, he stepped back and looked at her.

"Amazing, you managed to stay in one piece."

Carmen smiled at him, exhausted.

"Barely."

At that moment, Richard entered the hall. When Carmen saw him, her smile grew bigger, and she embraced him.

"Father! I was so worried about you."

Richard breathed in his daughter's hair and hugged her tightly. He squeezed her with yearning. He was finally reunited with his daughter. His daughter whom he did not even know was alive for sixteen years, and whom he saw just once, on the day she was born, was now in his arms. A single drop of tear fell from his eye. The suffering he had experienced… It was all over. He was happy now. He was holding his daughter in her arms.

"I dreamed of this moment so many times…" he said, smelling his daughter's hair.

Suddenly, the castle was shaken by the sounds of the bells. Carmen let go of Richard. Ron came over to Carmen.

"It is official now."

Carmen smiled as she looked over at the people around her. They had really succeeded. She had done it! She saw the dead bodies lying on the ground. Sadness filled inside her. They had died because of her. Then she saw a familiar face lying on the ground. Dean's face… Derick's face… He had such big dreams just a few minutes ago but was now dead. Life was so short. She turned and looked at the throne. It was no longer teasing her. It just obediently nodded, waiting for its new owner to rule it. Carmen closed her eyes for a few seconds. She listened to the silence. There were no clanging swords, no shouting. She opened her eyes. The throne awaiting her. She smiled as big as she could. Everything was over now.

Everything…

SETTLEMENT OF DAKLASHAVEN – BALENAUS

Situated far from the castle, Kamilla was tired out, lying in her room in the settlement of Daklashaven, where she had just finished her training for the day. She was a tall, slim woman in her 30s with puffy black hair and dark brown eyes. She had found herself here when one of the elders of Daklashaven adopted her because she had no family. Here they were taught to live for a single purpose:

To Kill Anka and Serve Inca!

She was thinking about her day while lying on her bed. As she did every day, she got up at five in the morning and started training. As usual, she knocked out all her opponents today. Kamilla had been trained since childhood and was a much better fighter than most. She was proud of herself. She smiled with arrogance as she was lying on her bed. Suddenly, a black wisp of smoke entered her from her mouth, and she was left breathless. She hadn't even noticed anything enter the room. Her eyes dimmed as she struggled with her demons in bed. She tried to speak, to ask for help, but was unable to utter a sound. It was as if a force was possessing her from within. Suddenly, everything ended as fast as it had begun. Unable to figure out what had happened to her, Kamilla got out of bed. As she tried to regulate her breathing, she looked around to understand what had happened. The pain had disappeared completely. Kamilla looked at her hands in disbelief. Then she clenched them into fists and burst out laughing. She was chortling with delight.

Kamilla got out of bed and looked out her window. Her friends were training outside. Friends who were training to serve Inca… Her arrogance intensified. She held her head up like a true leader. They would all serve her now! All Crictus would be hers now!

Far from Daklashaven, Carmen believed everything was over. In fact, this was just a beginning…

TO BE CONTINUED…

Dictionary

CHARACTERS

Caleb: The ancient emerald of fire during Anka Juliet's era.

Carmen: Carrier of the Noble Soul Anka. A Zirkus native who grew up on Earth, the true heir to the Crictus throne, daughter of Crictus-born Juliet and Richard, adopted by Earthlings Susan and Ryan.

Dean: A guard working in the castle.

Derick: Carrier of the Noble Soul Inca. The Biological younger brother of the soul hunter Edmund.

Eddie: Resistance friend of Ron.

Edmund: The last living Soul Hunter and the King of Crictus for the past sixteen years.

Geir: A guard working in the castle.

George: Earthling friend of Carmen who has feelings for her.

Hahim: The name of Matthew's Edram. Meaning: Wind.

Juliet: Carmen's biological Mother from Zirkus, previous carrier of the Noble Soul Anka, wife of Richard.

Klaus: Wealthy friend of Ron.

Lilian: Servant working in the castle.

Liz: Carmen's closest friend from Earth.

Margaret: Head servant of the castle.

Mason: Ron's younger brother.

Matthew-Maha: A villager living in Katablana Village, known as Maha in the Ankasuana (Anka language).

Richard: Carmen's biological father, husband of the former Anka Juliet.

Ron: Carrier of the Water Emerald, one of Anka's four emerald protectors. Son of Mier and Sonda, older brother of Mason, leader of the rebellion, born in Zirkus.

Rudolf: Ron's father's and Sonda's sword master friend.

Ryan: Carmen's Earthling father, husband of Susan.

Susan: Carmen's Earthling Mother, wife of Ryan.
Waldorf: Head guard of the castle.

TERMS

Abron: A type of bird that feeds on fabric; it has white eyes, red, bright green, white feathers, and a long tail.

Alti Magic: The simplest form of magic on Crictus, performed solely through spoken words. While less dangerous than other forms of magic, extended use can lead to illness.

Ankasuana or Anka Language: An ancient language spoken on Crictus, still used in villages and sometimes in cities.

Anka and Inca: The twin immortal spirits born when the Great Phoenix Bird touches the womb of Queen Kayra. They are heirs to the Crictus throne. After death, they fly across Crictus to find suitable bodies, ensuring their eternal lives.

Barelan: A large creature with a snake-like face, lion's mane, and red eyes, forms a bond with its owner.

Crictus: The name of the planet, sharing many similarities with Earth. It has three satellites.

Crictus Throne: The throne of Zirkus, the capital where the eleven kingdoms are ruled, and the seat of power for all of Crictus. It's also the throne of Anka and Inca.

Devara: A creature resembling a horned, white, long-toothed deer.

Edram: A horse-like animal with brown fur, a slender face, breath holes on its body, black eyes, and claw-like hooves.

Whisper stone: A magical stone that, when whispered a name, calls the person it belongs to.

Jolast: One of Crictus' three moons, the purple moon. Due to its distance, it appears close to Crictus every few years.

Klaush: A poultry bird with a taste similar to turkey.

Soul Hunter: The term given to individuals who feed on souls. The Werth Tribe turned themselves into soul hunters using the power of Se Uirvan to avoid annihilation by Anka and Inca. The soul hunters were made extinct by the former Anka Juliet. The last known representative is King Edmund.

Srilan: A predatory animal similar to a tiger, with black and red-striped markings.

Zirkus: The capital city governed by a system of eleven kingdoms, formerly known as Kallonus. It's the city of Anka and Inca, and the location of the Crictus throne.

Emeralds: They are the protectors of Anka. According to the legend of the Phoenix, they came into existence through Inca's desire to split Anka's power among four separate emeralds. They carry the powers of the four elements, and as most loyal guardians of Anka, the source of their power is Anka. They are indestructible. They choose their carriers and embed themselves in their hearts to transfer their powers. When their carriers die, if not immediately removed, the emeralds teleport to another part of Crictus for many years. Only when four emeralds are completed, Anka's and Inca's powers are equalized.

www.ingramcontent.com/pod-product-compliance
Lightning Source LLC
LaVergne TN
LVHW090911131224
799041LV00013B/202